the king's prey

the king's prey

saint dymphna of ireland

susan peek

Cover photo courtesy of Anne Mawhinney
Cover Design: Silver Fire Publishing

ISBN-13: 978-0997000573
ISBN-10: 0997000570

seven swords publications

www.susanpeekauthor.com

"In many chapels,

reddened by the setting sun,

the saints rest silently,

waiting for someone to love them."

These words, penned by an unknown priest, long dead,
were the inspiration for this series on the lives of saints
who have fallen deep into the shadows of obscurity.
My hope is that, in reading their heroic stories,
you will make the acquaintance of some of

God's Forgotten Friends

Susan Peek

To broken families everywhere.

And to Saint Dymphna and Saint Gerebran,

with the prayer that they will find

"someone to love them."

Introduction

What is the point of this book?

Why did the author (as it happens to be, my wife) work so hard to write it? She will tell you that it took all of three years. As her husband, I go a little further back. This story has haunted her. Almost begged to be written.

I read the first draft over fifteen years ago. In those days, Dymphna was portrayed as the classic production-line saint. No real personality.

Things are very different now in the pages you are about to read. Dymphna has come alive.

She is the Patron Saint of anyone suffering from any kind of psychological or emotional disorder. This is very apt for these times. We would all like to say, *not me!* But we all know someone. Don't we? A spouse. A parent. A child. A brother or sister. The neighbor next door. The boss. The in-laws. Oh yes, we all know someone who could use a little help along those lines. That is why the Catholic Church has given us Saint Dymphna. She is the champion of any soul hurting in mind or heart.

Before going to print, my wife sought and received differing views about this novel. Nonetheless, she has finally achieved her goal. Because, whether you love it or hate it (it really doesn't matter which), there is one thing I personally guarantee:

Read it . . . and you will never, till the end of your days, ever forget the name Dymphna.

And THAT, dear folks, is precisely the point of this book.

Dymphna, from Heaven, for the most part unknown and ignored, is waiting for us in this modern age of confusion to call upon her. Her time has come. Now it is up to us to make good use of her. But we can't love someone we don't know.

After finishing these pages, you will love her.

Saint Dymphna, pray for us all.

Jeffrey Peek, A.T.C.L., A.I.R.M.T.(N.Z.)

1

the kingdom of oriel
ireland
628 a.d.

Turlough never intended to shatter his brother's life. He only wanted to keep Brioc alive, to find a way for him to be safe and warm and fed every day. Winter drew near, and as the two of them tramped across the lonely windswept hills, all Turlough knew was that unless he did this terrible thing, his younger brother wouldn't survive. There was only so much hunger, so many freezing, fearful, and desolate nights the little boy could take. Turlough had no choice.

"Slow down," Brioc begged. "Please, Turlough. You're going too fast."

Turlough stopped on the rugged path so his brother could catch up. He didn't mean to hike so quickly. He had to keep reminding himself there was a big difference between his own endurance at fifteen and Brioc's at ten. It didn't help, of course, that neither of them had eaten since yesterday.

Brioc reached out a hand to steady himself as he climbed the steep slope. As he did so, his sleeve rode up his arm, revealing the scars. Even after all these months, Turlough's breath still caught with horror every time he saw them. Brioc clung to his miniature harp with his other hand. He'd been lugging the thing since they'd left home this morning. No wonder he struggled to keep pace.

"You look exhausted. Need to rest?"

Brioc reached him, shaky and breathing hard. Tugging his ragged cloak tighter against the cruel wind, he gazed at the cliff ahead. His face was a mask of despair. "Are we climbing that?"

"Of course not. A trail winds around and comes out back. We can't see it yet." Why were these places always built in the most inaccessible areas? It was one thing to want solitude, but to live on a veritable cliff top? Seriously?

"Let me carry your harp. I know you can't bear to part with the thing, but you've been hauling it all morning."

"But you're carrying everything else."

Everything else. Brioc made it sound like a lot. A few shirts that once belonged to their brothers, two pairs of patched trousers that wouldn't fit Brioc for at least another year, and a couple blankets. That was it.

Oh, and the tiny statue of Saint Brigid that Mam had loved.

Every night before blowing out the candle, she had traced a cross upon the forehead of each of her seven children and whispered the same ancient blessing: *May Saint Brigid keep you safe beneath her cloak.* Mam had blessed them and said that prayer to her dying day. Every night. Without fail. Turlough had packed the statue at the last minute.

He pushed the painful memory away. "Just give me the harp, will you?"

Brioc handed it over, gratitude filling his eyes. "If you're sure."

"I'm sure." Turlough took the instrument, relieved he hadn't sold it after all. God knew how tempted he'd been. It was the only thing they owned worth money, and it would have given him enough to buy a sword. But that little harp was his brother's lifeline, the thing that held Brioc together.

Well, not quite. *They* held each other together, and had for two years now. But the harp helped.

Turlough hoisted the bundle of clothes over his shoulder so it wouldn't bump against the delicate instrument. As he did, the bundle knocked against his hip and dislodged the hunting knife on his belt. It dropped to the ground.

Brioc automatically reached for it and picked it up. He gazed at it, his eyes filling with sadness.

The knife had been Daid's.

Funny how such a small object could bring back a flood of memories. But memories were lethal for Brioc. Turlough should know that by now. He should have hidden the knife, not slipped it so carelessly into his belt. Anything could set Brioc off. He held out his hand, a silent command to return the knife.

Brioc obeyed, as always. The wind whipped a strand of hair across his cheek and he shoved it away. A lump rose in Turlough's throat. Gosh, he looked so much like Mam. Brioc was the only one who had inherited her striking dark hair. Aislinn would've had it too. Turlough had been cursed with Daid's sandy-colored mess, just like Branduff and Raghnall and — *Stop.* Today was painful enough. Forget the past.

He jammed the hunting knife back into his belt and yanked his shirt down over it. Thank God it hadn't set Brioc off.

Starting uphill again, Turlough's eyes searched for the trail that would go around the cliff. Now that they were so close, he felt an urgency to get this over with. Just thinking about what he was going to do made him feel sick.

Brioc scrambled to keep up. "Turlough?"

"Hmm?"

"Where are we going?"

The question was bound to come sooner or later. Turlough's insides twisted. Incredibly, this was the first time Brioc had asked. Even when he'd watched Turlough collect their clothes this morning and cram them into a sack, Brioc hadn't questioned him. He'd looked bewildered when Turlough told him to fetch his harp, then led him outside, past the seven mounds with their carved wooden crosses and away from their ramshackle cabin and towards the hills. But even then, he obeyed with never-failing trust. The farther they had gone into the woods, the more nervous Brioc had become, and when they reached the waterfall — the one of his nightmares — he froze with terror. But Turlough was used to that by now, so he gently but firmly steered Brioc on, holding his hand until the sound of rushing water was behind them, promising Brioc the whole time that nothing would happen, that the wolves only came at night. Brioc had nodded, but his rapid breathing and the vice-like grip of his small hand in Turlough's betrayed his fear. Yet even then, he hadn't asked where they were going. Or why.

It was always like this. So unwavering was Brioc's trust in him that Turlough could tell him to do anything and Brioc would obey without a word. Order him to jump off a mountain and he would probably do it, all the while with that innocent trusting look that said he knew Turlough would catch him before he died.

Being your little brother's hero was the hardest job in the world.

Turlough sucked in his breath, unwilling to tell Brioc where they were going.

Brioc startled him by blurting, "I know! We're going to Gheel, aren't we?" His face lit up. "That's where, isn't it?"

In Brioc's mind, Gheel was a magical land. A place where hunger and cold and fear didn't exist, and dreams came true. Turlough felt a knife through his heart.

"No, we're not going to Gheel. I've told you a hundred times, it's in Flanders, on the other side of the sea."

"But if we buy a boat —"

"Forget Gheel." The words came out harsher than Turlough intended. *A boat.* As if. He couldn't even afford a crust of bread. He blinked back threatening tears.

Brioc went quiet. Turlough shifted the harp to his other shoulder, trying not to think of the sword he could have bought if he'd sold it. But if Brioc already needed music so desperately, how much more would he need it by tonight.

The gray-bearded minstrel must have sensed something like that when he gave Brioc the harp a year ago. Turlough couldn't even remember the old man's name. Just some carefree wandering musician from Gheel, passing through Ireland, full of laughter and song and endless stories to tell. Brioc heard him play in the village and was so entranced by his melodies that the man, having compassion on the little orphan, gave him the tiny harp right then and there. It was the first time Turlough had seen Brioc happy, radiantly happy, since disease had swept the region two years ago, claiming in death not only their parents, but their four brothers and baby sister too. The kindhearted minstrel even stayed around long enough to teach Brioc how to play. By the time he left, both boys had picked up a smattering of the man's strange language, and after that, all Brioc talked about was going to Gheel someday and becoming a wandering minstrel himself.

Turlough knew he would never get there. Neither of them had traveled farther than the woods around King Daemon's fortress, let alone to Flanders beyond the sea. Traveling was for the rich and noble, not for sons of a dead woodcutter without the means left to buy a scrap of food. But Brioc was entitled to dream.

For Turlough, there were no dreams left. Just survive another winter.

"If we're not going to Gheel, why'd you bring our clothes?" The trust in Brioc's eyes thrust the knife deeper. Turlough knew he'd have to tell him eventually. Might as well do it now. There was no way out.

"I'm taking you to a monastery."

There. He'd said it. The most awful words of his life.

Brioc's dark eyebrows squished together in confusion. "A monastery? We already went to Mass this morning. Don't you remember?"

"We're not going there for Mass." A chunk of ice formed in Turlough's stomach. "You're going to live there from now on."

"We're going to live at a . . . monastery?"

"Yes. I mean, no. I mean, *you* are. I'm dropping you off there. The monks will take care of you." Turlough picked up his pace, this time on purpose. He couldn't bear to see his brother's face.

Brioc scrambled after him and grabbed his sleeve, forcing Turlough to stop and face him.

"But . . . you're going to live there with me, aren't you, Turlough? We'll still be together, right?"

"No. I'm too old. I need to find work. I'm going to try to join King Daemon's army." The violent life of a soldier was the last thing Turlough wanted, but he could see no choice. Survival was survival. He didn't even know if Captain Barrfhoinn would accept him so young. His only hope lay in that he looked older than fifteen. Heaven knew he felt it. Fifteen going on fifty.

"You mean, I'll be alone? Without you?" Brioc had been petrified of separation ever since he'd seen the little girl eaten near the waterfall a few months ago. Turlough feared leaving him alone for more than a couple minutes, in case Brioc had one of his . . . turns. The nightmare-things. Flashbacks, awake-dreams, whatever they were. Turlough didn't even know. But they were terrifying to watch. And the scariest thing was, anything could trigger them.

"Please take me home. *Please.*" Brioc was close to panic. Turlough knew the signs. He saw them every night when the wolves prowled outside their cabin. Brioc would fly into Turlough's bed, so scared he could barely breathe. Not that Turlough could blame him, with scars like that. All he could do was hold Brioc tight until the pack wandered away. His heart ached for his brother.

He knew he had to keep Brioc calm, lest a flashback was triggered, right here on the steep hill. He groped for something to say to make the monastery sound attractive. "The monks will teach you to read and write. Imagine that. None of the rest of us ever got learning. Daid would be so proud of you."

Lame, lame, lame.

Brioc's gaze flew towards the unseen monastery, holding back tears. "I don't want learning. I want to stay with you."

"I bet they'll teach you music."

"I don't want to live there."

"Brioc, listen — "

"I won't stay without you. I won't." Brioc gulped in breath after breath. "I'll run away. I'll sneak out at night when the monks are asleep and search all of Ireland until I find you."

Turlough was aghast. "Don't you dare."

"I will. You'll see."

Horrifying images leaped into Turlough's mind of his brother wandering defenseless through the wild countryside, searching for Daemon's army. He'd be dead within a week. Even if he did find the troops, Turlough could never let him stay. Daemon's soldiers were for the most part pagans, like the king himself. They were the roughest and most violent men in the kingdom, and even for Turlough it would be risky at fifteen. He shuddered to think what men like that would do for sport to an innocent little boy.

"I swear I'll run away and find you."

This was getting out of hand. Fast. Turlough had to say something – *anything* – to prevent Brioc. He said the first thing he could think of.

"If you run away, the wolves will get you."

Instant terror leaped into Brioc's eyes. But his very survival depended on this, and if anything would keep him safe with the monks, it would be his paralyzing fear of wolves. So, hating himself for it, Turlough said, "If you run away, they'll eat you. Just like that little girl."

He couldn't believe he was saying these things! The tragedy near the waterfall had traumatized Brioc beyond words. Not only had he seen the girl killed, but he'd barely escaped with his own life. It was only because the wolf was away from its pack and already wounded that Brioc got away at all.

He had gone that first week into a kind of shock, a strange numbness in which he couldn't remember the attack, at all. That alone frightened Turlough.

Then came the flashbacks, the *reliving*. The memories so overwhelmed his little brother that Brioc believed the attack was actually happening again. He seemed to be in two places at once, and when things got that bad he didn't even register his surroundings. Sometimes Turlough had to physically tackle him and hold him down to prevent him from harming himself in his panic to get away from an imaginary wolf.

Thus to bring up the little girl herself, devoured alive before Brioc's eyes, was the cruelest thing Turlough could do. But the brutal words were already out. He cringed, bracing himself for Brioc's reaction.

But . . . it didn't come. At least not the reaction he expected. Instead, to his amazement, Brioc drew in a deep breath, squared his little shoulders, and said the most incredible words of his life.

"I'll still run away and find you."

Dear God, even the wolves couldn't keep them apart!

It was Turlough's turn to panic.

"Brioc, stop this. I mean it. I'm taking you to that monastery and you're going to live there and that's all there is to it." He snatched his brother's wrist, feigning anger as his only defense, and started to haul him along the path.

Brioc jerked his arm away and the dam holding back his tears burst. "I won't stay. You're my brother and I'm not living without you."

Turlough hadn't bargained for any of this. His mind reeled. "You can't run away because . . . because . . ."

Think of something! THINK!

Then it came. In a headlong rush, the lie tumbled out.

"You're staying with the monks because I don't want you with me. Ever thought of that? Maybe I don't want you anymore."

Brioc froze.

Once started, it was impossible for Turlough to stop. Desperation for his brother's survival swept him away in the tide of nauseating lies. "Maybe I'm sick of taking care of you. Maybe I've had enough." His voice rose, the voice of a stranger, someone Turlough didn't know, spewing forth such cruel words to the brother he loved. "We're separating and I'm joining the army and that's all there is to it."

Brioc could not have looked more dumbfounded if Turlough had whipped out Daid's hunting knife and started stabbing him. In his shock, even his tears stopped.

Then it happened. The last little light remaining in the child's eyes went out. Flickered with incredible pain and died, just like that. Like blowing out a candle whose flame was already too fragile.

Everything in Turlough wanted to scream, *No! I didn't mean that! We're*

8

brothers and I want to stay together as much as you do! But he couldn't say those things because then Brioc would threaten again to run away to find him, and it would start all over again. So, with that iceberg inside him growing bigger and colder and more monstrous with every step, he silently led the way up the hillside.

Brioc hung his head, shriveled up in his cloak, and silently followed. Neither said another word all the way to the monastery.

An elderly monk opened the door, bent with age and obviously hard of hearing. Turlough had rehearsed a hundred times how he would explain, but now that they were actually on the doorstep, he was too distraught to say a thing. Not that the monk could hear anyhow. Turlough could only manage to relay Brioc's name, then, knowing he himself was on the verge of breaking down, he rushed away before his tears could come. The monks would figure it out. They'd keep Brioc alive.

But Brioc was already dead. Gone from Turlough forever, just as truly as the seven in the grave.

As Turlough wound his way alone down the windswept hills, he knew he would never forget the shattered look in his brother's eyes as he handed him his harp and the ragged bundle of clothes and hurried away. There were no good-byes. Brioc merely cowered behind the white-haired monk, as if Turlough had beaten him, and wouldn't say a word.

Everything had become a nightmare.

eleven years later

2

If she didn't move, didn't breathe, maybe he wouldn't find her. Dymphna burrowed deeper into the musty hay, her fists clenched so hard it felt like the bones might crack. In all her fifteen years, she had never known such terror.

She heard him stomp across the floor directly below the loft, searching the barn, cursing and screaming, enraged that she had gotten away.

Jesus, Jesus, don't let Daidi find me.

They were alone here, not another soul within a mile. The dilapidated barn was hidden deep in the woods, overgrown and abandoned. If Daidi spotted the ladder in the corner, if he managed to heave himself up the flimsy rungs and discover her cowering in the hay, she would have no escape. If he found her, he would . . . he would . . . No, don't think of it! She squeezed her fists tighter, her palms slick with sweat. Night had plunged the barn into darkness; she prayed he would not see the ladder. She held her breath for so long it seemed her lungs would burst.

"Odilla!" he screamed in rage. "Come out! Come to your husband this instant!"

Go away, go away. I'm Dymphna, not Mamai. She's dead. You know Mamai's dead. Tears streaked her face and sharp prickles of hay stabbed her, but she didn't dare move.

Running away from him earlier on the path had unleashed his fury, a rage beyond anything she had ever seen. Below the loft, something banged. Something else crashed. He stormed through the barn like a savage beast, completely out of control, ransacking everything, slamming and hurling objects across the cavernous space.

"Odilla! I know you're in here! I want you! I will find you!" His voice rose.

Through the wild pounding of her heart, Dymphna heard his animal grunts, imagined his deranged movements a few feet below her. When she'd entered, an ax had been leaning by the door, rusted and sticky with cobwebs. If only she had grabbed it. But in her frenzy to scale the ladder, she left it behind — only to see through the cracked floorboards that Daidi snatched up the weapon when he barged inside after her. He was using it now. The thud of splintering wood echoed through the barn as he slashed and destroyed everything around him. It sounded like he was ripping chunks out of the walls, as if he thought she might be hiding behind some loose board.

"I know you're hiding!" he screamed. "You're mine and I'm going to have you!"

Another splintering crash. A curse and a grunt as he dislodged the massive ax from the wall.

Then . . . silence.

She huddled in the hay, drenched in cold sweat.

Seconds ticked by, stretching out to eternity.

Minutes passed.

Only ominous silence.

Her heart slammed in her chest, her breath came in choking gasps. *What was he doing down there?* His sudden silence was more terrifying than even his rage.

It was so quiet now she could hear his uneven breathing below her. Could he hear hers? The moldy hay pressed against her face. Strands of damp hair clung to her cheeks and she tasted the salt of sweat mingled with tears.

A soft creak of floorboards. She swallowed. A few tentative footsteps clomped towards the corner of the barn.

Don't move. Don't breathe.

"Odilla? Odilla, are you up there?"

Dear God, he'd spotted the ladder.

3

Seventeen-year-old Ethlynn burrowed deeper beneath the blanket and yanked her pillow over her head in frustration.

Bang!

Squeeeak.

Four seconds of silence.

Bang!

One . . . Two . . . She held her breath and counted . . .

Three. . .

It's coming . . . Wait for it . . .

Squeeeeeeeeeak . . .

Four . . .

BANG! Right on time.

With a frustrated groan, Ethlynn gave up. She dumped the pillow on the floor and looked with exasperation at her husband, peacefully snoring beside her. How could he *sleep* through this? The angels could be blaring the apocalyptic trumpets and he would snore his way through Judgment Day. Were all men like this? The only sound she knew that could wake her husband was the howl of a wolf. Never mind if it came from three miles away, Brioc would still leap awake and fly through the ceiling. But a gate slamming in the wind a few feet outside their door? Not a hope.

Bang-BANG.

Twice this time. The wind must be picking up. *Squeeeeeak . . . BANG.*

BANG-BANG!

With despair Ethlynn heard the next thing. *Scratch. Scritch-scratch.*

Then a whine.

Wonderful. Now Samthann was pawing at the door, trying to get inside. Brioc must have forgotten to let her back in before bed. That was unusual. He never forgot Sam. It showed how much he had on his mind. Not that Ethlynn could blame him. With Queen Odilla dead, Brioc was out of a job. King Daemon had dismissed all the Christians who'd been in his wife's service, and as court minstrel Brioc was the first to go. Daemon hated his beautiful harp music. He'd even threatened to take away their cottage, which would leave them not only destitute, but homeless too. Ethlynn knew Brioc was worried sick.

Sam's whining escalated to a bark and she scratched the door furiously. Ethlynn sighed, loathe to get up and leave the warm bed. Although it was spring, the night air was chilly. Besides, if she moved, the nausea might return.

Bang --- squeeeeak! Scratch, scratch!

Woof!

This was cacophony. *Bang-scratch-squeak-woof. Snooooore.* Like a torturous song. The only thing missing in the chorus was the nanny goat's *baa.*

Ethlynn bolted upright. The goat! Oh no! It had probably escaped through the open gate! She suddenly remembered she had forgotten to tie the nanny up after milking. This was the third time this week.

She tossed off the blanket, swung out of bed, and winced when her bare feet touched the cold dirt floor. She scampered to the door on tippy-toes, praying wildly she'd find the goat still in the yard. It was their only source of milk; if it went missing, Ethlynn would feel awful. What would they do for milk and cheese? They already had too little to eat.

The second she unlatched the door, a hurricane of fur and muscle exploded inside. It launched into the air and sailed towards the bed, plunging straight on top of Brioc. Ethlynn heard a thud and a creak as the bed nearly collapsed, followed by a sharp gasp of pain. She looked over and saw by a beam of moonlight that her husband had vanished beneath his giant wolfhound. Samthann's tail wagged so fiercely that her whole backside wiggled with it, rocking the entire bed. Her tongue was going crazy. Ethlynn knew Brioc was buried alive under the mountain of fur. It was just a question of where.

Incredibly, Brioc never seemed to mind this unusual form of torture. In fact, after his initial gasp of pain, he only partially woke up, just enough to shove the huge slobbering beast off his face so he could breathe again. Then he ruffled her head affectionately, mumbled, "Hi, Sam," in a groggy voice, and rolled over to go back to sleep.

Sam turned three wild circles on the bed, smearing enormous muddy paw-prints everywhere, then settled down happily beside him, her chin on his shoulder, right in the spot Ethlynn had just vacated. Within ten seconds both were sound asleep.

Ethlynn let out a sigh, wondering just which female her husband loved more.

She dismissed the jealous thought. How silly. Of course Brioc loved her best. He loved her more than the whole world, just like she loved him. Let him sleep with the dog. Ethlynn feared she would be up the rest of the night anyhow.

At least the months of nausea had finally passed, though she still could hardly force any food down. She hoped Brioc wouldn't notice her growing bump or wonder why she was so tired all the time. She hadn't told him about the baby yet. By her calculations she was nearly seven months along, but being her first, she was carrying tiny and only recently starting to show. Just as well. She would have to tell Brioc soon, but for now he had more than enough to worry about. No job and their food running out.

Food.

Milk.

The goat!

Ethlynn suddenly remembered why she stood turning into an icicle in the doorway in the first place. She took a reluctant step outside, shivering, and peered into the moonlit yard.

The gate creaked open and banged shut, every four seconds on the dot, except when a gust crashed it sooner. Leaves and debris fluttered across the grass. Apart from that, the yard was empty. Not a hoofed creature in sight.

Oh dear.

Ethlynn stepped back inside, wondering what to do.

"Um . . . Brioc?"

Man and beast snored on.

"Brioc? Sweetie?" she asked a little louder. She hated doing this to him.

Sam's ears perked, and she raised her head to look at Ethlynn. Her tail thumped the bed.

"Brioc, are you awake?"

He stirred. "Hmm?" he moaned, half asleep.

Ethlynn felt awful. "Guinevere's missing."

Brioc sleepily propped himself up on one elbow, glanced at the occupant on the bed beside him, and noticed for the first time that his wife had mysteriously been replaced by his dog. He looked confused until he found Ethlynn standing by the door.

"What are you doing over there?"

"Guinevere's missing. I think she escaped." Ethlynn bit her lip. "I forgot to tie her up again. I'm so sorry."

Brioc groggily sat up and ran a hand through his mussed-up hair, trying hard to wake up. Ethlynn's heart fluttered. He looked so handsome with his dark hair sticking up all over the place.

"Don't worry," he said sleepily. "I'll go find her."

"I'm sorry," Ethlynn said again. "You're not angry with me, are you?"

He gave her a tired smile. "I could never be angry with you. It's my own fault for not fixing the gate."

Ethlynn knew why he hadn't fixed it. He spent all his time searching for work to keep them alive.

With an effort, Brioc forced himself up. The second he moved, Samthann leaped to the floor and vigorously shook herself. Puffs of doggy-dust flew everywhere. Sam was giant, at least three feet at the shoulders, not even counting her massive head. One good shake meant the whole cottage would need dusting. Ethlynn sighed as the wolfhound bounded to the door, her tail swishing with such excitement that it knocked over one of their chairs. Sam must have sensed Brioc was going somewhere.

While Brioc pulled on his boots and lit a lantern, Ethlynn stood on tiptoes at the open door and strained her eyes to see through the darkness outside, hoping to catch sight of Guinevere.

Squeeeeak . . . Bang. The loose gate kept crashing.

BANG! The sudden gust of wind nearly blew Ethlynn over.

Brioc came to the door, fully awake now. "Stay inside," he said. "It's cold out there." He was so protective of her. A warm gushy feeling rushed through her veins, and for a second she nearly got all romantic. But, really, it wasn't a good time.

She expected Brioc to go straight out the door, but to her confusion he stood in the threshold for a long moment, hesitating, as if he had to gather his courage before stepping out into the night. Samthann was the opposite. After all her clamor to get inside a few minutes ago, she suddenly couldn't wait to go out again. Her tail slapped against Brioc's legs and she looked up at him expectantly and barked.

Brioc didn't move. He sucked in his breath. The color had drained from his cheeks.

Ethlynn suddenly realized something out there frightened him.

"Promise me you'll stay inside. Please, Lynnie."

"Why would I go out?" she asked. She had no intention of doing anything other than brushing Sam's fur off the blanket and trying to get some sleep.

Brioc didn't answer. His face was deathly pale.

"Um . . ." She hated to ask, but she really was desperate for sleep. "Can you stop the gate from banging before you leave? Please?"

He snapped out of his trance. "Oh. Of course I will." He leaned in to kiss her, but in his distraction he caught her left nostril instead of her lips. He didn't seem to notice. Through the fabric of his shirt, she could feel his heart galloping. It must be slamming a million times a minute. Obviously not from passion. *Was he alright?*

As he stepped into the night with Sam lolloping loyally beside him, Ethlynn realized there were so many things about her new husband she didn't know. Tonight, for example. This wasn't the first time she had sensed his reluctance to go outside after dark.

And what about the nightmares he had, when he'd bolt awake in a cold sweat of terror? And his refusal to talk about his family, or his past? Ethlynn didn't even know where Brioc came from, although she suspected it was somewhere around here. Sometimes he hiked to a tiny graveyard by an abandoned cabin in the forest, but for some reason he would only go there when he was certain the king's soldiers had ridden out of town, as if he were trying to avoid them.

Not even to mention those shocking scars all over him. The first time she'd seen them, her voice had abandoned her. Later, she'd gently asked what had caused them, but he froze up and wouldn't tell her.

And there was his music, too, which, for all its breathtaking beauty, was always so sad.

In fact, all Ethlynn really knew about Brioc — apart from the fact that she loved him more than life itself — was that he was an orphan raised by monks. Two years ago, Queen Odilla had brought a donation to the monastery, as she had every year, and she'd heard him play his harp. Instantly she fell in love with his music and invited him to come to the castle as her private minstrel. He accepted. The queen later twisted her husband's arm and arranged for Brioc to live in this little cottage by the meadow.

Ethlynn herself had met him ten months ago, when she was sixteen and he twenty. She'd come with her daid, a horse dealer down on luck, to King Daemon's village. He'd been trying to sell a pair of stallions, but no one was interested and they'd returned home to the Kingdom of Mide a week later, poorer than when they'd left. During the trip, more was lost than Daid's money. Ethlynn lost her heart. It had taken five minutes with the Queen's minstrel. She'd fallen hopelessly, helplessly, head over heels in love.

Back at home, she couldn't do anything. Not eat, not sleep, not concentrate on shoveling the stable floor. The pile of fresh manure would either end up in the water trough, or worse — on top of Daid's tools. She couldn't help it. Her brain wouldn't cooperate anymore. It was capable of one thing only — daydreaming about Brioc.

When he showed up at Mam and Daid's doorstep ten days later, she nearly passed out. He'd been so quiet at the castle that she hadn't realized he liked her. Had he really been thinking about her too? He must've been, otherwise he wouldn't be in Méifne asking Daid if he could court her.

Having no dowry for his ninth daughter, Daid was only too happy to give her away. Within a month Ethlynn found herself back in Oriel, floating in the clouds. No bride had ever been happier. Impossible.

Yet after the whirlwind of romance, Brioc had become withdrawn, bewildering Ethlynn completely. Whatever the reason, losing his job had little to do with it. Something else was going on inside him, something awful. Why wouldn't he confide in her? As horrid as the scars on his body were, the scars inside him must be much worse.

They were destroying him.

Ethlynn felt powerless to help. Maybe someday God would send someone who could.

4

Dymphna heard the wood groan and creak as Daidi tested the first rung. He was middle-aged and out of shape, and the ladder was old and cracked in several places. Would he try? Could he ascend with a lantern in his hand? What about the ax? Would he leave it below? She listened, every muscle strained. She clenched her hands so tightly they'd gone numb.

As in a nightmare, she heard him climb. His breathing sounded ragged with exertion as he slowly clambered upward, step by precarious step. Then suddenly he was there, standing in the loft, not three feet away.

The pale glow from his lantern revealed the toe of his boot under his scarlet cloak. Dymphna held herself in a tight ball, heart hammering. Could Daidi see her? Did a corner of her dress stick out through the hay needles in a bright splash of color?

I'm not here. I'm not here. Go away.

Panting, breathless from his climb, Daidi rested the heavy ax head on the floor with a thud. She could make out his shadowy bulk leaning against its handle. For the longest time he stood there. His eyes must be adjusting to the deeper darkness of the loft, roaming the space for a sign of her presence.

Perspiration trickled down her back. She bit her lip so hard she tasted blood.

His boot disappeared. The floor creaked as he moved away, ax in one hand, lantern in the other. He prowled the loft, a beast stalking prey. Something crashed as he violently kicked it aside.

"Odilla!" he screamed, smashing the ax into the wall in blind fury. Tears streamed down Dymphna's face. Daidi grunted and snorted like some hideous wild pig. He hurtled chunks of wood across the loft.

Something small and swift darted out of the hay and scuttled across the floor. She jerked involuntarily, her breath catching in her throat, before she realized it was only a mouse.

Had Daidi heard her gasp? She froze.

"Odilla! I know you're in this barn! Come out right now!"

Jesus, help me.

"I'll find you!"

His footsteps clomped across the floor, back near her haystack. Dymphna couldn't breathe. Then, to her great relief, he returned to the corner with the ladder.

He huffed his way back down, experimenting with each flimsy rung before surrendering his full weight. With his descent, the dim glow from the lantern disappeared. Dymphna stayed clamped in her tight ball.

Another minute of crashing below, then a sudden gust of cold night air told her the door was flung open. It slammed shut, plunging the barn into silence.

Dymphna slowly let out her breath, not daring to move. Had Daidi left, or was he pretending, waiting outside the door? Too afraid to crawl out from her hiding place, she lay there trembling, teeth chattering uncontrollably. She waited for a sign, a definite sound of his departure.

Somewhere a wolf howled. Branches scratched against the barn roof. Something that sounded heavy enough to be a rat scrabbled back and forth across the rafters above her head.

The agonizing minutes ticked by.

* * * * *

Dymphna had no idea how long she remained buried in the hay, an eternity it seemed. Finally she allowed herself to move enough to push the hay from her face. She gazed around the loft. The shadows across the floor had shifted drastically with the moonlight. At least an hour had passed. Maybe two. Was Daidi outside?

As if in answer to her question, the door below crashed open and slammed into the wall with a thud. A scream caught in her throat. The door swung back and forth a few times, then banged shut. The wind. *Just the wind.* Dymphna let out her breath.

The cramps in her muscles tormented her. She needed to move. She needed fresh air. Brushing the loose hay aside, she staggered to her feet. Her legs, numb from ankle to thigh, shook as she tried to stand. How could she possibly descend the ladder without making a sound?

She groped through the dim light towards the hole in the floor. Trembling, she lowered herself onto the top rung of the ladder. She clambered awkwardly downward, legs wobbling, fear racing through her veins.

Her foot missed a rung and she fell with a clumsy thud to the bottom, landing hard on the floor. Horror surged through her. Her eyes snapped to the door. Was Daidi on the other side, his face twisted in a grotesque hungry smile? If he'd heard her, she was trapped.

Trust in God. Trust! She'd consecrated her life to Him already, hadn't she? He would protect her.

Taking a deep breath, she summoned her courage and, praying her legs would stop shaking, tip-toed across the floor. Never had she been so grateful for such soft doe-skin shoes. At least they made no noise. But the door stood a hundred miles away. *Don't panic. Slowly. Just get to the door . . .*

She reached it and quietly nudged it open, inch by torturous inch. A narrow wedge of bright moonlight sliced across the dirt floor. She peeked out. The night air chilled her through her sweat-soaked dress. Tree branches swayed in the shrieking wind, their shadows dancing wildly across the ground. She strained her eyes and ears for a sign of Daidi and, seeing none, crept outside.

Something screeched and exploded above her head.

She ducked in terror. A black object swooped down at her. The thing cast a wild flapping shadow from the eaves of the barn and let out an earsplitting shriek. Then it flew past Dymphna with a flurry of feathers, and disappeared into the night.

An owl. Only a harmless owl, startled from its nest in the barn. Dymphna exhaled, the relief so great it made her dizzy. She steadied herself against the door and tried to regain breathing. But she had to move, and quickly. Daidi could be anywhere, hunting for her in these dark, isolated woods.

Trembling, Dymphna gathered her flowing skirt off the ground — and ran.

5

By the flickering lantern light, Brioc nervously gazed around the dark woods. The wind sent shadows dancing in mottled patterns across the forest floor. Chilly fingers raced up the nape of his neck. He strained his ears for the tinkle of Guinevere's bell. Surely the wind would make it ring. Instead he only heard the lonely hoot of an owl and a frog gurumphing somewhere in the dewy grass.

He'd been searching for close to an hour. How could such a small goat have wandered so far? It became harder to remain calm with every step. Could a wolf have found Guinevere? He blocked the image and moved closer to Sam. A dog of her size and breeding could take on a small pack. She'd protect him.

Besides, he had fire. Wolves feared fire. If one appeared, he knew what he would do. Throw the lantern at it and pray the woods caught fire. Insane idea. Terrifying in itself, but the only thing Brioc could think of. Anything, even death by burning, was preferable to being shred again by fangs.

If only he'd fixed that broken gate.

He took another wary step, his legs shaky. What kind of a man feared something that wasn't even there? He strained his ears for the tinkle of a bell or the sound of bleating. And that's when he heard rushing water.

The waterfall.

His chest constricted and his lungs froze. The gentle cascading water grew louder and louder, thunderous, deafening, crushing him with terror. And with no warning, the deadly beast inside awoke.

Not now, he begged. *Please no.* This couldn't happen tonight — not with Lynnie counting on him to find their goat.

She didn't even know about the flashbacks. Brioc had never told her.

The sound of the falls overwhelmed him and the beast inside sprang. He dropped to one knee and desperately grabbed for Sam, yanking her close, his mind clamping down against the memory. Suddenly nothing else mattered. Not Guinevere, not even Lynnie. He knew only that he must fight the monster being unleashed inside him.

Sam must have sensed his panic. She pressed her huge body protectively against him and whined.

Please God. Please, please.

He couldn't allow the pain to swallow him again. It had already claimed years of his life, six years of mute darkness he could hardly remember, as if his brain chained up that part of his childhood to prevent the pain from killing him.

Sam licked his hands, then his face, trying to help. She was the one who'd pulled him out of his private hell in the first place, as a tiny abandoned puppy. Sam — and Dymphna, his two most loyal friends, to whom he owed whatever sanity he had left. Slowly, *slowly,* the warmth of the dog's rough fur calmed him, anchored him to the present moment. *The little girl wasn't here. That was years ago.*

Brioc said it over and over again. *She's not here. She's not here. There is no wolf.*

Sam nuzzled him, licking him with her huge sopping tongue. Gradually the sound of the waterfall receded to its place in the distance, returning to a bubbling murmur far away.

Brioc felt numb. His hands tingled. He struggled to fill his lungs with air.

But the flashback had stayed at bay. Thank God. It had actually stayed away.

Shakily he forced himself to stand, ashamed of himself, ashamed that he was trembling so badly. And over what? Over the gurgling of a distant waterfall.

Something was wrong with him. Seriously wrong. And the flashbacks were getting worse lately, not better. They were becoming more frequent, like when he had been a child. Stress always made him vulnerable, but this was getting out of hand. Guilt for not telling Lynnie stabbed him.

He must tell her. She was his wife. She had the right to know.

He didn't want her to know. She might stop loving him.

Sam barked, the sound jerking him back to now. Disoriented for a second, he struggled to remember where he was.

The woods. Of course, the woods. He was looking for Guinevere. The instant he remembered where he was, he thought of wolves. The waterfall grew louder again. The panic rose.

Dear God, he wasn't normal. He needed help.

Sam's wild barking turned into a whine. She crouched forward, upset by whatever she saw. Brioc's gaze flew in the direction she was looking.

Guinevere!

Her head poked through the trees about twenty feet away. The moonlight reflected off her little bell.

Brioc squinted, trying to understand what he saw. Something about her head didn't look right. Sam must've noticed it too. Distressed, the wolfhound pawed the ground, inched forward then back two steps. Chills crept up Brioc's spine. Samthann looked at him and whined.

Something was terribly wrong.

6

Dymphna groped her way through the maze of trees, fear slamming through her. A sliver of moonlight streamed through the lattice of dark rustling leaves overhead, her only source of light. Where was Daidi? Behind every black tree trunk lurked a man with an ax. Everything inside screamed at her to run, but she forced herself to move slowly. She prayed that the howling wind would drown out any noise she made.

Another knotted root tripped her but she grabbed a nearby branch and managed to stay upright. She'd already fallen twice, bruising her knees and scraping her hands. She wiped her clammy palms on the skirt of her dress and fumbled her way through the twisted branches. A clump of clouds pushed across the moon, sheathing the forest in sudden darkness.

Her mouth went dry. With arms outstretched in front of her, she reached into black space. An overhanging leafy branch slapped her in the face and she jumped. Clumsily she moved around a thick tree trunk. Something threadlike and sticky wrapped around one hand. She jerked back, stifling a scream. Images of hairy black spiders crawling up her arm flashed across her mind and she frantically swatted at the huge spider web.

A tiny tinkling noise flitted on the wind. She stumbled past the spider web and stopped to listen. What was that? A bell? Far away, water tumbled against rock. The waterfall must be nearby. A dog barked, sounding close. A rush of hope pulsed through her. If there was a dog, there might be a person. Her heartbeat quickened.

The patch of clouds made its way past the moon and a wedge of yellow light reappeared. She took a step, and the ground squelched beneath her shoe. Another step and she slipped, both feet shooting out from under her. She landed hard on her backside in a puddle of mud. Sharp brambles ripped her hands.

Eyes stinging, she scrunched up the edge of her skirt and clumped it in one fist, trying to push herself up off the ground with the other. She managed to scramble to her feet.

And saw the ax.

* * * * *

Brioc stared at Guinevere's head lodged in the tree. Blood smeared the animal's face.

The rest of her was missing. Her little bell tinkled in the wind. Samthann sniffed the ground and whimpered, her fur on edge. Light from the lantern revealed more blood dripping through the branches and puddling near Brioc's feet. A dark crimson trail led into the woods.

He lifted the lantern and followed the path of blood with his eyes. Something that looked like an animal carcass lay a few feet away. A table-like object was set up beside it. *A table — in the woods?* He warily moved closer. Someone had balanced a large plank between two tree stumps. Burnt candle stubs had toppled onto the ground in front of it. Dark wet stains streaked the plank's top.

As Brioc realized what he was looking at, a sick feeling slithered into his gut. It was a pagan altar. Despite the efforts of Father Gerebran and the other priests, worship of the sun-god Dagda remained strong in the area. Suddenly the presence of evil felt so tangible that goosebumps prickled Brioc's skin. Samthann must have sensed it too. She backed away from the altar and growled.

Reluctantly he stepped closer to the carcass. Sure enough, it was a headless goat. He nudged the body with his foot, already knowing what he would see. He was right. The heart was carved out.

Someone had sacrificed Guinevere to Dagda. A twig snapped in the darkness beyond the altar. Brioc froze. Something rustled through the leaves back there, punctuated by heavy breathing.

Samthann pushed against his legs, whining, as if begging to leave. Brioc couldn't agree more. He half expected to see a demon burst through the forest and fly at them.

Then a shadowy figure flitted through the trees and Brioc could've sworn he heard a man's voice.

"Dymphna."

The princess? What? Surely she couldn't be back there?

Filled with dread, Brioc sucked in a breath and headed toward the sounds.

* * * * *

Dymphna spotted the ax a split-second before she saw Daidi. It was leaning against a tree, its blade and handle slathered with blood. Then Daidi stepped out from behind the tree.

She stumbled back, a scream rising in her throat. But sheer terror trapped the scream in her throat and no sound came.

"Dymphna."

His voice sounded . . . perfectly normal.

27

He stepped closer. "Where have you been, my daughter? I have been so worried."

Her eyes bugged. Everything inside her reeled. Apart from what looked like blood streaking his clothes, he seemed completely normal. As if the last few hours had never happened.

"I —" Her voice failed.

"What are you doing out here? It is the middle of the night." His face suddenly spasmed and for a second his eyes rolled in opposite directions. He regained control. "Let me take you home." He extended a hand. She recoiled. Did he realize his shirt had smudges of blood? What had he killed with the ax? Was it human? *Did he even remember?* Leaves crunched in the darkness. Daidi's eyes shot over her shoulder. Dymphna whirled around as a man with a huge dog emerged through the trees.

Relief flooded her. It was Brioc, and his wolfhound Samthann. As soon as Samthann spotted Daidi, the dog froze, her fur visibly on edge. She seemed unwilling to come closer. Then she did something Dymphna had never seen her do before. She poised to attack. A threatening growl emitted from her throat and she bared her deadly fangs at Daidi. Dymphna gasped.

Brioc's gaze flew to his wolfhound. Her behavior must have startled him too. She looked so savage that for a second Dymphna wondered if maybe it wasn't Sam at all, but another dog, a wild one.

"Sam." Brioc sounded unsure of himself, unsure of the situation, unsure what he wanted his dog to do. Or not do.

She remained in guard position, ready to lunge at Daidi, teeth bared. *Was it Sam?*

Daidi took a startled step back. Instinctively so did Dymphna.

Brioc glanced between his suddenly vicious pet, and Dymphna and Daidi, obviously having no clue what he was expected to do. His eyes widened as he took in Dymphna's ripped, mud-splattered dress and the blood streaking Daidi's clothes. Dymphna prayed he'd spot the ax against the tree.

"What — are you alright?"

That strange little bell-like noise continued to tinkle on the other side of the trees. *What was that?*

"My daughter got lost in the woods." Anger edged Daidi's voice. "Call your dog off." Without waiting for the outcome, he turned back to Dymphna. "Come, Dymphna." He grabbed her hand.

His was sticky with blood and she jerked back at his touch. He snatched her by the wrist and tears filled her eyes. But at least he was acting normal. And calling her *Dymphna*, not Mamai's name.

Samthann snarled, and Brioc quickly bent down to restrain her. Not that he stood a chance should she decide to attack.

Dymphna tried to make eye contact with Brioc, but it was too dark. She needed to make him understand that Daidi was insane! If he knew what had happened in the barn, he would never hand her over to Daidi like this. But Daidi was the *king*, not exactly the man to be crossed by a peasant. Besides, Brioc had no way of knowing anything of the last hours.

So he moved out of their way, pulling Samthann with him. As Daidi dragged her past him, Dymphna managed to meet his eyes with a desperate look. For a second their eyes locked and Brioc gave her an almost imperceptible nod. He may not understand what was going on, but between all the blood, her torn dress, and the ax — if he had seen it — he surely guessed something was wrong. She felt sure he would follow them from a distance and make sure she got safely to the castle. But that would be as far as Brioc could go. Once Daidi got her into the fortress and bolted the doors, she would be on her own.

As he hauled her through the trees, she almost wished he would snap and do something awful. Something that would *force* Brioc to rescue her. Even from the king.

But nothing happened.

Her only consolation was that Daidi no longer called her Odilla. She was his daughter again.

For the moment.

7

Brioc reluctantly extinguished the flame of his lantern, ignored the violent pounding of his heart, and followed from a distance as the king escorted Princess Dymphna back to the castle. He remained in the shadows, motioning for Sam to stay quiet. Thankfully she settled down and obeyed once Daemon was no longer so near. Her reaction had been unlike anything Brioc had ever seen. Sam never turned vicious. *Ever.* What was it about Daemon?

Queen Odilla had always allowed Brioc to bring Sam inside the castle when he played his harp for her. The kind queen inevitably had a dog treat waiting, a juicy bone or meat scraps from the kitchen. And Princess Dymphna showered the wolfhound with even more attention. Samthann basked in their affection and loved them both. But Sam had never been in the presence of the king. Her reaction to him tonight was not only unexpected, but unprecedented.

As Brioc quietly followed through the eerie woods, he couldn't shake the feeling that something was terribly wrong. His worry for Dymphna temporarily pushed even wolves to the back of his mind. Why were Daemon's clothes smeared with blood? Had that been an ax leaning against that tree? Difficult to tell in the dark, but it certainly looked like one. Had the king killed Guinevere? He must have.

How did Dymphna fit into it? Daemon said she'd been lost in the woods. Maybe she'd been sneaking food to the poor. She'd told Brioc she did that sometimes, which made him nervous. A young girl shouldn't be alone in the woods at night. He had tried more than once to talk her out of it, but she insisted God would protect her. So what had gone wrong tonight? Why did she look petrified?

Too many questions. Too much felt wrong.

Before Brioc knew it, Daemon and Dymphna reached the castle, and vanished behind its ominous wooden doors. He sucked in a breath and nervously watched from the shadows a few more minutes. After the heavy bolt clicked into place, no more sounds came from inside.

Not knowing what else to do, he headed back home to Lynnie, deciding not to tell her about Guinevere. She loved that goat. She'd cry.

Please, dear God, please keep Dymphna safe.

As he groped his way through the darkness, he tried not to think of the pagan altar, of Guinevere's severed head and sacrificed heart. He especially tried not to think of wolves. Even though Sam's protection was more than sufficient, he felt vulnerable and afraid without the flame of the lantern.

He forced his mind to prayer, begging God to keep the princess safe.

His memories flew back to when he'd first met her.

He had been sixteen at the time and she nine. It was a few weeks before he found Sam, abused and starving in the woods. Queen Odilla had brought her customary donation to the monastery, begging the monks' prayers, as usual, for her husband's conversion. This particular day, her face looked haggard and her step weary. She kept dabbing her eyes, and even from a distance Brioc could tell she was crying. She'd come without servants, which was in itself strange. Even more unusual, she'd brought her little daughter. Maybe for some reason she didn't want Dymphna left alone at the castle. While the queen went into the parlor to speak with the prior, the young princess was left outside with an assortment of toys. Queen Odilla stayed in the parlor a long, long time.

Brioc remembered that day clearly. He'd been alone in the rock-strewn vegetable garden, battling weeds. The rocky terrain was not ideal ground. A prickly stem stabbed his palm as he wrestled its root from the ground. He dropped the weed, brushed the dirt from his hands, and lifted his gaze.

A little girl stood across the yard, capturing his attention. Dark brows over big eyes, long hair the color of honey that fell in waves around her pixie face, a serious countenance. Brioc's breath caught. The child was a miniature Queen Odilla, identical in every way. He couldn't help but stare. She had a little wagon with a doll propped inside. Its two spindly arms, made from twigs, stuck straight out to the sides, and a huge silly smile was charcoaled onto the cloth face. The doll wore a dyed green dress, obviously an off-cut from the princess's own exquisite gown. Brioc was staggered by how expensive the material looked. He'd lived his whole life in rags.

Dymphna hummed to herself as she poured imaginary drinks into imaginary cups. Lost in her game, she didn't notice Brioc in the garden. Which was fine with him. He didn't speak back then. He'd lived in silence for six years, somehow losing his power of speech on the day he lost his brother. So he'd gone back to fighting the monks' weeds while Dymphna played with her doll.

Then something dislodged the toy wagon's wheels. Brioc never found out what. Maybe a hare darted past, bumping against it. Or perhaps it rested on uneven, slanted ground in the first place. Whatever the cause, while the princess had her back turned, pretending to pour drinks, her wagon started to roll downhill. It quickly picked up speed, bouncing and jostling along, faster and faster, the doll escaping with it.

Right towards the edge of the cliff that he and Turlough had skirted all those years ago on their way up.

When Dymphna turned and noticed her precious load missing, she looked around in confusion. Spotting the runaway wagon, she leaped up to chase it. It all happened so fast Brioc had no chance to think, let alone move to prevent her.

Thick bushes hid the drop, and travelers who approached by the road instead of the trail wouldn't necessarily realize it. But Brioc knew. He couldn't count the times he'd slipped away when the monks weren't watching, only to stand at the cliff's edge, wondering how it would feel to step off. Sometimes the urge was so overpowering he would dangle one foot over the drop, wanting so much to plunge into the abyss. No one would miss him. Not really. The monks said they cared about him, and maybe they did, but that didn't compare to a family loving you.

So Brioc would stand at the edge and think about jumping. A few times he almost did it for real. But something always stopped him. Sometimes an image popped into his mind of the Blessed Virgin watching from Heaven with a stricken look on her face. Other times he saw Mamai with incredible pain in her eyes. They were only pictures in his mind, but they always came right before he jumped, and suddenly sorrow of making the Blessed Mother and his own mam sad replaced the desire to kill himself. So he would carefully back away from the edge and tell God he was sorry for such sinful desires. He would thank the Virgin Mary for stopping him from committing suicide, then he would go on living another day, unloved and unwanted.

But now he watched in frozen horror, as Queen Odilla's little daughter tore headlong down the hill after the speeding wagon, right towards the same hidden drop. Her arms milled as she tried to keep her balance. She stumbled and would soon slip and fall.

She did.

Now she rolled wildly in the grass towards the precipice.

He snapped out of his stupor and flew after her. She cried out as she tumbled down the hill, her body rolling helplessly over and over, the stones and undergrowth scraping her and ripping her dress.

The out-of-control wagon crashed through the barrier of bushes, its sides noisily grating against the branches. Then it plunged over the cliff into nothingness, an eerie silence following in its wake.

Still rolling helpless, picking up speed, Dymphna neared the bushes, only a few feet behind her ill-fated wagon. If she broke through, she would sail over the abyss in seconds.

Brioc half ran, half skidded down the hill, terrified he wouldn't reach her in time. One little girl had already died because of his cowardice. He would not let it happen again. He was nearly there, when all of a sudden the princess smashed into the bushes and for a split-second they slowed her fall. That's all the time he needed. He scrabbled for the nearest bush, caught a fistful of branches, and slid to a stop, desperately reaching for her with his free hand. He managed to grab her sleeve, mere seconds before she plummeted off the precipice.

The ledge crumbled beneath her, sending loose stones and dirt cascading down. She dangled over the edge. For a heart-stopping moment, neither of them dared breathe. She stared up at him with wide, petrified eyes, probably not even knowing where he'd come from.

Brioc had never prayed so hard in his life. He begged God that her sleeve wouldn't rip off, begged that the flimsy branch he clung to wouldn't snap and send them both to their deaths.

God heard. Both held. The princess managed to grab one of his wrists, and ever so carefully he pulled her upward, scrambling back to solid ground and safety.

Apart from a bruised little face and arm, and a dirty, rumpled dress, the princess seemed fine. And more importantly, she was alive. Brioc hadn't left her to die, like that other girl with the wolves. He had saved her.

A weight lifted inside. *He had saved her.*

Later, after she'd calmed down, he tried to make her a new doll. It was a disaster. He'd never made a doll before. The arms wouldn't stay in place and the top-heavy head hung to one side. But, in the end, Dymphna's tears were replaced by giggles, which soon turned into laughter. Brioc laughed too, and realized it was the first time he'd laughed since coming to the monastery. He still couldn't speak, but Dymphna didn't mind. In fact, she seemed to understand. She grasped his lopsided attempt at a doll against her heart, told him it was perfect, then asked if she could help him weed the garden. They spent the rest of the afternoon together. By the end of the day, they were friends for life.

After that, Dymphna always accompanied her mother when she brought donations to the monks. Over the years their friendship had grown, although there had never been anything even remotely romantic between them.

There was something so good and pure about Dymphna. She talked about God a lot, which at first surprised Brioc. But she didn't do it like other people did, spouting cliches and preachy maxims. No, Dymphna spoke about God like others might talk about their family, or their daily tasks, or the things they enjoyed. God seemed present to her at every second and her love for Him simply radiated. It was hard to explain, but by the time she left that day they'd met, something inside Brioc had changed. Some of the searing pain had gone, and God seemed strangely closer than He ever had before.

Right before she left, Dymphna stunned him by throwing her arms around his neck, giving him a huge, innocent hug, and saying something he would never forget.

"I wish you were my brother."

Brioc never stood at the edge of the cliff again.

If anything happened to Princess Dymphna tonight, there in the castle with the blood-soaked king, Brioc would never forgive himself.

He crossed himself and prayed harder than he had when she'd been dangling from that ledge.

8

Dymphna scooted her stool to the window where the bright morning sunlight streamed into her room and sat down. Arranging the swath of cloth on her lap, she chose a needle from the basket at her feet. She must keep her hands busy. It was the only way to stay calm, to stop dwelling on the terror of three nights ago in the hayloft.

At least she'd managed to avoid Daidi since then. When they returned home, he'd locked himself in his bedchamber on the other side of the fortress. As far as she knew, he was still there. From the fluster and worry among the servants, it seemed he hadn't come out, not even once in three days, and no one knew what to do. Dymphna tried not to imagine what he was doing alone in his room. Slicing his arms with his hunting knife? He did that sometimes. Or maybe he was playing with the dead rats in the jars under his bed. Dymphna shuddered, took a deep breath, and attempted to thread her needle. It took six tries.

Things couldn't go on like this. She needed to talk to Father Gerebran. He'd know what to do. But he was away in another village, visiting his sister, who was the prioress of a convent of nuns. After that, he'd probably stop at one of his many missions. He could be gone for weeks. He'd left his curate, Father Rian, in charge. Father Rian was nice, but young and inexperienced. He hadn't even met Daidi. How could Dymphna begin to explain? Would the new priest even believe such a bizarre story? Something inside told her to wait until Father Gerebran returned. She prayed she could hold out that long.

Should she go to someone else for help? But whom? She could only think of Brioc. But what could he do? Besides, his cottage was a few miles away. That would mean traveling the isolated trail she had been on when Daidi chased her the other night. She'd been sneaking food to the poor, something she could only do under the cover of darkness, now that Mamai was dead.

Memories of the barn crowded in.

She swallowed. If only she knew what to do! Venture out at the risk of Daidi catching her alone again, or stay in the castle with him right downstairs? Both options terrified her.

At least servants lived here. Pagans, yes, but they were better than no one. The presence of other people afforded some measure of protection. Right? Staying here was probably safer than wandering off alone.

She focused on stabbing the needle through the material. Her hands trembled. Was Daidi playing with the rats?

He'd saved over a hundred since Mamai died. Dymphna had once seen them, to her horror. Daidi mummified them, preserving the rodents in some putrid liquid that made her nearly throw up. She tried to block the morbid image. *Dear God, please make Daidi's sickness go away. Please!*

"Enough!"

The enraged voice came out of nowhere. Dymphna's eyes snapped to the door.

Daidi loomed in its frame. At the sight of him in her bedroom, so sudden and unexpected, she dropped her sewing in alarm and leaped to her feet so quickly her stool crashed to the floor.

"I have come," he fumed, "to take him away. This must stop. Do I make myself clear?" His eyes burned with fury.

Dymphna stepped backwards. "Take . . . take who away?" Her gaze flew around the room, fear coursing through her. There was no escape. Other than the door. His body blocked it.

The tangle of hair on the left side of his head lay flat and plastered against his cheek, as if he'd spilled something sticky on the floor then fallen asleep on top of it. Was it the rat liquid? The thought made her stomach lurch.

"You must be punished, daughter. Your treatment of him is insupportable and must stop immediately."

"What are you talking about, Daidi?" She tasted fear in her mouth like bile. He came at her, crossing the room in long strides.

He seized her wrist and she recoiled. "Get him out. Get him before I kill you." His breath reeked of garlic and stale onions. And whatever it was that glued his hair to his face. He smelled like a corpse.

"Please, Daidi. I don't know what you're talking about."

"Get him," he screamed.

He dragged her across the room towards her bed. Dymphna gagged on his foul stench. She pressed her sleeve over her nose and tried to stop her stomach from heaving. She struggled to pull away. Daidi gripped her tighter.

He shoved her hard and she fell to her knees by the bed.

"Take him out!"

Her mind reeled. What was he talking about?

He moved behind her. Goosebumps danced up and down her spine.

He was close. Too close. He was breathing down her neck. *Don't touch me,* she silently begged. *Please don't touch me again.*

"Wh-what do you want me to do?"

He huffed. "What do you think? Pull out the trunk."

The trunk? He must mean the wooden chest under her bed. It contained childhood possessions: old toys, dresses that no longer fit. Why did he want the

36

trunk? *Dear God, what was in the trunk?*

Her hands shook as she fumbled with the rusty latch. After a few clumsy tries she managed to lift the heavy lid.

"Now. Finally." His voice sounded calmer. "Release the piglet."

The piglet?

She sensed him moving and risked a glance over her shoulder. He sank to the floor and curled his knees up to his chest. Dymphna watched, frozen. He began to rock back and forth on the floor.

Back and forth, back and forth.

"Mucmuc," he murmured. He rocked harder.

"Mucmuc!" He rocked harder still, until his back crashed against the wall. Over and over. Smack! Smack! Smack!

She sucked in a breath. "You . . . you want me to get . . . Mucmuc?"

Mucmuc had been Dymphna's favorite childhood toy. The piglet was six inches tall, made of dyed pink cloth and stuffed with sawdust. It had been packed away since she was three years old.

Daidi looked like he was about to cry. "Poor Mucmuc! Poor piglet!"

A tear slid down his cheek. His back pounded against the wall. "You've been grossly neglecting him for years and I am profoundly ashamed of you. He told me last night he is starving. Starving! He needs to be fed!"

Dymphna whipped her gaze back to the trunk and dug frantically through it. Daidi sniffled on the floor. Her fingers brushed something soft buried at the bottom. She jerked the object out. *Please let it be Mucmuc.*

It was.

Stay calm. Act like everything is normal.

"Here, Daidi. Here he is." She stood and held out the piglet at arm's length, not wanting to go closer to him than she had to. He stared straight ahead, not seeming to notice the stuffed animal in her hand. Something about the sight of him, vacant and rocking, ripped Dymphna's heart. Tears stung her eyes.

This was her Daidi, after all. He had once been normal. Memories of piggyback rides and peekaboo games and Daidi 'galloping' around the castle with her on his back when she was a toddler, squealing with delight, made her heart ache. Daidi had never believed in God, which saddened her profoundly, but he once had been a loving father. And he'd doted on Mamai.

And he had been handsome! Mamai once said that when she wed him, Daidi had been her fairytale prince.

What happened? Where did that Daidi go? A tear slipped down Dymphna's cheek.

She watched him rocking on the floor with the rat liquid plastering his hair, eyes empty. Part of her wanted to kneel down and hug him, to somehow force his sickness to go away by the sheer force of her love. But she didn't dare touch him. The terror of the hayloft was too fresh. Daidi was unpredictable.

Jesus, I'm sorry. Forgive my cowardice.

She moved as close to him as she dared. Then something inside her screamed a warning, *Get out of here, before he springs.* She dropped the stuffed toy in his lap and leaped back toward the door.

Daidi stared straight ahead, rocking. The toy pig lay unnoticed in his lap. She wondered if he might eat it later, like he had once eaten a corner of Mamai's blanket.

Fighting the urge to run, she stepped into the hall and hurried in the direction of the kitchen. At least servants would be there. Only pagans were left since Mamai had died, but the presence of anyone right now would feel like protection. If only Brioc still worked here. But Daidi hated Mamai having a minstrel, especially one who played such beautiful music. Brioc had been the first to go.

Dymphna turned the corner in the corridor and stopped dead.

Oh no. Faidh. Her blood froze.

Faidh was the high druid of Oriel, the one who sacrificed to the sun-god Dagda. Apart from Daidi himself, Dymphna feared no one more. Faidh was evil incarnate.

He stood at the end of the hall, conversing with three other men. Two of them Dymphna recognized as Daidi's councilors, although she didn't know their names. The third was Captain Barrfhoinn, in charge of Daidi's army. Thankfully all four had their backs to her. She flattened herself against the wall, relieved that the light was dim.

"It's our only option," Faidh said. "He has lost his grip."

They must be talking about Daidi.

"This is the most ridiculous plan I've ever heard," one of the councilors said. "No one looks exactly the same."

"Then we shall hunt until we find someone," Faidh insisted.

What was going on? Dymphna pushed herself harder against the wall and strained to make out Faidh's next words. His voice was too low. The second councilor whispered and Captain Barrfhoinn shook his head, muttering something in reply. She thought she heard the name Cenél Eóghain, which was a region up north where some of Daidi's troops were stationed.

More snatches of sentences she couldn't catch. It looked like everyone was growing impatient with each other. Then she caught the Faidh's words, loud like an order. "Send out soldiers. Search the kingdom."

Mumbling followed, none of which Dymphna could understand. Finally the four of them dispersed down the corridor, still muttering. Dymphna let out her breath.

She had no idea what was going on, but at least one thing was consoling. It couldn't possibly have anything to do with her.

9

After eleven years in the army, Turlough thought he'd seen everything a soldier could possibly see. Today proved him wrong.

He crossed his arms and leaned against the fence, watching with amusement and curiosity as a dozen or so men from his troop struggled to mount five enormous wooden cages onto the back of ox-drawn wagons. The cages didn't fit and kept sliding off, inevitably onto someone's foot, and by the swearing that followed, they must've weighed a ton. Turlough was glad he hadn't been chosen for that project — whatever the heck it was. It was awfully entertaining to watch but looked like tough work, and he was in no mood to be in the hurricane path of Captain Barrfhoinn's fury. No thank you. He'd been there more times than he cared to recall. It was bliss to have at least one day off.

Across the road, a door slammed in the breeze, followed by a burst of high-pitched giggling. Turlough glanced away from the cages. Another soldier had exited the tavern, females draped all over him. The cut of their attire instantly made Turlough's temperature rise twenty degrees. After a split-second struggle, he looked away. Even if he hadn't recognized Neill's long dark hair and the ragged four-inch scar across his cheek — both impossible to miss — Turlough would have no doubt whom the soldier was. The girls gave it away, every time. And Neill called himself a Christian. He must have a funny definition.

Neill glanced across the road, his gaze connecting with Turlough's, then he extricated himself from his giggling girly gaggle. He wandered over, grinning widely. Wonder why. When he noticed the ridiculous struggle going on with the troop and the cages, his amused grin grew wider.

He reached Turlough and gave him a bone-jarring whack on the back. Then he jerked a thumb towards the cages and asked, "Looking forward to our hunting expedition?"

"Depends. What are we stalking? Bears or wolves?"

"Neither." Neill raised a devilish eyebrow. "Women."

Talk about a seriously one-track mind. Turlough said, "Do you ever think of anything else?"

Neill laughed. "Rarely. What else is there to think of?" Then he cleared his throat. "But we are. Hunting women, I mean."

Turlough frowned and broke his gaze from the struggling soldiers. He stared at Neill. "Huh?"

"Not just any ol' women, mind you. Only the stunners." Neill's grin broadened and he winked. "Never knew we were huntsmen, did you? You thought all along we were just boring old soldiers. Surprise, surprise."

"What on earth," Turlough asked, "are you talking about? Sounds to me like you've been in that tavern too long."

But Neill didn't look drunk. Didn't smell drunk either.

"Don't tell me nobody's told you? Captain Barrfhoinn's sending us on a wife hunt. That's what the cages are for."

Turlough rolled his eyes. "And your grandfather was a leprechaun, right?"

"I'm dead serious. We're capturing girls. If you don't believe me, go ask the Captain. I'm sure he'll tell —" A heavy thud cut him off.

Both their gazes snapped to the cages. Another had slipped off its cart. Turlough cringed as he watched its edge splinter and a cracked piece of wood nearly impale the nearest soldier's thigh. The man let out a howl. With angry shouts, the others dragged at the toppled cage while the soldier clutched his gashed thigh.

Captain Barrfhoinn stood watching the scene, straight and unflinching as a slab of carved oak. He pierced the unlucky victim with those unblinking black eyes of his, which reminded Turlough for all the world of frozen stones. At his frigid glare, the soldier paled with fear, swallowed hard, and limped back to work, blood pouring and all.

Neill said, "Well, what are you waiting for? Go over there and ask him."

Turlough cleared his throat. "I'd rather not."

Rumor had it that Captain Barrfhoinn was spawned by a witch. Turlough had no trouble believing it. The man possessed exceptional ability to strike even the bravest hearts with terror.

"Seriously, Neill. What are the cages for?"

"I already told you. We're going wife hunting."

Turlough turned away from the drama unfolding around the toppled cage and looked at Neill. It was hard not to smile. "So, the Captain's heartthrob finally left him, has she? After all these years. Can't say I blame the poor thing. I'd stay clear of Barrf too, given a choice."

Neill snorted. "Name me one person who wouldn't." He fished around on his belt for his wineskin. Unfastening the top, he took a deep swig, then lowered the skin. "Actually, the little lady isn't for Barrf. Bet she'll wish she was. It's the demon who wants her."

Turlough's amusement vanished. "The king? We're looking for a new wife for Daemon?"

"Not just us. Every soldier in Oriel." Neill let out a loud belch, then swiped a sleeve across his mouth. "And here's the interesting part. His new queen has to be identical to his first. And I mean *identical*."

"But, that's . . . that's insane."

"So is our king. Or haven't you noticed?" Neill moved closer and lowered his voice. "Don't tell me you didn't hear what went on at the fortress after the queen died?"

"Haven't heard a thing."

"Daemon went wild with grief. Completely lost his grip. He refused to let anyone take her corpse away, insisting she was only sleeping. Apparently he forced his daughter to visit her every day and tried to bring her meals and brush her hair and everything."

"Whoa. That's sick. Poor Princess Dymphna."

"It went on like that for about a week. The stench in the castle was unbearable. Finally Daemon's councilors stole the body and buried it."

Turlough looked at him dubiously. "Are you making this up?"

"No." Neill solemnly placed a hand over his heart. Not that it meant anything, Neill being Neill. "I'm telling you, Turlough, this truly happened."

Despite himself, Turlough was fascinated by the morbid story.

Neill went on. "When Daemon couldn't find her body, he thought she'd run away. Then he changed his mind and decided she'd been captured by pirates."

"*Pirates*?"

"Only now she's appearing to him. He claims he saw her in the woods one night, and chased her into a barn, then she vanished again. He thinks she's playing games with him."

This was too wild. "You've got to be making this up, Neill."

"I'm not. Things were getting desperate. So Faidh came up with a plan."

"Faidh? Who's Faidh?"

"You know." Neill waved an impatient hand. "The kingdom's high druid. That creepy fellow who sacrifices to the sun."

"Oh, you mean the skeleton." Faidh's skin had a grayish hue and was stretched so tightly over his face that he reminded Turlough for all the world of a skeleton sporting a blob of thinning hair. His eyes protruded impossibly from his head and always looked empty, like there was no actual person living inside his body — which added greatly to the skeleton effect.

Neill let out a laugh. "That's Faidh alright. The king goes to him for everything. So the mastermind druid managed to convince him to take a new wife, hoping that'll end all the drama over Odilla. Daemon agreed on one condition."

"Which is?"

"He'll only marry someone who looks and acts exactly like she did." Neill gave Turlough a funny look and added, "I can't believe you haven't heard any of this. It's all everyone's talking about. Do you live down a rabbit hole, or what?"

"Let's just say I keep to myself." Turlough looked back at the cages, which were finally mounted on the carts, ready to go. The thought of what would soon be trapped inside appalled him. "So we're meant to *catch* the new queen? Hunt her down like an animal or something?"

Neill took another swig from his wineskin. "Only the Odilla look-a-likes. If we can find any."

Turlough frowned. "You're not going to do it, are you, Neill?"

"Do what?"

"Capture ladies."

Neill smirked. "It's my specialty. Always has been, always will be." When Turlough didn't laugh, Neill said, "Of course I'll do it. Easiest money we'll ever make."

Anger surged through Turlough. "Well, I'm not locking any innocent girl in a cage."

"Oh? Plan to eat next month?"

Ha. As if Neill knew anything about hunger. Turlough said, "I still won't do it."

"Yes you will. Barrf will make you. You'll see." Neill punched his arm. "Lighten up, would you? This whole thing might be fun. Imagine — cartload after cartload of Ireland's most gorgeous lassies. Doesn't sound too penitential to me. Odilla *was* beautiful, after all." Neill jiggled his eyebrows. "You might even find something pretty to keep for yourself. About time you got yourself a sweetheart, Turlough. Would do you a world of good if you ask me."

"Strange, I don't recall asking you."

Neill was one to talk. He might not know about true hunger pangs, but he sure knew about sweethearts. Had dozens of them scattered throughout the kingdom, and not particularly virtuous ones at that. They were no doubt stunning beyond words, every last one of them, but Turlough suspected beauty was the only quality they possessed. Not at all the type he himself would go for.

"I don't need advice about females, Neill. Even if I did, you'd be the last person on the planet I'd consult."

"Oooo, touchy, aren't we? Must've hit a raw nerve there." Neill crammed his empty wineskin back into his belt. "Fine then, stay monkish till the day you drop. Makes no difference to me."

He whacked Turlough on the back a second time and swaggered away.

10

Turlough watched Neill go, suddenly depressed. It wasn't that he didn't want to get married. Of course he did. He was nearly twenty-six, after all, years older than most men who'd taken a wife. It would be wonderful to fall in love and raise a family. Heaven knew how lonely he was. But how often would he even be home for his wife and children? Maybe three times a year, four if he were lucky. Soldiering wasn't the job for a husband and father, at least not a good one, and he refused to condemn some sweet little bride to a miserable life like that.

Besides, he barely made enough to keep himself alive, let alone anyone else. People ate food, and food cost money. Turlough already knew what a second mouth to feed was like.

Did he ever.

The sudden memory of the brother he'd failed thrust a dagger through his heart. He shouldn't be surprised his thought process worked this way. Hardly a day went by that he didn't think of Brioc, and how he'd killed him on that cold, windswept hillside. For that's what he'd done to Brioc — in keeping him alive, he'd slain him. Simple as that. The agony of his mistake still tortured him, even eleven years later.

Turlough tried to halt the dangerous thought process, but it didn't work. It never did. Now that he'd thought of the hillside, his memory latched on to Brioc's face cowering behind the wrinkled old monk. Of course all the other horrible memories followed in its wake.

Turlough had returned to the monastery three times after that day. It turned out to be three times too many.

The first was when he was eighteen and had saved as much of his meager pay as possible. He couldn't leave the army, but planned at least to take his brother home to the family cabin. Brioc was thirteen by then and would be able to find a job, and Turlough had money. Between the two of them, he figured they could eke out a living, however humble, and be together again.

But apparently, as he neared the monastery, Brioc spotted him coming and hid. He was missing deep into the night, by which time the monks were frantic. That's when Turlough learned that Brioc hadn't spoken a word, *not one single word*, since the day Turlough dumped him at the doorstep. Brioc had locked himself up in some inaccessible region of darkness where none could reach him, not even the monks with all their patience and prayers.

Even more chilling, the monks told Turlough that day that Brioc was suicidal. They'd often caught him at the edge of the cliff, ready to jump. Turlough's blood had run cold. When they couldn't find him, everyone thought he'd finally done it. It was the longest day of Turlough's life. When Brioc was finally found cowering in the wine cellar, he refused to come out until Turlough left.

Ten months later, gathering his nerve, Turlough had tried again. Similar story.

His last attempt was a couple years later. It was a catastrophe. That's when the prior gently told him to leave and not come back.

Sickening memories. Just thinking of them made Turlough feel ill.

The only consoling thing that had come from his final visit was that he learned Brioc was speaking again. Apparently he'd run across an abandoned wolfhound pup in the forest, nearly dead. That day Brioc spoke for the first time, timidly asking the kitchen brothers for a few food scraps to bring the starving puppy. He'd named her Samthann. She brought him back from the brink.

Samthann. Just thinking of the smelly beast set Turlough's teeth on edge. He shouldn't hate the dog so much. He knew he shouldn't. But really, he couldn't help himself. He and Brioc rarely crossed paths, but they'd run into each other a few times in the village, and it had taken Sam a whopping five seconds to figure out they were brothers (was it the scent, or what? Turlough knew nothing about dogs). As soon as she realized that, her affection for Turlough bordered on life-threatening. It was one thing to be greeted with an enthusiastic tail wag and a stick dropped at your feet, as a normal dog would do, but another thing altogether to be charged by one-hundred-and-forty-pounds of rock-solid muscle, knocked flat on your back, and asphyxiated by a huge slavering tongue. Turlough had never *actually* had his hands bound behind his back while his face was mopped with a dishrag dripping with doggy drool, but if anyone ever tried to do it to him, he would know exactly how it was going to feel: R-e-v-o-l-t-i-n-g. Not to mention those enormous muddy paws. Turlough always needed a bath after running into Sam.

Those hounds were bred to hunt wolves, not murder people with affection. Maybe Brioc better tell her that.

Yet deep down, Turlough was awfully grateful for the rotten mutt. At least Samthann forced Brioc to talk to him once in awhile, which would never happen otherwise. Their conversations were always limited and usually went something like:

"Get her off me! *Help! I can't breathe!*"

"Down, Sam! Leave him alone!"

End of conversation.

Turlough sighed. They were brothers, once so close, and now their vocabulary to each other consisted of less than fifteen words (not counting the swearwords which Turlough occasionally let slip in the heat of attack.)

The only one who now loved Turlough was a smelly slobbering wolfhound. How bad could it get?

If only he could find a way to apologize. But it was hopeless. Even if he ever managed to corner Brioc and try to explain that fatal day on the hillside, his explanation would sound like a lie after so many years. The thought slashed another dagger through him. He would give anything to have his brother back. *Anything.*

If only Neill hadn't come over and reminded him of his loneliness.

The thought of Neill made Turlough suddenly remember something. He spun in the direction Neill had gone. "Wait!" he yelled. "Neill! Hey, come back here!"

He wanted to kick himself. Neill had been standing right here, hardly a minute ago. How could Turlough have forgotten again?

Across the street, Neill hesitated, then reluctantly turned around. He must've guessed what was coming.

"What about my money?" Turlough called out. "You said you'd have it today."

Neill cupped a hand over his ear, pretending not to catch the words. "What was that?" he called back.

"The money you owe me!"

Neill stood there with this fake look on his face like he didn't understand, then raised his hands helplessly. "I can't hear you!"

"My money! I lent it to you over two months ago."

"Sorry, still can't hear! Tell me later. I'm in a hurry!" He swiftly ducked into the closest building — which turned out to be the tavern again — and conveniently disappeared.

Even if Neill *did* have Turlough's money, he wouldn't have it by nightfall. Not with all those girls waiting in the tavern.

Turlough sighed.

Life in the army just got better every day.

11

Brioc was a child again. He pounded through the woods, gasping for breath, enveloped in black terror. A gray wolf, impossibly big, exploded from the earth in front of him. He screamed and tried to swerve around it. The wolf bared its fangs, and the razor sharp teeth crashed down like prison bars on every side of him. He slid in the mud and stumbled. Fell hard. The fangs disappeared and giant trees uprooted all around him, toppling and blocking his path.

The wolf shrank to normal size and ran after him. A giant claw came out of nowhere and swiped down his back. Pain seared his flesh and he cried out and flung himself into the river. The wolf appeared in front of him now, its fangs ripping the front of his shirt. His chest opened and filled the river with blood. He splashed through the crimson water, blinded from agony. Blood filled his throat and he choked. Keep running! The cliffs streamed with blood like waterfalls.

No one to help. Blackness surrounded him. The woods were so dark.

"If you run away from the monastery, the wolves will eat you."

A stone's throw away, his brother stood in a glow of warm light. Relief coursed through him. He ran towards Turlough, the wolf flying behind him, at his heels. Brioc crashed into the safety of his brother's arms. The wolf exploded into a million pieces and vanished.

Turlough smiled, then said, "They'll eat you."

"I don't care! I'll still run away! I'll run away and find you!"

The cliffs closed in on them and turned into seven towering graves reaching to the sky. He clung to Turlough with all his strength. Blood poured from his wounds, staining the ground. "Don't leave me! You're all I've got left!"

"But I'm sick to death of taking care of you! I don't want you anymore!" Turlough's mouth twisted into a sneer. "I DON'T WANT YOU!" he screamed. Brioc recoiled in shock. His brother grew fangs, still holding Brioc in his arms.

Brioc bolted awake, lungs exploding. Sweat pooled down his back. His soaked shirt clung to him, wet like blood. *Was it blood?* Shivering and groping for his shirt, Brioc fought down irrational fear. The room was pitch dark. *Why was it so dark?* Shaking uncontrollably, he threw out an arm and reached for Lynnie.

His hand hit something hard. Cold. What — *Where was Lynnie?* He sat up, trying to get his bearings in the dark. Heart racing, he explored the cold object beside him with both hands. A sharp sliver stabbed his palm. He winced and jerked his hand away. He touched the thing again, more carefully this time.

Wood. It felt like logs, stacked on top of each other.

He was in the woodshed.

How did he end up here? The terror of the nightmare lingered, making his surroundings feel surreal. Heart still slamming, throat dry, he gulped in breaths of air. Every muscle ached from sleeping on the hard uneven ground. His face hurt from pressing against the kindling. He ran a shaky hand through his hair. It was damp with sweat and flecked with wood chips. How long had he been in the shed?

He staggered to his feet and floundered in the dark for the door. What time was it? Did Lynnie even know he was missing? Had she woken up and watched him sleepwalk from their cottage?

No, she couldn't have. She would have followed him, right? She wouldn't just leave him here to sleep in the wood pile.

Unless she couldn't wake him up. Or had been too afraid, and not known what to do.

The thought of Lynnie seeing him like this stabbed him with horror. Someday she would discover how messed up he was. He couldn't hide this forever — the nightmares, the flashbacks. She would stop loving him. Maybe she would even return to her parents' home in Méifne. The thought of living and dying without Lynnie was unbearable. She was all he had left. She, and in a much lesser way, Sam. Not even his harp mattered anymore.

Lynnie had the right to know he was so unstable. She was his wife, after all. He had to tell her.

No. He couldn't. She would stop loving him.

Agony and guilt churned in his stomach. How long could he keep hiding all this?

He found the cold, splintering wall of the woodshed and followed it with his hands toward the door, careful not to trip on wood chunks scattered on the floor. Why were the episodes triggered so easily lately? Was it because Turlough was hanging around? True, Brioc hadn't spotted him in several weeks now, and usually Daemon's troops were away from the village, but he'd seen big brother more times lately than he had in all the previous years combined. To make things worse, the troops often rode straight through the meadow right in front of his cottage when they went to the castle. Thankfully, Brioc had managed to duck inside every time, and Turlough didn't seem to realize he lived here. But just spotting him in the distance always left Brioc drenched in cold sweat, and, without exception, a flashback would come within days.

Samthann didn't help matters. The traitor. Of all the people in Oriel, she *would* have to fall in love with his brother. Maybe they had the same scent, who knows? Whatever the reason, every time Sam spotted him in the village, she went crazy, jumping and yelping and racing across the road to bowl him over and lick him half to death. A few times, horror of horrors, Brioc was forced to physically go over and haul his giant wolfhound off. Try doing *that* while pretending not to recognize your own brother and struggling to keep your last meal down.

Stop thinking about it. Just get out of the woodshed.

Locating the door, he shoved it open. He blinked in the gentle light. The first hesitant rays from the rising sun crept over the horizon, brushing the meadow with gold and slowing his heartbeat. His gaze fell on the quiet cottage. Peaceful. Lynnie must have slept through his sleepwalking.

He took a deep breath of the fresh morning air to clear his head. That's when a distant rumbling noise reached his ears. Horses. Lots of them. Hoof beats and whinnies and men's voices soon drifted across the meadow.

Daemon's army? At this hour?

Oh no! Was his brother with them?

Without waiting to find out, Brioc scrambled back into the woodshed and hid.

What a coward.

12

There was an art to sleeping on horseback, and a soldier had to learn it awfully fast if he planned to last for any length of time in Daemon's army. It had taken Turlough less than a month to master it, way back when he was fifteen years old. He had realized quickly that if he slept only when the captain allowed them to dismount and set up camp, he would hardly ever close his eyes. The men under Barrfhoinn lived on their horses, so that's where you dozed.

The soldier riding beside him woke him up with a nudge that nearly sent Turlough tumbling from his saddle. "Wake," the speaker informed in half-intelligible grunts. "Now."

Turlough glanced over and up. *Way* up. No wonder the man couldn't create a sentence. It was the cave-dweller.

Well, at least that's what Turlough called him. Behind his massive back, of course. His real name was Gruagh, which meant *giant,* and did his parents ever know a thing or two when they named him. Nearly seven feet tall with muscle hard as steel, Gruagh lacked anything remotely resembling a brain. Turlough was positive he was something left over from prehistoric times. The kind of thing that might eat you if you weren't careful. Knowing Gruagh, he wouldn't even have the sense to spit out the bones.

Veering his horse a safe distance from the giant, Turlough drowsily straightened in his saddle. The first rays of sunlight streaked the horizon. It must be nearly morning. Where were they?

With a sick feeling, he remembered. Of course. Returning home from Daemon's perverted wife hunt. It was finally over. Even Barrf had given up. They were back in Oriel; Turlough recognized the meadow ahead. The one just beyond the king's castle.

He stretched and rubbed the sleep from his eyes, feeling like a wreck. After three grueling weeks of this, the soldiers had collected only six pretty girls. They huddled together in one cage, having hysterics, while the four other cages remained empty.

Queen Odilla, apparently, didn't have many twins. Hardly surprising.

Even the six females they had caught didn't resemble her. At least not to Turlough. But he might be wrong. Face it, most soldiers had never even seen the *king* in person, let alone his wife. Not one man in this troop even had a clue what kind of eyes they were searching for. Of the six lassies in the cage, three had green, two had brown, and the last had bags. But they actually made her look kind of cute, in a sad puppy dog way, so maybe that's what excited Daemon. Everyone knew he was strange.

Neill alone knew what Queen Odilla had looked like. The result, Turlough suspected, of years of assiduous flirting with her serving girls. But Neill, being Neill, had maliciously kept the details of her appearance to himself. The most he'd say was, "Just picture her daughter, only older, and that's exactly how Odilla looked." Fat help that was. Turlough had never seen the princess up close either. He wouldn't recognize Dymphna if she were staring him in the face. Neill told the soldiers he would sell the queen's description for a price. And it wasn't cheap.

The few who were desperate enough to buy it likewise sold the information for a profit. Despite the fact that they only ended up with six sobbing girls behind bars, the whole thing had turned into a sideline business, a fast way to make a cheap dollar on the road.

Money.

Neill.

Wait! That rat still owed him!

He craned his neck around Gruagh's bulking frame and scanned the horsemen in the pale morning light. All one hundred and twenty of them. Great. Where was Neill? Turlough hadn't seen him in days. No doubt Neill was avoiding him. Wonder why.

Aha, over there, among those riders up ahead. Neill's unmistakable long black hair cascaded down his back.

Weaving his way past the cave-dweller, Turlough rode through the rows to catch up with him.

Neill gave a sleepy glance in Turlough's direction, then his eyes snapped open. He straightened and faced forward, jabbing a boot into his horse's side, urging it to a quicker pace. Too late. Turlough wedged his own horse beside Neill's, blocking his path, and grabbed his reins.

"Pay up, Neill."

Neill rolled his eyes and let out a martyr's sigh.

"I mean it. I've had enough. I want my money."

"Alright, alright." Neill fished around in his saddlebag and produced a small pouch. Grudgingly he handed it over.

Turlough looped both sets of reins over his arm and opened the bag. He emptied the coins into his hand.

"What are you doing?" Neill asked.

"What do you think I'm doing? Counting them."

"What, you don't trust me?"

"Guess."

That's when Turlough noticed the strange imprint on the coins. He held one up in the dim light and studied it. He frowned.

"I've never seen money like this in my life. Where's it from?"

Neill shrugged. "No idea. I got it from some foreigner in a tavern a few days back."

Annoyance rippled through Turlough. "Is it even valid currency here?"

"It's twenty coins, isn't it? That's the amount I borrowed and that's the amount I'm paying back. Just how picky are you?"

"I suppose it wouldn't occur to you that I want money I can use?"

"You can use it." Neill shifted uncomfortably in his saddle. "I swear. A fellow bought a drink and the tavern-keeper didn't look twice."

"Ha. He probably didn't look once either."

"It's money, alright?"

"Are you *sure* it's valid?" Frustration edged Turlough's voice.

"Sure I'm sure. I give you my word." Neill solemnly placed a hand over his heart.

Turlough sighed. If he didn't accept these strange coins, he'd likely never get paid at all. "Oh, alright." He was too tired to argue. He re-counted the pieces, just to make sure, then stuffed them back into the pouch and released Neill's reins.

He was about to ride away, when Neill said, "Hey, Turlough?"

"What?"

Neill cracked a grin. "Can I borrow some money?"

Turlough glared at him, then couldn't resist a little smile.

"No."

"Please? Just half of it? Ten measly coins. That's all I ask."

"Nup."

"Five? I'll pay you back next week. I promise."

"I said no."

Neill leaned over and this time *he* tugged on Turlough's reins, pulling their two mounts back together. He lowered his voice and said, "You hid ladies."

Turlough froze.

"Those pretty ones in the last hamlet, you helped them get away before they could be captured. And you did it in nearly every town. Think I didn't notice?"

Turlough's chest tightened. "So?"

"What do you think Barrf will do to you if he learns you're playing the hero?"

They both knew exactly what the captain would do. Run him through with a sword, that's what.

Neill said, "Be a shame if he found out."

Turlough sucked in a breath. "So, blackmail, is it?"

"Of course not." Neill tossed him an innocent smile. "I'd rather call it a loan between friends. And on second thought, make it eight."

Eight coins! Turlough couldn't believe this. "That's weeks of my wages!"

Neill shrugged. "It's not my problem you hid the girls."

Seething, Turlough dug into the pouch and counted out eight coins. As he handed them back over, it took all his restraint not to make Neill's already scarred face even more interesting. For a moment he struggled with the delicious temptation, then jerked his reins and cantered away before he could give in.

All he had left now was twelve measly coins — foreign ones at that — and the possibility of instant death if Neill decided to tell Barrfhoinn anyhow.

Another magnificent day loomed before him.

13

Dymphna rattled through the cupboard in the cooks' quarters with a flickering candle, hastily shoving leftovers from last night's meal into a basket. She'd regained her courage and was determined to sneak food to the poor in the outlying hamlets, like she had done before. But now, instead of doing it at night, she would do it at the earliest morning light, before the servants arrived in the kitchen. Daidi usually stayed locked in his room till well into the day, so the chances of encountering him on the path were slim. She tried not to imagine what he did in his bedchamber.

She was dropping handfuls of nuts into the basket that already contained rolls and carrot stubs, when voices floated through the window from the courtyard beyond the door, startling her.

"Is this all of them? Not one of them is right. *Not one.*"

Dymphna's breath caught. Daidi's voice. He was never up this early! She quickly snuffed out the candle.

"But Sire, these are the best we could find. We searched the kingdom. And beyond." Captain Barrfhoinn this time, an edge of anger to his voice.

"You failed me," Daidi's tone was calm, but fury lurked beneath the words. "*Failed me. Do you understand?* Get your troops back on that road and find her. Find my queen or I'll saw your head off and mount it on the wall."

Find . . . his *queen*? Troops on the road? Dymphna remembered the strange conversation she'd overheard in the corridor several weeks ago. Faidh had said something about soldiers being sent out. What did that have to do with Mamai? She was Daidi's queen. How could they find her? She was dead.

Feeling guilty for eavesdropping, but not *too* guilty, Dymphna tiptoed across the room and pressed her ear against the door. Other noises came from the courtyard too. Horses snorting, men talking in the background.

And . . . what? *Crying?*

She cracked the door open a couple inches. Silent as a meadow mouse, she gazed into the courtyard. The sound of sobbing grew clearer. Not just one individual crying, but several. Dymphna squinted into the rising sun and searched for the source. She could make out the forms of Daidi and Captain Barrfhoinn standing about twenty feet away. A skinny figure joined them. Faidh? It must be. No one else was that skeletal. The three of them stared at something farther back in the courtyard, but the glare of the sun blinded Dymphna, making it hard to tell what they were looking at.

"Sire, at least take them out," the captain urged. "Examine them. You're bound to find one that pleases you."

"I don't want one that *pleases* me; I want one *identical.* I thought I made that clear!"

Faidh's voice took over. "You've hardly seen them, my lord. They'll look better in daylight."

"I don't need to examine them!" Daidi screamed. "I can see through the bars, and none look anything like her!"

Bars? What bars?

"None of them!" He stomped his foot like a child bursting into a tantrum.

Careful to remain hidden in the kitchen shadows, Dymphna risked poking her head farther out. Five other men, near ox-drawn carts, came into her range of vision. Soldiers, obviously. She squinted, trying to see which ones.

The giant was there. He was impossible to miss, towering a head taller than everyone. All Daidi's soldiers frightened Dymphna, but especially him and the captain. In fact, only one soldier didn't make her skin crawl, although she wasn't sure why. Probably because he looked so much like Brioc. Sure, his hair was lighter and he was obviously a bit older, but apart from that, they looked amazingly alike.

But he wasn't in the courtyard. Neither was the soldier who hung around with him, the one with long dark hair and that awful scar across his face. Dymphna knew both were Christians, because she spotted them at Mass whenever the troops were in town. The one that reminded her of Brioc would pray and go to Holy Communion. The other would lean against the back wall of the church the whole time with his arms folded, watching the women and grinning. He often slipped into the castle to flirt with the servant girls.

As Dymphna pressed deeper into the shadows of the doorway, she found herself wishing one of them was in the courtyard. Somehow the presence of a Christian soldier would make her feel safer, even if it was the flirty one. But neither of them were there.

Blinking through the glare of the rising sun, she strained to see the strange structures mounted on top of the ox-drawn carts. They almost looked like — she stared, unable to believe what she was seeing. The carts were mounted with *cages.* All were empty except one. Inside that one were . . .

Impossible.

Dymphna raised a hand and shielded her eyes. There were girls barred up inside! She quickly counted. Six, huddled together in one cage, sobbing.

There was a flurry of movement. Faidh approached the captives, steering Daidi by the arm, taking control of the situation as he always did. Dymphna shrank back deeper into the shadows.

"This one, Your Majesty." Faidh sounded smooth, convincing. "Give her a chance."

"She is a hag." Daidi's voice rose.

"One week, my lord. Try her for one week. If we rearrange her hair and put that royal scarlet gown on her, I'm sure she'll — "

"This — this *thing* — could be my great-grandmother! Look at those bags under her eyes!" Daidi shrieked at the top of his lungs. He pounded his fists against the bars of the cage. Dymphna cringed in the doorway. The ladies cringed in the cage, grabbing each other in terror. Faidh wiped his forehead. Even the group of soldiers threw wary glances at each other and backed away from Daidi, as if seeking escape.

"I want my wife found!" he screamed with rage.

Captain Barrfhoinn — the only one who didn't cower — stood tall and unflinching. Dymphna couldn't see his face, but imagined him rolling his eyes.

Faidh pleaded, "Sire, be reasonable. No one looks exactly like Odilla. You must face facts."

That's when the giant lumbered toward the captain, his wild hair matted and muscles bulging beneath his filthy shirt. "Uh, 'scuse me," he grunted, his deep voice rumbling through the courtyard.

Barrfhoinn glanced at him impatiently and snapped, "What do you want, Gruagh?"

"Whaddabout the prin-cess?" He spoke in monosyllables and had an animal grin on his face.

Dymphna's heart pounded. He was talking about *her*. She swallowed hard.

Barrfhoinn glared at him with disdain. "What about Princess Dymphna?"

The courtyard fell quiet. The captives stopped crying, the soldiers froze; even the oxen seemed to hold their breath. All eyes locked on the giant. His grin broadened, and he puffed out his chest with pride, as if he'd just come up with the first idea of his life.

"She look like queen. Why not king make wife of her?"

14

Paralyzed with horror at the giant's words, Dymphna at first couldn't move. It was as if her legs no longer obeyed her brain. She had to get out of here! *Please, God, please.* Lurching back into the kitchen, she forced her legs to work, stumbling towards the corridor.

Jesus. I have to see Jesus.

She moved faster and faster, picking up speed, till she was running through the hall towards the chapel. But when she burst into the tiny room, she stood aghast. The doors of the tabernacle hung loosely open, empty, devoid of Jesus. The Blessed Sacrament was gone, and had been for weeks.

How had she forgotten? After Mamai's death, Daidi forbade Mass to be said at the castle. Father Gerebran had taken Jesus away! A sob rose in her throat. Where to now?

She frantically looked around the bare room that had for years been her little Heaven on earth. Would Daidi think to search for her here? With Jesus gone, Dymphna visited the larger church in the village these days when she wanted to pray. Maybe Daidi wouldn't look in here.

Besides, this was the opposite side of the castle, as far from the courtyard as Dymphna could get.

Shakily she knelt on the hard floor near the stripped altar. God was here regardless of the empty tabernacle. He was everywhere. He lived in her soul. She whispered the words over and over to herself. *Jesus is with me. He's here, He's here.*

It was in this same spot, a little over a year ago, that Father Gerebran had allowed her to consecrate her virginity to Christ. He had opened the tabernacle door. Kneeling at his feet in front of the Blessed Sacrament, Dymphna had vowed never to marry. As the daughter of a king, entering a convent was out of the question, but she had promised to shun human love and give herself to God as fully as she was able.

Trembling, she clasped her hands together now and squeezed her eyes shut, renewing her vow with all her heart. Surely Jesus would protect her from Daidi's evil designs. He had to! She was His spouse now! She was sure of it.

Gradually her breathing slowed and her heart stopped slamming against her ribs. Sweetness enveloped her as she was pulled deeper into prayer. Her surroundings vanished. She forgot about Daidi, forgot about the soldiers and the cages. She was alone with her Beloved. His presence wrapped around her and her heart radiated with joy, love pulsing through her soul. Everything disappeared except the thought of God.

Something tickled her nose.

She startled and jerked out of prayer. Her eyes flew open. Shapes and shadows and light came into focus. Where was she? Then she saw what was shoved in her face, touching her nose.

A rose.

Her eyes raced to the one who held it. *Daidi!*

She bolted to her feet.

Daidi's hand clamped around her arm. She struggled and he gripped her tighter. *Don't touch me,* she silently begged. *Please don't touch me.*

He laughed. As if reading her thoughts, he stroked her face. "Odilla," he whispered with sick, maudlin affection.

He had combed his hair and donned his most kingly clothes. He'd even shaved off his matted beard, as if in an attempt to look twenty years younger. Strong perfume mingled with the odor of his sweat, making her nearly gag. She pulled back, frantic, as his fingers caressed her cheeks.

"Daidi, please don't —"

He cut her words off, cupping her chin painfully in his hand. Lifting her face, he gazed into her eyes.

"You have the most beautiful eyes, Odilla. You always have. They are like sapphires, glistening in the moonlight."

Something inside warned her not to move. If she rejected him, it would make it worse. So she stood there rigidly, hot tears stinging her eyes. Daidi took a lock of her hair and twirled it tenderly through his fingers. "I love you," he breathed, his voice husky.

Dymphna recoiled, a whimper escaping her. "I'm not Mamai!"

A muscle on his face twitched in fury. His eyes flamed.

"You are Odilla. Do I make myself clear?"

She swallowed, too terrified to move.

His rage drained and he lifted her lock of hair and smelled it. A sigh of pleasure escaped him. "So soft and silky." He clasped it to his lips and kissed it. Then he repeated firmly, "You are my wife."

The first tear trickled down her cheek.

"My little lily on fire," Daidi continued. "That's what you are, Odilla. My flaming white lily." He gently tucked the rose behind her ear, arranging her locks around it. "We were made for each other."

"No!" she cried. "Never!" She tried to push him but he grabbed her other arm too, locking her in his strong grip.

"You're sick! Get away from me, Daidi! Get away!"

He smiled, amused. "You refuse me? You refuse your husband?"

"I'm not your wife!"

"Then become her."

"No!" Dymphna screamed. She wriggled to free her arms. "You're insane! Let go of me!"

Her struggle made him laugh. "Ah, the games lovers play. I know you love me, Odilla. I know you want me. I will make you my queen again. My beautiful golden lily queen." Before she could resist, he clasped her in a sickening embrace.

Jesus, help me!

Adrenaline surged through her. She lifted one knee and shoved it hard into him. *Very hard.* He groaned with pain and his grip went slack. Dymphna staggered backwards. She turned towards the door to run.

He flew after her and grabbed her waist from behind. Tears poured down her cheeks. She kicked backwards and jabbed with her elbows, battling with all her might. He was too strong. She couldn't fight him, she couldn't reason with him. A voice inside whispered, *Change tactics.* Her guardian angel? *Stall for time.*

Her mind spun. She forced herself to stop struggling. Relax. Breathe. *Lead him on.*

"Wait, Daidi. Wait." She gasped for breath. Tried to slow her words. Tried to sound normal, calm. *Don't show fear.* "Let's . . . let's plan this properly."

Please God, please, please.

It worked. Daidi froze, obviously startled by her sudden change in attitude. He loosened his grip and Dymphna turned to face him.

Sweat trickled down her back. She shakily brushed a strand of hair from her damp cheek and forced a smile. Her heart banged against her ribs. *Act calm. Act happy.*

"I love you too, Daidi."

It wasn't a lie. He was her father, the one who'd given her life. To not love and honor him in the way God intended would be a mortal sin. But to love him *that* way? She would rather die!

"You — you do love me?" His eyes grew wide with delight.

She swallowed and nodded.

"Then . . . you'll marry me? You'll be Odilla?"

His brain was sick. Keep stalling . . .

"I — I need time. This is too big, too sudden, becoming Mamai just like that. I need time to . . . prepare." She wiped her sweaty palms on her skirt, her heart hammering.

"I need to make a wedding dress. I can't just wear any old thing." She batted her eyelids, imitating the serving girls she'd seen flirting with the soldiers.

His face melted with affection. "You'll do that for me, sweetpea? You'll sew yourself a new dress?"

She nodded and swallowed hard. "But it's going to take awhile. To make it pretty and appealing."

A smile spread across his pasty face and he clasped his hands together. "Of course, darling. How much time?"

Dymphna's mind raced. If she escaped — tonight — how many days would it take her to get far enough away? It couldn't be too many, or he'd get suspicious. Where would she even go?

Father Gerebran. Get to his cottage.

She threw out a number. "Fifty days."

Daidi frowned. Rage lurked behind his eyes. "Too long."

"Forty?" she fumbled. "I — I can make a beautiful dress in forty days."

Daidi rubbed his stubbly chin where his beard had been, considering. She held her breath. The seconds ticked by.

"Alright. That sounds fair. You have forty days to become Odilla."

Five weeks. How far away could she get in five weeks? She'd sneak to Father Gerebran's cottage tonight after dark and —

"Until then, you will be locked in your room."

She froze.

"You may gather your sewing materials, and anything else you may need."

Before she could react, Daidi strode to the door and stuck his head into the hallway. "Barrfhoinn!" he bellowed at the top of his lungs.

Footsteps instantly sounded in the corridor.

"Escort my daughter to her room, and find soldiers to guard her door. Immediately."

At the realization of what she'd done, a wave of dizziness overwhelmed her. She reeled to the side and grabbed the wall for support.

She was doomed.

15

Dymphna waited four days to see if the soldiers posted in the hall outside her room would eventually leave. Daidi had assigned two at a time. Only two. But how could she possibly get past them?

The first day she stayed with her ear pressed against the door, listening with a pounding heart. Every time footsteps creaked up the wooden stairs, hope pulsed through her. Maybe whoever was out there would be called away. But it didn't happen. Instead new voices joined the old, followed by several minutes of crude banter and ribald jokes which burned her ears with shame. Then the last set of guards would stomp down the stairs, leaving the fresh pair to watch.

Finally she'd lain down and dropped into an exhausted sleep, full of nightmares.

The second day, she tried to drag the bed against the door, which took nearly an hour because she wanted to do it quietly. She moved it inch by painstaking inch. Then it scraped against the floor, only once, but obviously loud enough to be heard. The door flew open and the guards barged inside. That frightened her so much she didn't dare move anything again.

By that night, she figured out the same six soldiers took turns around the clock. No doubt handpicked by Captain Barrfhoinn. She had no hope of getting past them, nor moving them to compassion. Her only consolation was that none of them would dare touch her. Daidi would kill them if they did.

The third day, someone must have remembered she needed food, because a servant arrived with a platter, piled with meat and pastries. On the side of the tray Daidi had placed a bouquet of roses. Dymphna stared at it with horror, then dumped it out the window. Although her stomach rumbled with hunger pangs, she couldn't get down more than a few bites of food.

Thirty seven days till the wedding, and counting down.

Blessed Virgin Mary, what will I ever do?

On the fourth day, she prayed a war would break out. Nothing big or serious, just an itsy-bitsy battle, enough to force the soldiers outside her door to leave. Of course it didn't happen. Neither did the fire she asked for, nor the earthquake, nor the end of the world.

On day five, she stared at the window frame for three hours, trying to summon her courage. With a sinking feeling, she arrived at the conclusion that the tiny hole was her only hope of escape.

It would be a tight squeeze and a thirty foot drop to the ground. A tall oak with sturdy, outstretched branches stood several feet from the window. If she found a way to reach it, she could potentially climb down. Her brow furrowed in thought. Finally she had an idea.

Knotting three of her shawls and a blanket together, she managed to fashion a rope. Then she tied a loop at one end. It took nearly forty minutes and as many tosses, but eventually she snagged a branch with the loop.

She pulled hard. It held. Her heart leaped. Maybe this would work!

The next phase took nearly an hour.

Tiptoeing back and forth to each side of her heavy bed, she alternated between dragging and pushing it to the window. Once it was close enough, she tied the other end of her shawl-rope to it.

Now came the scary part. She would have to climb out her window and go hand over hand across the rope to the tree, like the little monkey she'd once seen with a traveling circus troupe. It wasn't that far, but one chance was all she'd get. If she lost her grip, or if the shawls ripped apart, she would plunge thirty feet to serious injury. Or death.

Of course, she preferred either option to marrying Daidi.

She waited a few hours till the soldiers changed shift outside her door, for that was when they made the most noise. She whispered a prayer and scrambled out the window. Firmly clutching the shawls, she squeezed her eyes closed and swung towards the tree.

Please Holy Mary . . . let me make it.

Her legs crashed against a thick limb and pain jolted through her knee, making her gasp. She let go of her rope with one hand and grappled for a hold among the leaves. She caught a branch and held on for dear life. For a terrifying moment she dangled in the air, one hand gripping the homemade rope, the other a tree limb. *Could she do this?* Fear squeezed her heart at the thought of letting go of the rope with her other hand. *Don't look down! Don't!*

She must have made more noise than she realized because suddenly she heard her door crash open. A soldier said, "What's going on in — Hey, where'd she go?"

Footsteps. Commotion. Yelling. A soldier's head poked out the window.

"Hey!"

Adrenaline surged through her and she relinquished her hold on the shawl and leaped into the tree. She had to climb down! She'd never climbed a tree in her life! She fumbled her way through leaves and twigs, reaching for anything resembling a branch that she could hold on to. Half climbing, half falling, she bumped and slid her way down. Sharp twigs scratched her, drawing blood. Tears stung her eyes.

Her left ankle got wedged between branches. She was stuck! The soldier's head out her window was joined by his arm, as he contorted and squirmed to get his shoulders through. Fortunately, he was too big. The other guard probably rushed to the stairs. Dymphna twisted her leg one way, then the other, struggling to free her foot. As her ankle slipped free, her shoe fell off and dropped through the branches. She watched in dismay as it plopped its way down in slow motion, limb to limb, until it snagged on a twig several feet below her, where it hung limp and useless. She had no time to retrieve it. Summoning all her strength, she shimmied as far down the trunk as she could, then jumped to the ground.

She landed hard. Pain shot through her, but there was no time to care. She had to run! Shouts came from the castle. She scrambled to her feet and tore into the woods.

At least she had a head start. And she heard nothing behind her, no soldiers in pursuit yet. She ran as fast as she could with only one shoe. Awkwardly she swerved through the trees and splashed across a stream. Five minutes later, she plunged into a thicket of bushes.

Breathless, she squirmed deep into the foliage. Her bare foot cut and bleeding, her dress ripped, she couldn't go on.

She huddled in the bushes. And prayed her heart out.

16

Brioc hadn't planned to come to the graves today, but somehow that's where he and Samthann ended up. Maybe it was because he would give anything to be able to talk to his parents and ask them what to do. Food was running out, he had no job, Guinevere was dead and Lynnie always sick – and now the king threatened to take away their cottage.

What else could possibly go wrong?

He knelt on the grass before the wooden crosses and wondered what Daid would have done. Would he have packed up their family and gone to another town in search of work? Or would he have stuck it out here as a woodcutter and simply trusted in God to provide? How had Brioc's family survived in the first place, with six growing boys, a baby girl, and never enough to eat?

Brioc didn't remember much about those years. He was only eight when they died. All he really remembered of his early childhood was being supremely happy. Poor, yes, but happy and safe and loved. And wanted.

That was a million years ago.

He pushed the thoughts away. Memories were dangerous ground. Like walking unarmed into an enemy camp, just begging to have your throat slit. Normal people were safe with their memories, but he wasn't normal. So better just finish his prayers and get away from these graves. And away from that cabin. *Enemy territory.*

He crossed himself and whispered a *requiem aeternam* for his parents and four brothers. Aislinn didn't need prayers. She'd been a toddler when she died and would have gone straight to Heaven. Brioc tried to picture her — what she had looked like, the color of her downy hair. Turlough had once told him her hair was dark, like his own and Mamai's, but Brioc couldn't remember anything. The memories of his little sister had been sucked down the same black hole with everything else.

He couldn't even remember the funerals. Had he been here when they were buried? Incredible, but he didn't even know. For some reason, it filled him with guilt. Not even remembering the funerals. Just how sick was he?

He drew in a breath and rose from his knees. It was always painful to visit the graves, all seven in a row, but almost worse to know the abandoned family cabin was down that slope, hidden by the trees. Brioc couldn't bear to look at it. For two years he and Turlough had lived there alone, trying to survive. Most days they'd gone hungry. Many nights they froze. Plenty of times Brioc had broken down and cried, especially in those early months after being orphaned. Once he even found Turlough crying in the woodshed, although Turlough never knew he saw.

The wolf and that little girl had done something awful inside Brioc, but even after the killing, he continued to feel safe and loved and wanted, as much as anyone could with those terrifying flashbacks. Back then, he'd never dreamed for a moment that his brother didn't love him. Turlough acted like there was nothing he wouldn't sacrifice for Brioc. Many days Turlough would chop wood for sixteen or seventeen hours, trying to do alone what even Daid had needed three strong sons to help with, until his hands bled and he staggered in so frozen and exhausted he'd practically collapse, then insist he wasn't hungry so that Brioc could devour most of the meager meal he'd managed to buy from selling the logs. Usually it was watery turnip soup flavored with some strange herb, which made Brioc gag, but Turlough forced him to eat it because it was healthy. And no doubt cheap. Bread was a luxury. Cheese a treasure. Still, never an hour passed without Brioc's stomach rumbling.

He had tried, in his own childlike way, to help earn money too. He'd even wandered around the village busking a few times with his little harp, but no one gave him a penny. He was young and obviously useless, so his main role eventually settled to stirring their soup, keeping the cabin tidy, and staying out of trouble. Oh, and trying not to think of wolves, which gave his brother an *awful* lot of problems. With a fiercely loving and loyal heart, Brioc *really* tried.

He'd obviously failed. Turlough deserted him.

Brioc hadn't stepped near the cabin since.

If the waist-high weeds choking its entrance, the door dangling precariously by a solitary hinge, and the matted animal nests peeking between rotten boards were any indications, Turlough never went inside either.

Brioc shook himself, trying to break free from enemy ground. To linger at these graves was asking for trouble. Besides, he needed to get back to Lynnie. She'd looked pale and tired again today; the very least he could do was help with a few chores. When he'd left, the washbasin on the table had been stacked with dirty dishes. It was selfish of him to leave it all to her when she was sick.

Was it normal for someone to be exhausted all the time? Before they were married, Lynnie had all the energy in the world. What if something was wrong with her, *really* wrong, and she was dying? The thought stabbed him with fear. Should he find a doctor? If only his parents were alive, he could ask them. If only he could ask *anyone*. But he couldn't, so he'd better just get home and see what he could do.

Not allowing his gaze to fall on the cabin, he turned the opposite way to leave.

"Sam. Let's go."

The dog didn't hear him. She was asleep on Maedoc's grave.

"Sam, come."

Suddenly her ears perked, but it wasn't because of him. She ignored him completely, focusing instead on something behind him. A twig snapped and dead leaves crunched.

Brioc spun around.

Sam let out a bark of pure joy and bounded to her feet. Before Brioc realized what was happening, she sailed through the air and crashed straight into the person emerging from the trees.

Brioc winced as Sam bowled her unsuspecting victim backwards. Both man and beast tumbled into a clump of bushes and turned into a wild blur of flailing arms and scrambling fur as Sam went wild with bliss.

Oh no. His heart plunged. Sam treated only one person this way. The very person Brioc would rather die than face. He'd heard somewhere that animals had a sixth sense about people. It must be true. Samthann had figured out very quickly that he and Turlough were related. Brioc wished she hadn't. No one else knew he had a brother. Not even Lynnie.

"*Get her off me! Get. Her. Off!*" Turlough yelled from somewhere in the bush. It sounded ominously like he was suffocating. Sam stood on her hind legs now, her backside wriggling frantically as she pawed her way deeper into the foliage. Loose leaves fluttered to the ground. Brioc didn't even want to imagine what her tongue was doing in there.

"Sam! Bad girl! Come back here!"

She was too excited to obey.

"*Sam!*" Brioc feared he would have to go over and haul her off. Again.

To his relief, she squirmed backwards out of the bush. A whole tangle of branches came out with her. She shook herself, barked twice, then raced around in circles, no doubt looking for a stick that Turlough might be willing to throw. Within seconds she found one and loped back to the bush. She waited, tail thumping wildly, stick dangling from her mouth, while Turlough staggered forth in a daze. Brioc held his breath.

Sam deposited the stick at Turlough's feet and barked again.

But Turlough didn't . . . uh . . . look in the mood to play. He wiped her slobber off his face and brushed the dead leaves from his hair. Then he glared at Sam and her stick like he'd love to ram the thing straight down her throat. "That mutt of yours. One of these days I swear I'm going to — " He stopped himself in time and let the sentence hang.

Brioc cringed and tried to console himself with the thought that it could be worse. At least Turlough's shirt wasn't ripped this time. Well, not much. There

66

was a little tear on the sleeve. Maybe Turlough wouldn't notice. Or, even better, maybe the rip had been there before.

"She . . . um, likes you." Brioc swallowed. "You're the only one she does that to."

"Silly me. I never knew I was so privileged." A lone twig dropped from Turlough's hair and snagged on the cuff of his sleeve. He reached to swipe it off and just *had* to notice the rip.

A trickle of sweat ran down Brioc's back. He had an irrational urge to run. Turlough stared at the sleeve in dismay, but thankfully let it go. He tried to wipe Sam's muddy paw prints off his chest.

They didn't come off.

Brioc stood there like a moron, trying to breathe. Apart from literally fleeing, he didn't know how to get away. Served him right for coming to the graves today. He'd seen soldiers in town. He shouldn't have taken the risk when Daemon's troops were around. Too late now. The moment he'd been dreading for eleven years had arrived.

And of all places, outside the old cabin.

17

Ethlynn was up to her elbows in flour. She kneaded the lump of dough, singing the only lullaby she knew at the top of her lungs, swaying and twirling around in a full circle every time she got to the chorus. Well, it wasn't technically a lullaby. It was too jaunty for that. But it was cheerful and would make any baby goo with glee. She couldn't wait till their child was born. She would have to learn more songs before then. Babies loved songs. Everyone knew that. Hmm, maybe Brioc could teach her some more.

She instantly stopped singing and frowned. No, not a good idea. For starters, she still hadn't told Brioc she was pregnant. He had so much on his mind that he hadn't even noticed the tiny round bump on her tummy. Or if he did, he didn't bother mentioning it. Besides, his music was too sad. If his harp always made *her* want to cry, what effect would it have on a little baby? How strange that a minstrel should play nothing but gloomy melodies. Sure, everyone loved a good tear-jerker once in awhile, but *all the time?* And forget about getting Brioc to sing anything. She humphed. Maybe a Requiem Mass.

Her cheerful mood vanished. *What was wrong with him?* She attacked the dough with sudden vengeance, pounding it to a pulp. Every day her husband seemed more depressed, more withdrawn and distant. Half the time she had no idea what he was thinking. Or even where he went. Like today. He'd taken off somewhere with Sam, leaving her alone.

An awful thought hit her. She froze.

What if Brioc was tired of her? What if he regretted marrying her?

While that horrid-beyond-horrid thought churned in her head, someone banged on the door. The sound was so sudden and violent that she jumped and nearly dropped the ball of dough.

"Brioc, are you in there?" someone called. "Help me, please help me!"

It was the voice of a young lady. It sounded frantic. *Who on earth?* No one ever visited their cottage. Brioc was such a loner and Ethlynn herself hadn't had time to make any friends in the few months they'd been married.

A female? A . . . girl? Looking for Brioc? Ethlynn's frown deepened.

"Hold on. I'm coming." She wiped her floury hands on a towel and tossed it on the table. "Just a second." Tucking a loose strand of hair behind her ear, she headed to the door.

When she opened it, she did a double-take. A girl stood there, perhaps a year or two younger than she was. She wore a dress smeared with dirt and ripped at the hem. Tears smudged her face. She gasped for breath.

"Please," she sobbed. "I need Brioc! I need to see him!"

Oh my gosh, whoever she was, was she ever pretty! Even with all that grime all over her. Ethlynn stared.

The girl threw a glance over her shoulder, then looked back at Ethlynn, her eyes wide with terror. Suddenly Ethlynn spotted the dainty shoe grasped in the girl's hand. One shoe only; where was the other? But that one shoe, it was made of the most *beautiful* doe-skin. Only someone extremely rich could —

Her eyes popped and she looked again at the girl's dress. Beneath the dirt the material was exquisite, the type of cloth Ethlynn could only dream about. Leaping leprechauns, this must be Princess Dymphna! Of course Brioc would know her. He'd been her mother's minstrel. Ethlynn's heart did a back flip. The king's own daughter, right here on their lowly doorstep!

As she stared, dumbfounded, the princess burst inside and slammed the door. She frantically struggled to secure the latch to lock them in, but her fingers trembled too badly. "Hide me, please!"

The princess's fear was contagious. Ethlynn whipped past her, snapped the latch in place, then flung herself as a blockade in front of the door. She hadn't a clue what was out there, but she was suddenly terrified nonetheless. If only Brioc were home! He could handle anything. Face Ethlynn with an emergency and she knew she would faint. Especially if blood was involved. *Dear God, anything but blood.*

Then her gaze snapped to the princess's left foot and she gasped. It was bleeding!

"Hide me, please! If my father finds me, he's going to —"

"You're running from . . . *your father*?"

That meant THE KING! Ethlynn's blood pressure shot through the roof.

Princess Dymphna's gaze darted around the room for a place to hide. "He's looking for me. He wants me to marry him and —"

"Marry him?" Ethlynn reeled. "*Marry him?*"

"I'm so frightened. Please help me."

Had Ethlynn heard right? King Daemon wanted to *marry his own daughter?* God have mercy!

"He locked me in my room. I escaped, but his soldiers are looking for me."

Someone banged on the door. Ethlynn leaped out of her skin. The princess flew across the room and flung herself behind the bed. Ethlynn bolted after her. She almost squeezed into the hiding place next to Dymphna, but realized with a dreadful sinking feeling that hiding would never work.

"Open this door!" a man shouted.

Ethlynn frantically dumped an armload of blankets on top of the fugitive, her heart pounding so hard she thought she'd pass out. *Brioc, come home,* she silently begged. *Please. PLEASE.* She tossed an extra blanket on top of the already ridiculous pile. Then, for safe measure, threw a pillow on too.

She saw how stupid it looked.

"I said, open this door!"

She grabbed the pillow off. Put it back on. On, off. On, off. She had no idea what to do!

Brioc, come ho-o-o-o-o-me!

"Lady, I know you're in there. Let me in or I'll be forced to kick your door down."

Through the slamming of her heart, Ethlynn called, "Um, who is it?" She wildly hoped her voice sounded natural. It didn't.

"King's business. I need to search this house."

18

It took all of Brioc's willpower not to flee. *Act like an adult. Running is childish.* If only he could breathe. "I guess you came here to pray," he got out. "I was just leaving. Come on, Sam, let's go."

"No!" Turlough blurted, way too fast.

Now what? Brioc didn't know what to do, so he just stood there, his palms starting to sweat. His stomach coiled into a tight knot and he prayed he wouldn't lose his breakfast.

"I didn't know you were here," Turlough said, as if showing up at his own parents' graves called for an apology. "But I'm glad you are."

"I really have to leave."

Don't throw up, you idiot. Whatever you do, just don't.

"Can't you stay a minute?" Turlough's words rushed out in a pleading tone. "Please?"

Brioc squirmed.

"I mean, you don't —" Turlough had to clear his throat to finish the sentence, "you don't have to go just because I came." What was *he* nervous for?

They stood there, in the world's most awkward silence. Finally Turlough cleared his throat again and knelt at the graves, obviously pretending that being here together was perfectly natural. Which it should have been, but wasn't at all. Brioc didn't know what to do, so he reluctantly returned to his knees as well, kneeling as far from Turlough as he could without being outright rude.

To his shame, he didn't pray this time. No prayer would form. Instead his mind spun. So did his stomach. His hands started tingling. Every alarm bell clanged in his head, screaming at him to get away from here, and fast.

But how could he? Apart from leaping up and running.

Samthann loped around them with the stick in her mouth, hoping one of them would play. When neither did, she gave up and plopped down, this time on top of little Aislinn. She probably chose that spot so she could lie near Turlough. She obviously didn't realize it was a one-sided friendship. Not that Brioc could blame her. There was a time he hadn't either. Ignorance sure was bliss.

After what seemed an appropriate time of fake prayer, Brioc shifted his weight to get up. To his dismay, Turlough swiftly prevented him. He would. He did it by asking a question.

"The writing on the crosses. Was that you?"

As if anyone else would have written on their family's graves.

Brioc was caught half way between kneeling and standing, and didn't know which way to go. So he stayed on one knee. Turlough remained on the ground before the graves, but he sat back on his heels. This was bad. Really bad. Did Turlough seriously think they could have a conversation? Brioc could barely drag enough air into his lungs.

"Yes, I wrote it." It was a miracle his voice didn't crack. One of his hands shook now, so he jammed it under the knee he was kneeling on, trying to hide the trembling. "I thought it might be nice to write their names and the year they died."

It had never occurred to him that his brother might someday ask about it. If he'd known that, he never would have written a thing.

"Is that what it says? Their names and the year? I guessed it was something like that, but I've never been sure."

Bewildered, Brioc tried to understand what he meant. Then he remembered. Of course. Turlough couldn't read. He'd forgotten that fact. Brioc took reading and writing for granted. The monks had taught him.

"How come Mam's grave only has the second half? You left off the first part."

One of Brioc's legs was jerking now. *He had to get away.*

"I only wrote the year because . . ." Shame assailed him and he grappled for words. "I . . . well . . . I never knew her name." Heat crawled up his face. "She was always just *Mamai*. But it would be stupid to write that."

To his surprise, Turlough's eyes misted. "That would not have been stupid, Brioc," he said softly. "It would have been a beautiful thing to write." When Brioc made no reply, Turlough told him, "Her name was Brigid."

Brigid. Brioc thought about it for a minute, tried to imagine people calling her that. For some reason thinking about their mam calmed him a little, and his leg stopped jiggling so violently. A memory zipped through his mind, something he hadn't thought of for years. "There was a prayer. Something about Saint Brigid." He tried to latch onto it, but the memory slipped away.

A sad smile touched Turlough's mouth. "*May Saint Brigid keep you safe beneath her cloak,*" he recited. "Mam said it every night when she blessed us before bed. So you remember her doing that too?"

Brioc didn't want to admit he hadn't, not until now. Without thinking, he asked, "Was that why we had that statue of Saint Brigid on the shelf? Because it was her name?"

"Yes. Daid made it for her."

"He made it? I never knew that."

"It was his wedding gift to Mam. Well, that's what Branduff told me anyhow." Turlough gave him a lopsided grin. "But you know Branduff. He could make things up. So who knows if it's true."

It was strange to hear Turlough talk about their oldest brother. Brioc couldn't remember Branduff much either. He'd been sucked down that black hole with Aislinn. Brioc realized, with a kind of shock, that the very shirt he was wearing had belonged to Branduff. It was one of the few things Turlough had stuffed into their bundle on . . . *that* day. Every time Brioc wore it, he thought of the brother he hardly remembered but knew he'd loved. All he recalled about Branduff was that he was always smiling, always teasing everyone. He used to give Brioc piggyback rides and take him fishing at a little water hole, which made Aedh and Maedoc terribly jealous. But Branduff would cuff them on the side of the head, tell them to stop whining and go help Daid and Raghnall and Turlough with the wood, and take Brioc anyhow.

Brioc hadn't thought of these things in years. He felt an unexpected pang of sadness. What would things be like if Branduff had survived instead of Turlough? Would Branduff have discarded him at the monastery too? He couldn't imagine Branduff doing something like that. Then again, as much as Brioc had loved their oldest brother, he had always loved Turlough more. Turlough was the one he had hero-worshiped. Even now, Brioc struggled to shake off those feelings. Incredible.

"I still think you should write *Mamai*," Turlough said, startling him from his thoughts. Then, just like that, he whipped out a hunting knife and reached it out towards Brioc.

Brioc stared at it, dread gripping him. "You mean now?" He swallowed hard. "You want me to write it . . . *right now*?"

"Sure. Why not?"

He *couldn't*, not with his hands shaking so badly! He would drop the knife, he would make a fool of himself. "I . . . I can't."

"You mean you can't spell it?"

"No, of course I can spell it. It's just that —" Brioc blinked. *The hunting knife.* Another snippet of memory flashed across his mind, then just as quickly vanished. Where had he seen the knife before?

Turlough waited for him to take it.

Something close to panic took hold. Brioc didn't want to remember why he recognized the knife. It had something to do with that day on the hillside. He had to get out of here. *Now.* He groped for an excuse, his face growing hot.

"Listen, I really have to be going." He wiped his sweaty palm on his trouser leg. His other hand, under his knee, had gone completely numb. "I'll write it another day." He jumped up, desperate to get away.

"Another day." Turlough muttered the words under his breath, like he didn't believe them.

Was he angry? Brioc shot him a glance to see. To his surprise, Turlough only looked incredibly sad. Brioc watched him sheath the strangely familiar hunting knife and rise to his feet as well.

Without thinking, Brioc asked, "Was I here when . . ." His chest constricted. ". . . when they were buried?"

He couldn't believe he'd just said that. He couldn't believe he was talking to his brother *at all*, let alone coming out with something like this. But he had to know. The not-knowing was torture.

Turlough stared at him. He opened his mouth as if to say something, then closed it again. By the look on his face, he didn't know how to react to the question. Brioc regretted asking it. Turlough already thought he was an idiot. He'd just made it a hundred times worse.

"You mean, you can't remember?" Turlough's voice came out strangled.

Brioc cringed. "I . . . No." His own fault for asking.

Turlough blew out a breath. His eyes darted from the graves back to Brioc. He ran a hand through his hair.

"Yes," he finally said. "We were together."

Brioc's hand trembled like crazy. He could no longer hide it, so he gave up even trying. Turlough's eyes filled with compassion. Or was it pity? Brioc really, *really* wished he hadn't asked the question. He suddenly felt three inches tall. Now his brother knew how messed up he was. Why hadn't he kept his mouth shut? Not knowing what to say now, he muttered, "I need to get home. My wife is sick."

Turlough seemed as relieved at the change of subject as Brioc was. In fact, his face lit up with surprise. "Brioc, that's . . . that's wonderful! I didn't know! I'm so happy for you."

"You're . . . happy my wife is sick?"

"No! No, that's not what I meant!" Flustered, Turlough tried to correct himself. "I meant, I didn't know you were married. That's . . . that's so amazing! Congratulations!"

So amazing. Amazing that someone could love him?

Hardly was the word out when Turlough must have realized how it sounded. "What I mean is, that's wonderful! It's . . . amazingly wonderful." He cringed at his own words and his face reddened. He struggled to cover it up. "Is she anyone I know?"

"I doubt it. Her family's from Méifne. She's the youngest daughter of a horse dealer over there."

"Méifne. Sounds familiar." Turlough's forehead crinkled in thought. "I think I've been there. In the Kingdom of Mide, right?"

Brioc's heart nearly stopped. *Oh no! Please don't let Turlough know Lynnie's family!* He threw a desperate glance at the path, dying to leave. He wondered how rude it would be to just start walking.

Turlough was waiting for his answer. Who cared where Méifne was; would Turlough just *please* leave him alone? But no, Turlough obviously wouldn't give up. "Does she happen to, uh, have a name?" He grinned mischievously, suddenly looking like Branduff. "Or did her parents run out of ideas by the time they got to her? Gosh, must be a huge family."

Turlough was making fun of him. That's all he was doing.

"Her name is Lynnie," Brioc said quickly. He felt like adding, *May I go now?*

"Hmm, you're right. Guess I don't know her. But I bet she's awfully sweet."

Gosh, Turlough was a master at this — pretending to be genuine. If Brioc didn't know better, he would fall for it. But he didn't dare. Turlough had proved beyond a shadow of doubt that he'd never loved him. Why were they even having this conversation?

Brioc clammed up.

"Lynnie's a lovely name," Turlough said, still trying.

Oh no! Brioc wanted to kick himself. Why had he told Turlough her name was Lynnie? No one called her that except him. He should have said her name was Ethlynn! He felt like he'd spilled out something special, something his brother had no right to know. But it was too late to take it back.

Turlough gently punched his arm. "You deserve someone extra sweet. I mean that, Brioc."

"She is. She's the best wife I have. I mean, know! I mean . . ." Brioc let the jumbled sentence trail off. *This was a disaster.* Couldn't he say anything to his brother without sounding like a total moron? Desperate to get the subject off Lynnie before any *let's-have-supper-together-so-I-can-meet-her* plan was launched, he blurted, "What about you? Are you ever married?"

Good grief. He was butchering everything!

He shoved his wildly trembling hand into his sleeve. Turlough mercifully pretended not to notice. "Nah," he answered, equally ignoring Brioc's last jumbled sentence. "Away from home too much to make something like that work out." He tried to sound casual like it didn't matter, but Brioc suspected he was trying to cover up, like everyone does who's lonely.

Brioc threw a longing glance towards the path. *Leave,* he ordered himself. *Now.* "Listen, I really need to —"

"Brioc?" The fear in Turlough's voice jerked Brioc's gaze back. In the space of a heartbeat, Turlough had turned deathly pale. He was taking a wary step backwards. Brioc frowned. Since when was Turlough ever scared of anything?

"Why — why is your dog looking at me like that?"

Brioc's eyes flew to his huge wolfhound. Sometime during their conversation, Sam had woken up. She was crouched now, deadly fangs bared. She gave a deep, menacing growl. There was no mistaking it, she was preparing to attack. Brioc's heart leaped into his throat.

"What do I do?" Panic edged Turlough's voice.

An icy sensation raced over every inch of Brioc's flesh. He could hardly get the words out. "She's not looking at you."

"*Oh-yes-she-is.*" Turlough was ready to bolt. Brioc couldn't blame him. From where Turlough stood it would appear as if Sam was eyeballing him with every intention of going straight for his throat. But she wasn't looking at Turlough. Something else held her attention. Something out there in the woods beyond.

Sam had turned vicious only once. That night with Daemon. But Daemon wasn't here. And there was only one thing Brioc could think of that would make a dog of her breeding turn savage.

An awful trembling crawled up his body, melting his legs, turning his stomach into a writhing mess and strangling his throat. There had always been wolves around here. He remembered them prowling outside their cabin at night, their stealthy, hungry presence so tangible he'd bolt for the safety of Turlough's bed.

That same raw fear gripped him now. There must be a wolf nearby, so close Sam could smell it.

Or see it.

"She's your dog. Tell me what to do," Turlough begged in an urgent whisper.

"Shh. It's not you." Brioc could barely speak. He was vaguely aware of having grabbed onto his brother's arm, but was so frightened he couldn't let go.

"Brioc, what is it? What's going on?" Turlough sounded confused, and hearing him like that made things a hundred times worse than they already were.

The beast inside. It was coming alive. Without warning, Brioc's vision blurred. Cold water suddenly sprayed his face. He recoiled. *The waterfall . . . it was right in front of him. How could it be here?* Everything inside him screamed, *Run.*

Too late. The wolf appeared, and the little girl. Her pleading eyes seared through him. Within seconds, her screams shredded the roar of the thundering waterfall. She thrashed about, the wolf's fangs buried in her flesh, her small body thrown and pulled into grotesque positions. Sprayed blood splattered Brioc's face, but he couldn't move, couldn't wrench his gaze from the horror.

The girl's screams turned to whimpers. Then then she fell silent. Limp. Blood ran everywhere. The wolf turned towards Brioc. He whipped around — and ran for his life.

Something crashed into him. He fell heavily and rolled onto his back as the deadly weight of the wolf landed on top of him. Teeth sharp as daggers ripped open his arm and chest. Eyes closed, pain pulsing through him, he fought to push down the icy waves of terror turning his body to mush. A ragged sound, barely human, forced its way from his throat.

Blood hammered in his ears, the sound so loud it drowned out the waterfall. He clawed at the wolf with all his strength. He managed one strike before the beast pinned his arms down. He bucked and twisted beneath the creature, fighting and kicking and screaming.

The wolf was too strong, too heavy. It would eat him, it would —

"Brioc, stop! It's alright! There's no wolf!"

Who was speaking? Where was — *Whack!* The stinging slap to his face stunned him. Everything stopped.

The world grew suddenly quiet, the only sound the gentle chirping of a cricket and his own ragged breathing. Where did the wolf go? What happened to the pain?

What was this weight straddling his chest?

"You mean this still happens to you?" The voice sounded horrified, yet compassionate.

Turlough? How'd he get here? Where were they? Something still pinned his arms. His brother? *Oh no! This couldn't be happening!* Brioc waited for the earth to open up and swallow him.

"If I let you go, you're not going to — Are you even back?"

Brioc moaned. He didn't want to answer. Exhaustion prevented him from even giving a nod. But it was only fair to let Turlough know it was over. He cracked his eyelids. Sunlight stabbed his eyes. He squeezed them shut again.

Turlough released his arms and climbed off. Brioc's hands instantly flew to his chest, expecting to find his shirt saturated with blood. The material was dry. He dragged air into his lungs. His head felt heavy. Groggy, like coming out of sleep. So did the rest of him for that matter. His spine slumped closer to the ground. His eyelids weighed a ton, so he kept them closed.

"Well, is he going to get up? Or lay there all day playing dead?"

A new voice entered, laced with scorn.

19

Ethlynn's sole consolation was that the man demanding entry into the cottage said he was here on king's business, which meant he couldn't possibly be the king himself. He must be a soldier, which was unnerving enough, but if it had been Daemon in person, Ethlynn would keel over and die.

She made her way to the door, shaking so badly she had to lean against the frame for a moment before lifting the wooden bar. She undid the latch.

The soldier rudely shoved the door the rest of the way open and barged in. Bald with a shaggy beard, did he ever look mean. The kind of man she'd run from if she met him alone after dark.

She prayed he wouldn't notice she was hyperventilating. Prayed even harder he wouldn't find anything unusual about the jumble of blankets on the floor behind the bed.

Brioc, come home. I need you!

The soldier stood there, sharp eyes roving around the room. He seemed to take in everything.

"C-can I help you?" Ethlynn's heart thudded with fear.

"The king ordered the village searched. Mind if I look around?" There was sarcasm in his voice, as if he needed her permission.

If she was the bold type, she might have pointed out that their cottage wasn't part of the village. It was in the meadow. But getting sassy didn't seem like a good idea. Besides, this muscular man with the mean scowling face and a sword hanging at his side scared her terribly. She didn't dare ask what he was searching for. She already knew. It was buried under a mountain of blankets less than six feet away.

Ethlynn gulped in air. "No, th-that's fine." Her voice came out an octave too high.

The soldier nodded and walked around the cottage. It took about seven seconds. There was only one room and hardly any furniture, so he didn't have much to search. Ethlynn held her breath.

He paused in front of her long winter cloak hanging by the door and frowned. He jerked it aside and looked behind it. It suddenly occurred to Ethlynn that she could have hidden the princess in its heavy folds and she thanked their guardian angels neither of them had thought of it. There wasn't much else for him to go through, so he merely asked, "Anyone else on the property?"

Ethlynn shook her head, not trusting herself to speak.

"Who else lives here?"

"Just my husband." She sounded like a mouse trying to find its vocal chords. What would he do, she wondered, if she fainted at his feet? "But my husband's not home," she added.

Immediately she wished she hadn't. Maybe if the soldier thought Brioc was outside, he would leave.

That's when the soldier's eyes moved to the bed.

Ethlynn's gaze shot to where he was looking. To her horror, she spotted Dymphna's little shoe on the floor. The princess must have dropped it in her haste to hide.

The mean, nasty soldier strode straight over and picked it up, the frown on his face deepening. Ethlynn held her breath while he examined it.

"This yours?"

She didn't want to lie. That would be a sin. Her mind raced. "Um . . . well . . . kind of." The shoe was in her house, after all, and she was sure the princess would give it to her if she asked. In fact, the princess was hearing this whole conversation from behind the bed, and Ethlynn could imagine her wildly nodding her head saying, *I'm giving it to you right now. It's yours, all yours.* So Ethlynn got bold and said, "Yes, it is mine."

The soldier glanced down at Ethlynn's feet, then at the shoe in his hand, and back at her feet. She could see him mentally calculating whether or not it would fit. She was calculating the same thing, and didn't think it would.

"Doe-skin," he said. "Rather fancy for a peasant girl."

She couldn't think of anything to say other than, *Excuse me, I'm about to go into a coma,* so she said nothing.

That's when he asked, "You seen Princess Dymphna anywhere?"

The coma was mere moments away.

"I – I haven't left the house all morning," she managed to squeak out. It wasn't a lie. She indicated her floury apron and the lump of dough on the table. "I've been here m-making bread."

"I thought I heard voices."

Ethlynn gulped. "I was singing."

"I didn't hear singing. I heard talking."

"I, well, I sing terribly off-key."

"Is that so?" He squinted one eye, as if not believing a word of it.

"Yes." She bobbed her head up and down, trying to look convincing. "I do it all the time. I'm practicing lullabies." Visions flooded through her head of the creep marching straight to the nearest neighbor and demanding if her off-key singsong voice carried on the breeze every time she kneaded dough. She prayed they'd say yes.

The seconds dragged as the soldier studied her. Beads of sweat trickled down her back.

Finally he said, "If you see the princess anywhere, report immediately to Captain Barrfhoinn. Do you understand?"

Ethlynn had no idea who Captain Barrfhoinn was, but she nodded anyhow. Her voice had abandoned her.

He kept standing there in a way that her gave her goosebumps. She wished more than anything she hadn't admitted her husband wasn't home.

After an eternity he turned to leave.

But not without saying the most terrifying eight words Ethlynn had ever heard in her life.

"Anyone found hiding the princess will be executed." He smiled at her then. "Just thought you'd like to know that, Miss."

As soon as he was out the door, she slammed it shut and fell breathless against it.

They were as good as dead. Herself, Brioc, Princess Dymphna. They would all be killed!

That horrid soldier had taken the doe-skin shoe.

20

Brioc forced his eyes open, half expecting to see the girl's mangled body lying in a pool of blood beside him. Instead he saw his brother, kneeling on the ground where the little girl should have been. A trickle of blood streaked Turlough's cheek, and Brioc realized he must have scratched him when he thought he was the wolf. Brioc's own face stung where Turlough had slapped him.

Ashamed and confused — still not sure what had happened — Brioc slid his gaze away. Where did the second voice come from? And where was Sam?

He spotted her a few feet away, tense, her fur still bristling. Her fangs bared in warning. She was still guarding them. But not from a wolf. From Captain Barrfhoinn. It must have been him that she'd seen through the trees. She'd reacted the same with King Daemon.

Brioc vaguely wondered why she hadn't attacked Turlough when he slapped him. Had she understood somehow? She was only an animal, but she'd been with Brioc during plenty of flashbacks. He'd even come out of them with Sam licking him or nudging him with her huge body, trying to help. If she wasn't a dog, she'd probably slap him across the face too. It worked, after all.

"Well?" Barrfhoinn scoffed. "Are you going to just lie there?" He didn't seem intimidated by the huge, threatening wolfhound. The man must be crazy. His black-eyed gaze locked on Brioc, glinting with derision.

Turlough got to his feet, then reached out a hand to Brioc. "Come on," he said softly, "get up."

Heat crawled up Brioc's neck to his face, but he had no choice. His shaky legs wouldn't allow him to rise by himself, and the last thing he wanted was to fall back down. Burning with shame, he took Turlough's hand and let him pull him to his feet.

Judging by the way Turlough glared at the captain, he would've preferred a ravenous wolf pack. Samthann acted like the captain *was* a wolf. If Brioc hadn't been so groggy, her deadly fangs and low threatening growl might've unnerved him. After all, there wasn't much difference between Samthann now and a bloodthirsty wolf. But he could never be afraid of Sam.

"Sam, come here," he said, meaning to give a command. But to his embarrassment, his voice came out a wobbly croak. Everything about him felt wobbly. Hot and shivering at the same time, he didn't trust his sick brain not to slam him back to the past again with the screaming girl and the waterfall. Turlough must have realized that, because he reached over and squeezed Brioc's arm. Hard enough to make it hurt and anchor him to the present.

Part of Brioc wanted to jerk away. He didn't want his brother touching him. He didn't want his brother anywhere *near* him. But another part of him was grateful. A second flashback right now would really be the pits.

He forced himself to take slow, deep breaths. When he trusted his voice, he tried again. "Sam. Come." He had no idea what the captain thought of all this, or why the man was even here.

Turlough kept squeezing his arm.

Sam hesitated, obviously torn between her habit of obeying him and some primal instinct to attack the captain. She let out a little whine, as if to say, *But I want to rip this creature's throat out. Please let me.*

"Sam. No."

Reluctantly she returned to Brioc's side, but remained poised to lunge if necessary. Brioc bent down and sank his arms into her thick, warm fur, clasping her around the neck. Not that he'd be able to stop her if she decided to attack, but holding onto her drained some of his own tension.

It wasn't until he was firmly clutching Sam that his brother released his arm. But Turlough stayed close, which made Brioc annoyed and embarrassed and relieved all at the same time.

He concentrated on *annoyed*, rather than the other jumbled feelings. His insides churned with mixed emotions. It was actually a relief when the captain broke the silence.

"Either of you seen the princess?"

It sounded like a threat.

Brioc shook his head. "No."

Turlough said, "No, sir."

Barrfhoinn broke his scornful gaze from Brioc. His black eyes turned to Turlough. They seemed to burn a hole through him. "You lying to me, soldier?"

"No, sir," Turlough said again. Was it Brioc's imagination, or did he sound nervous?

Barrfhoinn glared for the longest time. The hostility between the two soldiers hung in the air, almost tangible. Sam must have sensed it too, because her enormous muscular body tensed. Brioc clasped her tighter. Now that the attention had switched away from him, he felt relief. Granted, a bit of guilt laced it. But relief none the less.

"I've heard rumors about some of the ladies." Barrfhoinn's hole burned deeper and Turlough shifted uneasily. "Up north," the captain continued, "near Cenél Eóghain. Know anything about that?"

A bead of sweat formed on Turlough's brow. The words seemed trapped in his throat. "No, sir."

Something about the way he said it made Brioc sure he was lying. Incredible, after all these years, he could still pick it. He wondered who the ladies were and what his brother had done to them.

On second thought, he didn't want to know.

The captain continued glaring at Turlough, but his next words were thrown at Brioc. "You sure you haven't seen her around, minstrel?"

Brioc couldn't remember what they'd been talking about. It felt like thick syrup had been poured into his brain. The flashback had drained him so much that it took a few seconds to register the question. "Seen who?"

The captain shot him a look as if Brioc were the village buffoon. But, really, who could blame him? Brioc *had* put on the ultimate comedy show, thrashing around on the grass believing he was being eaten by a wolf.

Barrfhoinn rolled his eyes. "Prin-cess Dymph-na," he said, clipping each syllable as if he were speaking to someone without a brain. "She's miss-ing. Dae-mon's look-ing for her."

Turlough's eyes flared. "We already told you, we —" He never got to finish his sentence. The captain grabbed him by the collar and slammed him against a tree.

Sam snarled and lunged, struggling against Brioc's grip. He had an inexplicably delicious urge to let her go. The feeling shocked him. Why should he care what happened to his brother?

But he did care, and that confused him more than anything.

The captain pinned Turlough by his throat against the tree. "You smart-mouthed piece of Christian filth." A glint of steel suddenly flashed in his free hand. "Talk to me like that again and I'll carve your tongue out and make you eat it for breakfast. Understand me, soldier?"

Brioc's grip wavered and he nearly let Sam go.

Turlough said, "Yes, sir," and Barrfhoinn jerked his hand from Turlough's throat, roughly releasing him. Turlough stumbled forward and almost fell, but caught himself in time.

Out of the blue, Barrfhoinn said, "And what have we here? A cemetery?" His attention had shifted to the seven wooden crosses on the ground as if noticing them for the first time. His mouth twisted into a sneer.

Turlough's eyes said, *None of your business.* But out loud he said, "Our family's buried here."

Sam growled again. Just a reminder.

Barrfhoinn ignored her. He must be as insane as Daemon. He narrowed his eyes and glanced from Turlough to Brioc, then back to Turlough. "Your family? You mean you're related?"

Brioc stared at the ground.

Turlough said, "We're brothers."

"Is that so?" The captain's sardonic tone said he didn't believe a word of it. Gosh, he must *really* think Turlough was a liar. Why would anyone invent a sibling? Especially a sibling he didn't want.

"I've never seen you two together."

Brioc didn't dare raise his eyes.

Turlough said softly, "That doesn't make us not brothers." His voice sounded strangely sad.

Brioc tugged Sam closer and concentrated on the ground with all his might. Mamai's grave was the closest, so he focused on its little cross, the one with no name, and tried to block out the captain and his brother, the way he used to detach from reality at the monastery. Seeking that blackness now, on purpose, was insane and sent a bolt of terror shuddering through him. Did he really want darkness to imprison him again? That black pit was deadly, it had been hell, yet at the same time, it had been his only refuge for years. It had been either that or suicide.

He was going mad. What was wrong with him? This shouldn't be happening anymore. He couldn't let himself be sucked back down.

Too late. The edges of his mind slipped dangerously towards darkness. Outside him, far away, the silence deepened.

Horrified, heart racing, Brioc crushed Sam against him, trying to pull himself out, stunned that he was succumbing. *He couldn't!* He had Lynnie to take care of! He couldn't plunge back into that silent abyss. That terrifying *nothingness*.

He became aware of Sam's soft whine. She licked his face. He shook himself, forcing his eyes to focus. His mind instinctively flew to prayer, begging Heaven. God mercifully heard. The blackness slowly dispersed. Mamai's grave re-entered his vision. He noticed that his hand was shaking violently, although he couldn't feel it. It was as if his hand had taken a life of its own. For the millionth time, he crammed it up his sleeve, mortified that the others would see.

A voice reached him, as if through a clearing fog. The captain. He must be talking to Turlough.

"If I find out you're lying to me, about anything, the three of us will be back here with a nice big shovel. You can dig each other's graves, before joining your dear departed."

A flash of memory zipped through Brioc's mind. *Standing in this spot, huge clumps of dirt at his feet. Cheeks wet with tears. His brother standing in a deep, frightening hole, gripping a heavy wooden shovel.*

Terrified of remembering more, Brioc jerked his eyes away from their mam's grave and back to Turlough and the captain. He had to return to the present, fast, before the beast came back.

84

He yanked Sam closer, desperate now. She nuzzled him and licked his cheek, then his hand.

"Do I make myself clear?" Barrfhoinn asked.

Turlough said, "Yes, sir."

Brioc was confused by the question, but the captain was glaring at him, as if expecting an answer, so he managed a nod.

"You," the captain snapped at Turlough, "get out there with the others and hunt for the princess."

"Yes, sir."

The captain threw Brioc one last scornful look, then spun on his heel and stalked away.

Neither moved until he'd disappeared through the trees. Then Turlough audibly let out his breath and Brioc reluctantly released his hold on Sam and straightened. His legs wobbled and he prayed he wouldn't collapse. Heat burned his face. Had Turlough seen him blank out a few minutes ago? Desperate to appear normal, he cleared his throat and said, "Nice man."

"Oh the sunshine he brings. You don't know what you're missing. You ought to join the army."

Whew, he must not have noticed anything.

"But you really let me down, Brioc."

Brioc froze. *What —*

"I was sure you would let Sam go. Why didn't you?" But a smile played behind his eyes, and Brioc realized with relief he was only joking.

"I admit it did cross my mind."

Now Turlough tossed him a wicked grin. "Next time. Do mankind a favor. Let Sam take him out."

And for one magic moment it felt like they were brothers again.

Then Brioc remembered what a fool he'd made of himself with the flashback, and instantly the magic vanished. His stomach re-knotted and he wrapped his arms tightly around himself, shuddering. "I really need to get home." He turned and headed towards the path as quickly as he could without actually running.

Sam didn't come at first. No doubt she was saying good-bye in doggy language, which probably meant scrabbling onto his brother's chest on her hind legs and licking his face all over again. Turlough must've shoved her off because she loped to Brioc's side.

"Brioc, wait!"

His heart plunged.

He turned back around with dread.

Turlough's brow was creased, his eyes now filled with worry, and Brioc realized to his horror that he *had* seen him blank out a few minutes ago. How could he have missed it? Turlough's words spilled out too quickly. "I'm home for a few weeks. So, if there's anything you . . . you need, just let me know. Anything at all." His voice cracked. "Please, Brioc?"

As if Brioc could possibly need anything from him. All he needed was for Turlough to vanish from his life. But he couldn't actually say that, so instead he tried to look casual and said, "Thanks."

"You know where I live, right?"

Brioc didn't know and didn't care.

"It's that shack about a mile north of here, right at the edge of the woods. You can't miss it. It's the one about to topple over. One decent gust of wind and I'll have to move out."

Despite himself, a ghost of a smile tugged at Brioc's mouth. "Sounds just like my place."

A bit of the tension seemed to drain from Turlough's voice. "So if you turn up and find the house blew away, just look for me in the shed down back."

If I turn up. Right. When hell freezes.

"Thanks," Brioc repeated with fake cheerfulness. Then, fast as he could, he spun and hiked away. As soon as he got out of the line of his brother's vision, he broke into a run.

He couldn't imagine anything that could force him to his brother's doorstep.

21

The whole way home, Brioc's insides twisted as if something alive and deadly looped and rolled in his stomach, frantic to get out and kill him. He stopped running when he hit the meadow and slowed to a clumsy walk. His rubbery legs nearly made his knees buckle. How could he let Lynnie see him like this? Both hands were numb, and his cheek still stung where Turlough had slapped him. Was there a bruise? Unlikely; Turlough hadn't hit him that hard. But what if there was and Lynnie asked questions? As he staggered through the broken gate into their tiny yard, his mind spun with all the things he could tell her.

I tripped and fell.

Stupid.

I wasn't watching where I was going and ran into something. That sounded even more lame. Ran into what, a tree? The side of a barn? How does a person bruise his cheek on the side of a barn?

I got in a fight.

No, definitely not that one. Lynnie would be horrified and ask with whom, and why, and it would release a flood of questions that he wouldn't be able to answer.

Besides, they were lies. Every explanation he could come up with was a black and white lie. And he couldn't lie to Lynnie. He simply couldn't bring himself to do that.

Yet nothing in the world could get him to tell her the truth.

See, I watched my family die in agony one by one, then there was this little girl I allowed to be eaten by a wolf, and it tried to eat me too, then my brother who I really really loved told me he hated me and shoved me off on strangers, and this black hole swallowed me up and now I have these . . . spells.

He could picture Lynnie's face with those beautiful green eyes of hers going all big.

So every once in awhile some monster that lives inside me comes alive and hurls me back to then and I lose control of everything and thrash around on the ground, thinking I'm being eaten by a wolf . . . and I'm totally messed up and abnormal, and by the way, what's for supper?

Right. That would go down great. Just what every young bride wants to hear.

Brioc sighed and reached for the door, his hands shaking. All he could do was pray there was no bruise on his face. He pushed the door open with dread.

As it turned out, he didn't have to explain anything to Lynnie.

She wasn't there.

The moment he stepped inside, he sensed something was wrong. It wasn't because Lynnie was nowhere to be seen — that in itself wasn't unusual; she could be drawing water from the well or off at the river washing laundry. What set the alarm bells clanging in his head was the chaotic state of their cottage.

Lynnie's heavy winter cloak had somehow been knocked off its hook and lay limp at his feet just inside the doorway. As his gaze roamed the room, his shock increased. Unshapely lumps of half-kneaded dough were rising, abandoned, on the table. Lynnie's apron had been discarded, not over the chair where she usually tossed it, but dumped on the floor, which was strangely sprinkled with flour. The vase on the shelf had mysteriously toppled, its flowers scattered in a spill of water. Brioc's chest tightened. What happened to his wife?

Then he noticed the mound of blankets on the floor behind their bed. *What on earth?* Sam padded around the room, sniffing everything, as if she, too, sensed something was wrong. She never sniffed like that. She must have discovered a foreign scent. Someone had been here.

Had Lynnie been captured? The mere thought made Brioc stumble to the wall, where he slumped against it for balance, trying to breathe. Blood pounded in his ears. *Dear God, please let Lynnie be safe.* The thing in his stomach coiled tighter.

Suddenly Sam was there, scrabbling onto his shoulders with her front paws, in order to lick him. How did she always know? Brioc gratefully ran his hand through her fur, forcing himself to breathe slowly, deeply. Maybe Lynnie hadn't been *taken* anywhere. After all, who would abduct her, and why? Maybe she simply left of her own accord. But that made even less sense. Why would she dump stuff all over the floor, then walk away?

A horrid thought rushed upon him. She'd returned to her parents! She must have witnessed one of his flashbacks. She realized he was unstable, some freak of nature, so she ran away and —

No. Even if she did leave him, why would she trash their cottage first? And she would've at least taken her cloak, right?

Besides, what about the strange scent Sam had obviously found? Lynnie had been with *someone.*

Brioc's mind reeled. How many terrible things could happen in one day? His gaze darted around the room for a clue, *anything* to explain. That's when he spotted a strange white square, about the size of his palm, sitting in the middle of the bed. What was that? Gently pushing Sam's front paws off his shoulders, he made his way unsteadily across the room. Sam dropped to all fours and followed him. He stared at the object on the bed, bewildered.

It was a piece of dough, pressed flat to make a sort of tablet. Lines had been etched into the soft surface, probably with a knife. With surprise, Brioc realized the shapes made the letters *F.G.*

Who wrote this? It couldn't have been Lynnie; she could read and write no more than his brother could. Who in the village knew letters? The only people around here with an education were the priests. And the monks who'd taught him — but they were miles away, over the hills. Besides, why would a priest or one of the monks come all the way here, mess up their cottage, and take his wife away? It made no sense.

It had to be someone else. Brioc breathed slowly, *in and out, in and out,* desperate to keep his brain from seizing up. *Think. Who could read and write?*

The only other person who came to mind was Queen Odilla. But she was dead.

No, wait a minute! She'd taught her daughter. Dymphna could read. Brioc had seen her countless times in the castle chapel with her mother's greatest treasure, a precious little book of the Gospels. The monks had given it to Queen Odilla as a gift. Brioc had been there when Father Prior presented it to her, his way of thanking her for her generous donations throughout the years. And when the queen died, Dymphna inherited the book.

Hold on. Hadn't Captain Barrfhoinn said Dymphna was missing? Maybe she'd been here with Lynnie. Brioc couldn't imagine why. That would be incredible. The two didn't even know each other. And why would they mess up the house then leave together?

He stared at the letters etched in the square of dough.

F.G.

Initials? Obviously. But of what? A place? A person? It could be anything.

He picked up the square and examined it. A tiny cross was cut above the two letters, signifying something holy. A church?

As soon as the thought crossed his mind, it occurred to him that Father Gerebran's name would make the initials *F.G.* Maybe the princess, or whoever had been here, wanted to tell him to go to the priest. But why hadn't they written Father's whole name? Why keep the message cryptic?

Unless whoever wrote it needed to deter others from figuring it out.

Well, there was only one way to find out.

Brioc tried to collect himself. "Come on, Sam," he said. He somehow made his way to the door. "Let's go see if Father Gerebran is home."

22

Huddled on the floor of the tiny, pitch-black closet, with the hems of vestments dangling in her face, Ethlynn felt Dymphna clutch her arm. "Shh. Listen," the princess whispered. "Someone just entered the church."

Fresh fear coursing through her, Ethlynn clasped Dymphna's arm in return. They were already squashed so closely together they could hardly move. The cramped compartment behind the altar where the priests stored their vestments was barely large enough for one person to squeeze into, let alone two. But it was the only place Father Gerebran could think of to hide them in haste.

"I didn't hear anyone come in," Ethlynn whispered back.

"I'm sure the door squeaked a second ago. And listen. Father's talking to someone."

All Ethlynn could sense was the blood hammering in her head and her heart thumping. She strained her ears and caught muffled voices drifting from somewhere in the church. A whimper formed in her throat and she slapped a hand over her mouth to keep it inside.

"Stay calm," Dymphna breathed. "I bet it's Brioc this time." Her soft, warm hand found Ethlynn's and she squeezed. The gesture was no doubt meant to be reassuring, but Ethlynn felt her tremble. "It has to be Brioc," the princess repeated, as if trying to convince herself. "They're talking too long. Father must be explaining everything."

Not that Father Gerebran actually knew what was going on. They had tried to tell him, when they'd barged into the priory half an hour ago, but they had both been so frantic that all the priest received was a jumbled, incoherent story. He must have gotten the gist of it, though — at least the part about the king wanting to marry Dymphna — because he had hidden them lightning swift.

"What if he's talking to another soldier?" Ethlynn's voice came out strangled. In the last ten minutes, at least five soldiers had barged through the heavy wooden doors of the church. Somehow Father Gerebran had steered them away from the closet.

"Shh," Dymphna said again. "Brioc will come soon. I know him, too. He'll figure out my note. I'm sure he will."

For some reason, jealousy shot through Ethlynn. It was silly, of course, but the thought of this royal princess exchanging cryptic notes with her husband — notes she herself was unable to read — made her burn.

"It's him!" the princess blurted. "I was right. Sam's barking outside."

The princess even recognized her *bark*? And called her *Sam*? Ethlynn thought she and Brioc were the only ones that shortened Samthann's name. Was Princess Dymphna really *that* familiar with her husband and his dog?

She chewed her lip. It was wrong, of course, but suddenly she didn't like the king's daughter. So what if everyone said Princess Dymphna was sweet? Maybe she was, but she was also pretty. *Way* too pretty. No one had the right to be that gorgeous. Especially no one who hung around Brioc. And the only reason the princess's hands were so soft and warm was that she'd never worked a day in her life. Never shoveled horse manure, never kneaded bread, never —

Footsteps, then the door behind which they were hiding flew open. Panicking, Ethlynn pushed further into the hanging vestments, practically ending up in Dymphna's lap.

A wedge of light from the church revealed a tall, middle-aged figure in a priest's robe standing in the threshold, a bundle of clothes in his arms. Ethlynn let out her breath. It was Father Gerebran.

"Quickly, come out. We need to disguise the both of you."

Brioc appeared behind him. Ethlynn shot out the tiny door, pushed past the priest, and sailed straight into Brioc's arms. "They're going to kill us!" she shrieked. "They'll find us here and murder us and —"

Brioc pulled her hard against him, cutting off her sentence. She buried her face in his warm shirt and felt his heart galloping. "Thank God you're alright," he breathed, holding her so tight he nearly crushed her.

Dymphna must have crawled out of the hiding place after her, because she barged into their private space. "I was at your house," she sobbed, her voice on the verge of hysteria, "and the soldier took my shoe and —"

"Shoe?" said Father Gerebran. "What shoe?" His voice remained calm, completely in control. "What has that to do with —"

"My other shoe! It fell off in a tree."

"A tree?" Brioc said, confused. "How did your shoe get in a tree?"

Ethlynn's head shot up from his shoulder and she took over, terrified Dymphna would mess up the story. Who cared about a tree? A tree had nothing to do with this! They were going to be killed and Dymphna was blabbering about a *tree*! "He took it from our house and said he'd kill us, then —"

"Wait. Wait! Who's *he*? Lynnie, slow down. Who was at our house?"

"A soldier!" Dymphna blurted. "And the other one fell off outside my window, and —"

"A soldier fell out your window?" Father Gerebran's bewildered gaze shot back and forth between them. "Was he hurt?"

"No, my shoe."

Brioc's brow creased in a frown. "I thought you just said it was at our house."

"It was!" Ethlynn nearly screamed. "But he took it with him!"

"Lynnie, shh. Keep your voice down. The village is crawling with soldiers."

"They'll find my other one in the tree," Dymphna cut in, her voice rising, "and realize it's a pair. Daidi will find me and make me marry him and —"

"*Marry you?*" Brioc's voice rose. "What the —"

The priest took charge. "Girls, take a deep breath and get a hold of yourselves. You can explain all this later. Right now, we need to get you disguised and out of this church safely, before more soldiers show up." He glanced at Brioc. "These are women's clothes." He indicated the bundle he held. "They're from my sister. But, on second thought, I'm going to run back to the priory and gather men's clothes. I think they'll be safer dressed as boys."

"What are we going to *doooo?*" Ethlynn wailed.

Father said, "Escape. After dark."

At the word *escape*, Ethlynn's blood ran cold. "You mean, we have to leave town?"

"I'm so sorry!" Tears rolled down Dymphna's cheeks. "This is all my fault. I didn't mean to drag you all into this."

"Stop. It's not your fault. Nothing's your fault." Brioc reached over and pulled her lightly against his shoulder, almost absently, as he said to Father, "I have clothes at my place. I can go get them."

Ethlynn's eyes popped. Brioc had *hugged* her? Alright, so it wasn't an actual hug, as in a *hug* hug. It was a simple gesture of comfort, something a brother would do. *But still!* She glared at Dymphna. Unfortunately, Dymphna's eyes were too full of tears to notice Ethlynn's scathing look.

"No," Father was saying. "Stay away from your cottage. As soon as someone figures out the princess was there, your lives will be in danger too."

Outside Samthann howled. Everyone's gaze snapped to the door.

"Someone might recognize Sam," Dymphna gasped. "They'll know we're in here."

The priest's eyebrow shot up and he looked at Brioc. "Is that your dog?"

"Yes."

"Hurry. Bring her inside."

Brioc rushed down the aisle to the door, which gave Ethlynn another chance to glare at the princess. Even with tears streaking her face, a muddied dress, and blood smeared all over her foot, Dymphna was still beautiful. Ethlynn's heart sank. If they had to flee for their lives with another female, couldn't they at least be stuck with one who had warts and straggly hair and crooked teeth? Every other person Ethlynn knew had *some* natural defect. Not the princess. Ethlynn couldn't even spy a tiny lone pimple. Fresh tears stung her eyes. It wasn't fair.

Father held out the armload of clothes. "Here. Go through these dresses while I run to the priory. It should only be necessary to disguise you as boys until we're far enough away. After that, you can wear these. Hopefully something fits."

Dymphna accepted the bundle. Confusion crossed her perfectly unblemished face.

Father smiled. "I know what you're thinking. You're wondering what a priest is doing with a small armory of dresses, right? My sister is the prioress of a convent and every time a postulant takes the habit, she sends me their old clothes." Amusement twinkled in his eyes. "I keep asking her what I'm meant to do with all this female attire, and she keeps insisting I never know when a parishioner will need a new dress. Lo and behold, she was right."

Ethlynn leaned over Dymphna's shoulder to see the clothes, an involuntary twinge of excitement racing through her. A new dress! She hadn't had one in years! The princess knelt down and dumped them on the floor, and Ethlynn dropped down beside her.

Dymphna held up a drab brown scarf. It was the ugliest thing Ethlynn had ever seen. She screwed up her face in disgust, about to comment on its atrociousness, then — *Wait! Maybe Dymphna would choose it!*

As soon as Ethlynn imagined Dymphna wearing the thing, she felt herself sprouting horns. She couldn't help it. She made herself gasp with delight. "What a gorgeous scarf! It would look lovely on you!"

Dymphna looked dubious. "Really? You think so?"

Ethlynn nodded gravely. "Absolutely. It brings out the highlights in your hair."

"It does?"

"Mm-hm." Ethlynn bobbed her head up and down. She threw a quick glance towards the priest to make sure he wasn't noticing any of this. Fortunately, Father was busy with some sack on a pew. Probably more supplies he'd rushed in. Ethlynn snapped her gaze back to Dymphna. "Truly, it will look so pretty on you!"

Dymphna's face lit up. "Well, if you're sure. Unless you want it?"

"No, no, really. You saw it first. I'll find something else."

Ohmygosh, was she sinning? And with the Blessed Sacrament hardly ten feet away! Guilt stabbed her. *Jesus, I'm sorry. I just don't want my husband to notice her!* She tried not to gloat at the thought of what the princess would look like with that horrid rag covering her honey-colored locks.

To rid her mind of the totally uncharitable thought, she fumbled through the pile herself. It was impossible not to ooh and ahh at some of the clothes. That convent obviously drew nobility. Several dresses looked exquisite. Ethlynn's baby bump limited her choices, of course, but with any luck she would find something prettier than Dymphna did.

What in the world was she thinking? The soldiers were going to kill them, and here she was having a fashion contest with the king's daughter! The second she remembered why they were ratting through discarded clothes in the first place, her excitement returned to terror.

Brioc re-entered, Sam trotting up the aisle after him. She had her nose to the floor, sniffing the pews and the kneelers, exploring everything, tail swishing.

Sam spotted the heap of clothes.

Toys!

The dog galloped across the church, wild with excitement, and snatched a laced bodice in her teeth. Before anyone could stop her, she dragged her discovery straight to Father Gerebran's feet, plopped down, and started chewing its straps.

The priest turned five shades of red.

Brioc hurried over. "Sam, no!" He snatched the embarrassing article away and flung it back into the pile.

Ethlynn dived for it before Dymphna had a chance. If she sucked in her stomach, *really* sucked it in, then maybe it would fit.

Father said, "I'm afraid we can't take the dog."

Ethlynn froze. Her eyes flew to Brioc. He froze too.

"She'll slow us down," the priest said. "Besides, it'll be difficult enough finding food for ourselves. I'm sorry. The hound stays behind."

Dymphna's eyes widened. She dropped the dress she'd been holding up for size. "We can't leave Sam!"

Everyone stared at Brioc. Ethlynn held her breath.

After an agonizing silence, Brioc said, "Father's right." His face had paled. One hand slightly shook.

Dymphna bolted to her feet. "No, please," she begged, "we can't just abandon her."

"Do you know anyone who could take her?" Father asked Brioc. His tone was regretful, but matter-of-fact.

The princess looked nearly as dismayed as Brioc did. She glanced back and forth between the two men, as if beseeching Father to retract his decision.

Ethlynn said, "Sam could never live with anyone else. She would die without Brioc!"

What she really meant was her husband would die without his dog.

Brioc hid his trembling hand in his sleeve. For a second it looked like he couldn't breathe. Then he said, "She's just an animal." His voice nearly broke. "A hundred soldiers will be looking for us by now. If we have to leave her, we have to leave her."

Father nodded. "I'm sorry. But we can't take the risk of a pet slowing us down."

Tension and fear hung in the air.

"But who can you give her to?" For some reason, Ethlynn felt like her heart was ripped out.

Father Gerebran offered, "I could ask Father Rian if he knows anyone."

"Sam could never adjust to a new owner," Ethlynn insisted. "Brioc's the only one she loves."

Brioc looked like he struggled with some great interior battle. Finally he said, "I know one person she'd be happy to live with. Whether or not he'll take her is a different story."

Ethlynn frowned. *Sam would be willing to live with someone else? Impossible.* "Who?" she asked.

Brioc didn't answer. He averted his pained gaze and said to Father Gerebran, "I'll be back."

The priest hesitated, then nodded. "Be quick. And for God's sake, be careful."

Brioc trudged to the church door like a man on the way to his own funeral.

Oblivious to her fate, Samthann romped after him.

23

Half dressed, his mind churning, Turlough grabbed a towel and ran it through his wet hair with one hand, foraging through his clothes pile with the other. Where was a clean shirt?

It had taken six trips to the river with a bucket, half an hour stoking the fire, and another forty minutes heating water for a bath, but there had been no way in the world he was going to bed tonight smelling like Samthann. It took even longer soaking in the tub, before he was certain he'd removed every last trace of doggy stench. At last, he felt human again. What a waste of a free afternoon.

Just find a shirt, then maybe he could relax.

But he knew he wouldn't. He was worried sick about his brother.

And disgusted with himself.

He'd blown it. Brioc had been there, *right there*, actually speaking to him — a real conversation with real words — for the first time in eleven years. And Turlough hadn't even made an attempt to apologize. He couldn't find the words. All he'd done was say the wrong things, making Brioc feel stupid and useless.

And that flashback! He couldn't believe Brioc still had those! Not even to mention when he'd blanked out a few minutes later with that frightening, vacant look in his eyes. And the huge gaps in his memory. He seriously couldn't remember the funerals? That alone was . . . . not normal. Way not normal. Brioc was unstable. He desperately needed help.

Guilt ripped through Turlough like the fangs that had once ripped through his brother. This was his fault. Brioc's flashbacks, his memory loss, all the unspeakable damage. Turlough had heard of things like this, of people being so traumatized that half their memory was wiped. Or worse, they lost touch with reality. From what the monks had told him, it sounded like Brioc might have gone that far at the monastery, at least for awhile. Was he still that fragile? The thought filled Turlough with horror. *No, Brioc wasn't that far gone anymore.* Everyone blanked out once in awhile, right? He'd just been drained after the flashback. That was all. It was nothing to worry about, nothing to —

A knock on the door startled him, jerking him from his disturbing thoughts.

He hesitated, then decided to ignore whoever was there. He was only half dressed, and his hair was dripping. Besides, it would be Neill. It was always Neill, and always for the same reason. To bludge money. Turlough wasn't in the mood. He continued digging through his clothes pile, hunting for a shirt that Samthann hadn't yet ruined.

Neill knocked again.

"Go away," Turlough yelled. He forced his thoughts away from his brother. Hey, a miracle! A shirt, fully intact! He pulled it on.

Neill pounded again.

"I said, go away! The answer's no."

He spotted a black smudge on the shirt's sleeve. The exact shape of a paw. Great. With a sigh, he yanked it back off and rummaged for another.

Neill knocked a fourth time. Persistent little beast, wasn't he? Turlough had the sudden urge to march out there and rearrange the elements of his face. He owed Neill a few. Blackmail. It made his blood boil.

Another tap on the door, timid this time, like Neill was finally having second thoughts. Oh, he'd have second thoughts alright by the time Turlough was through with him. He snatched a random shirt from the pile and stormed to the door. He yanked it open, his hand already balled into a fist. "If you don't get lost, you rat, I swear I'll —"

His mind did a back-flip.

Brioc, not Neill, stood at his door. His gaze snapped to Turlough's fist, his eyes opened wide, and he stepped back. "Sorry. I'm leaving."

"No, wait! I thought you were someone else!" For a split second, Turlough debated which was more urgent: climbing into the shirt or dragging his brother inside. He did both simultaneously.

Hardly had he pulled the shirt on, than Sam blasted through the door.

She crashed into him at ninety miles an hour, knocking the air from his lungs. He stumbled backwards, struggling to keep his footing as giant mud-caked paws landed on his shoulders. Standing on her hind legs like this, Samthann was as tall as he was. He tried to block his face with an arm. No use. The attack was full on, a wild battle against her tongue and her scrambling paws.

"Get her off! She's suff —" The dog suddenly dropped down to all fours, noticing there was a whole fascinating room to explore. Squiggling with excitement, she loped off.

" — ocating me." Turlough drew air into his lungs and wiped her sticky drool off his face. He looked at his shirt in dismay. Paw prints were stamped onto both shoulders.

Brioc cringed. "I'm sor—"

SPLASH! Water sprayed everywhere as Sam dived into the tub. The whole basin rocked, then capsized. Both wolfhound and soapy water cascaded to the floor. Sam slid across the room on the slippery suds, her legs splayed in four different directions. She collided with a chair and crashed to a stop. The chair toppled.

Its wooden seat cracked in two.

Tantalizing images of nooses and hunting knives danced in Turlough's mind. This dog was a goner.

Sam clambered to her feet, her sopping gray fur clinging to her sides. Her head twitched and she prepared to — Oh no! He tried to dodge. Too late. Dirty water sprinkled his face and flecked onto his clothes as the giant animal vigorously shook herself dry.

Turlough's temperature spiked.

Brioc looked like he wanted to die. And so he should.

Sam padded to the table, eager to continue exploring. Turlough tried not to glare at her.

"I . . ." Brioc winced. "I . . . . well, had a huge favor to ask you. But, on second thought — " He let the sentence trail off.

Wait. He came to ask for a . . . *favor?*

Turlough's heart leaped. Asking a favor implied trust, right? Brioc was *trusting him?* Suddenly Samthann and her wake of destruction didn't matter anymore.

"Of course, Brioc. Anything I can do, anything at all."

Something out of his range of vision crashed to the floor and shattered into a million pieces. Turlough's gaze flew to the table. It was overturned and laying on its side. Pieces of stoneware and chunks of meat and turnip littered the floor. Sam's tail wagged furiously as she gobbled up his supper.

He watched with sinking heart as the wolfhound cleaned up his stew, then she trotted across the room, leaving a path of gravy paw prints in her wake. Which hardly mattered, because the pool of sudsy bath water was spreading in that direction anyhow. She stretched up on her hind legs to investigate the top shelf of his pantry, dumped over a sack of flour, and partially vanished in a puffy white cloud. She re-emerged, her back half dusted white.

With a painful effort, Turlough ripped his murderous gaze from the wolfhound and turned back to his brother. He tried hard to look casual, like having his home destroyed by a wolfhound on the rampant was commonplace, something that happened every day.

"So, what's the favor? Anything, Brioc, really. Just name it and it's — "

"Sam! Get down from there!" Brioc pushed his way past and hurried across the room.

Dare Turlough look?

Bracing himself, he did.

Brioc was engaged in a titanic battle to lug Samthann off the bed. He finally managed to drag her back onto the gravy-spattered floor. Turlough saw with despair the damp outline of an enormous dog imprinted on his blanket.

"I'm so sorry. I didn't know she was going to jump up there. She's used to sleeping on our bed."

"She sleeps on . . . *your bed*?" Turlough's mind reeled with images of cuddling up to a smelly canine every night. And he'd thought sleeping on a horse was bad. "Uh, can I ask where you put your wife?"

Brioc returned to the door, looking bewildered, like that was the most ridiculous question he'd ever heard. "She sleeps there too. Where else would she sleep?"

Turlough tried hard to keep a straight face. Interesting marriage. Just how big was their bed anyway? Must be a whopper. "So, what's this favor you came to ask?" He was starting to hope it wouldn't take too long. Sam was suddenly quiet — way too quiet — and it took all his willpower not to glance over his shoulder and check what she was doing now.

"I . . ." Brioc floundered. "I don't know how to ask this." His hand started shaking, like it had at the graves.

Turlough's heart clenched with compassion. "Just ask," he reassured. There was a noise across the room and he nearly added, *Hurry!* but stopped himself in time.

Brioc crammed his hand up his sleeve and his eyes flicked over Turlough's shoulder in the direction of Sam. He looked like he was having serious second thoughts. "I shouldn't have come over. I better find someone else."

The words made Turlough panic. He wanted the dog to leave, but not his brother. "No! Please, Brioc. Whatever the favor is, the answer's already yes. I promise."

Brioc sucked in his breath, as if gathering courage. He shifted his gaze back to the floor. It took at least a full minute for him to squeeze the words out. "I need someone to take Sam." He dared to look up and there was begging in his eyes. "Would you take her, Turlough? Please?"

Did he say, *take Sam?*

Take SAM?!

Uh-uh, no way. Absolutely not. Out. Of. The. Question. Give him anything: martyrdom, torture, the rack. *Anything but that dog.*

"Sure," he found himself saying. "No problem. I can babysit her for a few hours." He had no idea how these incredible words could be spilling from his mouth. "I'm not doing anything this evening anyhow. Would you like to pick her up later, or should I drop her off at your place, or what?" If this wasn't proof of brotherly love, nothing was.

Brioc squirmed. Now his other hand shook. He looked so nervous Turlough wondered if his brother might pass out.

"That's not what I meant. I, um, need to find a new home for her."

The earth stopped spinning. The roof caved in. The floor opened up. "A new

99

home?" For some reason Turlough's voice came out sounding high-pitched. He cleared his throat. "You mean . . . *permanently?*"

Brioc shrank in the doorway until he was again a malnourished ten-year-old. The two of them were suddenly back on a cold, windswept hill. "Please take me home, Turlough. *Pleeeease.*"

Only now the words were, "Please take Sam, Turlough. *Pleeeease.*"

Turlough blinked, and Brioc was transformed back to adulthood. He was saying, "There's no one else who would want her."

"Really? That's — " Turlough shook his head, "— that's staggering. I can't begin to imagine why."

A metallic clang made them both jump. They whipped around to see a pot spinning across the floor. Sam chased it as it circled and banged its way noisily towards the bed. Her rump was powdered with flour, making her look like two different dog breeds mixed in one. Gravy tracks and gloopy mud and soapy water criss-crossed the floor. One of Turlough's boots, its lining newly shredded, lay limply in the dirty suds.

He closed his eyes and massaged his forehead. A headache was coming on. Funny, that.

He sighed, opened his eyes, and forced a smile. "Of course I'll take her, Brioc. It'll be a pleasure."

No one, absolutely no one but Brioc could get away with this.

Brioc's eyes first widened with surprise, then filled with such gratitude they practically glowed. "Really? You'll take her?" For a second, he was speechless. Then he got out, "I . . . I don't know how to thank you."

"It's fine. Honestly. Sam and I will get along just . . . great."

"I promise she'll behave." Brioc looked across at her. "You'll be a good girl, won't you, Sam?"

Hearing her name, the stupid hound perked her ears and abandoned the pot, which had come to a standstill. She galloped back to the bed. Turlough watched in despair as she clamped his blanket in her mouth and dragged it off. Her wet outline could still be seen in its folds. She pulled it across the room, straight through the gravy trail, and deposited it at their feet. Then she barked, tail thumping. Either she thought Turlough was finally going to play with her, or she expected him to tuck her into bed. He didn't know which one.

Brioc bent down and patted her. His eyes dampened. "Promise you'll be good for my brother," he said. Then his face twisted with sorrow and he dropped to his knees, pulling Sam tight against him. She licked his cheeks and he let her, then he buried his face in her fur. The way he hugged her, one would think he was never going to see the pest again. The sight should have been ridiculous. Except it wasn't. Somehow it was tragic and Turlough nearly had to look away.

But the thing that wrung his heart even more was what Brioc had just said, probably without realizing it. Brioc had called him '*my brother.*' He felt his own eyes sting. "Hey," he said, trying to sound cheerful, "it's not like this is good-bye forever. You can visit Sam any time you want. You know that, right?"

Brioc ignored him. He kept clinging to Sam like a life-line, too cut up to speak.

Turlough tried again. "She'll always belong to you. Come over anytime. Day, night, whenever. I mean that." In fact, thinking about it, wasn't this an answer to prayer? Alright, so Sam herself would be purgatory, but imagine having Brioc stop by. He might come over once a week. Maybe more. And Turlough could walk the useless beast over to his place once in awhile.

His imagination ran away with him and he pictured himself standing at Brioc's door being introduced to — *what was his wife's name?* He couldn't remember. But no doubt she was sweet and shy. She'd welcome him with a glowing smile and insist he join them for supper. Turlough would hedge and Brioc would say, "Oh, come on, you have to stay!" and the three of them would sit by the hearth for hours chatting and laughing, and he'd have a family again and . . .

Forget it. More likely the girl would say, "Oh, so *you're* the evil big brother!" and slam the door in his face.

Turlough sighed. Dreams never came true. He should know that by now.

Brioc released his hold on Samthann and stood, dusting flour off his clothes. His face was streaked with tears and he brushed them away, which only smeared the flour across his cheeks. "Thanks for taking her, Turlough." He swallowed. "I can't tell you how grateful I am."

"It's nothing. I'm happy to help."

Brioc hesitated, then awkwardly said, "Um." He stared at the floor. Beads of sweat broke out on his forehead. He looked even more nervous than he had a couple minutes ago, which was saying something. Like he thought Turlough might hit him. Or stab him. Or gobble him up. Or all three. Finally he squeezed out the words, "Can I ask you something?"

Turlough's chest tightened and he suddenly couldn't get enough air. *This was it.* Brioc was going to bring up the monastery. He was going to ask why Turlough hated him, and Turlough would fumble to explain and everything would come out all wrong, and the explanation would sound like the biggest lie Brioc had ever heard in his life. Whatever Turlough said would make things worse. Infinitely worse.

He looked at Brioc with a mixture of dread and terror and the deepest despair. How was he ever going to explain? He braced himself and waited for the conversation he had dreaded for over a decade.

24

"What would make a person throw up every day?"

Turlough stared at Brioc, dumbfounded.

"Huh?"

"Lynnie. I'm really worried about her." Everything of Brioc's was twitching now. Both hands, one leg. "She's sick all the time." His voice came out strained.

Turlough blinked, confused. Who was Lynnie, and what did sickness have to do with the monastery? Brioc was about to bring up the monastery, right? Wasn't that what this question was about? He frantically tried to rearrange his thought process. *Who on earth was Lynnie?*

Then he remembered. Brioc had said his wife's name was Lynnie. So . . . wait . . . *this wasn't about the monastery?*

Brioc took a breath. "I think she's dying."

Whoa. That snapped Turlough's brain into action.

"She can hardly keep food down and is always exhausted. It's been going on for months." Brioc's voice cracked. "Is that what . . . I mean, when Raghnall and Aedh got sick — "

"No," Turlough assured him quickly. "They had fevers." Raghnall and Aedh had been the first two to die. "They were burning up, then a strange rash appeared. Besides, it happened fast. Within days, not months."

Brioc's shoulders slumped and his tension visibly drained. Some of the shaking lessened. "Lynnie doesn't have anything like that."

Turlough tried to think. "You say she's throwing up?"

"Well, that part is starting to go away. It went on for, I don't know, two or three months. But she's always pale and tired, like she has to drag herself around all day. And it's really strange; she's gaining weight even though she barely eats."

A new bride, nauseous, tired and gaining weight. Turlough bit his tongue to stop from laughing. He struggled to keep a straight face.

"I really don't think you need to worry about her dying, Brioc." Turlough couldn't stop the smile. "Ever occur to you that your wife might be, uh, pregnant?"

Brioc's eyes widened, as if for some reason this was the last thing in the world he needed to hear.

"Women get sick when they're expecting. It's normal. Don't tell me you didn't know that?"

The second his last sentence was out, Turlough could've kicked himself.

Here he was, making Brioc feel stupid again. Of course his brother had no way of knowing these things. He was raised in a monastery, for heaven's sake. And Brioc had been so young when their mother had carried Aislinn. He wouldn't remember. In fact, it was very possible that Brioc had never encountered a pregnant woman in his life.

"Your wife will be fine, honestly. Mam got sick every time she was expecting. Especially with you. You made her live in the outhouse."

Why'd he just say that?

"I mean — It wasn't just you." *Think of something. Tell a lie, fast.* "Branduff told me I was as bad. I was Mam's hardest pregnancy by far." Their oldest brother had never said anything of the sort, but it kept tumbling out. "You weren't half as difficult. With me, she nearly —" *Just shut up.*

Why couldn't he engage in a normal conversation with his brother? Must he always mess up and lie to fix things? He instantly resolved to go to confession. Not sure what to say without making things worse, he punched Brioc lightly in the shoulder. "Hey, congratulations. You're a daid. That's wonderful."

Brioc didn't seem to be listening. He stood there with a kind of stupor stamped on his face. Obviously an approaching baby was not good news.

Suddenly it struck Turlough why. Of course. It was the same reason he needed to get rid of Sam. It was the same reason everything in life went wrong. Money. Always money.

Or rather, never money.

"Wait. Hold on a minute." On impulse, Turlough crossed the room to where he kept his gear. He noticed with relief that Sam had fallen asleep behind the upturned table. She was cuddled with the blanket she'd dragged off his bed, the color of her fur making her practically invisible behind its wet folds.

He rummaged through his saddlebag, found the money pouch from Neill, and returned to Brioc. He held it out. "It's not much, but maybe it'll help a little."

Brioc came out of his daze. "What is it?"

"Just a few coins. I wish I had more. I'm sorry."

From behind the table came a strange moaning sound. Turlough frowned. *What the* — Then he realized it was only Sam yawning. She shifted position on the floor. It might as well be an earthquake. Good grief. Even asleep she was going to be a pain in the neck.

Brioc shook his head. "I can't take your money."

"Yes you can. It's the least I can do."

That's it. The guilt was killing him. He couldn't live this way any longer. It was now or never. Apologize.

"Brioc, about that day. When I brought you — "

Brioc stiffened.

Turlough lost his nerve. *Tread carefully.* Brioc had been suicidal, after all. For all Turlough knew, he still was. He started again, fumbling for words. "Brioc, please let me explain. I know you believe that I —"

"What a mess! Look at this place!" Neill's sudden voice made Turlough jump. He dropped the pouch of money. Coins spilled out and rolled everywhere.

Neill stepped through the doorway. "What happened, a hurricane pass through your house?" He surveyed the damage with open fascination. "Do you know there's a lake on your floor?"

Turlough glared at him. "Did I invite you in?" He could strangle Neill for showing up. Now of all times. But there were more urgent things to do than break the Fifth Commandment. Like collect these scattering coins.

"This is amazing. Who broke all your furniture?"

Ignoring Neill, Turlough knelt down and swiped up the closest coins before they spun away. He managed to grab ten. The other two rolled into the soapy water and out of sight. That's when he saw a second pair of legs appear behind Neill.

He straightened. It was another soldier. Some beady-eyed brute named Cahir that no one liked.

Turlough stood. Brioc had visibly frozen at the sight of the two soldiers.

"The captain's wondering where you are," Cahir said. "You're supposed to be hunting for the princess."

"Tough. I had something else to do." *Like take a bath,* Turlough thought. *And soon a second one. Thanks a lot, Sam.* "Besides," he added, "I don't even know what the princess looks like."

Neill's eyes traveled past him. "What's that under your table?" He squinted. "Looks like mashed turnip."

"Get out there and help us," Cahir growled. "Just look for some girl in a fancy dress. That's all the rest of us are doing."

"It doesn't take a hundred soldiers to find one missing girl. Get out of my house. Both of you."

"She hasn't been found yet." Cahir stepped forward and got right in Turlough's face. Probably trying to scare him. Sorry. Didn't work. "Someone's hiding her, and Daemon's out for blood."

Turlough laughed. "What? You think she's in here?" He swept a hand around the tiny room. "By all means, drag her out."

Neill broke his gaze from the wreckage and said, "Seriously, Turlough. Barrf's going wild. If he finds you in here doing nothing, you're history."

"As if you care about my skin. You and your blackmail. Get out."

Neill raised his hands in surrender. "You're the one who called it blackmail, not me. In fact, help us find the princess so we can all relax, and I'll pay you back today. I promise." Then, in typical Neill-fashion, he steered the subject from the money he owed and asked, "What's the minstrel doing here?"

Brioc backed towards the door, as if wanting to flee.

Neill raised his eyebrows at Turlough. "Wait, don't tell me. You're taking music lessons." He glanced at the water pooling by their feet and frowned. "Or is it swimming lessons?" He turned to Brioc. "Do you swim?"

Turlough gave him a dagger of a look. "Good-byyye, Neill," he warned. He grabbed Brioc's hand and forced the ten coins into his palm, tossing him a *take-them-or-else* look. Brioc obeyed, probably because he didn't know what else to do with the two soldiers watching.

Neill grinned and thumped Brioc on the back. "And I thought I was the only one who borrowed money from him." He winked, as if the two of them belonged to some secret clan.

Cahir said, "We have orders to kill anyone hiding the princess."

"Good for you. Enjoy. Now this is the last time I'm going to say it. Get out of my house."

Brioc swallowed. "Speaking of that, I was just leaving." Beads of sweat glistened on his brow. He dived for the door.

Cahir clamped a hand on his shoulder and stopped him. "You seen Princess Dymphna anywhere, sonny?"

There was an awful silence as Brioc and Cahir stared at each other.

"I . . . saw her a few days ago."

Neill sighed. "That's what everyone's saying."

"If you run across her, bring her to the fortress. Understand, minstrel?"

Brioc's color drained. He nodded and Cahir released him. He shot a split-second glance in Samthann's direction, something like anguish flickering in his eyes. But he wasted no time escaping. He was out the door and gone before Turlough could even say good-bye.

Neill gave him a funny look. "Why'd you give the minstrel all your money? Do you two know each other?"

"He's my brother," Turlough said without thinking.

Neill's jaw dropped. "The minstrel's your *brother*?"

First Barrf, now Neill. What was this, the theme of the day?

Turlough took both Neill's arms, spun him around, and steered him to the door. "Out."

"Alright, alright, I get the message. But . . . really? Your *brother*?"

"Actually, he's my grandson. Have a great day, Neill." He smiled at Cahir. "Nice seeing you too." He gave Neill a shove out the door.

While he'd been busy removing Neill, Cahir had picked up one of the two stray coins. It must have landed near his feet. He squinted at it with interest.

"Look at this, Neill."

Neill turned back around, his brows knit in a frown. But he wasn't paying attention to Cahir. "Now that you mention it, you do look incredibly alike. His hair is darker, but apart from that, you could be twins."

Turlough said, "The coins are foreign. Can't you tell?" He scowled at Neill. "*Supposedly* it's real money."

Neill laughed. "You're still worried about that? I already told you, the money's real."

Turlough glared at him, then turned to Cahir and held out his hand, palm up. Cahir shrugged, dropped the coin into it, and headed outside.

Neill said, "I hope it was swimming lessons. Looks deep in there. Don't drown."

He turned and walked away. Cahir barked, "Just get out here and look for the princess." Their voices faded — Neill muttering something about how amazing it was that Turlough had a brother, and Cahir grumbling about the princess being lost — until finally they disappeared.

Turlough closed the door and slumped against it. He opened his hand and stared at the coin. He'd given foreign coins to Brioc. Were they real?

He gazed at the floor for the second one. Spying it in a puddle, he sloshed over and swiped it up. He crammed both coins into his saddlebag.

A strange rumbling noise filled the room. Then he remembered, his new roommate.

A paw the size of a sawed-off log stuck out from under a corner of his blanket behind the upturned table. Sam had somehow managed to tuck herself in, and was snoring her stinking head off.

Speaking of stink — Turlough sniffed his shirt — he reeked again of unwashed dog.

Forget Princess Dymphna. The others could find her. What he needed to find was a clean shirt.

25

Getting dressed in a church seemed irreverent to Dymphna, but she knew God would understand. After she and Ethlynn had selected outfits from the pile and stuffed them into a sack to wear later, Father Gerebran brought in men's clothes from the priory. Now he waited outside, while they fumbled in nervous silence with the unfamiliar straps and ties, trying to figure out which direction the trousers were meant to go, and how to fasten their strange floppy shirts. To Dymphna, the whole situation felt surreal.

Beside her, Ethlynn struggled to clasp a belt around her waist. Her hands trembled so badly she couldn't manage.

"Here," Dymphna offered, "let me help." She stepped across the aisle to Ethlynn and grasped one end of the belt. She was about to latch it in place when she noticed Ethlynn's bump. She gasped.

"You're pregnant!"

Ethlynn blinked, startled, and Dymphna realized how rude it was to blurt it out like that, especially to someone she had known hardly an hour.

"Yes," Ethlynn answered in a small voice. Her eyes brimmed with tears. She must've been petrified. Fleeing for her life while carrying an unborn baby would be terrifying. Dymphna felt awful for dragging Ethlynn into this mess.

"I'm so sorry. Please forgive me. I should never have gone to your house."

Ethlynn grabbed her arm, eyes wide with alarm. "Listen! The door!"

Dymphna's heartbeat accelerated. The church door squeaked open and Father Gerebran's voice boomed in the silence. "Of course you may search the church. Do come in."

He all but yelled it, no doubt wanting to warn them. Dymphna dived into the vestment cubby, snatching Ethlynn inside with her. She quietly pulled the closet door shut and they huddled in silence, hardly daring to breathe.

Footsteps echoed in the church. Father said something, but with the door closed, Dymphna couldn't make out the words. Another voice replied. Heavy boots stomped across the floor. Objects scraped as soldiers shifted them. A third muffled voice said something indiscernible.

Dymphna clung to Ethlynn. Ethlynn clung back.

After an eternity, the heavy footfalls clomped back down the aisle towards the church's entrance. The soldiers were leaving. Suddenly Dymphna wanted more than anything for night to fall. She longed to be as far away from here as possible. What was taking Brioc so long?

A horrible thought flashed through her mind. Had he been captured? Killed? *Please Jesus, no!*

The church door closed again as Father Gerebran presumably escorted the soldiers back outside. Ethlynn let out her breath. "I think they're gone," she whispered, still clinging to Dymphna.

Dymphna prayed it wouldn't cross Ethlynn's mind that Brioc was taking too long. "Let's finish getting dressed," she said, forcing her voice to sound natural. She opened the door to let the dim light in, and they tiptoed out.

They fumbled to finish dressing in the ill-fitting boys' clothes then helped each other tie up their long hair. They both crammed on hats. The church door opened one last time, and two unfamiliar priests entered. Dymphna stared, bewildered, as the two strange clerics approached.

Whew. It was only Father Gerebran and Brioc, both in disguise. Father had miraculously aged thirty years — the result, Dymphna realized, of gray ashes sprinkled through his hair. Brioc wore the garb of a young priest, his dark hair cropped shorter than it had been when he'd left with Sam.

Ethlynn audibly let out her breath and rushed forward, straight into his arms. "Who did you give Sam to?" she asked.

Brioc didn't answer. His gaze traveled to her tummy, no doubt to the unborn child she carried. He said nothing, but a kind of tender desperation filled his eyes. Something about his expression made Dymphna wonder if he hadn't known before now that his wife was pregnant. Was that possible?

Father Gerebran picked up the sack that held their chosen dresses and hid it under a pew. "There are too many soldiers searching the area," he said. "We'll wait till night before we sneak out."

Dymphna bit her lip. "Where will we go?"

"I'm not sure. But we need to get out of Oriel. If we can reach another kingdom, we'll appeal to its king for protection." Father rubbed his chin in thought. "I have connections with the monastery in Begerin. I'm leaning towards heading there."

"Where's Begerin?" Dymphna asked, feeling shaky just hearing this.

"Southern Ireland, near the east coast, in the Kingdom of Laigin. I know several of the monks there. They may be able to give us temporary refuge." Father paused, then added, "Although that's a long distance to travel, and it might prove awkward housing young girls at a monastery."

"Maybe we can think of somewhere closer," Brioc suggested.

Ethlynn's eyes lit up. "I know! My parents' house!"

Brioc shook his head. "No. That would put them in danger."

"How? Nobody knows where my family lives. The soldiers will never find us there." Ethlynn searched their faces, hope in her eyes. "It's not as if I have friends here who know where I came from."

Father asked, "Where do your parents live?"

"Méifne."

Dymphna felt a spark of hope. She liked the idea of being safe with a family. "Where's Méifne?"

"The Kingdom of Mide," Brioc told her.

Father said, "Mide is the same direction as Laigin. Only nowhere near as far."

Ethlynn bounced on her toes. "Please? All of my sisters are married. Their husbands can help us." She looked at Brioc with begging in her eyes. "You can get a job there. They love music. And I'm sure my brother Angus will let us stay with him temporarily." Her pleading gaze went back and forth between Brioc and Father Gerebran. "The soldiers would never find us there."

Dymphna realized how much Ethlynn must miss her parents. Probably as much as she herself missed Mamai. She wondered what it would be like to have a big, loving family, and felt a pang of anguish. If only Daidi wasn't sick. If only he was normal and didn't want to . . . marry her.

Father Gerebran pursed his lips, considering. "Mide," he repeated. "Well, it is another kingdom, so Daemon has no power there."

"It's not far," Ethlynn persisted.

Father looked questioningly at Brioc, who said, "It would take us a few days to get there. Two, maybe three."

"And you're certain nobody knows your parents live in Méifne?"

"No, Father. I've never told anyone. Who would I tell?"

The priest rubbed his forehead, some of the gray ash fluttering from his hair. His brows knit with indecision. Dymphna was likewise unsure. This whole thing was awful, and it was her fault.

Father turned to Brioc again. "What do you think?"

"Lynnie's family are good people. They're poor, but I'm sure they'll do what they can to help."

Dymphna tried to think of how she could be useful in Mide. She loved children. Maybe she could help Ethlynn's sisters. "I can find work too," she offered. A plan started forming in her mind, bringing a twinge of excitement. "Maybe I can start a school there. I know how to read and write."

Silence hung in the air as everyone waited for the priest's decision. At last he said, "Alright. It should be safe enough. If things don't work out there, for whatever reason, we can rethink the plan. We'll keep the monastery at Begerin in mind, as a backup."

26

Samthann was amazing. For every mess of hers that Turlough cleaned up, she managed to make two more. Demolishing his house was obviously the ultimate doggy game. As he watched her pad around the room, leaving a wake of destruction, he tried to remind himself that she couldn't possibly be tormenting him on purpose. She was nothing but a dumb animal, with no free will.

Why was that so hard to believe?

By the time he'd mopped up the pond on his floor, fixed the seat of his one and only chair, scooped up the gooey remains of his turnip stew, and laundered his last shirt at the river, he was more than ready for bed. Looking after Samthann was going to be exhausting. Brioc must have incredible reserves of energy.

Finally, just when Turlough felt he couldn't take anymore, Sam had mercy on him and settled beneath the table, where she promptly fell asleep. Relieved, he tiptoed past her and gingerly climbed into bed, trying not to make any noise. He hoped it wouldn't get cold tonight, because he no longer had a blanket. There was no way he was going to wrap himself up in the one she had dragged across the floor earlier. In fact, the blanket was still under the table with her. Looked like she'd staked her claim on it, along with everything else in his house.

He blew out his flickering candle, softly set it on the floor by the bed, and lay down, trying not to think about the fact that Sam's sopping-wet, flea-ridden body had stretched out on this same mattress a few hours ago. He could hear her gentle, even breathing across the room. Good. Hopefully she'd sleep the night. He closed his eyes, trying to relax. He started to drift off.

Wait! He sat bolt upright. He'd forgotten to take her outside before bed. When was the last time she'd . . . done her job? Come to think of it, he hadn't taken her out since Brioc dropped her off hours ago. Great. He cleared his throat. "Sam?" He felt ridiculous even talking to her. "Sam, do you need to go outside?"

Across the room, her huge hulking body shifted slightly on the floor, but she didn't wake.

"Hey, you, dog," he said, louder. "I've got to take you out."

He reluctantly got up and walked over to her. "Hey." He nudged her with his foot. "Get up."

She stretched and let out an enormous yawn. Then her head shot up and her tail slapped the floor. She let out a playful yap and leaped to her feet. Turlough threw his hands out in front of him to fend her off before she had the chance to jump up and lick him. "Don't you dare."

She barked, her whole backside wiggling with her tail.

"Let's go. You need to do your thing." He led the way to the door, opened it, and waited.

Sam stood there, looking up at him with doleful eyes.

"Go on. Go outside."

She didn't budge.

"Go!" He gave her a gentle kick in the rear. "Hurry up. I want to go to bed."

She still didn't move.

Rolling his eyes, he stepped through the door. She immediately followed. Then she ran around the yard in circles, until she found a stick. Within seconds, she deposited it at his feet.

"No. No playing. Just do your job." Turlough picked up the stick and hid it behind his back. "I'll throw it — *once!* — but only after you've done something."

He couldn't believe he was talking to an animal, let alone trying to reason with her.

She trotted around him, attempting to get the stick. He twirled around in a circle, trying to keep it out of her reach, holding it securely behind his back. "No," he blew up. "Bad girl."

His tone seemed to startle her. She stopped in her tracks and her tail drooped. Then she slunk off into the yard away from him, looking forlorn, and sat in the grass, moping.

Turlough broke the stick in half, chucked the pieces inside the door, and folded his arms. He waited.

And waited.

Ten minutes later, she was still sitting in the grass, pouting. She hadn't moved an inch. No jobbie in sight.

He huffed. "Alright then, stay there and feel sorry for yourself all night. Suits me fine." He stomped back into the house and closed the door.

Within seconds, a thump sounded on the door, then whining and scratching.

"Serves you right," Turlough said. He climbed back into bed and closed his eyes.

What if Brioc found out?

He rolled over, trying to push the disturbing thought away. What a stupid thing to worry about. How could Brioc possibly find out? It wasn't as if the wolfhound could go and tell him.

He had let the cold air in by having opened the door. Great. Goosebumps prickled his skin. He wished he had his blanket.

Sam barked and pawed at the door. Turlough buried his head under his pillow. "Shut up," he called.

She kept scratching and barking.

Turlough sighed. He threw his pillow down, hoisted himself out of bed, and went back to the door. The second he opened it, Sam charged inside and ran around the room as if she had never seen the place before.

Maybe she had done something before she'd come to the door. Turlough would at least pretend she had, so he could sleep without worrying about it.

He headed back to bed for the third time. Thankfully, Samthann returned to her spot under the table, curled up, and settled down.

He let out his breath, closed his eyes, and forced himself to relax.

WHOMP! A suffocating weight dropped on him, crushing his body. The bed creaked and sank and almost collapsed. His face was buried in fur.

Enough was enough. Frustration surged through him and he shoved the dog off, hard. She fell to the floor with a thud. Turlough jumped up as Sam tried to scramble back to her feet.

He glared. "Ever heard of a thing called a shed?" He grabbed a fistful of fur behind her neck and tried to drag her towards the door. She whimpered in self-pity, her claws clicking on the floor as she scrabbled for a foothold. The battle posed more of a challenge than he thought it would. He used every ounce of his strength, but couldn't manage to haul her forward. This was one big dog.

It wouldn't work.

He glanced around the room. His eyes fell on the broken stick. Perfect. He'd lure her out. Releasing her fur, he marched over and swiped it up.

He put on an enthusiastic voice and slapped his thigh. "Come on, Sam! Good puppy! Let's play!" He raced out the door and through the yard. Magic. Sam shot after him. Turlough ran all the way to the shed behind the cottage, whipped open the door, and threw the stick inside.

Sam flew in after it. Fast as lightning, Turlough slammed the door.

Whew. He slapped his hands together, and headed back to the house.

Sam howled and scratched on the shed door.

He ignored her. He needed sleep.

27

They had been walking only a few hours, but to Dymphna it felt like forever. The combination of navigating unfamiliar farmland by a sliver of moonlight, wearing men's clothing that didn't fit and boots that killed her already-bleeding feet, plus her mixture of fear and tiredness, made the hours seem endless. As they awkwardly tripped along the rutted path that could have been a road, Father Gerebran's normally calm face was creased with concern, and Brioc jumped at every noise in the dark. Right now, neither man filled Dymphna with much confidence. Not that she blamed them. They were tired too, and no doubt worried sick.

Surprisingly, Ethlynn was the exception to the gloom. She didn't seem to notice her husband's nervous glances around the dark woods. In fact, Dymphna suspected Ethlynn wasn't noticing much of anything. Maybe that's what happened when you got to ride the only horse, which belonged to Father Gerebran.

As soon as they had gotten beyond Daidi's village and out of immediate danger, Ethlynn had started chattering about her family, going on and on about how wonderful it would be to be back home in Méifne with her parents and eight older sisters and one brother. She rambled nonstop, making their life-threatening escape sound like a holiday. Dymphna couldn't actually classify it as conversation, since Ethlynn was the only one talking.

It wasn't long before Dymphna pined for the silence of their first hour. Eventually Ethlynn's chatter blended with the hooting owls and crickets and became background noise. It was rude, of course, to ignore her, and Dymphna felt mean. But it already took every ounce of strength to not burst into tears thinking about Daidi wanting to marry her. The last thing she needed was to hear how perfect Ethlynn's family was.

Brioc must have realized that, because every once in awhile, when he wasn't peering nervously around them, he would throw Dymphna an apologetic glance. Even Father Gerebran sighed once or twice. And *he* was a saint. That said a lot.

Yes, the hours dragged indeed.

Things finally came to a head. Everyone was overtired and their nerves were fraying. Dymphna's pinky toe was bleeding from her ill-fitting boot, Father stepped in a hole and stumbled, dropping his bundle in the mud, then Brioc realized the other three bundles with their remaining belongings had somehow been forgotten the last time they'd stopped to rest. No one could remember who was supposed to be carrying them, or where they had been left. This meant a retracing of their steps half a mile back to search for the missing bags. Right when it seemed like Brioc was ready to explode, and even Dymphna herself was on the brink of tears, Ethlynn, cozily astride the one horse, launched into the life story of . . . Angus.

Angus, so her claim went, was the most loving and loyal of big brothers who'd ever graced the earth. He was eight years older than Ethlynn and treated her like a queen. She stopped briefly in her monologue to ask Father Gerebran if he had a brother.

"No," he replied, his voice maintaining its eternal patience. "Only my one sister, in the convent." He smiled at her and managed to sound deeply interested. Dymphna marveled. Yes, the priest was definitely a saint.

"I know the princess doesn't have a brother," Ethlynn went on, "and of course Brioc doesn't, so I'm the only one." And for the next twenty minutes, as the rest of them battled ruts and brambles and slippery mud, Ethlynn expounded on what they were missing, and how brothers, especially older brothers, and *especially* her older brother, Angus, was the most magnificent gift God could give to anyone.

Without warning, Brioc exploded. "Lynnie, would you *please* shut up?"

Everyone froze. Father Gerebran froze, mid-stride. Dymphna froze, boot in hand, about to nurse her sore foot.

Brioc never lost his temper. Never.

Ethlynn stared at him with wide eyes, looking as if he had slapped her. Even Brioc seemed stunned by his outburst. For a second, no one moved.

Dymphna squirmed. Even eternally-calm Father Gerebran frowned. How many times these last hours Dymphna had been tempted to blurt the same mean words to Ethlynn, and possibly so had Father. But for *Brioc* to say them — Brioc, who was so kind and gentle and quiet, and would never hurt a bug, let alone his pregnant wife — was shocking. What was it about big brother Angus that lit his fuse?

Within a skipped heartbeat, he repented. "Lynnie, I'm sorry. I'm so sorry, dear. I didn't mean —" Too late. She burst into tears.

It was suddenly too much. Dymphna's own tears started to flow as well. She crumbled, right in the middle of the road, and sat down, covering her face with her hands as tears spilled down her cheeks. *Why couldn't Daidi be like Ethlynn's daid? How could he want to marry her?* It was so sick and sinful it made her heart shatter.

Somewhere in the back of her mind she knew it was selfish to sit here, blubbering her eyes out, while Ethlynn did likewise. Ethlynn had a right to cry. She was with child and terrified, which was probably the reason she was talking so much in the first place. People acted differently when they were scared. Dymphna should show her compassion, listening to her stories and trying to look interested, like Father Gerebran had done. Instead she'd been rude and had ignored the girl. *Jesus,* she thought, *I'm sorry.*

She sniffed and wiped her eyes with the back of her hand. Through tears she saw that Ethlynn had dismounted and stood crying on the side of the road. Brioc tried to give her a hug, but she pushed him away. Father Gerebran looked lost, unsure, something like despair stamped on his face. The poor priest had not only one, but *two* sobbing females on his hands. His expression was so dismayed it was almost funny, and suddenly Dymphna smiled. It was just a tiny smile, but it made her feel better. She took a deep breath. She could do this.

Or rather, *God* could do this. God would make her strong.

She brushed away her tears with her sleeve, stood up, and went to Ethlynn. Brioc stepped aside, giving Dymphna a pathetically helpless look. He seemed only too relieved to have someone come to his rescue. Another female to take over the situation.

Dymphna gathered Ethlynn into a hug and let her cry her eyes out. "Angus sounds wonderful," she said, holding Ethlynn tight. "I can't wait to meet him, and your sisters. They'll be so excited when you show up."

It was a silly thing to say, as Angus was totally irrelevant, really, but it seemed to calm Ethlynn. She sniffled and wiped her eyes and nodded. She opened her mouth to say something, but she never got the chance.

Because just then, a wolf howled.

28

If there was one thing Turlough hated, it was waking up with a dagger to his throat.

The blade against his neck hadn't actually been the thing to pull him from slumber. Rather it was the foul-smelling breath inches from his face, like a blast of air from a line of outhouses upwind on a hot day. He wrinkled his nose in disgust. *Sam?* How had she gotten back in? He groaned, still groggy, and started to sit up to shove the dog off his chest. Something pushed him back down, hard. It was a hand. Cold steel pressed against his throat, its edge razor sharp. His eyes shot open.

"Where is he?" a voice snarled in his face. It was too dark to see the man's features, but did he ever reek. "Answer me, or you shall die."

Turlough swallowed. The action, tiny as it was, forced the knife's blade a fraction into his flesh. A drop of moisture trickled down his neck. Blood. *His.* He froze, not daring to move another muscle. One twitch and it would be bye-bye.

"Answer me!"

How? If drawing a breath would be fatal, there was no way he could speak. Besides, where was *who*? What was Stinky even talking about?

A second voice, from the doorway, cut in. "Your Majesty, perhaps I should take over."

Your . . . Majesty? Did he say *Your Majesty?* Turlough's mind reeled. *This was King Daemon! Whoa!*

As his brain frantically tried to process that terrifying tidbit, he caught a movement from the corner of his eye. A person near the doorway, presumably the one who had spoken, strode across the room. He came into view, taking up position directly behind the king. Now *this* was one man Turlough had no trouble recognizing, even in near-darkness. It was jolly old Captain Barrfhoinn. The man himself. This didn't hold promise for a good day. Turlough could be wrong, of course. It was just a gut feeling.

Suddenly he thought of Samthann and could've slit his own throat. Why-oh-why had he locked her in the shed? Remembering how she'd acted towards Barrf at the graves, the one-hundred-and-forty-pound wolfhound would come in very handy right now. Especially her bright sparkling fangs. Turlough made a mental note to let Samthann sleep inside in the future. In fact, she could have the bed. He'd be glad to sleep under the table for the rest of his life.

If he had a rest of his life.

Then the dog started barking from the shed. He realized she'd probably been at it all night. Come to think of it, the sound of barking had invaded his dreams.

Barrf said, "My lord, if I may?" He spoke as if to a child.

Amazingly, the king relinquished the dagger. As the blade moved away from his throat, Turlough dared to let out a breath, although he wasn't sure yet if Barrf holding the weapon made his situation better or worse. Daemon stepped away from the bed, thankfully taking his hygiene problems with him. Before Turlough could suck enough clean air into his lungs, Barrfhoinn leaned in and pressed the knife to his throat again. Only this time it didn't cut into his skin. Presumably, so he could answer questions.

There was movement outside his line of vision. Murmuring voices. How many men stood crammed in his doorway?

"It would be to your advantage," the captain told him, "if you tell us where he is."

Turlough was careful to move as little as possible. "Where who is?"

First Dymphna goes missing, now someone else. Must be the day for missing people.

Barrfhoinn's lips curled back, making Turlough think again of the four-legged killing machine locked in his shed. The captain got up close.

"Your brother."

Brioc? An icy chill swept over him. *They were looking for Brioc?*

The captain glanced at the king, and whoever else stood at the door, then back at Turlough. As if in answer to his unspoken question, Barrf said, "Your brother took something that belongs to King Daemon. Something precious. And the king wants it back."

Brioc stole something from Daemon? The mere idea was ridiculous. Under any other circumstances, Turlough would've laughed.

A strange sound came from behind the captain — from King Daemon? Out of the corner of his eye, Turlough saw the king collapse to the floor snarling like a wild animal. Turlough froze. In fact, even Barrfhoinn froze. A flurry of movement ensued as someone rushed across the room to the king.

While whoever it was dealt with whatever that was, Barrfhoinn managed to regain his composure. "Where's your brother?" he asked again. "Answer me."

The king kept growling like a dog. Turlough wished he could see what was going on. The sounds reminded him of Sam locked in the shed.

Bodies shuffled to the king. Voices commanded, pleaded, but the bizarre noises continued. And Barrf ignored it all. It was distracting, to say the least.

"Tell me!"

"How should I know where my brother is?"

Barrfhoinn grabbed him by the collar and shoved the knife so hard against his throat that it again pierced the skin. "You gave him money to get away. You know where he's headed."

What?

Then Turlough remembered the coins. Neill and Cahir had been there. He'd told them Brioc was his brother. But that didn't mean he knew where Brioc had gone, and he certainly didn't know what he'd taken from the king. He couldn't imagine Brioc stealing anything.

Was that why he'd given Sam away?

The thought hit him hard. His blood ran cold. Why hadn't he realized his brother was in trouble? Brioc would never give away Sam unless he was desperate. And the way Brioc had looked when Neill and Cahir had shown up, like he could barely breathe at the sight of the two strange soldiers.

If only Turlough had known what was going on, he could've helped.

Barrfhoinn slapped him hard across the face. He wanted an answer.

"I don't know where my brother is. Even if I did, you think I'd tell you?" To drive home the point, Turlough did something he'd fantasied about for years. He spit in Barrf's face. And it felt good. He was dead anyhow, so he might as well go out in style.

The captain wiped the spittle off his face and his eyes flared. Surprisingly, he released Turlough's collar.

"Gruagh," he said calmly, "teach this soldier a lesson."

The giant was here?

Oh no!

Turlough didn't even see the cave-dweller coming. One second he was on his bed with the dagger to his throat, the next second he was yanked to his feet. A fist the size of a battering ram slammed into his jaw. It felt like being kicked in the face by a warhorse. His head exploded in pain. He stumbled and sank to his knees. Then Gruagh gave him another one. Bright lights flashed across his eyelids and he went down.

For a few merciful seconds the world blacked out. Then the giant's fist smashed into him a third time. Darkness pulled him under. But not long enough. Somehow he found himself face down on the floor. The cave-dweller planted a foot on the back of his head, as if threatening to grind his face into the ground. Thankfully, before he could, Barrfhoinn spoke. His voice sounded a million miles away.

"Would you care to tell me now where your brother is?"

Turlough grit his teeth. "No."

Gruagh changed tactics and jerked his arms behind his back, twisting them. It felt like the bones would snap.

The Captain said calmly, "Changing your mind?"

Gruagh wrenched his arms till tears burned Turlough's eyes.

"Never! You can go jump off a —"

"I'm going to give you one more chance. You gave him money to get away. Therefore you know where he went. And if you don't know where he went, I have every confidence you can figure it out. Agree to lead us to him, and I will order Gruagh to heel."

Gruagh pulled his arms tighter behind his back. Pain shot through him.

"I didn't hear your answer." Barrf sounded amused. "Will you find your brother for us?"

Turlough clenched his teeth. It took all his strength to get one tiny word out. *"Never."* It came out more of a whimper.

He squeezed his eyes shut, bracing himself for his arms to be broken. And probably his skull shattered afterward too. He could picture the animal grin on the giant's face as he no doubt waited eagerly for the captain's command to end it all.

Nothing happened.

Turlough waited, breathless, heart slamming.

Silence. The only sound was Sam barking in the shed. Somewhere amid all this, the king had stopped his own canine noises. Turlough hadn't noticed when. For all he knew, the king was gone.

The ominous silence unnerved him.

Then he heard Barrfhoinn sigh, like he knew he was beat. It gave Turlough a very small thrill of satisfaction.

Footsteps crossed the room. Flickering light came into the edge of his vision, like a large flaming torch above his head. Someone consulted in a low voice with Barrf. It sounded like Faidh, the druid.

Turlough's insides froze. What were they going to do? Sweat poured down his back. A trickle of blood slid down his face. *Brioc, what did you take from the king? Why didn't you tell me you were in trouble?*

Gruagh kept holding his arms, awaiting orders. In the shed, Sam howled her head off. *Come on, mutt! Do something! Break down the door or — or anything!* Turlough surprised himself by wondering who would take care of Samthann when they killed him. Because they were going to kill him. No doubts there.

He knew an Act of Contrition was in line about now, but the familiar words blurred in his mind. The only prayer he could think was, *Don't let them find Brioc. Please, God, don't let them kill him too.*

He'd never even apologized to his brother. Never told him how sorry he was for shattering his life that day on the hill. He suddenly realized the trickle of blood on his face was mingled with tears.

Faidh gave him one last chance. "Will you help us find your brother?"

Turlough shook his head, and said what he knew would be the last word of his life.

"No."

29

Dymphna couldn't sleep. She'd tossed and turned for over an hour, trying to get comfortable, but the hard, uneven ground beneath her made every muscle ache. She realized with shame that, unlike her three companions, she'd never slept on anything other than her warm bed in the castle, with a soft duck-feather pillow beneath her head. Beside her, Ethlynn breathed softly, deep in sleep, despite the prickly grass and the chill in the air. Several yards away, Father Gerebran snored his head off.

Brioc was the only other one awake. He sat by the fire. For some reason he had thrown way too much wood on it. It was practically an inferno, blazing so hot that Brioc had both sleeves rolled up and his cloak dumped on the ground beside him. Even their horse, tied not far away, seemed nervous by the huge shooting flames, as any animal would be.

Dymphna frowned. Why would Brioc build up the fire so much, only to sit there sweating? As she watched, he glanced nervously into the woods, then threw on yet another log. What was he doing? Her frown deepened. Brioc had been acting strange ever since they'd heard that wolf a few hours ago.

The wolf hadn't even sounded close. Its howl came from miles away, only carrying because of the stillness of the night. But Brioc's reaction had scared the living daylights out of Dymphna. And probably out of Father Gerebran too. She'd never seen anyone launch into full fight-or-flight mode like Brioc had. Thank goodness Ethlynn had been too busy sniffling and wiping away her tears to notice. Brioc had turned to bolt, terror in his eyes, as if he saw something no one else did. But Father Gerebran had grabbed him. For a few seconds, it was like Brioc's mind wasn't even there.

Just remembering it made Dymphna shiver.

A shocking thought hit her. Was Brioc's brain sick? Like Daidi's?

She gasped. No! He wasn't like Daidi at all! She tried to push the appalling thought away.

But . . . something *was* wrong with him. She'd known that from the first day they met. Brioc wouldn't even speak all those years ago, which definitely wasn't normal. And the monks had said something to Mamai about him being suicidal. Dymphna didn't know what that word meant back then, but now the thought filled her with horror.

Swallowing hard, she sat up. She reached for her shawl, careful not to wake Ethlynn beside her. Fortunately, they were both back in dresses now. Wearing men's clothes those first few hours had been awful. Thankfully after the danger passed, Father Gerebran had let them change. He'd washed the gray ashes out of his hair and let Brioc stop being a priest. Dymphna found some comfort in having everyone back to normal.

She got to her feet and pulled the shawl around her. It was an ugly article in the daylight, just as ugly as the dress and scarf Ethlynn insisted Dymphna take from Father's bundle of leftover convent clothes. Ethlynn had cooed over them with wide adoring eyes, assuring Dymphna they were gorgeous. Really? Dymphna had been surprised, but Ethlynn was older and did know more about fashions. Besides, she was *married*. Surely she could judge a pretty dress when she saw one. Still, Dymphna found it disconcerting to discover that her own taste in clothes had been so completely wrong all these years.

Ethlynn's new gown, on the other hand, seemed beautiful. Dyed a soft pink, with delicate embroidery, it surpassed in loveliness any dress Dymphna had ever owned. But Ethlynn told her it was only a rag, and, besides, it had a stain on the hem, so Dymphna couldn't possibly wear it because she was a princess.

Oh Jesus, my Beloved, what am I thinking? Daidi wants to wed me, and here I am, worried about clothes! Ashamed, Dymphna crossed herself and asked forgiveness.

She tiptoed past the sleeping form of Ethlynn and made her way to the fire. Overwhelmed by its heat, she immediately shed the shawl.

"I can't sleep. May I sit here with you?"

Startled, Brioc glanced up. Quick as lightning, he jerked both his sleeves down. But not before Dymphna saw the ghastly scars running up his arms. She gasped, horrified. What had made those?

Brioc composed himself and scooted over on the ground. "Of course, Princess." He brushed away a few stones and leaves to clear a place for her to sit down. He tugged his sleeves down further.

Suddenly Dymphna felt awkward, not sure what to say. Had Brioc heard her gasp? Did he know she'd seen the scars? She had glimpsed them for only a second, but that was enough. Biting her lip, she lowered herself to the ground and arranged her skirt, pretending to take her time about it while she decided what to say. Should she say anything at all?

Brioc remained silent. He kept glancing around the dark woods, looking like he could hardly breathe. A moment later, he jumped up and threw another log on the already raging fire.

"Are you alright?" she asked softly.

He didn't answer. Maybe he hadn't heard. He tossed yet more wood into the flames. Log after log. The nearby horse whinnied and pranced nervously, frightened by the fire. Dymphna stared at Brioc. What on earth was he doing?

His gaze darted into the woods every couple seconds.

She watched, bewildered, as he dumped more wood on the fire. For some reason goosebumps prickled her skin.

Had Daidi ever done that at the fireplace in the castle? She strained to remember.

No, she'd never seen him do that before. Still, she wished Brioc would stop. His strange behavior frightened her.

"Um, it's awfully hot. I don't think you need to add any more."

Brioc looked at her and hesitated. Then, thank goodness, he sat back down. Dymphna let out her breath.

She couldn't get those ghastly scars out of her mind. Whispering a prayer for guidance, she risked asking about them. After all, he probably knew she'd seen.

"What did that to you?"

"Did what?"

"Made those scars."

Brioc froze. He quickly averted his eyes.

Suddenly Dymphna thought of Daidi sitting on the castle floor, eyes vacant, slicing his arm with his huge hunting knife. Her heart stopped. She slapped a hand over her mouth, trying to stifle another gasp at the thought. *Oh Blessed Mother Mary,* she begged, *please not Brioc too!*

Stay calm. Keep an even voice.

"Would it help to talk about it?" Her voice trembled anyhow.

Brioc glared at her. "No." Unexpected harshness edged his voice. "You should be asleep, Princess. Tomorrow will be another long day."

She bit her lip. "I can't sleep. The ground's too hard. I've never slept outside. And it's chilly. I mean, over there."

She hadn't meant it to be a hint, but her words were already out. He picked up his cloak from the ground and, before she could object, draped it around her shoulders. Now she would really swelter near this fire! But it seemed to distract him for a moment from shoveling more wood on the flames.

In fact, the presence of someone with him must have made him relax a bit. He stopped glancing into the surrounding darkness quite so much. He actually smiled a little and said, "I can't do anything about a bed, but when we get to Méifne, I'm sure Lynnie's brother Angus will make you one. He can obviously do anything." It wasn't said sarcastically. Well, not *too* sarcastically. He sounded normal.

Relief flooded her.

"Lynnie doesn't usually talk so much," he went on. "I apologize. I'm sure you didn't need to hear about her wonderful family when your daid is . . ." He stopped himself, and ended with, "Lynnie's really scared right now. Forgive her if she said anything that hurt you."

"I'm the one who should apologize. I dragged you both into this. I never should've gone to your house. I've ruined your life." Oh no, tears welled in her eyes. She pushed her fist against her mouth, trying to stop the flow of sobs before they started.

Brioc noticed. "Hey." He rammed his shoulder into hers. "Not the tears again. I've got Lynnie to deal with; at least *you* can have mercy on me."

She laughed a little and sniffed and wiped her nose.

"Do all girls cry this much?"

She shrugged. "I don't know. Probably." She picked up a dead leaf and twirled its stem between her fingers. The dry leaf crumbled into tiny pieces and fluttered away. Kind of like her life right now. Crumbled into a million pieces.

But Brioc seemed much calmer than when she'd first come over. He startled her by saying, "I had a little sister. She would've been exactly your age. Well, a few days younger."

"Really?" she asked, surprised.

Brioc had never offered information about his family before. Dymphna had only known he was an orphan. Even that knowledge hadn't come from him, but from Mamai. The monks had told her.

"What was her name?"

"Aislinn."

"What a pretty name!"

He was probably trying to distract her from thinking of Daidi. She was grateful.

"What was she like?"

"I don't know." He said it like it was a perfectly natural answer.

She frowned, perplexed. "What do you mean, you don't know?"

Brioc shrugged. "I don't remember anything about her. Except that she was born a few days after you."

Dymphna did a quick calculation. She had lived fifteen winters, so Brioc would have been seven or eight when his sister was born. Children that age could remember things. Lots of things.

"I only remember when she was born because the whole village was celebrating your birth." Brioc gave her a weak smile. "The castle servants set up tables in the field outside, with more food than I had ever seen in my life. When my mother went into labor, everyone scrambled to get me out of the way, so my brother Tur —" He abruptly stopped. Dymphna waited. Brioc sucked in a breath and continued, "One of my brothers took me to the festivities, and I ate so much I got sick."

She tried not to giggle. "Oh no."

"He kept warning me to stop, but I didn't listen to him. Funny, because I always listened to him. Not that time. I threw up all night."

"Oh no!" she said again, trying to hide her smile. "I guess your parents weren't too thrilled. I mean, with a newborn and all."

"Not thrilled isn't the word. Daid was furious." Brioc shook his head, but she saw his tiny smile. "It was my own fault for not listening to my brother." He looked away then, the smile suddenly gone, and added quietly, "He took the blame anyhow. He always did that for me."

What a good big brother. Brioc must miss him.

Brioc concluded with, "And that's the whole extent of my memories of Aislinn."

"Really?" Dymphna couldn't believe that. Surely Brioc could remember more. "You mean, you don't know what she looked like or anything?"

"No. Nothing at all. My brother told me she had dark hair, like mine." He shrugged again, as if this was normal.

Dymphna fished for something to say.

"What about your brother? You obviously remember him. What was his name?"

Brioc stiffened, and Dymphna realized she'd unintentionally hit a raw nerve. One of Brioc's hands trembled slightly, and he crammed it beneath him. She instantly regretted her question.

Finally, when she was sure he wouldn't answer, he said, "I had a few brothers. I remember bits and pieces. Not much."

"I'm so sorry. It must be awful to have lost them all."

Now it made sense. No wonder Brioc reacted so unexpectedly when Ethlynn raved about her brother Angus. It must have brought back great pain to make him blow up like that.

"I'm sorry," Dymphna said again.

Brioc shrugged, as if it didn't matter.

"Well," she announced, trying to break the awkwardness, "I have a brother."

Startled, he stared at her. "*What?* You mean, your parents had another —"

"No, silly." She smiled. "It's you."

Well, that got a smile out of him. Although, to her disappointment, only a halfhearted one.

"Shh, don't tell your wife, but I think you're a thousand times better than Angus."

Brioc shook his head but genuinely smiled this time. "Go get some sleep, Princess. You're overtired."

"You aren't allowed to call me that anymore. If anyone hears you, they'll know it's us, and Daidi's soldiers will find us." Without warning, tears filled her eyes again, a flood of regret and fear with them. She tried to stop them, but couldn't. "They're going to kill you and Ethlynn and Father Gerebran, and Daidi'll force me to marry him."

"Stop. They're not going to find us." Brioc held her gaze. "I promise, Dymphna. Your daid won't get you. You're not going to marry him or anything sick like that. We'll take care of you, no matter what."

Tears blurred her eyes. "What happens if they follow us to the Kingdom of Mide?"

"They can't. No one knows Lynnie is from Méifne. They'll never think of looking for us there."

Dymphna nodded, trying to be brave. "I'm just so scared," she whispered, and without further warning, the dam burst. The tears came, spilling down her cheeks. She buried her face in her hands as sobs wracked her body. Her heart was breaking.

She thought she heard Brioc sigh, then he reached over and put his arm around her. He pulled her against his shoulder. "Please don't cry, Dymphna."

She sniffled a few times and wiped her eyes with the cloak he'd earlier wrapped around her, trying hard to stop. His gesture was brotherly and innocent, and for a moment she felt safe and consoled. Then she suddenly remembered her vow to God. Ashamed of herself for letting a man touch her, she jerked away.

He jumped, confused, then scooted aside as if he'd done something wrong. "I'm sorry, Princess. I truly didn't mean —"

For some reason Dymphna's gaze flew to Ethlynn, asleep on the ground.

Only she wasn't asleep anymore. She was propped on one elbow, staring straight at them.

She had seen the hug.

30

Turlough shut his eyes and prayed, bracing himself to be killed. Sweat trickled down his face, mingling with the drops of blood on the floor. Would Gruagh just hurry up? Because if he didn't, Turlough feared his courage might shatter.

Nothing happened.

He opened his eyes, managing to turn his head just enough to see Faidh and Barrf standing above him, still consulting in whispers. Light from the torch the druid held illuminated their scheming faces. Daemon was nowhere to be seen.

Barrf nodded at something Faidh said, then motioned for the cave-dweller to release Turlough's arms. The giant obeyed.

They must be planning some torture.

At least his arms were free. They hurt like anything, but the bones weren't broken. He stayed on the floor, not daring to sit up or move.

The tight pale skin across Faidh's face stretched into a diabolical smile. It made him look for all the world like the living dead. Then the druid did the last thing Turlough expected. He turned on his heel and walked out the door. Just like that.

Gone.

Barrf and Gruagh followed him out. They closed the door behind them.

No way.

Turlough struggled to sit up. He leaned back against the bed. Everything ached. His head pounded. Blood streamed into his eyes. He fumbled in the dark for something to wipe his face with. The simple motion sent bolts of pain through both arms. Settling for the closest thing he could reach, the tail of his shirt, he gingerly mopped it across his bruised face.

He strained to hear sounds outside. There were no voices. No noise at all, except Samthann's continuous barking. They were planning something. Maybe they would torch his house. He had to get out of here.

Holding onto the bed for balance, he staggered to his feet. They would return any minute now, with more flaming torches or whatever they had gone to fetch. He didn't have much time.

He lurched to the corner where he kept his gear and groped in the dim light for his hunting knife, the one that had belonged to Daid. He found it and crammed it into his belt, along with the near-empty pouch that held last week's pay. He'd forgotten to give it to Brioc with the other money. Probably just as well; he would need it himself. Then he grabbed his sword and saddlebag. Get

Sam. *Quick. Move.* He had to find his brother before Barrf and Faidh did. They'd kill Brioc for sure. What had he taken from Daemon that deserved this?

He stumbled to the door, every muscle screaming in protest. Pain seared his face.

Wait. The statue! The little Saint Brigid that had belonged to Mam. For some reason, he felt compelled to take it. He'd had that same strange urge eleven years ago, the morning he and Brioc had left the cabin. They had never returned. Maybe Mam was nudging him, from wherever she was, to take it now.

He hurried back across the room and swiped the figurine off the shelf. Again, something made him pause. He should say a prayer. He hastily crossed himself. The prayer sprang straight to his lips, as familiar as if it were a part of him, as if it had been there all along, just waiting to be spoken.

"May Saint Brigid keep us safe beneath her cloak." He squeezed his eyes shut, silently begging protection for himself, and especially Brioc, from the saint that Mam had so loved. If Saint Brigid had worked so many miracles with her cloak when she walked upon this soil, how much more powerful she must be in Heaven.

Turlough added a hasty prayer for his parents, then his four brothers. He reminded Branduff and Raghnall that, as the two oldest, they had a duty to rescue their youngest brother. Then he threatened Aedh and Maedoc, as *their* older brother, that if they didn't help too, he would kick their backsides, hard, when he entered eternity, so they better not mess around up there as they had on earth. All of his brothers had received Extreme Unction before they'd died, so hopefully they lived in Heaven. But even from Purgatory they could intercede. A priest had told Turlough that after the burials.

Lastly, Turlough prayed to little Aislinn, but with reverence, because she was definitely with God, and therefore a saint.

Having finally covered the whole family, *whew,* Turlough shoved the wooden Saint Brigid with her tiny folded hands and carved cloak into his saddlebag and returned to the door. For some reason, he felt a little calmer.

He drew his sword and paused, free hand on the latch, listening.

Silence.

He inched open the door. No one was in sight. They most likely would ambush him. But all he needed was a few seconds. Ten at the most. Just enough time to run to the shed and reach his weapon.

The ultimate killing machine.

Samthann.

31

Turlough gripped the shed door. He suspected what would happen the second he opened it. As he scraped the door back Sam sprang to her hind legs, her front paws crashing on his shoulders. He braced himself for the fresh pain of her tongue on his raw wounds.

The dog paused, tongue suspended in front of his face, then, unbelievably, dropped back on all fours. Her tail shot between her legs, and she whined. Then she nuzzled against his leg, as if she somehow understood he was hurt.

He blinked. Really?

Tentatively he put out one hand, and she licked off the blood. Gently. After a moment, she scrabbled back onto his shoulders. She hesitated, as if asking permission, then carefully licked his face.

"Yuck." He shoved her off. "Get down."

She obeyed, stunning him anew.

"We have to be quiet," he whispered. "We need to find Brioc."

At his brother's name, her tail went wild. She wiggled back and forth and barked, shivering with excitement.

He cast a look out the shed door into the darkness. "Shh. I said we have to be quiet. Come on, let's go." He motioned for her to follow. She pressed so closely against him that with his next step he tripped on her paw and nearly fell.

Stupid mutt.

Once out of the shed, he bolted across the yard towards the safety of the dark woods, Samthann at his side, then hid in the even darker shadows of a cluster of trees. He glanced at Sam, checking her reaction. Judging by what he'd seen at the graveyard, the dog had sensed Captain Barrfhoinn's presence long before he'd come into view. Surely if he were nearby now, Sam would react the same way.

She stood beside him, her tail wagging.

Apart from leaves rustling in the breeze and the noise of night bugs, the woods were quiet. No person in sight. No flickering torches in the distance. Where had they gone? *More importantly, why?*

Nerves on edge, he tried to stay calm. Sam was here. She would have no trouble defending him from a handful of soldiers and a brainless caveman.

So, where to now? Brioc's house? Where did Brioc even live? That would've been the first place Daemon's henchmen had searched, so obviously Brioc wasn't home. But it might reveal some vital clue to where he had gone. Or why.

Turlough knelt next to Sam. "Home, Sam. Show me *home*."

She must have understood, because she took off at a trot.

* * * * *

Samthann led him to a tiny cottage at the edge of the meadow. Turlough stared in disbelief. He had passed this way countless times with the troops, on their way to the castle, and had never realized his brother lived here. The knowledge brought a fresh pang of sadness.

Stepping through the broken gate into the yard, he glanced around to make sure no one hid in waiting. But he wasn't too worried; Sam would alert him if a third party lurked nearby. Without bothering to knock, he pushed open the rough wooden door and entered the cottage.

Dim light from the rising sun filtered into the room from a small window, revealing a mess.

Samthann plodded inside. Immediately her tail sagged and her ears drooped, as if disappointed at not finding Brioc. She sniffed around, then hopped on the bed, where she curled up and fell asleep within seconds. Considering she'd barked all night in the shed, she must be exhausted.

Turlough looked around. Brioc and Lynnie must have left in haste. A lady's cloak, presumably Lynnie's, and a flour-dusted apron, were dumped on the floor. A lump of dough lay on the table. Next to it stood a jug of water, a towel, and a small basin, its bottom stacked with dirty dishes. Someone had piled a strange mound of pillows and blankets behind the bed. Wilting flowers spilled from a toppled vase.

None of this told Turlough anything.

Then he spotted Brioc's miniature harp in the corner and his pulse raced. For some reason the abandoned instrument disturbed him more than everything else. Brioc would never leave it behind. But he had, which showed the urgency of his flight.

Fear mounting, Turlough stepped over Lynnie's cloak and made his way to the cupboard. Praying it would be empty, he yanked it open. A handful of vegetables, half a block of cheese, and a quarter loaf of bread met his eyes. Admittedly it wasn't much, but food was food and Brioc hadn't taken it. Ice formed in Turlough's stomach. His brother must have fled in a desperate hurry.

Brioc, what did you get yourself into?

Fighting down fear, Turlough's gaze swept the room. There must be a clue, somewhere. One of Sam's huge paws twitched, drawing his attention to the bed. A small, strange object lay on the blanket next to her.

"What's that?" he said, walking to the bed. He picked it up—a flattened square of dough. Someone had etched strange lines into it. He frowned. Having no idea what the symbols meant, he put it back down.

Think. Where would Brioc go?

To his sorrow, he didn't really know his brother anymore. But they'd had a conversation — no, *two* conversations — just yesterday. Turlough sank to the edge of the bed and lowered his pounding head into his hands. A few drops of blood still dripped from his face. He wiped his hand on his trouser leg and sighed. *Forget the pain. Just think.*

Had Brioc said anything that might give a clue where he'd go? What could he have taken that Daemon found so precious he would kill to retrieve it? The object was obviously small enough for Brioc to carry. Did it fit in a sack? A tiny pouch? Or had he lugged it away in a wagon? Turlough's mind reeled. The thought of Brioc stealing *anything* was beyond comprehension.

Hmm. Maybe Lynnie was the thief. Turlough found it more comfortable imagining a faceless, unknown sister-in-law stealing from the castle, rather than his brother. Perhaps she snitched a piece of jewelry, or a valuable trinket that had belonged to the queen. Maybe a tapestry?

Turlough shook his head. None of this made sense. Alright, forget what Brioc had taken. The object itself wasn't important right now. Just figure out where he and Lynnie had fled. Where did people go when they were in trouble?

The answer was obvious. Normal people turned to their families, right?

If only Brioc had turned to him. Turlough sighed. Well, Brioc hadn't, so there was no point moaning about it. Just find him.

He lifted his head from his hands and nudged Sam's shoulder. "Hey, snoozeball. Where does Lynnie's family live?"

The wolfhound opened one eye and halfheartedly thumped her tail. Then she yawned, changed position, and fell back asleep.

"Great help you are."

Turlough massaged the back of his neck, hoping his skull wouldn't cave in. A patch of his hair was matted with dried blood, his shirt wet and sticky. He stood and went back to the door. There was no way Gruagh — or Barrf or Faidh, or anyone, for that matter — could attack him here and live to tell the tale, not with Samthann on that bed, but he'd better lock the door regardless.

He fastened the latch, then hunted through Brioc's clothes for a clean shirt. That seemed to have become the story of his life lately. Finding one, he brought it to the table where the jug of water stood. He fished the dirty dishes out of the basin and, bracing himself for fresh pain, stripped off his own blood-streaked shirt. He leaned over the basin, wincing as he poured the pitcher of icy water over his head and face. The water in the basin ran red.

Mide.

The word flashed through his memory like a bolt of lightening.

They'd been standing at the graves, talking, and somehow a town in Mide had come up. What had been said? Turlough shook the freezing water from his hair and gingerly wiped his face on the floury towel that had been left beside the basin.

What had Brioc said about Mide?

Shivering with cold, Turlough scrubbed the towel through his hair and tried to replay the conversation in his head. No good; his mind drew a blank. He'd been nervous, and so had Brioc. Their conversation had been disjointed, to say the least. Apart from the word Mide, he couldn't remember any other place names.

He glanced heavenward, imploring his family. *Come on, all of you up there, help me out!*

Prayers heard. His graveside conversation with Brioc came back in a flash.

"Is she anyone I know?"

"I doubt it. Her family's from Méifne. She's the youngest daughter of a horse dealer over there."

Yes! Méifne was in the Kingdom of Mide!

"Sam, wake up!" Turlough scrambled into the clean shirt. A sense of urgency gripped him, sending goosebumps racing down his spine. He had to get to Méifne before Barrf figured it out!

The dog sleepily lifted her head, but didn't move. Turlough rushed to the bed and yanked her by the fur of her neck. "Move, dog! We've got to go!"

Samthann yawned, leaped to the floor and shook herself. Turlough snatched his saddlebag, hurried to the cupboard, and swiped all the food off the shelf into it. His gaze fell on the pile of blankets behind the bed. He grabbed one.

Now he simply needed to sneak into the soldiers' stables without being detected. If he could snitch a horse, he'd be in Mide in a couple days. He might even be able to cut Brioc and Lynnie off on the road. If, that is, they'd taken the highway and were on foot. Even if they were taking a different route, he could still arrive in Méifne before them.

And if he was wrong, and they weren't heading to Lynnie's family for help, then hopefully one of her siblings might have an idea where they would flee. Turlough had no other leads.

He swung his saddle bag over his shoulder and breathed a prayer he was right. "Come on, Sam. It's a long trip ahead of us."

He reached the door, then stopped in his tracks. *Wait. Brioc's harp!* The extra burden wouldn't slow him much, especially if he was on horseback. He rushed to the corner where Brioc had abandoned the instrument. His gaze fell on the intricate designs carved in the wood of the harp and for a moment Turlough paused, memories spilling over him. He'd forgotten about those carvings. As a youngster he wouldn't have appreciated the delicate etchings, but now he ran his fingers lightly over them, amazed at the craftsmanship of whoever had made it. Carefully he wrapped the little harp in the blanket.

As he hoisted everything else over one shoulder in order to carry the delicate instrument, the memory of having done this before punched him hard in the gut.

In trying the first time to save his brother's life, he had killed him. He couldn't mess up again.

This time he would keep Brioc alive.

Or die in the attempt.

32

On their third day of travel, the truth dawned on Ethlynn. She was poking at the flickering fire with a stick, awaiting the others' return so they could eat breakfast, when it hit her like a battering ram. In shock, she dropped the stick.

Brioc didn't love her anymore! He loved Dymphna!

The realization hit her with physical pain. She clutched her stomach and melted into the sand, where she sat in horror. It was so obvious! Why hadn't she realized it before?

The way Brioc and Dymphna walked together, while she sat alone on the horse. Sometimes they talked in quiet voices near the fire in the evening. And the night Brioc had given her his cloak, then put his arm around her and hugged her!

Brioc loved the princess! Dymphna was so beautiful with her flowing hair, her perfect face and petite figure; what man wouldn't fall head-over-heels for her? And Brioc had known her for ages; they were *'friends'* he claimed. Wedding the king's daughter was, of course, out of the question for a peasant. So, after a mere fleeting crush on a strange girl from another village — *her* — Brioc had gone ahead and gotten married. But now he was bored with her. He regretted it. He had loved Dymphna all along!

Tears welled in Ethlynn's eyes and she rubbed her sleeve across them, trying not to bawl. The unborn baby inside her wiggled and gave a tiny kick, which normally delighted her. But now she protectively wrapped her arms around her tummy.

What would she do? Homeless, a child on the way, and a husband who didn't love her!

Thinking about it, this explained everything. Brioc's depression, his secrecy. All the times he took off somewhere with Sam. Ethlynn's heart pounded. Maybe the nightmares he had were bad dreams about having married her!

Oh Blessed Mother, tell me what to do.

Approaching voices and the rustling of branches made her look up. The other three emerged through the trees. Father Gerebran and Brioc each held three squirming fish, and Dymphna walked between them, chatting and smiling.

She spotted Ethlynn. "Look, Ethlynn! Look what they caught us for breakfast! Can you believe it — without a hook or a line or anything!"

Ethlynn sniffed and miserably wiped her eyes with the cuff of her sleeve. She pushed herself off the sand and stood, hoping her face didn't reveal her pain.

"You should've seen it." Dymphna hurried towards her through the trees, hair bouncing, beautiful skin glowing. "Father and Brioc found a way to corner the fish where the water was shallow and made a little pool and they actually just waded in and —" She frowned. "Are you alright?"

Brioc had reached her by then too. "Sorry it took us so long, Lynnie. You must be starving."

Ethlynn refused to look at him. He leaned in to give her a good-morning kiss, but she stiffened and stepped to the side. Then, just to make sure he got the message, she flipped her hair back defiantly. "I'm not hungry," she announced and stomped away.

"Lynnie, wait. What —"

"I said, I'm not hungry." She turned and threw a glare at Dymphna. "Enjoy your fish." Then she hurried away before her tears could flow.

Low, bewildered voices immediately broke out near the fire. She heard Brioc say, "What's going on with Lynnie?" and Dymphna said, "Want me to go over and try to —" and Father Gerebran cut them both off with, "Maybe it's best to leave her alone for awhile. Give her some space. She's frightened and . . ." Their voices trailed off as she pushed her way between overgrown bushes, cutting her own path into the woods to be away from them.

Fine, let them gossip. Why should she care what they thought? Why should she care about anything anymore? Her husband didn't love her.

Her lip quivered. Oh no. She was about to cry.

She stumbled to a large rock. The dam broke and tears slid down her cheeks. She groped her way to sit down, tears blinding her eyes. She buried her face in her hands and cried her heart out.

She had no idea how long she sat there, sobbing. Part of her longed for Brioc to come and console her, while the other part of her thought that if he did, she'd slap him across the face. And Dymphna. Don't even get her started on Dymphna! Her and her perfect unblemished skin and gorgeous honey-colored hair! Ethlynn would love to . . . to . . .

Oh that would be a sin. Besides, she had nothing to shear it all off with.

She cried and cried, not even trying to stop.

Until an awful thought hit her.

Stress could bring on early labor! Her baby could be born too soon! *Oh no! Stop crying!*

She rubbed her eyes, sniffled hard, fumbled for the tiny cloth in her pouch and blew her nose.

Mam had warned her, on her wedding day, that if she ever got pregnant she must remain calm and happy throughout.

Mam had never fled for her life. Mam had a husband who loved her.

Ethlynn sniffed again and stood up. *Don't cry, don't cry.* Stay calm.

BE HAPPY!

She crept back the way she'd come. Firelight flickered in the distance but her view of their camp was blocked by the trees. Were they still talking about her? Was anyone worried about her? Or was she out of sight, out of mind?

Why wouldn't Brioc come over and give her a big hug? Fresh tears threatened.

She tramped closer and peered around a tree trunk.

Father Gerebran tended their horse, adjusting its bridle, checking its hooves, preparing it for another day of travel.

Dymphna was packing their scattered belongings back into bundles. She had temporarily taken off the ugly scarf, and her impossibly luscious hair cascaded down in perfect waves. Not a strand out of place. Even in the drab brown dress, she was a heartthrob. A fairy princess. Ethlynn's lip quivered.

Near Dymphna, a few feet away, Brioc doused the fire. Ethlynn stretched her neck to see his expression. Yes! Her heart leaped! He looked hurt! Bewildered! Worried!

Oh good. Any second now he would dash over here and swoop her into his arms, swing her around, and wipe away her tears. He might even pick a blossom off some bush and tuck it into her hair. She glanced around for a blossom.

Clusters of tall grass, unruly green bushes, gnarled tree trunks . . . no flowers.

Disappointed, she frowned.

Oh well, let her husband find the blossom. She quickly combed her fingers through her hair, trying to get the knots out, and straightened the wrinkles from her pink dress, just in case. She peered around the tree again to see if he was running over to her yet.

Her heart sank. Brioc hadn't moved from the fire pit. He knelt and picked up something from the ground. She strained her eyes to see. It was the hunting knife Father Gerebran had lent him. Brioc had left his own at home, of course, but Father had two. Brioc wiped the knife in the grass to clean it, his expression still pained. He was racked with inner turmoil. Ethlynn could tell.

Suddenly Dymphna turned to him and said something Ethlynn couldn't hear. Brioc let out a little laugh and swiveled towards the princess. He said something, then she said something else, and they both smiled. Father Gerebran glanced at them and chuckled. For a few seconds the three of them joked around, then the priest turned back to the horse and Brioc got up to help Dymphna finish packing.

How. Dare. He.

Well, so much for his inner turmoil! Ethlynn turned away and flipped her hair, even though no one would see it. Humph. If Brioc wanted her to rejoin them, he would have to come over here and beg her. Maybe even on bended knee.

She balled her hands into fists.

Calm and happy, her foot.

She blinked back the new round of tears and stomped to the top of a small nearby hill. From here she could see the road by which they would travel to Méifne. At least she would soon be with Mam and Daid. And Angus. She'd tell Angus everything. He would find a way to get rid of Dymphna. Maybe stick her in a convent, or marry her off to some prince somewhere. Angus would think of *something* so Brioc would never see her again. Then Ethlynn's sisters could help scrounge for pretty clothes and fix Ethlynn's hair in an exciting way and Brioc might find her attractive again.

A movement below arrested her attention, breaking off her thoughts.

A man on horseback rounded a bend in the road and came into view. He was too far away to see her up here on the hill, but she instinctively stepped back. A wolfhound trotted beside him. She stared.

Sam?

She blinked, then squinted, trying to see the dog better. They were too far away. She couldn't make out the man's features, let alone the dog's. Should she run and get Brioc?

Wait, no. She wasn't speaking to him anymore.

She stared at the wolfhound. Was it Sam? She craned her neck and bit her lip, trying to tell.

Of course it's not. Ethlynn shook her head, dismissing the silly thought. Ireland was full of wolfhounds. Besides, what would Sam be doing way out here, with some strange man?

Hmm. Who had Brioc given her to? He'd never said.

"Ethlynn?" a kind voice said behind her.

She spun around. Father Gerebran stood at the foot of the little hill, gazing up at her through eyes heavy with worry.

"Are you alright?"

She drew in a quivering breath and nodded.

He came closer. "Brioc told me you're with child. Is anything wrong?"

She hesitated, then shook her head.

"Is there anything I can do? Anything you want to talk about?"

Another tiny shake of her head.

"Just tired?" he asked gently.

"I . . . I guess so, Father."

"We saved some fish for you. You should try it." He smiled. "It turned out surprisingly well."

She shook her head. "I'm not hungry."

137

He hesitated. "Whenever you're ready, everything is packed and set to go."

She gave a nod. "I'm ready now."

The priest must have seen the damp streaks on her cheeks and her puffy eyes, because he added, "I'm here if you need me. You know that, don't you?"

She nodded again, scared she would cry if she tried to speak.

"Come join us when you're ready."He hesitated for another second, then headed back to their camp.

Ethlynn glanced one last time at the road far below.

The rider with the wolfhound had vanished.

33

As Turlough rode into the village, a group of little boys charging around a field by the roadside came into view. They shouted and brandished sticks at each other, occasionally falling in the grass, clutching their chests in theatrical death agonies. A few flung wooden boards in front of their faces — shields, Turlough gathered. It wasn't difficult to guess at what they were playing. He'd played the same game himself at that age, with Branduff and Raghnall. He hadn't known then how brutal the life of a soldier truly was.

Still, the children looked so gleeful as they stabbed and maimed and slew one another with their blunt little twigs, giggling the whole time, that Turlough couldn't help but smile. Oh the innocence of youth. He reined in near their battlefield and watched the skirmish. Sam sniffed the grass near his horse, circled a few times, then plopped down. Her tongue hung out as she panted. She must be tired. Turlough was amazed how well she'd kept up. In fact, the wolfhound seemed to have more endurance than his horse.

At last, a lull descended upon the warriors. "Hello," Turlough called out with a friendly wave, "is this Méifne?" He'd been through the Kingdom of Mide once or twice, but not for years. Besides, after awhile, every village looked the same.

The boys noticed him. A dozen or so lowered their fearsome weapons and wandered over.

"Yes," one of the boys answered. "This is Méifne."

Another said, "I like your dog. He's huge. Can I pet him?"

"Sure. Only it's a she."

Suddenly the memory of Sam's viciousness towards Captain Barrfhoinn at the graves flashed through Turlough's mind. Horrified, he was about to retract his permission, but the boys had already gathered around the giant wolfhound. Six of them stroked her fur, while the others crowded in, waiting their turns. To Turlough's relief, Sam stood and wagged her tail. She was taller than some of the children. She eagerly licked all the hands held out to her.

What was it about Barrf? Could dogs sense evil?

"What's her name?"one boy asked. Another fell into peals of laughter as Sam mopped his face with her enormous tongue.

"She's Samthann."

"Hi, Samthann."

Others pet her ears, sticking their faces straight into hers, trying to make her shake hands. One little boy pulled her tail. Another tried to climb on her back.

Sam squirmed with happiness, basking in the children's attention.

"She's nice. We owned a wolfhound once, but he died."

"My daid won't let us get a dog. He says they eat too much."

"Does Samthann eat too much? Where'd you get her from anyhow?"

"Actually, she belongs to my brother." This was it, Turlough's opening. "Maybe you've seen him come into town. He looks a lot like me, but with darker hair. Anyone run into him, perhaps earlier today?"

As soon as his words were out, he realized how ridiculous they were. Thanks to Gruagh, he probably didn't resemble Brioc much right now.

The children exchanged blank glances. Some shook their heads; others shrugged.

Turlough added, "His wife is with him." He looked down at the group hopefully.

"Uh, what does she look like?"

A pang of sadness stabbed him. "I don't know. I never met her. But her daid is the horse dealer. Her name is Lynnie." He glanced towards a cluster of houses, wondering which one belonged to her parents.

A tallish boy with an unruly shock of red hair said, "I know the horse dealer, but he doesn't have a daughter named Lynnie."

Turlough frowned. Really? Was this the wrong town? Maybe Brioc hadn't said Méifne at all. Had he gotten mixed up with some place that sounded similar?

"Is that a sword?"

The word was magic. Apart from two tiny fellows, who took turns scrambling onto Sam's back, the rest of the group abandoned the wolfhound and converged instead around Turlough's horse.

"Is that thing real?"

"Of course it's real, stupid," the tallish redhead said to another tallish redhead, rolling his eyes. The two looked identical.

Someone asked, "Are you a soldier?" to which another lad, presumably a sibling, shot back, "What does he look like to you, birdbrain? A monk?"

There was jostling and gawking and crowding around as everyone tried to glimpse the sword at his side.

"Did you get in a battle?"

"Is that what happened to your face?"

One youngster's eyes widened in alarm. "Is there a war going on?"

"Shut up, Nollaig. You ask the dumbest things."

Turlough couldn't keep up with their rapid-fire questions, but he assured the one named Nollaig that there was no war, then indulged them by unsheathing his sword for them to admire. A dozen hands reached up to touch it. Before someone got hurt, Turlough leaned over in his saddle and passed it down to one of the redheads, who looked big enough to handle it, while the others erupted into envious oohs and ahhs.

"Careful," Turlough said. "It's sharp."

Its weight must have come as a surprise to the boy, because he nearly dropped it. But his face lit up as he hoisted the thing up with both hands. Then he grinned and swiped the deadly blade through the air, so clumsily he lost his balance and came within inches of impaling little Nollaig's thigh. Turlough almost had heart failure. The redhead lowered the weapon and tossed his twin a smirk. Then, as if the privilege of holding a real sword had aged him ten years, he said, all grown-up like, "My name's Kinnard. Nice to meet you." He extended one hand to introduce himself, and as he did so, the end of the sword clunked downward and scraped against the ground.

Turlough tried not to wince. He quickly shook Kinnard's proffered hand and forced a smile. "I'm Turlough. Uh, maybe I better have that thing back."

To his relief, Kinnard relinquished it. He handed it up, but blade first, instead of the hilt. Turlough managed to take it without slicing his palm.

Clearing his throat, he said, "Are you sure the horse dealer doesn't have a daughter named Lynnie?"

Kinnard glanced at his twin. Their identical faces held the same bewildered expression. Kinnard said, "We're sure. The horse dealer is our grand-daid. We don't have an Aunt Lynnie."

Turlough's heart sank. All this way for nothing. For all he knew, he wasn't even in the right kingdom. Wonderful.

He tried to smile at the boys. "Guess I got the wrong town."

Now what?

His tired body rebelled at the thought of riding on tonight. Sam must be exhausted too. She'd kept up with his horse the whole way, but the last few hours she'd seemed strangely agitated. Probably just lack of sleep. It was unfair to push her farther without letting her rest.

"I don't suppose there's a place to catch a nap around here?"

Kinnard said, "There's no inn, if that's what you mean. But our Uncle Angus lives alone. Maybe he'll let you stay with him. We could ask him if you want." He turned to his twin. "Hey, Darragh, any idea where Uncle Angus is now?"

"He was at Grand-daid's house an hour ago. I bet he's still there."

Kinnard turned back to Turlough. "Darragh and I will take you there. Wait till Uncle Angus sees your sword!"

* * * * *

The stew was steaming hot and delicious. Turlough hadn't realized how famished he was until he took the first bite. Finally, the first real meal in three days. The horse dealer's wife had insisted he sit down and join them, since he'd obviously barged in with Kinnard and Darragh right in the middle of lunch. Excellent timing.

As they ate, the kind woman moved around the tiny hut, first stirring a pot over the fire, then collecting a plate with meat scraps and a bone.

"May I give these to your dog?" She nodded towards the door. Knowing the damage Samthann could do to a place, Turlough had commanded her to stay outside. She had actually obeyed him. The woman continued, "She must be hungry too."

"I'm sure she'd love some food. Thank you."

The woman cracked the door open and Sam tried to wiggle past her and get inside. "No," Turlough ordered her sharply. "You, hey. Stay outside."

With a smile, the woman shoved the dog with her legs and set the plate down. Sam gobbled up the scraps in the blink of an eye, then settled down happily to chew the bone just beyond the door. Her tail thumped with delight.

For a moment, the woman watched her fondly, then she closed the door and returned to the table. She sat down, a smile playing on her lips. "One of our sons-in-law has a wolfhound too."

The boys' Uncle Angus chuckled. "Now *his* is one big dog. Only glimpsed her once, but she was massive. Must be the hugest wolfhound in Ireland."

The woman added, "She was friendly too. Can't remember her name." Her brow wrinkled in thought. "Sandie? Was that it?" Her frown deepened. "It was something like that." She glanced at her grandsons for help.

"Never met her," Darragh said, shoveling a spoon of stew into his mouth.

Across from him, his twin shrugged. "Me neither."

The woman turned to her husband. "You know the one I'm talking about. Eth's husband. What was his dog's name?"

The horse dealer looked bored. "Who cares, dear? Just another wolfhound. They're everywhere."

Turlough snorted, agreeing with the man.

The woman gave up. "Oh well, it doesn't matter. It's just that your dog reminds me of her." She pushed the pot of stew across the table towards Turlough. "Would you like more?"

"I've had plenty. That was delicious. Thank you." Turlough gratefully let her take his empty bowl.

Kinnard leaned forward, his eyes snapping open wide. "Hey, you promised you'd show them your sword! You've got to see this, Uncle Angus!"

Turlough hesitated, but Angus lifted his eyebrows with interest.

Kinnard and Darragh scraped their stools back and jumped up with excitement, crowding in.

Just as Turlough unsheathed the weapon, the door flew open and a tiny freckled girl skipped into the house. She clutched a bowl overflowing with bright red berries, half of which spilled to the floor as she dashed to the horse dealer's wife.

"Grand-mam! Look how many berries I collected!" She grabbed the older woman's hand, trying to drag her out of her chair. "Can we make caithne syrup? Please?" She hauled her willing grandmother away from the table and across the room.

"Of course, dear." Throwing a glance at Turlough, the woman explained, "Caithne syrup is Ciara's favorite."

The little girl, presumably Ciara, followed her grandmother's gaze and spotted Turlough and his sword. Her eyes widened. "You mean there's another one?" she asked.

Before anyone could ask another *what*, Darragh begged, "Can I hold it? Please? You let Kinnard."

Turlough's attention whipped back to the sword. He didn't want another near-maiming incident like in the field. He hesitated, not knowing how to refuse without hurting Darragh's feelings. Thankfully, Angus intervened and reached to take it. Relieved, Turlough passed him the sword.

Angus examined it, letting out a low whistle. "Some blade." He carefully ran his finger along the razor-sharp edge. "We don't get many soldiers passing through." He looked up, curiosity in his eyes. "So what brings you to Méifne?"

Across the room, pots and pans clattered as the woman and little girl fussed over bright red berries.

"I'm looking for my brother," Turlough said. The thought of Brioc in danger while he sat here relaxing made the stew swish uncomfortably in his stomach. "Unfortunately, I got the wrong town."

The little girl, who must have been listening all along, twisted her head around. She popped a red berry in her mouth, then spoke as she chewed. "Mamai lost my brother today too. Only it turned out he was playing next door." She nodded gravely as if her sage words would solve everything.

"Well," the horse dealer said, pushing back his chair and standing, "I need to get back to work."

Turlough took it as a hint to leave. He took his sword back and sheathed it.

The old man turned to Angus. "There's a pair of geldings I want to look at in the next village over. Can you come? I'll need a second rider if I buy them."

"Sure, Daid." Angus rose.

Turlough stood too, and again thanked his hostess.

Then Kinnard blurted, "Uncle Angus, can Turlough stay at your house? I told him you'd let him."

Turlough winced. "If you don't want me —"

"Certainly. It's fine," Angus said, giving him an easy smile. "My place is just down the road." He turned to the twins. "Show him which one."

"I'm indebted. Thank you."

"Make yourself at home. There's a hitch outside, and some hay for your horse. Bring your dog inside too if you want."

"I won't stay long. If I can just catch a nap, I'll be on my way." Where would he head afterward? Back to Oriel?

"Sleep as long as you need,"Angus said. "I won't be back for a few hours. And if I don't see you again, all the best finding your brother."

"Thanks."

As Turlough followed Angus, the horse dealer, and the redheads out the door, Grand-mam called over her shoulder,"Before you leave town, do stop back in to taste Ciara's syrup."

"I will. Thank you." Turlough didn't want to waste time returning, but he couldn't be rude.

What a nice bunch of people.

He sighed. If only this had been the right town and the right horse dealer.

Alas, it wasn't.

34

Bone-tired and weary, Brioc spotted the cottage that belonged to his father-in-law. Thank goodness, they were finally in Méifne. Maybe now he would find a chance to be alone with Lynnie.

She hadn't spoken to him all day. She'd avoided eye contact too, riding near Father Gerebran the whole time and acting like Brioc and Dymphna didn't exist. What was going on with her?

Brioc sighed. Obviously he'd done something wrong, something to upset her. Would he never stop messing up? First his brother, now his wife. Couldn't he ever do anything right? Well, he'd apologize for whatever it was as soon as he could get Lynnie alone. Hopefully soon.

He was nearly at the cottage when he noticed how quiet it seemed inside. Strange. The only other time he'd been here, when he'd asked Lynnie's daid if he could marry her, their house had been teeming with a million grandchildren. Something about the silence was ominous and disturbed him.

Then Brioc saw the thin dark stream seeping from underneath the door. He stared at the trickle. *What was that?*

For some reason, his heartbeat accelerated. He twisted his head to consult with Father Gerebran, but the priest and Lynnie weren't there. Confused, Brioc looked around, then spotted them at a watering trough a couple hundred yards away. Father Gerebran must have stopped without Brioc realizing it. Father leaned against their horse, holding the reins limply in one hand as the animal drank. Lynnie slumped forward on its back, her head resting on its neck, obviously asleep.

Dymphna had halted a little ahead of them. She was shaking a pebble from her shoe.

Brioc turned back to Lynnie's parents' door with that strange liquid pooling beneath it. The color of it sent alarm bells clanging in his head. His insides cramping, he stepped closer.

Blood? His throat constricted. He threw the door open and burst into the house.

His heart stopped. The floor pooled with blood. At his feet lay — *No! No! It couldn't be!*

The little girl!

He stumbled backwards. It was happening again. Out of nowhere, icy water sprayed him. The hissing, roiling waterfall appeared in front of him, its roar

145

deafening. Brioc lurched and slipped on a wet rock. The girl's body was at his feet. A wolf materialized on top of her. She screamed. Brioc whipped around to run, blind panic swelling inside him.

Get away, get away! It would kill him, it would — He spun and crashed hard into something.

The cliff? Was it the wall of the cliff? Seized with terror, he tried to scramble around it. He couldn't get around! The cliff was in the way! Something pounced on his back, snarling. Fangs ripped his flesh as the wolf — Everything suddenly stopped.

Brioc stood face-to-face with a wall. Inside a house.

No wolf was in sight.

Disorientated, legs threatening to collapse, he turned around.

The little girl was still there! In a puddle of blood!

Dizziness washed over him. The room tilted. Brioc groped for the wall to steady himself, fearing he would pass out.

Then the corpse moved. It straightened on the floor and assumed a kneeling position. In one hand it clasped a rag, dripping with blood. The little girl's wide, startled eyes stared at Brioc.

"Oh, I thought you were that soldier coming back in."

Brioc stared at the girl, the room whirling around him.

"Is . . . is that *you*, Uncle Brioc?" The child's face scrunched up in confusion. "I didn't know you were around. Is Aunty Eth with you?"

She must be one of Lynnie's thousand nieces. Brioc was too off balance to recognize which one. But she was alive and unhurt.

So why was she kneeling in a pool of blood?

The door opened and Dymphna stepped in, confusion stamped on her face.

"Careful!" the little girl yelped. "Don't step in the syrup! You'll get your shoes dirty!"

Syrup? So it wasn't blood?

The child glanced at the door through which Dymphna had just entered. "Grand-mam is getting more rags from the stable to wipe it up. I accidentally spilled the whole pot." At her last words, her voice quivered and her face fell. "And we spent hours making it." She looked like she would cry.

"Here," Dymphna said, "let me help you clean it up." She tiptoed through the spreading gooey liquid towards the tiny girl, and that's when a word registered in Brioc's mind.

"Did you say *soldier*?" His voice came out strangled.

Dymphna froze at the word. She cast him a frightened glance.

"Yes. One of them said he's coming back."

"You mean," Brioc's voice was a croak, "there's *lots* of soldiers?"

146

Dymphna's eyes widened in alarm.

The little girl nodded. "I saw a bunch of them in the woods. I think they're playing hide-and-seek, because they were behind trees and things. Turlough must be *It*. He's the only one not hiding." She returned her gaze to the syrup all over the floor and blinked back tears.

Brioc's mind spun. "*Turlough?*" The word got stuck in his throat. "His name is *Turlough?*"

"I . . . I think that's what Kinnard called him." She glanced back up. "He looks like you. I was sure you were him at first."

Turlough had brought Daemon's soldiers here?

Brioc tried to grasp the unthinkable. His brain couldn't wrap around it.

Wait, how would Turlough even know where they went?

'Her family's from Méifne. She's the youngest daughter of a horse dealer over there.'

Saints above, Brioc had told him! Turlough must have told the king!

"He came here searching for his brother," the little girl added. "He had his sword out."

Turlough had barged into Lynnie's house looking for him . . . *with his sword drawn?*

At first, Brioc didn't even register the physical danger. The pain of betrayal overwhelmed him, not allowing his mind to grasp anything else. It was as if a dagger slammed through his heart. He staggered back, his mind grappling with the realization that his brother not only didn't love him, but actually *hated* him. Hated him enough to want him dead. Enough to kill him with his own sword!

And he'd trusted him. Given him Sam. After Turlough had been so nice at the graves, Brioc had dared to think that maybe, just maybe his brother didn't hate him after all.

Everything inside him crumpled, started to die. Like a huge steel hand reached inside him and crushed out his life.

"What do we do?" Dymphna's terrified voice hardly registered.

Fingers dug into his arm. Someone seemed to be yanking him across the floor. He blinked, confused, fighting to focus.

Dymphna was pulling him by his sleeve towards the door. "It must be Daidi's soldiers! They'll capture us! We've got to go, we've got to go!" Fear laced her voice.

Brioc's brain could hardly function. He fought to snap out of his stupor.

"Come on, Brioc! We have to find Ethlynn and Father!"

Lynnie! Oh my gosh, she was still outside! Turlough would kill her too!

Adrenaline surged through him and he bolted for the door, the princess still clutching his arm in terror.

35

Turlough rolled over again and his eyes snapped open. It was useless trying to doze. He was overtired, and worried sick about his brother. He'd been lying here for nearly two hours, desperately willing himself to sleep, but no luck so far.

He had to hit the road again, had to somehow find Brioc before Daemon did. How could this be the wrong town? He was *sure* Brioc said Méifne.

Frustrated, mind churning, he sat up on the blanket he'd spread out as a bed on Angus's floor.

Across the room, Samthann must have sensed his movement. Her head shot up, then the rest of her body. She stretched, shivered, then vigorously shook herself, sending dust in all directions. She trotted to the one tiny window and climbed onto her hind legs. Front paws resting on the windowsill, she stuck her head out as far as it would go, ears perked and tail swishing.

While Sam watched the birdies and the butterflies, Turlough tidied the havoc from her exploration of the cottage. Then he wrapped Brioc's harp back in the blanket, strapped on his sword, and glanced around for his boots. He thought he'd left them near the door with the rest of his gear, but he couldn't see them there. Bewildered, his gaze roamed the room.

Ah, there they were, under Angus's table. Sam must have snuck them while he'd had his eyes closed, trying to sleep.

He was half way to his boots when Sam went berserk.

She barked, then whined, then barked again. Her paws frantically scrabbled against the windowsill, her whole body squirming and shuddering as she tried to climb through the tiny window.

Turlough stared, horrified, not knowing what to do. She would get stuck! She would break the windowsill or pull down Angus's whole wall!

"Whoa, Sam! What's going on?" He raced to the window, grabbed her backside, and tried to haul her back into the room. She barked and scrambled and twisted to get through the hole, her tail wagging so madly it whacked him in the face.

He struggled to pull her in while she struggled to climb out. She would never fit! He had to stop her!

Letting go of her rump, he dived for the door. He jerked it open. Sam yanked her head out of the window back into the room, crashed down on all fours, and shot out the door.

Turlough stood in a daze, staring after her.

* * * * *

Dymphna felt Brioc grab her hand as they raced down the street, away from the little girl and the cottage. "Run!" he shouted, half dragging, half propelling her along. His panic amplified hers.

He ground to a sudden halt and she smashed into him. He scanned the road, searching. "Where's Lynnie? Where's Father? *Where did Father take Lynnie?*" His voice verged on hysteria.

It was all happening too fast. Dymphna's mind whirled with fear.

"There! Over there!" She spotted their horse in the shade of a tree near the watering trough. Father Gerebran peered up and down the row of houses, confusion stamped on his face. He was probably wondering which cottage she and Brioc had disappeared into. Still mounted on the horse, Ethlynn looked groggy, like she'd just woken up a second ago. Her hair stuck out in a thousand directions, her pink dress was askance and rumpled. She yawned and twisted in the saddle, stretching her arms.

Brioc must have spotted them because he started running in their direction, jerking Dymphna with him so abruptly her arm nearly popped out of its socket. She stumbled to keep up. She couldn't run that fast; she was going to trip. "Slow down! Brioc, please, I can't —"

Out of nowhere, an enormous wolfhound exploded onto the scene, right between them and the horse. It sailed towards Brioc, closing the distance with lightning speed. A second later, a man burst from a doorway in the direction the dog had appeared. He was dressed in normal clothes, but a huge sword hung at his side. He must be a soldier! No one else carried swords. At least not that big!

"Sam!" he yelled. "Stupid mutt! Get back here!"

Sam? Dymphna reeled. Was that Samthann?

The dog kept coming. The soldier ran into the road, then sprinted after the wolfhound.

How did he get Sam?

And why was he in his socks? Didn't Daidi pay them enough to buy shoes?

Brioc stopped dead in his tracks, so suddenly that once again Dymphna's arm was nearly wrenched from the rest of her body. The oncoming dog and the man running in his socks blocked their way to Father and Ethlynn. Brioc started to swerve one way, then changed his mind and went the other, jolting Dymphna's arm afresh with every move. He obviously didn't know where to go or what to do.

On the other side of the running soldier, Father Gerebran suddenly snapped from his leaning position against the tree, his gaze locking onto something off to the side, hidden behind a row of houses. Dymphna couldn't see what it was. His expression was nearly as panicked as Brioc's. The priest hesitated for a split second, then leaped on the horse in front of Ethlynn. He looked both ways, as if somehow trapped, then jerked the reins, kicking the horse into a full gallop. They flew down the road the opposite direction and disappeared from sight. Were they being chased too?

Dymphna had no idea, because she couldn't see what happened next. For just at that second, the wolfhound crashed into her and Brioc. The force of the collision nearly knocked them clean off their feet. Brioc stumbled backwards, dropping Dymphna's arm as he raised his hands to shield himself. Dymphna heard what sounded like the thundering of a dozen hooves in the direction Father had disappeared with Ethlynn, but she couldn't turn to see what was happening to them. The dog leaped up, clamped her front paws onto Brioc's shoulders, and frantically mopped his face with her tongue.

He tried to swat her off. "Sam, get off! Get off!"

The dog was unstoppable, her tail wagging so fiercely the movement alone all but pushed Brioc over.

The socked soldier skidded to a halt about thirty feet away. Dymphna saw shock in his eyes, like he was seeing a ghost. His mouth opened, then closed. He looked speechless.

"Brioc?" he finally got out.

He must be one of Daidi's soldiers, but Dymphna didn't recognize him. Bruises covered his face, as if he'd been in a fight.

Sheer adrenaline must have given Brioc the strength to shove the wolfhound off. The dog landed on the ground with a thud. "Run!" Brioc shouted at Dymphna, spinning around. "The stable! Get to the stable! Go go go go!"

She had no idea where the stable was. Stumbling after him, heart drumming with fear, she managed to latch onto his arm. He reached for her hand, clasped it, and together they ran as fast as they could. Sam — *was it Sam?* — raced alongside them, barking excitedly, like this was a game.

"Brioc!" the soldier yelled behind them. "Brioc, no! Come back!"

Dymphna threw a glance over her shoulder.

The soldier charged after them.

They careened around the corner of Ethlynn's house. A woman with a handful of rags stood in their way, her eyes startled at their sudden appearance. Brioc practically bowled her over in his frenzy to reach the stable. He didn't even stop to apologize.

Dymphna couldn't keep up with him. She lost her footing and tripped, falling to her knees and slamming into a barrel set against the wall. It toppled and a million brown, rotting apples cascaded out and rolled across the ground, straight into the path where Daidi's soldier would follow. The wolfhound slipped and scrambled through the onslaught of what was obviously last year's crop. It slowed her for an instant.

"Get up! Hurry! Hurry!" Brioc pulled Dymphna to her feet so hard it brought tears to her eyes.

She caught a glimpse of the soldier. He swerved his way through the rolling fruit, then nearly collided with the astonished woman holding the rags. "Move, move! Out of my way!" He veered to the right; she accidentally did too. He stepped left. So did she. Back and forth, back and forth. After several seconds, he managed to navigate his way around the wide-eyed woman.

"Brioc!" he yelled. "Brioc, wait!"

At Brioc's name, the woman spun to look at them, jaw dropping, fresh astonishment on her face.

Brioc shot a look backwards. He must have seen how close the soldier was.

"Come on, come on, come on!" he yelled in Dymphna's ear.

They plowed into the stable.

With a flurry of squawks and feathers, half a dozen chickens raced out. Dymphna clumsily sidestepped them. She was out of breath. Her heart slammed against her ribs. Brioc let go of her hand and vaulted over the gate into the nearest stall.

While he loosed the horse and shoved the bit into its mouth, Dymphna scrambled to unlatch the stall door. Her hands trembled. Samthann stood beside her, barking her head off, as if this were the most exciting game she had ever played.

Dymphna couldn't believe they were stealing a horse, but Brioc obviously had no such scruple. Then again, it *did* belong to his father-in-law, which made it partially Ethlynn's horse as well, right? Besides, Brioc would somehow pay for it later; Dymphna knew he would.

He jumped on the animal's back and it nervously pranced out of the stall, almost rearing. Brioc swiped for Dymphna's hand. She managed to catch it and he yanked her on behind him. She landed clumsily on its back. Fear pulsed through her veins, blood pounded in her ears.

The soldier raced into the stable entrance just as Brioc jerked on the reins and kneed the horse savagely in the flanks. It bolted past the soldier and flew out of the stable at a dead gallop.

It was all Dymphna could do to hold on. She clung to Brioc for dear life as they raced down the road, Samthann on their heels, barking and yelping.

The soldier was shouting, "No! No, wait!"

His voice faded as they left him behind in a cloud of dust.

36

Ready to explode with frustration, Turlough wanted to swear. But he couldn't do that, because that woman he'd collided with a minute ago might still be in earshot. So instead he glanced around the stable for something to throttle. The victim of choice right now would of course be his stupid brother, but Brioc and Lynnie were already out of sight.

Why had they run from him?

To release his anger, he kicked the first thing in sight, a metal bucket on the ground.

Ouch.

He'd forgotten — he was in his socks.

Grabbing his throbbing foot, his hand wrapped around a clump of goo. Confused, he looked down. His hand was coated with horse manure from his sock, and some weird brown squishy mush.

What the —

Then he remembered. He'd run an obstacle course of rotting apples.

He sighed, suddenly feeling old and tired.

Sam straggled back to the stable doorway, her tail between her legs. Tongue hanging out, she panted from her sprint after the galloping horse. She looked up at Turlough with sad, forlorn eyes, as if begging him to bring Brioc back. If a dog could cry, Samthann would be sobbing her heart out.

"Don't look at me like that. I feel the same way."

For a split second Turlough considered grabbing a horse from the stable and pursuing Brioc and Lynnie. But that was stealing. He couldn't do that to the nice horse dealer and his wife.

There was only one thing to do. Rush back to Angus's, grab his gear, and follow with his own horse. At least he knew which direction they'd gone. He was better off than he had been yesterday, right?

Did Angus have a spare pair of socks?

Heaving a sigh, Turlough turned and saw the woman still standing in the same spot. Her expression was befuddled. The rags she'd been holding earlier lay scattered on the ground. She must have dropped them.

Oh no! It was the horse dealer's wife! Get out of here, before she asked questions!

Turlough slunk around the stable door, hoping she hadn't recognized him. As soon as he rounded the corner, he spotted a horse racing up a hill in the distance.

Two riders sat on its back. A man and a woman. Turlough's heart stopped. *Brioc and Lynnie!*

No wait. Impossible. How did they get way over there? They'd ridden in the opposite direction. There was no way Brioc could've turned the horse so quickly.

Nah, it wasn't them. Lynnie had been wearing some drab brown thing. That girl had a pink dress. Fancy color. Something a princess might own, or a noble lady. Turlough was about to turn away when a group of horsemen came into view on the hillside, about a quarter a mile behind the galloping couple.

It looked like they were chasing them.

Mildly curious, he shaded his eyes and watched.

Most of the riders were nondescript, but one wore a flowing scarlet cloak. Another man looked huge, like a giant.

Turlough stared, then blinked.

Could that be —?

He shook his head. No, of course not. Just a bunch of people, probably all friends, heading off to — *oh, who even cared? He was wasting precious time!*

He ripped his gaze away and broke into a run towards Angus's house to get his horse.

Sam raced at his heels.

37

Ethlynn clung with all her might to Father Gerebran as their horse tore up a hill at breakneck speed. She couldn't figure out where they were or what had happened. One minute she'd been asleep, dreaming about cuddling her baby and Brioc loving her again, and the next minute she had straightened up, yawned, and nearly been knocked off the horse as the priest leaped on in front of her and bolted down some village road.

The countryside whizzed by in a blur. She held on for dear life. What was going on?

Where was her husband?

Where was that . . . that *girl* who was ruining her life?

Why was Father in such a hurry?

Twang. Pfft.

Thwish.

A long stick-like object whooshed through the air, sailing past her head. *What was that?*

Another one. Another and another.

Pfft, fwooph.

Swoooosh. Swoooosh.

The sticks rained down, littering the ground. Ethlynn realized with shock what they were. Arrows!

Thwack-thwack-thwack-thwack! A million in a row.

Pfft. Thwick. Whoosh, whooooosh.

They turned into a swarm, arching through the air, swooping, then thudding to the ground. They seemed to be everywhere.

Father's body tensed. Ethlynn held on tighter.

The horse slowed as the hill steepened. Father kicked it, trying to urge it faster, faster. Hoof beats thundered behind them. The gallop turned to a lope as the animal struggled up the hill. The arrows kept sailing past.

Without warning their horse lurched and collapsed to its knees. Ethlynn soared from its back and landed with a bone-jarring clunk. Pain shot through her. Suddenly she was tumbling, pink material alternating with green grass in front of her eyes as she rolled down an incline.

Pink, green, pink, green, pink, green, *splash!* Brown, brown, pink, green, pink, green.

She crashed into something squat and leafy, and banged to a stop. Everything whirled around her. Stars danced before her eyes.

Somewhere in the back of her mind, she registered the sound of a horse screaming in agony. *Screaming?* Could a horse scream? She'd never heard a horse scream, but she was sure that was a horse, and sure it was screaming.

A hand clamped around her arm and yanked her to her feet.

She was face to face with a straggly blond beard and beady eyes.

Her legs buckled. She melted to the ground.

The man jerked her back up, supporting her so she wouldn't fall again. The earth tilted. The blond bearded face turned into two blond bearded faces for a second, then merged back to one.

"I have her, Sire."

Another tilting man jumped off a tilting horse. He stomped towards them. Something scarlet billowed behind him. A tent? What was he doing with a tent protruding from his back? The ground continued to sway as her head got lighter. She was going to faint!

She squeezed her eyes closed, praying the spinning would stop.

"In the name of God, let her go. Do not hurt that girl!"

Father Gerebran?

He sounded far away. Sounded like he was in pain.

She opened her eyes again. The man wearing the scarlet tent marched towards her. He mercifully stopped spinning. So did the blond bearded face.

More men dismounted, seven or eight of them. One was huge. Swords clanged at their sides. Were they *soldiers?*

The scarlet one came closer. His tent mutated into a cloak. "My foolish, foolish daughter." His voice was an animal growl. "You are coming back with me to —" He stopped dead in his tracks. He threw a bewildered glance around him, then his jaw twitched in what looked to Ethlynn like fury.

Someone out of her range of vision said with alarm, "It's not her."

Murmuring and frantic whispering.

The horse's screams turned into pained whinnies.

Father Gerebran ordered, "Let her go."

The blond man released Ethlynn's arm. Relief flooded her as the priest limped into sight. Dirt smudged his robe. One sleeve had a grass stain.

The whinnies stopped. Their horse fell strangely silent. Ethlynn dared to glance towards where its pitiful sounds had come from. The horse lay sprawled on the ground in a spreading pool of blood, riddled with arrows. She gasped and clapped her hand over her mouth, stifling a scream. Brioc! She needed Brioc!

Father Gerebran stepped protectively in front of her. Without warning, Ethlynn's stomach seized. For a wild, terrifying moment she thought she would collapse from the strange agony. The man in the scarlet cloak watched her impassively. Finally the pain peaked, then subsided. Ethlynn tried to catch her breath.

One soldier hung back from the others, still astride his horse. Dark hair cascaded down his shoulders. A deep scar ran the length of one cheek, yet despite that he was almost handsome. He stared straight at her, a frown furrowing his forehead. Had he seen her in pain? His eyes searched her face, then roved downward. When his gaze reached her baby bump, shock flickered across his face. Then something like understanding. Even compassion.

He looked vaguely familiar. Where had she seen him before? She was positive she'd never seen any of the others.

Without warning, her stomach cramped again, so painful that a cry escaped her lips. Could . . . could these be contractions? Mam said they would hurt. The thought that she might be going into labor sent fear bolting through her.

"Who are these people?" someone asked, sounding confused. Everyone started talking at once. They *all* sounded confused. Her agony passed as suddenly as it had come.

"You fool! You led us to the wrong —"

"It was Turlough. I know it was!"

"Then he took us on a wild goose chase!"

The scarred one sat in silence.

"Turlough knows where his brother is! He must!"

Who was Turlough? Who was his brother? What was going on?

And where in the world had she seen the one with the scar?

"Shut up, you idiots!" One man barged forward and took charge. "Head back to the village, you bunch of morons. Find Turlough. Follow him!" His eyes flared. "He'll pay for this."

The soldiers shook their heads, murmuring, and the group dispersed towards their mounts. A skeletal figure, the only one without a sword, stepped to the man wearing the scarlet cloak and took his arm. He steered him away, the other's jaw still twitching in silent rage. For a second it looked like his eyes rolled inside their sockets. Then the thin one led him to his horse.

Another sharp pain made Ethlynn nearly double over.

Father Gerebran stood protectively near her. Finally, her cramp passed. Sweat rolled down her back.

Soldiers swiped arrows off the grass and swung into saddles. The scar-faced man sat motionless on his horse, staring at their dead mount. He glanced away. Ran a hand through his hair. Looked at the man in the cloak, disgust in his eyes.

At Mass? Had she seen him at Mass? There was a man who stood at the back by the doors sometimes.

No, that wasn't possible. These men weren't from Oriel.

The others had all mounted. In a scattered line, they galloped away. The scarred one tugged his reins, as if to follow. But for some reason, he hesitated.

Ethlynn clutched Father's arm, frightened. What did he want?

The soldier, licking his lips, shot a glance over his shoulder at his retreating comrades, then back to their dead horse. He bent and detached something from his saddlebag.

Ethlynn held her breath. Father Gerebran spread his arms protectively in front of her. The man tossed something at them. It landed near Father's feet.

With a sympathetic look, he whipped his horse around and raced away to catch up with the others. Within seconds, he vanished from sight.

Father's brows came together. He stepped forward and picked up the object. A small bag. He opened it and emptied the contents into his palm.

The last sound Ethlynn heard was the chink of coins. Another sharp jab of pain, and her vision blurred to red, then black. She was about to faint.

The ground flew up to meet her.

38

After ransacking Angus's cottage for a pair of clean socks, Turlough whipped them on and stuffed his feet into his boots. He frantically collected his gear.

Why had he taken this cumbersome harp? What a pain in the neck, wrapping it up every time, trying not to knock it on his bag. What on earth had he been thinking? For a moment he wondered if he should leave it behind. It could pay for Angus's socks.

Heck, it could pay for the horse his brother had just stolen!

He sighed.

No, he couldn't do that to Brioc.

He hoisted the thing over his shoulder, dropped one of his precious coins on the table to pay Angus for the socks, then flew out the door.

His conscience nagged him. The horse. He really had to pay for that horse. *Brioc, I could kill you for this.*

He ran back in, fished around for more coins, and realized there was no way out of it. He would have to leave them all. Even that would be pathetically insufficient. He tossed the entire money pouch on Angus's table. He didn't allow himself to think of how he would get by now. Penniless.

Worry about it later.

Back out the door. *Hurry!*

Securing everything onto his mount, he swung into the saddle. He turned the horse east, the direction Brioc and Lynnie had gone, and kicked it into a gallop.

Sam raced excitedly beside him.

He figured Brioc had about a forty minute head start.

It could be worse.

Once he was out of the village, he forced himself to slow down. Keep a clear head. Don't overshoot.

As he rode, he put himself in his brother's mind: what would have been Brioc's thoughts as he blasted into a gallop and blindly fled, his young wife hanging on for dear life behind him?

Well, for starters, he probably wouldn't have reasoned, *Let's get off the main road.* Brioc had no experience with these types of life and death situations. He had never outrun an enemy. Emergencies like that didn't happen in a monastery, and playing a harp in a castle wasn't exactly a job fraught with danger. It would've taken Brioc awhile before the thought even occurred to him to cut into the woods. And Turlough would put money on it, not that he had any, that if his brother *had* thought of that, it certainly could not have occurred to him to cover their tracks.

In other words, Brioc was out of his element.

Perfect.

Turlough stayed on the road for just under three miles before looking for signs of Brioc's departure into the woods. He didn't know the condition of the horse his brother had taken, but presumably it was in decent shape, having been in the possession of a man who sold horses for a living. It was no nag.

Turlough did the calculations as he rode.

At a breakneck gallop, with two riders on its back, even a well rested horse in top condition would struggle to get a mile without slowing. Brioc hadn't had time to saddle the thing. Riding at a full speed would have been almost impossible for both Brioc and Lynnie to hang on without falling off, and having no saddle would have made it especially painful for the rider in the rear. Lynnie. And she was pregnant.

Turlough pictured the scene in his mind:

Brioc reining the horse down to a canter, a pace they may have maintained for three miles, but certainly no more. Brioc and Lynnie finding themselves trotting. Catching their breath.

The horse slowing to a walk. Brioc twisting to look down the road behind them, wondering if they'd been followed.

No one would be in sight.

What would Brioc have done when he'd perceived they were safe?

Turlough imagined him pulling the horse to a stop. Riding double was uncomfortable at the best of times, but Lynnie was with child. By now Brioc would need to let her dismount.

So, he swings off their horse first, then reaches up to help his wife down. She walks around a bit. Maybe stumbles to a bush or something. In a flash, Brioc realizes he should move off the road.

Thus, at three miles, Turlough steered his horse closer to the ditch and rode even slower, alternating sides of the road, searching for signs in the dirt of Brioc dismounting or having veered off into the woods.

It took him four minutes to find the spot.

Right there.

Turlough drew near to a patch of flattened grass and dismounted. Trampled, snapped branches lay on the ground. A clump of horse manure was nearby. Obviously fresh.

Yep, he found their trail alright. Sam sniffed the area, tail going crazy. The soft dirt was stamped with prints. Three sets. A horse's. A man's. And the other, smaller, definitely made by a woman. It looked like they'd walked for a few moments, probably trying to decide what to do, then the smaller footprints disappeared. Lynnie had remounted. Brioc would have led the horse. The prints headed into the woods.

Turlough looped the reins around his hand and followed them, leading his horse. He didn't want to miss anything vital.

The farther he walked, the more he was aghast. His brother could not have blazed a more obvious trail if he'd been trying. Footprints, broken twigs, trampled leaves littered the ground in a more or less straight path through the woods. Good grief. A seven-year-old could follow this.

If Barrf was out here searching, Brioc would be dead.

What on earth had he stolen from the king?

The more Turlough thought about it, the more bewildering it was. Brioc obviously didn't own the horse he'd taken from the stable. The horse dealer wasn't Lynnie's daid. So whatever Brioc had stolen, it wasn't stored on the horse beforehand. He must've had it on his person. In a pouch or something.

So it was small. Very small.

Turlough came to a place they had obviously stopped to rest. Lynnie's prints reappeared. A little space had been cleared in the dirt, as if Brioc had brushed aside leaves and undergrowth so Lynnie could sit down. Maybe they'd taken a drink from a waterskin or cut a few chunks of bread. Did they even have food? Turlough had seen no saddlebag, or bundle of any kind on the horse. They didn't even have a blanket.

He paced the area, worry making him feel sick. Brioc was in way over his head. He had no idea how to survive out here. And with a pregnant wife!

Blessed Mother Mary, let me find them. Before they die; before Daemon and Barrf figure out where they are.

Turlough rubbed the back of his neck and crouched by the many footprints. He stared at them, as if somehow the prints would hold the answer to what Brioc had stolen from Daemon.

What in the world could the object be? It wasn't on the horse. It wasn't in a saddlebag.

If he found Brioc, could he convince him to return the thing to Daemon? He'd have to try! What could be so precious that Brioc would risk his life? And the lives of his wife and unborn child? It was mind boggling.

To add to the mystery, why had Brioc told Turlough his wife was from Méifne, when no one there knew her? And why had he run from Turlough in the village?

Brioc had asked him to take care of Sam. That had been an act of trust, right? And Turlough had accepted, living up to the trust. He'd even given Brioc money. So why would Brioc flee from him, as if they were enemies?

Nothing made sense.

Turlough sighed and straightened. He remounted his horse and rode along the trail further into the woods.

Then he spotted a stream ahead, and his heart sank. Oh no.

Anyone with *any* sense at all, would know to walk in the water. Surely even Brioc knew that much! Wash away the scent, hide the tracks, throw the trackers. Basic as basic gets. Survival for dummies.

Part of him prayed Brioc knew that, while another part of him prayed he didn't.

He had to find him!

A hill sloped to the left, on this side of the stream. Turlough ran a hand through his hair. It looked steep. From the top, he would have a commanding view of the area. It was getting dark, but if he climbed quickly enough, there might be enough light left to actually see his brother.

He pulled the reins and trotted towards the slope.

Sam raced around in circles, then barked and followed.

39

"Is this enough wood?"

Dymphna dumped the armload on the ground next to Brioc. She'd never gathered firewood before and couldn't help feel a glow of satisfaction at how much she'd collected in such a short time.

"They're the biggest ones I could find," she added, slapping her dirty hands against the skirt of her dress. Then she shoved her sweat-damp hair back into her ugly scarf. That had been hard work!

Brioc didn't look up. He knelt in the dirt, in exactly the spot she'd left him twenty minutes ago, still attempting to light a fire. Her heart sank when she saw there was no hint of a flame. "You mean you haven't managed to get it going yet? Maybe I can help."

He threw her a look. "No, I haven't managed to get it going yet," he snapped. "And I doubt you'd be any better at lighting a fire without flint or tinder. If you can, please do."

Dymphna flinched. It was so unlike Brioc to be in a foul mood.

Then again, his wife and unborn child were missing.

She bit her lip. "I thought Father Gerebran brought a tinder box."

"He did. He still has it. It's on his horse. The horse we don't have. Remember?"

"Oh."

Actually, Dymphna had forgotten. Father Gerebran and Ethlynn had everything now. All she and Brioc had were his father-in-law's horse, the priest's extra hunting knife which Brioc had borrowed when they caught the fish this morning, and the clothes on their backs. Which were still wet at the hems, from that little stream they'd crossed forty minutes ago. They didn't even have blankets for tonight.

They really needed that fire.

She saw Brioc toss a distracted glance at the sticks she'd deposited beside him. He did a double-take, then his gaze snapped back to the pile.

He stared at it incredulously.

Dymphna cringed. *What had she done wrong?*

Brioc sucked in a breath. "I said *twigs*, not branches. Didn't you hear me?" He was obviously trying to keep his patience. "These things are hunking logs, Dymphna. You can't start a fire with — " He stopped himself, sighed, then stood up. "Alright, I'll go find them myself. You stay here and — and — oh I don't know what. Cook a meal or something."

Hot tears stung her eyes. She blinked them back. "You don't have to yell at me. I thought you said —"

"I said kindling. That means twigs. Little ones." He let out a frustrated sigh and rubbed the back of his neck. "And for the record, I didn't yell at you. I only said —"

"I've never had to light a fire before!" she blurted. "How was I supposed to know what kind of wood you wanted? I tried my best! My hands are cut and my arms hurt and I ripped the hem of my dress on some thorny bush and —" An image of Christ in His Passion, uttering not a word, pushed its way into her mind. She instantly clamped her mouth shut to stop her flow of defensive words. *Oh Jesus, forgive me.* She had no right to get mad at Brioc. He was risking his life to save her from a fate worse than death. *Marrying Daidi.*

Determined not to cry — knowing that if she started, she wouldn't be able to stop — she wiped her eyes with her sleeve and sniffled. Who cared if part of her dress was left in a bush? It was the most atrocious dress she'd ever seen in her life. How could Ethlynn think it was pretty? Dymphna hated it. She wanted her own clothes back and was so frightened and exhausted and terrified the soldiers would find them and . . .

Without warning, the dam burst. Tears poured from her eyes.

Brioc let out another sigh, but his voice softened. "I guess you've always had others to light a fire for you. I'm sorry, Dymphna. I apologize. Princesses aren't meant to . . . to do things for themselves. Still less for peasants like me. I had no right to ask you to gather wood in the first place. Forgive me."

Tears streamed down her cheeks. She stared at the ground, ashamed of crying in front of him like a baby. Even more ashamed of her uselessness. She'd never realized before how comfortable her life had been compared to the poor. Like the other night, trying to sleep on the hard ground without a blanket. No one else had a problem with that. Not even Ethlynn, pregnant and all. And there Dymphna had lain, feeling sorry for herself that she couldn't sleep in a soft goose-feather bed. She'd offered it up but it hadn't made it any more bearable.

And today, as they'd galloped away from the soldier, it struck her that she didn't even know how to ride a horse. Her whole life she'd traveled in horse-drawn carts, driven by servants. If Brioc had had time to loose two mounts in the stable, instead of only one, she wouldn't have even known how to steer the beast out the door. The soldier would have caught her in five seconds flat — if she hadn't fallen off first. She owed her life to Brioc. Twice. First as a child with the doll and the cliff. And now . . . all this.

And, to her mortification, no, she couldn't cook. If they had food, which they didn't, and a fire, which they also didn't, Brioc would end up making the meal.

Shame burned her face. Fifteen years old, and she'd never cooked in her life.

She would never survive without Brioc and Father Gerebran to take care of her.

The sudden thought of the missing priest increased her misery. Where was he, and Ethlynn? Were they still alive?

No wonder Brioc was exploding inside. That was his *wife.*

Dymphna furiously rubbed her eyes with her sleeve cuffs, trying to stop her flow of tears. If anything, *he* should be the one crying. Fumbling in the pouch of her ugly dress, she pulled out the small cloth she'd earlier found there. She wiped her eyes on it, then blew her nose.

Brioc ignored her. His impatience had drained as abruptly as it had flared. He dropped to his knees again by the pit he'd cleared for a fire and scraped the blade of the knife against a stone, trying to get a spark. He was so frantic he was shaking.

Dymphna watched his frenzied movements, the desperate determination in his eyes. He wanted that fire, needed it. Why was he so obsessed with fire?

Her own nerves frazzling at the sight of him, she sniffled and glanced up at the sky. Daylight had faded so quickly. But Brioc had seemed troubled even before the threat of night. The last few hours he had a haunted look about him. It reminded Dymphna of when she'd known him at the monastery, back when he couldn't speak. It must be something to do with that soldier.

How had Daidi's soldier ended up with Sam in the first place?

She had earlier asked Brioc about it, but his eyes had filled with pain and he'd remained silent. Experience had taught Dymphna that no amount of prying would get anything out of him. He was the master of silence, if ever there was one.

She stared, apprehension mounting, as he futilely scraped the blade against the rock.

"I'll go find more wood if you want," she offered in a tiny voice, mostly so she didn't have to stay here and watch.

"Thank you, Princess," he mumbled meekly. "Make sure they're twigs. Little dry ones. We really need this fire or we'll freeze."

Surely the prospect of cold couldn't put such terror in his eyes each night. Besides, it was spring. Yes, it was still chilly at night, but not *that* chilly. So what was wrong with him?

If only Samthann were here to calm him down. Funny how his dog could do what no human could.

As if in answer to Dymphna's thoughts, a dog barked in the distance, making her jump.

She looked at Brioc with alarm.

The dog barked again. It was far enough away that the sound was faint, but close enough to be ominous.

That soldier with Sam must be in the woods, looking for them!

Brioc shoved the knife into his belt and sprang to his feet. He ran for their horse.

Dymphna bolted after him.

40

Within seconds, Brioc had helped Dymphna onto the horse's back. The dog's bark sounded far away, but fear slammed through her nonetheless.

"Do you think it's him? That soldier with Sam?"

"I don't know." Brioc hurried to untie the horse from the tree. His hands shook, making it take twice as long as it should have. "Keep your voice down. Sounds carry farther at night." He said it in a whisper.

Dymphna hadn't thought about that, noise traveling at night. They'd been speaking in normal tones a few minutes ago. Had whoever was out there heard them?

Brioc seemed to take forever. Finally he grabbed the reins. He gave her an apologetic look. "We'll only ride double till we're away from here and safe. Then I'll get down, I promise." She felt bad, knowing why he said that. It was because of that first night, when he'd given her a brother-like hug. She hadn't meant to offend him by jerking away, when all he'd been doing was trying to console her. Yet ever since then, apart from their hurried flight from Méifne, Brioc had kept a noticeable distance and had not touched her once. She was grateful, but felt awful for having hurt him.

Nudging their horse into the fastest gait he dared, he headed deeper into the woods. The sun had disappeared over the horizon. Shadows sheathed the woods ahead of them.

"How did he find us?" she whispered. She wanted to ask again how he'd gotten Sam, but it wasn't the time for a million questions. "Do you think he can follow our tracks?"

"I . . . I don't know."

When they'd crossed the stream a few miles back, Brioc had been careful to lead the horse through the water for at least a quarter of a mile. He'd zigzagged from side to side, covering any scent in case they were tracked.

"It might just be some local with a dog." He sounded like it was getting hard for him to breathe. Fear? He urged the horse faster.

"Do you think Daidi's with him?" The thought filled Dymphna with terror.

"Shh. We don't even know if we're being followed. It could be anyone out there."

The sound of swishing water reached their ears.

Brioc jerked on the reins and froze.

Dymphna could feel him tense in front of her at the sound of the water. He didn't only act strange about fire, he had this thing with waterfalls too. She didn't know why. She glanced around frantically, looking for the water's source, but no falls were in sight.

Brioc sat rigid for a moment, no doubt every sense heightened to danger. Finally he must have realized there was no waterfall, because his muscles relaxed slightly and he cautiously moved the horse forward.

A minute later they came to a river, much bigger than the tiny stream they had earlier crossed. Perhaps fifteen or twenty feet wide.

Brioc rode along the bank, back and forth, searching for a shallow place to cross. Dymphna held her breath. What if there was no place? Being trapped on this side with the soldier, and maybe even Daidi himself, filled her with horror.

Please, Jesus, please please.

Brioc halted and quickly dismounted, hopping to the ground. Handing Dymphna the reins, he waded several feet into the river, testing the depth. It went up to his waist.

Then his chest.

Oh no. It was going to be too deep.

"Can we cross?" she called out to him as loud as she dared.

He couldn't hear her from the river. The water was too loud. He slowly and cautiously sloshed towards the opposite bank. At one point he lost his footing on something below the surface. He went down to his neck, then managed to right himself. The water got shallower. He made it to the other side.

Thank you, Jesus.

He turned around and waded back, then took the reins.

"There's lots of rocks. Especially as you come out on the other end. But if we go slowly, I think the horse will let me lead it across. Hold on tight."

She nodded. Sweat trickled down her back. She cast a nervous glance at the darkening woods behind them.

Nothing but trees and shadows.

Brioc carefully tugged the horse behind him into the water.

Dymphna squeezed her eyes shut and held onto the horse's mane so tightly the muscles in her hands cramped. Within seconds, the bottom half of her dress was soaked, her legs and waist completely under water. She shivered with cold.

The horse slowly pushed its way through the churning river. Thankfully the current wasn't swift. It was the hidden rocks and boulders that made the crossing treacherous. Dymphna's legs knocked one, then another, under the surface. She kept her eyes closed, her lips moving in silent prayer.

The whooshing of the water blocked out other sounds. Was the person with the dog following them?

The river abruptly became shallower. More and more of Dymphna's body emerged from the water, until only her ankles were under. They must be almost at the other side. She kept praying, eyes closed.

The horse lurched to a stop, jerking her forward.

Her eyes snapped open. They were three feet from the shore, in shallow water.

A bewildered look crossed Brioc's face. He tugged the reins, but the animal didn't move.

Couldn't move.

Brioc pulled sideways. No use. Tried to back the horse up. Didn't work.

He looked down at its legs. So did Dymphna.

Its rear left hoof was wedged between the rocks!

Brioc shot Dymphna a frantic look. She shot one back. The horse whinnied in distress, stomping with its free legs.

The dog barked again.

The horse neighed and stamped and suddenly struggled, splashing water everywhere.

"Shh," Dymphna begged the horse, holding on even tighter to stop from falling.

Brioc bent into the water and jerked at the rocks, fumbling to free the animal's hoof.

Dymphna threw another nervous glance behind her.

The water swished around them.

Whoosh, whoosh.

A glimpse of movement, on a hill. Something on all fours. Sam? She strained to see.

The thing disappeared.

Her heart hammered. *Please, please, please.*

She kept straining her eyes. Was that a man on a horse? It was hard to tell.

She gasped. It must be the soldier! A huge wolfhound came into view beside him.

"Brioc," she whispered, fear pulsing through her. "I think it's the soldier who chased us! There's a dog up there. It looks like Sam."

Brioc looked up with alarm.

"They're on that hill. Over there."

Brioc's gaze flew in the direction she indicated. The color drained from his face. "Has he seen us?"

"I . . . I don't know," Dymphna said. "I don't think so. He hasn't moved."

Brioc dropped to his knees in the water, clawing at the rocks to get the hoof free. Dymphna's eyes darted back and forth between him and the man on the hill. Her heart pounded.

The horse snorted and heaved and splashed, making an awful racket. It took all of Dymphna's strength to stay on.

The dog moved away and vanished.

So did the man.

Brioc looked up and bit his lip. "It's too stuck," he said. "I can't get it free."

The animal was going wild.

"What do we do?" She threw another look towards the hill. "Can't we just leave the horse and run?"

"No. He'll see it here. Besides, we need it."

"What do we do?" she asked again.

His eyes darted to where the man had been. *"Pray!"* he said, then bent back down.

Dymphna couldn't cook a meal. She couldn't light a fire. She had not one single survival skill. But she was good at praying. She loved prayer more than anything.

So she lowered her head and begged her heart out.

Brioc let out a gasp. Startled, Dymphna looked down.

The horse sprang forward onto the sandy bank, its leg free. Brioc stared at something on the rocks. He seemed rooted to the spot.

"Hurry," she finally whispered, realizing he wasn't going to move. "Brioc, come on, we've got to go!"

He stared and stared at the rock in the river, mouth hanging open.

What was he looking at?

Finally he ripped his gaze away and joined her on the riverbank, only to gape at her with shock and wonder. "Dymphna, you —"

"Come on!" she begged. "Before the soldier sees us!" She yanked his sleeve.

He came out of his daze and quickly pulled the reins, leading the horse into the nearest shadows.

Dymphna shot another look at the hill.

No one was there.

Brioc glanced back at her, his eyes filled with reverential awe.

41

Seeing nothing from the top of the hill, Turlough rode back down to the stream.

Alright, find where Brioc crossed.

This could take forever. Especially in the increasing darkness.

Dismounting, Turlough glanced in both directions. Upstream or down?

Think like Brioc.

In other words, do the obvious.

It had to be upstream. Down led back to Méifne. Of course if Brioc knew anything about hiding his tracks, he would go downstream first, then double back. He'd cut into the woods in several places, create false leads with footprints and debris, then backtrack, attempting to wipe away his tracks with a leafy branch as he did.

Brioc would never think of that.

Turlough slowly walked upstream, leading his horse, analyzing every pebble in the stream bed and every clump of grass alongside it. Brioc would have avoided staying in the water longer than he had to. The water was cold. Lynnie was pregnant. He wouldn't want her to catch a chill. The hems of their clothes would get soaking wet. Brioc would've gotten out as soon as he thought he'd gone far enough to throw the scent.

Perhaps quarter of a mile.

Turlough walked even slower when he'd gone that distance, all the while searching, scanning the area for fresh clues. Sam loped beside him, barking and sniffing everything, splashing in the water, having the time of her life.

It was getting dark. Soon he'd be unable to see.

He stopped and fumbled through his saddlebag for his tinder box, a rag, and oil. Then he looked around for a sturdy branch. Finding one, he wasted another fifteen minutes making a torch.

A flame burst forth, small at first but growing as the branch took fire.

He resumed pacing the riverbed, searching, searching.

Something caught his attention. He bent down. The rocks in the stream were green with moss.

All except one.

Its top was smooth. No moss grew. Turlough picked it up and turned it over. Sure enough, moss covered the rock's underside.

Something — *a horse hoof?* — had recently dislodged this rock, perhaps exiting the water onto dry land.

Turlough carefully scanned the area. Sure enough, a few yards away lay a clump of horse dung. Snapped twigs littered the ground. A pair of wet human footprints appeared, and a few feet away the ground showed clearly where they had sat to put their shoes back on. After that, the female prints disappeared again. Lynnie was back on the horse. Brioc kept walking.

"Found it," Turlough said to Sam. "They left the stream here."

Leading his horse with one hand and holding the torch with the other, he followed the tracks as darkness descended.

* * * * *

The ground became harder and harder to see with each passing minute, the trampled leaves and footprints blending with the shadows. Turlough knew the flame of his torch could be spotted miles away, if anyone was out there to see it. Should he extinguish the fire and stop for the night?

How close was he to Brioc?

The darkness heightened his senses, putting him on high alert, both for Brioc's safety and his own. Daemon had been out for blood; surely he'd sent out soldiers. Where were they? A hundred miles away, or five? Turlough had no way of knowing.

And what about wolves?

He shuddered. Just *thinking* what would happen if Brioc heard one, or, heaven forbid, stumbled across a pack, made Turlough nervous. Brioc would lose control. He might have a flashback, even hurt himself. Would his young wife know how to handle it? Did Brioc have them all the time, like he did as a child, or was the graveside incident a one-off? Turlough had been unnerved beyond anything that day. He'd hidden it well from Brioc and Barrf, but he'd felt shaky, almost ill afterward. So how would poor Lynnie react?

Come on, Brioc. Where are you? I've got Sam right here. Let us help you!

He was tempted to call out, to yell Brioc's name.

But Brioc wouldn't answer of course. He had run from Turlough in Méifne. Turlough had somehow managed to become the big bad enemy. *Again.*

He took a deep breath, carefully propped the burning torch against a large rock, and rummaged through his saddlebag. Thankfully he'd filled his waterskin at the stream. He pulled the top off, leaned against his horse, and drank as much of the cold water as he dared. He would leave some for later, just in case. How far was the next water source?

His stomach rumbled. The stew was a distant memory.

Wait. Where was Sam? Turlough glanced around. She'd been here a minute ago. Where did she go?

"Sam?" he called in a loud whisper. "Dumb dog. Where are you?"

There was movement in the trees. He strained to see.

Whew. It was her.

She trotted over, something dangling from her mouth. Dropping it, she flopped to her belly. She chewed her new toy.

"Hey, what is that?"

Turlough strode over and knelt beside her. He wrestled the object from her jaws.

A scrap of brown material.

Part of Lynnie's dress!

Sam whined, so he gave it back. "Good girl, you found something. Well done." He ruffled her head, then scratched behind her ears. Her tail thumped. She dropped the scrap of cloth and instantly rolled onto her back. The big hint. Turlough rubbed her tummy. She squirmed with delight.

"Where did you find this? Show me." He stood, and her doggy face fell. She whimpered, wanting him to keep rubbing her tummy.

Stupid mutt.

He sighed, then slapped his thighs enthusiastically, pretending he wanted to run. To play. He felt ridiculous. "Show me where, Sam. Come on, let's go. Let's go."

Samthann rolled off her back and shot to her feet. She raced in the direction she'd come. He swiped up his torch and grabbed the horse's reins, then jogged to keep up with her.

She led him to what was obviously intended as a camp site. Someone had made a clearing for a fire, and a pile of wood had been dumped beside it.

The size of the branches bewildered him. Logs, but no kindling.

That was strange.

Sam had her nose to the ground, sniffing everything. By the way her tail was wagging, she had Brioc's scent.

Turlough swept the area for any hint. Why had they abandoned the would-be fire? What had happened to Lynnie that ripped her dress? Most importantly, where had they gone from here?

He scanned the dirt for hoof prints.

Found them.

Followed as far as he could back into the forest until the sound of rushing water met his ears.

He hurried towards the bank and his heart plunged.

Ahead of him flowed not a mere trickling stream, but a surging river.

Despair crept over him. "Well, Sam, this is it. The end of the trail. We'll never find Brioc now."

He sank to the ground and Sam plopped down beside him. She whined, as if sensing his misery, and started to lick his hand.

He didn't stop her. Absently he tossed an arm around her. Her fur was warm. She snuggled closer to him. He let her.

"What do we do, Sam? Where to from here?"

An image flitted through his mind of his little sister. His brothers. Mam and Daid. Were they watching this whole mess? If they could see him, they could see Brioc too. Aislinn was certainly a saint. She had power with God. The others were at least in Purgatory. Surely they could pull *some* weight.

He crossed himself and gazed towards Heaven. The first stars had appeared, twinkling in the black sky.

"Come on," he begged. "Would you just help me out? What the heck are you doing up there? Sitting on your holy backsides the whole time?"

That last part was for the brothers, not Aislinn or Mam and Daid.

Sam barked and shot to her feet. She shuddered and barked at something across the river.

Turlough's gaze flew in that direction.

A dazzling golden ball of light glowed from a spot on the ground, on the opposite shore.

He stared. *What on earth?*

The light was brilliant as the sun, blinding, yet at the same time somehow gentle. He blinked, shielding his eyes.

A supernatural fear gripped him.

What was that?

He swallowed hard and slowly rose to his feet.

"Alright, alright," he whispered, throwing a glance heavenward. "I take that back."

With a mixture of awe and fear and hope, he waded into the river.

42

Shivering in her soaking dress, Dymphna clung to Brioc mounted in front of her. His clothes were even more saturated than hers. She squeezed her eyes shut, trying to pray, begging God to help them out of this mess.

Their mount crested a hill and Brioc exhaled, the tension leaving his body. Wondering what he saw, Dymphna opened her eyes and peered around him. A wave of relief, stronger than any she'd ever known, washed through her. The twinkling lights of a town lay in the valley before them.

"Thank God," Brioc said under his breath. It was the only thing he'd said since the river crossing. She had no idea where his thoughts were, except that he must be sick with worry about his wife.

What had he seen on that rock?

He urged the horse towards the blinking lights and they rode down the hill. Dymphna hoped it wouldn't take long to reach it. Freezing cold, miserable and scared, her teeth chattered and tears welled in her eyes. But after the firewood incident, she promised God not to complain anymore. Soft beds, warm fires and goose-down pillows were things of her past. Days with nothing more to do than embroider and pray in the chapel were gone. She was no longer a princess, but a homeless fugitive fleeing for her life.

At least there had been no further sign of that soldier with Sam.

Finally they entered the town. Brioc must have felt the danger, and therefore the need for speed, had passed, because he immediately dismounted to walk, leaving Dymphna alone on the horse. He led the mount past cottages, silent and dark. Where did all the lights go?

Then they turned onto what must have been the main road. Dymphna drew in an astonished breath. Wooden buildings lined the way, more buildings than she'd ever seen. Fires and lanterns flickered behind windows. It was night, but the place seemed alive. She gazed around in awe.

"What town is this?"

"No idea. But it looks big. Pray there's an inn."

Her heart leaped at the thought. She couldn't face another sleepless night on the hard ground.

"Can we get some food somewhere? Please? I'm starving."

Oops, there she was, complaining again. Sorry, Jesus.

"Of course we can."

An awful thought struck her. "Wait. We can't. We don't have money."

"Yes we do."

Her brow knitted. "Really?"

Brioc fished around in his wet clothes and pulled out a tiny bag. It jingled. He handed it up to her. "I have no idea how much it's worth. Hopefully it'll get us a meal and a couple of rooms somewhere."

His gaze briefly met hers and she saw something like reverence in his eyes. Why did he keep looking at her like that? What had she done at the river that had awed him? All she'd done was pray.

She took the bag and peered inside. Coins. "Where did you get these?"

He didn't answer. All he said was, "That looks like a tavern up ahead."

* * * * *

Dymphna huddled by the blazing fire pit in the center of the long, low-ceilinged room. She wrapped her arms tightly around herself, wishing Brioc would hurry and return. After he'd warmed himself by the fire for a few minutes, he'd told her to stay here and get dry, while he went across the room to buy some food.

Why was he taking so long?

The tantalizing aroma of roasting mutton and spiced honey and herbs made her stomach rumble at the same time as the heavy smoke nearly suffocated her. She glanced nervously at the benches lining the walls, hoping no one had seen Brioc leave her here alone. Rough looking men were scattered in groups, tankards in their hands or on the tables in front of them. Some stuffed food in their mouths with their knives or fingers, laughing and talking as they chewed. Their crude language and ribald jokes burned her ears.

She saw only two other females in the tavern, neither of whose presence made her feel any safer. One looked young and bored, weaving between tables with platters of steaming meat and sloshing vessels of ale. She wore a drab apron smeared with grease and had limp hair. One cheek was bruised and she had a black eye.

The other woman sat in a man's lap, laughing way too loud with a mouth painted way too red. Her dress made Dymphna blush. Dymphna looked away and her eye caught another man sitting alone a few feet away. He grinned, winked at her, and jerked his head, inviting her to join him. Heat scorched her face and she hurriedly broke his gaze.

Brioc, please hurry!

Her gaze roamed the room, trying to spot him through the heavy curling smoke. She couldn't see him. She fought to stay calm.

Then she glimpsed him and let out her breath. He had stopped the girl with the platter of food. With a bored expression, she lowered the platter and set it on the nearest table.

Dymphna bounced on her toes. *Hurry. Please.* She shot another look at the lone man sitting near by. He winked at her again and patted the bench next to him. She hugged her arms tighter around herself and stared at Brioc, silently begging him to get back here.

Brioc pulled out his money pouch and held out a coin. The girl in the apron was about to take it, then confusion crossed her face. She hesitated.

Brioc said something. The girl shook her head, obviously annoyed. He tried again. She glared at him and kept shaking her head, pushing away the coin he was trying to hand her. They exchanged more words. Finally she heaved a sigh and glanced around, as if searching for someone.

Dymphna held her breath. What was going on?

The girl snatched Brioc's coin and stomped around the tables towards an older man wearing an even greasier apron. They looked alike. Must be her daid.

Brioc watched them impatiently.

The man examined the coin and frowned. They consulted for a minute, then the girl tossed her head in Brioc's direction. They both walked over to him.

The man said something. Brioc made a reply. More frowns and head shaking.

What was wrong with the money? Why wouldn't they take it?

Dymphna crossed herself and prayed.

Finally Brioc indicated in Dymphna's direction. The aproned man looked over. Her damp dress and tired face must have moved him to some sympathy, because he let out a sigh and reluctantly accepted Brioc's coin.

Dymphna let out her breath. Finally, Brioc would come back!

But he didn't. He stood there forever talking to the man in the apron. The man bent down and started drawing with his finger on the table. Brioc leaned in, asking questions, then drew something himself. The man nodded a few times, then straightened and pointed out the tavern door and to the left.

Come on, Brioc, hurry!

At last he came back with two plates of food.

"Was there a problem?" she asked, staring at the food which looked less than appetizing.

"Something with the money. He didn't recognize it." Brioc looked around for an empty table. "Don't worry about it. He accepted it in the end. Let's sit down and eat."

They found a place far enough from the other patrons, but still close enough to the fire to feel its warmth.

Neither spoke as they dived into the meal: chewy slices of roast mutton, slathered in grease and strung with ropes of fat. The only thing Dymphna could taste was salt. Way too much. But hunger kept her from complaining.

"There's an inn down the road. We'll grab a couple rooms and get some sleep, then head to Begerin in the morning."

"Begerin?" She blinked. "Why?"

"Because," Brioc said, not sounding very confident, "I'm praying that's where Father will head with Lynnie. I don't know where else to go."

Of course. The monastery in Begerin. That had been their back-up plan.

"But how will we find our way?"

"The tavern owner gave me directions. I thought he might know."

How could *that* man know where Begerin was?

Brioc saw her confusion. "This is a big town. A lot of travelers must pass through. Tavern owners are famous for knowing things." He threw a glance towards the door. "Let's take the rest of this food to the inn. I don't like you being in this place."

She couldn't agree more.

They stood, piling the remains onto bread and clumsily folding it all up. From the corner of her eye, Dymphna caught a glimpse of that man who had motioned her over earlier. He gave her goosebumps. He was still staring at her, the look on his face leaving no mistake about his intentions. He winked at her and grinned. Dymphna blushed and instantly broke his gaze, her pulse quickening in fear.

Brioc must have seen, because he swiveled around to see what she'd been looking at. He couldn't possibly miss the man and the way he was staring at her. When Brioc turned back around, his eyes were dark with anger.

"Let's get you out of here."

"What if he follows us to the inn and —"

"Don't worry. I'll keep you safe."

Dymphna let out her breath. Of course he would. She couldn't doubt it for a second. *Thank you, God, for such a noble protector.*

As they headed to the door, they passed the girl with the limp hair and the platter of food. Dymphna tossed her a kind smile.

The girl gave her a look full of hate.

43

Turlough struggled to plow through the cold swirling water. It already came up to his chest. If it got any deeper, he would be forced to turn back. The slick rocks strewn beneath his feet made every step treacherous, and it was hard not to slip. It was like stumbling blindfolded across a battlefield, trying not to trip on the bodies. To make it worse, Samthann barked her head off from the shore, distracting him with the noise. Would she just shut up? His nerves were already on edge.

Shivering uncontrollably, he locked his gaze on the brilliant glow across the river, the only source of light in the otherwise darkened forest. Could he reach it without being washed away? He stepped on an uneven rock and it tilted beneath him. Pulse racing, his arms shot out and he fought to regain his balance.

Too late. His head went under and the world turned black. The sound of barking faded, replaced by the gurgling of water in his ears. Slipping and splashing, he managed to plant his feet on a steady rock and his head broke the surface. The glow across the shore came back into view.

Half-stumbling, half-swimming, he battled his way through the icy water. Coldness numbed him from head to toe.

Sam kept barking, the sound grinding down his nerves.

At last, the water grew shallower. Dropped to the level of his waist, then his thighs. Whew.

Finally it was knee deep. Sending up a quick prayer of thanksgiving, Turlough splashed to the source of the light. Despite its brilliance, he had no need to shield his eyes. The glow came from a clump of rocks. No, it was one rock in particular, pulsing with a beautiful, unearthly radiance beneath the rippling water.

He pushed his dripping hair from his eyes and dropped to one knee beside the rock. To his shock, the water was warm here. Rays of dazzling light danced and darted from the rock's surface, mesmerizing him. His heart thudded with a mixture of fear and awe. Dare he touch it?

He swallowed and flicked his gaze heavenward. "Um . . . Branduff?" he whispered. "Raghnall? This isn't funny, you know." He looked back at the rock. "Would you both please just —" The rock's light gently faded.

Dimmer. Dimmer.

Twinkle. Blink.

Gone.

Turlough now stared at a normal rock. The water turned icy cold.

Had he dreamed all that?

He threw a glance towards the opposite shore. Sam barked, as if to reassure him he was awake and this was real. Then she wagged her tail, bounded into the river, and started to swim.

Returning his attention to the rock, Turlough reluctantly plunged his hand back into the icy water. He wrapped his fingers around the rock and lifted it out.

His breath caught. Into its surface was embedded the perfect print of a horse hoof!

He blinked. The print was still there. Impossible! How could a hoof stamp itself into —

Sam reached him, soaking wet, her gray fur plastered to her body. She splashed past him to dry land.

"Sam, you're not going to believe this." Turlough's voice came out an awed whisper.

The wolfhound tilted her head, uninterested, and took one step back. She shuddered, then shook herself violently, spraying Turlough with cold muddy water and flecks of dirt. Well, that broke the spell. Instantly all feeling of the supernatural passed.

The rock tumbled from Turlough's hand of its own accord and splashed into the water. It landed with the hoof print visible. Turlough reached for it, grabbed it, and tried to lift it back out. He couldn't. The thing suddenly weighed a ton. *What on earth?*

Confused, he used both hands. The rock still wouldn't budge. He looked around, wondering what his brothers in Heaven were doing now.

The answer came like a flash. For some reason, God wanted the miraculous rock to stay here. Maybe a future generation would find it and venerate it. Perhaps legends would be woven around it, legends of an Irish minstrel and his wife who fled with . . . *something* . . . from an insane king.

Wait. Had Brioc taken a holy item? Turlough hadn't thought of that before. The idea grabbed hold of him as the only explanation that could possibly make sense. Maybe the thing Brioc and Lynnie had with them belonged to God or the church. Maybe they hadn't stolen it, but *rescued* it, before it could be desecrated by King Daemon. What in the world could the holy object be?

Would the legend of the fleeing minstrel have a happy ending? Or a tragic one?

Turlough blessed himself and whispered a prayer of resignation to God's will. This miracle hadn't happened for nothing. That much Turlough knew.

He also knew that Brioc had crossed here, with whatever holy thing he had in his possession.

More determined than ever, he rose from his knees and ran a hand through his wet hair. Time to start tracking again.

A neigh and a snort reminded him that his horse was still on the other side of the river. His heart sank. Oh no. He'd have to brave the waters again — two more times — to bring the animal across.

At least he had Heaven on his side. How could he doubt that now?

"Sam," he said, "wait here. I'll be back soon."

Gathering his courage, he stepped back into the freezing river.

* * * * *

Somewhere in the back of his mind, Turlough registered a chirping sound in the air. What was that? Half asleep, he pressed his hands to his ears, trying to block the invasive noise. He was so tired. The rough blanket beside him was warm, comforting. For some reason he had a pillow. Strange. He hadn't brought a pillow. Where'd a pillow come from? *Who cared?* It was soft and cozy. He snuggled deeper into it, reluctant to wake up.

The chirping wouldn't go away.

Shut up. I'm trying to sleep.

It sounded merry, cheerful.

He buried himself in the warm pillow.

Birdsong? Was that what it was?

He groggily opened his eyes. Bright sunlight stabbed them. *Huh? What time was it? Where was he?*

The warm pillow beneath his head heaved and squirmed. It shifted position of its own volition. The entire blanket moved too. Startled, Turlough bolted to a sitting position. *What the —?*

Sam cracked one eyelid, saw him, and thumped her tail. She eagerly sat up, nudged him, and licked his hand.

He'd . . . slept with her? Seriously?

"Well, good morning to you too." Confused, and a little embarrassed, he glanced around, trying to get his bearings. His horse grazed in the distance, untethered, the blanket with the harp still strapped to its saddle. The torch lay on the grass a couple feet away. Thank God its flame had burned out without setting the forest ablaze.

When had he even fallen asleep? He remembered sitting down sometime during the night, overcome with tiredness several miles beyond the river. He must've lain down and accidentally dropped off to sleep. Sam obviously had joined him.

She *had* been warm. He couldn't deny that. If not for her, he would've frozen. Especially since his clothes had still been wet from the river.

And she'd been soft too. Softer than anything he'd ever slept on.

He ruffled the fur on her head. "Hey, thanks."

She barked, then tumbled onto her back, sticking her enormous paws in the air. Her tail wagged furiously. She looked so ridiculous that a smile tugged at his mouth. "Stupid mutt," he said and rubbed her tummy. She squirmed with ecstasy.

He indulged her for a couple minutes, then, stifling a yawn, stretched and clambered to his feet. "Come on. We better hit the trail."

She popped up beside him and barked. She raced around in circles, then found a stick. A second later it lay at his feet.

"You want to play, do you?"

She barked.

"Alright. But not for long." He threw the stick as far as he could. She sailed after it.

Within seconds, she was back, eager for the next round. He rolled his eyes and laughed, tossing the stick again.

44

"Dymphna. Dymphna, wake up."

Brioc gently shook her arm, feeling terrible for barging in here and pulling her from slumber. From where he'd slept outside her door, he had heard her softly snoring all night. She must have been exhausted. But they needed to get out of here.

Dymphna rolled over in the bed. Her eyelids fluttered, but she didn't seem to see him. She closed them again and instantly dropped back to sleep.

Brioc hesitated, not wanting to touch her. But he had to wake her up. So, hating himself for it, he shook her harder. "Hey. Wake up. Come on."

She groaned. "Huh?"

"Get up."

She sleepily cracked her eyes open. This time she saw him. With a startled gasp, she fumbled for the blanket and whipped it up to her chin. There was no need. She was already fully covered and perfectly modest. He wouldn't have come in here if she hadn't been.

"We need to leave. Right now."

She sat up, still clutching the blanket to her throat. "Why? What's wrong?"

Brioc didn't want to alarm her, didn't want to tell her that when he'd gone outside to check on their horse a minute ago, he'd spotted a rider coming down that hill towards town. A huge dog had been romping in circles around the man's horse. It could be anyone, but something inside told him it was Turlough.

Brioc couldn't wrap his head around it. Was his brother really that bad that he would help Daemon hunt down an innocent girl, and for such a sinful cause? It was hard to believe. In fact, when Brioc had gone to Turlough's house with Sam, it had taken all his willpower not to pour out everything and beg his brother for help. Even after all that had passed between them these eleven years, Brioc still struggled to shake off his childhood hero-worship. Amazing.

Imagine if he *had* told him everything. Dymphna would be in her father's evil clutches, and Brioc would be killed by his own brother's sword. What had he done to earn such burning hatred from the brother he had loved so much?

"What's wrong?" Dymphna asked again, alarmed.

"Nothing's wrong." Brioc struggled to keep his voice even, so as not to scare her. "We both overslept. That's all. It must be nearly noon."

"Noon? Already? Are you serious?"

"Guess we were both really tired." Brioc threw a nervous glance at the bedroom door. They had to flee this town, before Turlough found them. "Come on, let's go."

She blinked. "Um, can't I have a minute?"

Brioc frowned. "A minute for what?"

"Well . . . um . . . you know."

Brioc didn't know. She was already fully dressed. They'd both slept in their clothes. What did she need a minute for?

She sat there, the blanket pulled to her chin, waiting for him to leave.

He stared at her, confused. Then he realized she wasn't going to budge from the bed until he left. Gosh, females were strange.

"Alright. I'll wait by the horse," he said, hoping she wouldn't take as long as Lynnie did every morning. It took Lynnie forty minutes to do . . . *stuff.* Brush her hair eighty times, mess around with her face. He loved Lynnie exactly the way she was, but she still took ages trying to *do things* with her hair and face.

The thought of Lynnie made his heart ache. Where was she? Father Gerebran better take care of her, because if anything happened to her or the baby —

Stop! He pushed the thoughts away. Of course the priest would keep her safe. Father Gerebran would sacrifice his life for her if necessary; Brioc had no doubt of that. Yet he couldn't help but remember with pain how he hadn't even had a chance to talk to Lynnie alone before they got separated. She had ignored him the entire time, alternating between glaring at him and bursting into tears. Every time Brioc went near her, she'd steer the horse away, and start chatting with Father Gerebran, as if Brioc didn't exist. Why would Lynnie be treating him as if he — In a flash, he got it. *She no longer loved him.*

A knife plunged through his heart.

"Brioc, um, are you alright?"

His mind snapped back to the present moment, to Dymphna in the bed with the blanket pulled to her neck. She stared at him with worry in her eyes. Or . . . wait. *Was it fear?* Was Dymphna afraid of him? He'd thought she'd yanked up the blanket because of her innate sense of modesty. That was so like Dymphna. But maybe . . . maybe she was scared of him! Maybe she thought he was about to mutate into her sick father, or that man in the tavern!

Oh no, he was doing everything wrong! His wife didn't love him, his brother wanted him dead. Even Sam was gone. And now Princess Dymphna no longer trusted him!

Brioc instantly backed away from the bed. Get away from her, get away.

He bolted from the room and into the hallway just in time. He slumped against the wall. Everything inside him shattered into a million pieces. No matter what he did, or how hard he tried, he made a mess of everyone's life. Why had God even created him?

He slid down the wall to sit on the floor. Closing his eyes, he silently begged the monster inside to devour him, to take him back to the blackness of years ago. It had been hell, but a safe hell. A place where pain couldn't reach him. A dark, silent place where nothing could touch him, nothing could hurt him, ever again.

Just die.

But . . . the princess. He could hear her on the other side of the door, scrambling out of bed, doing whatever girls did that took them so long. He couldn't abandon her. Her life was in danger. He must keep this poor innocent girl safe. At least get her to Begerin, where Father Gerebran could take over. Lynnie would be long gone by then, back in Méifne with her parents. Brioc would never see her again, or his child.

Hot tears stung his eyes. That huge steel hand reached back inside his chest and squeezed his heart to an agonized pulp.

But he had to get Dymphna to safety. Right now, that's all that mattered. Just focus on that.

After she was safe, the monster could rip him to shreds. He would actually find relief being sucked back into blackness.

He wished the wolf at the waterfall had killed him. The little girl might be alive if it had. Everyone he loved would be better off with him dead.

If only he had not run that night.

45

As soon as Turlough spotted the town in the valley below, his heart plummeted. He had already lost Brioc's trail an hour ago. The woods had thinned out, the soft dirt and fallen leaves of the forest floor replaced by grassy hills. All signs of Brioc's and Lynnie's passing had vanished.

He reined his horse to a stop and gazed with dismay at the busy, bustling roads of the town ahead of him. This place was too big. Too many people. Even if he headed the right direction, and even if Brioc and Lynnie *had* entered the town, he had almost zero chance of finding them.

Now what?

He glanced around for Samthann. She frolicked around his horse, stopping every few seconds to sniff something in the grass or chase an insect. Her tail wagged nonstop.

"Hey, Sam."

At his voice, she abandoned her game and hunted for a stick. Finding one, she raced with it in her mouth to his horse. She dropped it on the grass and barked.

"No, not now. I need your help. This is important. You know Brioc better than I do."

Her tail wagged furiously at his brother's name. She barked again.

"So, where would he go from here? Into that town," he said and nodded down the hill, "or stay off the main roads? Come on, tell me what to do."

Sam cocked her head as if thinking. Turlough couldn't believe he'd started treating her like a human these last few days. Gosh, he was seriously overtired. Either that, or losing his mind.

Sam barked again, then spied a moth. Within seconds, she was romping through the grass, nipping at the air, back in her own little doggy world.

Turlough shook his head. "Brainless mutt."

He blew out a breath and stared at the town, trying to decide. Should he backtrack into the woods and try to pick up Brioc's trail again? If only Sam were a scent hound. He suspected her breed tracked by sight, if indeed wolfhounds tracked at all.

His stomach rumbled. The last meal he'd had was at the horse dealer's house. He could use some food.

That decided it.

"Alright, dumbo dog. Let's hit the town."

* * * * *

Turlough found the tavern with ease. It lay directly off the main road near the entrance of the town. It wasn't the right hour to expect a meal, but Turlough tied up his horse anyhow, ordered Sam to wait outside, and entered the long, low building.

The light was dim inside, and it took his eyes a minute to adjust. Although the fire in the central pit had gone out, the smell of last night's smoke lingered heavily in the air, along with mouthwatering aromas of roasted meat. His gaze clicked from empty table to empty table. Apart from an obviously inebriated trio clustered near the extinguished fire pit, and a middle-aged man in a grimy apron wiping a table in the far corner, no one was in sight.

Turlough approached the fellow in the apron. "Hello."

The other glanced up briefly but said nothing. He continued rubbing the table with a greasy rag.

"I don't suppose you have anything left to eat?"

The man heaved a sigh, straightened up and turned towards an open door a few feet away.

"Dana!" he yelled.

A girl with a black eye and a stained dress appeared in the doorway. Dana, Turlough assumed. It looked like she hadn't brushed her hair in a week. Annoyance was written all over her face.

"What?"

"Any food left for this man?"

Her lips met in a thin line and she glared at Turlough as if he were the biggest nuisance in the world. Rolling her eyes, she disappeared back through the door.

"Um, do you have any bones by chance? Or meat scraps?" Turlough nodded towards the entrance. "I have a wolfhound. I'd like something for her too."

The man's shoulders slumped. "Dana!" he yelled again.

She materialized a second time in the door frame, eyes practically blazing. "What?"

"Find something for his dog."

The girl scowled at Turlough, her look saying she'd love to give him a black eye too, then she spun around and stomped back to wherever she'd come from.

Charming people.

The owner resumed wiping the table, his filthy rag smudging grease across the surface and making it dirtier than before. He ignored Turlough.

Clearing his throat, Turlough wandered to a nearby table to wait. As soon as he sat down, something slippery squished beneath him, nearly making him slide off the seat. He shot up and looked at the bench. A globule of meat fat in a puddle of ale lay smeared across the seat.

Maybe a meal here wasn't such a brilliant idea after all.

Hoping the drunken threesome by the fire pit weren't watching, Turlough slapped and swatted his backside to get rid of the blobs of beef lard, then he slithered towards another bench. He carefully inspected it before gingerly lowering himself onto the seat.

What felt like an hour later, Dana emerged from the backroom and marched towards him with a plate of food. She crashed it on the table in front of him.

Turlough stared at what looked like a mound of grizzle. Was this his or Sam's?

The girl shifted her weight to one foot and put a hand on her hip. She held the other hand out, palm up. "Well?" she snapped.

"Huh?" Turlough broke his gaze from the plate of gloopy leftovers. "Oh. Oh, of course." He fished around for his money pouch.

With horror, he remembered he had left all his money on Angus's table as payment for Brioc's horse.

Dana stared at him with impatience, palm still out.

Wait! He had two of the coins from Neill! The ones that had rolled across his floor when Neill and Cahir had barged inside.

"Hold on. I have money in my saddlebag. I'll be right back."

Turlough hopped up and hurried outside. Sam barked, about to jump on him, but he managed to shove her off. He fumbled through his saddlebag and found the coins. Grabbing one, he turned back around and nearly slammed into the girl.

"Oh, sorry." He didn't know she'd followed him out.

She glared.

Turlough handed her the coin. Her expression turned to surprise, then something like fury.

"Another one? You *have* to be joking."

Before Turlough could say anything, she spun on her heel and stormed back inside, straight for the man in the filthy apron. Turlough gave Sam a helpless look, mumbled, "Weird," and trailed after her.

"Look, Daid. You're not going to believe this." Fuming, she handed him Turlough's coin.

The man frowned. "Two in one day?" His eyes shot to Turlough. "I'm sorry. I can't accept this."

"I know it's foreign, but I'm sure it —" Turlough stopped, suddenly reeling. "Wait. Did you say . . . *two in one day?*"

"Yes. Some fellow came in last night with a coin just like this. Are you both playing some kind of a game?"

"What did he look like?" Turlough resisted the urge to grab the man by the shoulders and shake him. "Where did he go? Did he say his name?"

The man's eyes narrowed. "Why? Why do you want to know?"

"He's my brother. Please," Turlough begged. "I need to find him. His life is in danger."

Dana offered, "He had dark hair." For the space of a heartbeat her eyes wistfully lit up. Then her face hardened and envy flashed in her eyes. "He had a girl with him."

Turlough's pulse raced. "Was she young? Pretty?"

The man said, "Very." For the first time his mouth twisted into a grin. "A real looker, that one. You have one lucky brother."

Dana scowled. "Her dress was ugly."

Ha. As if *she* could talk. The girl couldn't even figure out how to comb her hair. Turlough bit his tongue. "Was her dress brown?"

"Yes. Brown and ugly." She stuck her nose in the air. "And wet. Smelled like she'd spent the night in a swamp."

Their tavern smelled worse than a swamp.

"Do you know where they went?" Turlough turned back to the tavern owner. "Please. Did he say anything? Anything at all?"

"He asked for directions to Begerin."

"Begerin? Why there?"

The man shrugged. "He didn't say."

"Did you give him directions?"

"Yes."

"Can you give them to me?"

With a nod, the tavern owner leaned over the grease-smeared table and drew a map. Turlough tried to memorize it, begging his guardian angel to help.

He thanked the man, hurried back and grabbed his plate, and took it to the door. He scraped the whole disgusting mess on the ground in front of Sam. She gobbled it up. Handing the empty plate back to Dana, who had followed him out, Turlough swung onto his horse and kicked it into a gallop. The tavern keeper was left with the coin, like it or not.

If Turlough was lucky, he might even catch up with Brioc before Begerin. The hard part would be getting close enough to talk. Brioc would probably run again, as he did in Méifne.

If only Sam could talk. Brioc would listen to *her.*

An idea slammed into Turlough and he jerked on the reins so suddenly his horse reared.

The map on the greasy table! Of course! There *was* a way Samthann could deliver a message!

Heart pounding, Turlough spun the horse around and flew back to the tavern.

46

"I don't want to stay here," Ethlynn said, gulping back tears. "I want to go to my parents' house."

"Now, now." The midwife, a middle-aged woman who had introduced herself to them as Laoise, gently guided her by the elbow to the bed across the room. "Lie down and get comfortable. Have you eaten? Would you like something to drink?" She threw a glance at Father Gerebran standing in the doorway, then looked back at Ethlynn. "Broth? Milk? I have stew. Tell me what you want, dear."

Ethlynn's lip quivered. "I want to go home. That's what I want. I want my mam."

The woman pushed back a loose strand of graying hair and helped Ethlynn sit on the edge of the bed. "I think warm broth is what you need," she said.

"I won't stay here." Ethlynn folded her arms. "I'm going back to Méifne, even if I have to walk."

Across the room, Father Gerebran let out a sigh. Ethlynn knew she was acting like a pouty child, but it was either this or burst into tears.

"I want my mam," she repeated. "And my sisters."

Actually, it was Brioc she wanted. Desperately.

"I'm leaving for Méifne right now. You can't stop me." Ethlynn popped up from the bed.

The woman gently pushed her back down. "Dear, you're not going anywhere. Not till your baby is born."

Father Gerebran strode to the bed and crouched in front of her. His eyes held compassion, yet his expression was unyielding. "Ethlynn, I know you're upset. I understand that. But I won't risk your child being born on the road. We're staying in this town — you here with Laoise, and me at the nearby monastery — until you've delivered your baby. Laoise is a midwife. She'll take care of you. And the fresh sea air will do you good." He gestured outside. "I can bring out a chair, and you can sit on the beach during the days and watch the fishing boats."

Laoise joined in, motioning to the window at the back of the room. "And if you're not up to sitting outside, you can see the ocean from here."

They were both trying, of course, to make staying here attractive. Ethlynn had never been to a coastal town and couldn't deny the ocean was breathtaking. But she still wanted to go home. Mam could deliver her baby, not this stranger.

"Please, Father. If we leave right now, I'm sure I can make it back to

Méifne."

"No. Absolutely out of the question. Neither of us are leaving this place until that baby comes, whether it's tomorrow, next week, or next month."

"I'll fetch some broth." Laoise patted Ethlynn's hand and disappeared through a doorway into another part of the cottage.

Ethlynn sniffled, miserable.

Father had earlier explained to her, as they rode in the back of the farmer's wagon that he'd managed to flag down, how she had been asleep on their horse when they had arrived in Méifne. That's when the four of them had become accidentally separated.

Accidentally.

Ethlynn wanted desperately to believe that. Her husband might not love her anymore, but he would never be actually unfaithful. Brioc was too good for that. He loved God. He'd never sin. No, he'd get Dymphna to safety, then leave her.

But that still wouldn't make him come back.

The dam burst and tears streamed down Ethlynn's face.

Father scrambled for something she could wipe her eyes on. He found a cloth on the table and swiped it up. "Now don't cry." He handed it to her. "You'll only get more upset, and that won't do anyone any good. Everything will work out. This village is on the road to Begerin. Your husband and the princess will head there. It was our back-up plan, remember? The farmer that gave us the ride cut through the fields, so we're probably a few days ahead of them. They'll eventually pass through this village, and when they do, we'll see them. Trust God to take care of everything."

Ethlynn wanted to tell the priest that her husband didn't love her, that she had seen him hug Dymphna, and that her own heart was breaking. Nothing would ever, ever be right again. But instead she rubbed her eyes with the hem of her sleeve, blew her nose on the cloth and said, "But even if they come this way, they won't know we're here."

"God is in charge. We'll see them, or they'll see us. The monks nearby said I can lodge with them. They'll all keep an eye out too. Besides, I know Princess Dymphna. She will spot their church with its tall stone bell tower and want to attend Mass. There aren't many churches, so she'll definitely notice it. She won't let Brioc pass through without at least stopping to pay a visit."

Ethlynn drew a trembling breath. Father Gerebran might be right.

"God will take care of everything." His words brought her some comfort. He was a saint. Charity radiated from Father Gerebran. "I want you to promise me that you'll rest," he went on. "The farmer who gave us the ride told me there is no better midwife than Laoise. She has agreed to let you stay with her until the baby comes. But it's up to you to take care of yourself. You're already in danger of early delivery. For your child's sake, you must stay calm and rest."

For her child's sake. Yes, Ethlynn could do that. She nodded, ashamed of her earlier tantrum. She sniffled. "But how will we pay Laoise?"

Gratitude lit up the priest's face. "The money from that soldier is ample. I know he intended it for a new horse, but I'm sure if we could consult him, he'd agree to this instead."

Ethlynn frowned. "I think I recognized him."

"You did. He sometimes attends my Mass back home. But I doubt he realized who we were." A hint of a smile twitched on Father's lips. "To most people, all priests look alike. Just men wearing this." Amused, he tugged the sleeve of his priestly robe for emphasis.

Ethlynn felt her eyes widen. "You mean, that soldier was from Oriel?"

Father looked taken aback. "They all were. I thought you knew. The man in the scarlet cloak was King Daemon. He obviously mistook you from a distance for Dymphna."

Speechless, Ethlynn stared. *Those were Daemon's soldiers?* Her mouth went dry. Thank God the bald one, the one who'd taken the princess's shoe from their cottage, hadn't been with them! He would've recognized her! The king would have killed her and Father Gerebran on the spot!

Before her mind could process this horrible new knowledge, the midwife stepped cheerfully back into the room with a steaming bowl.

"I want you to drink this all up, dear," she instructed, placing the bowl into Ethlynn's trembling hands. "I've added some special herbs. They taste nasty, but will help your body relax. We need to prevent more contractions. We can't have that sweet baby of yours coming early."

Ethlynn bit her lip and tried to focus on what Laoise was saying. It hadn't been nine months, had it? She actually didn't know for sure. If her baby was born now, would it even survive?

Father Gerebran gently laid a hand on her shoulder. "Don't fret. We're safe now. God protected us from the king, and He will continue to do so. Have trust, Ethlynn. God is the best of Fathers."

She meekly nodded, then the priest made the sign of the cross over her.

"Get some sleep now. I'll head over to the monastery and settle in, then I'll come back in a few hours." He winked. "God will set everything right. I promise you."

As he left the room, fresh tears welled in Ethlynn's eyes. She felt so alone. Imprisoned in a strange house with a woman she didn't know, pregnant with a baby that might come early and not survive, and with Brioc long gone when she needed him more than ever before.

To make it worse, he was with the most beautiful girl in Ireland . . . and in love with her.

How could God possibly set everything right?

47

"Excuse me. The tavern owner told me you're a scribe."

A stooped, elderly man with thinning hair and watery eyes glanced over from where he sorted objects on a dusty shelf against one wall. The tiny dim room was crammed with more clutter than Turlough had ever seen in his life. Funny little jars and strange smelling potions and what looked suspiciously like instruments of torture took up every inch of the shelf, overflowing onto a table, and even spilling to the floor. The scribe was also a surgeon of some sort, the tavern keeper had told him. From the odor of the concoctions and the rusted surgical blades, definitely not the type Turlough would let near his vitals. But apparently the doc could also read and write.

"Yes, I am a scribe."

"I need a letter written to my brother. Can you do that for me?"

"Perhaps." His watery eyes met Turlough's gaze. "It depends."

Turlough was prepared for that. He'd already brought in his last remaining coin. He held it out as payment, breathing a silent prayer the man wouldn't notice its foreign imprint. How he would make a journey all the way to Begerin with no money, he had no idea. He'd worry about that later.

The man shuffled across the room and took the coin from Turlough without examining it. *Thank you, God.* Then, with the speed of a three-legged turtle, he made his way to the messy table and cleared a space. It took him forever, stacking one toppling pile upon another, until it looked like the whole mountain of junk would slide to the floor. Turlough stifled a groan and a sigh and resisted drumming his fingers on a nearby table, trying not to show impatience as the fellow hunted through the rubble for a piece of parchment. Finding none, he scuffled slowly back to the shelf. A titanic search ensued. Turlough chewed his lip, feeling like ripping the place apart himself to find the misplaced writing materials. Every minute that passed, Brioc got farther away.

Just hurry up, would you.

What felt like half an hour later, the man dragged himself back to the table with parchment in one unsteady hand and a long feather in the other. It took another five minutes to lower himself comfortably into the wobbly chair, arrange the parchment at the perfect angle, and smear the tip of the feather with something from a weird-smelling jar.

Finally, feather poised, he cleared his scratchy throat and glanced up at Turlough. "What would you like me to write?"

Turlough had no idea how a letter was supposed to sound. How did one begin? How many words could fit on that square of parchment? He sucked in a breath and began. "Alright. To my brother Brioc. I know you don't understand what is going on, and I know you don't trust me, but you truly have to believe what I'm telling you. King Daemon and his soldiers want to kill you because of whatever you stole." Turlough stopped. "No, wait. Change that word to *took*, not *stole*, because my brother would never steal anything." Clearing his throat, he continued dictating. "I'm only tracking you to save your life. And of course Lynnie's life too." He paused for air as the man scribbled away with his feather."But I can't help you if you won't let me near you, so that is why Sam is bringing you —"

"Slow down." The man's eyes squinted at the parchment, his shaky hand scratching furiously with the feather.

Turlough waited, trying not show his impatience.

The man scribbled for several minutes.

"Um, can I go on now? With the rest of it?"

"You are going too fast."

Turlough leaned over the table, staring at the strange symbols on the parchment. "How far are you up to?"

". . . my broth . . . er . . . " he glanced up questioningly. "Sam, you said?"

"No. No. It's Brioc. Sam's my dog. I mean, his dog. You mean you're only up to his name?" Frustration welled up inside him.

The watery eyes were concentrating again on the parchment. "You are speaking much too quickly." He cleared his throat, wrote for another few minutes, then read back, "To my brother Bradan . . ."

"Brioc. His name is Brioc!"

"Brian?"

"No. Brioc."

"How do you spell that?"

Turlough couldn't believe this. "How should I know?"

A long swipe of ink crossed out several symbols in a row. Turlough sighed. He'd be here till lunchtime tomorrow.

"Bree . . . uck . . ." the man mumbled to himself, squinting as he scratched new weird shapes next to the long black line.

"Uh, can we do this, you know, a little faster?"

The man frowned and dipped the feather back into the stinky jar. Too much ink collected, which necessitated a hunt on the tabletop for a rag. Several moments later, finding one, he carefully wiped the excess ink from the tip's edge. Another lengthy pause as he mopped up the mess on the table too.

Finally, the feather was again poised over the parchment. He looked up. "To my brother Breeuck. What was next?"

Turlough couldn't remember what he'd said. "Um, I think it was, You don't trust me." He ran a hand through his hair, trying to think of what he'd said before.

"You mentioned about understanding. Or was it not understanding?"

"Oh right. You don't understand. Or you don't trust me. I can't remember which one."

They looked at each other, befuddled.

"A king? You said something about a king? Your brother doesn't trust a king?"

"No, it's me he doesn't trust. He doesn't trust the king either, but — oh, look, let's forget all that part."

A nod of agreement. "So, to my brother Breeuck . . .?" The scribe waited patiently.

Every minute they wasted, the distance lengthened on the road between him and Brioc. Daemon's soldiers could be anywhere by now. Might be a good idea to keep this short and simple.

"How about, I'm tracking you down to save your life. If you don't let me help you, the king's soldiers will kill you and Lynnie."

Another nod. More deep concentration and shakily scrawled loops and lines.

After repeating the two sentences endless times — the exact words being forgotten and changed with every attempt — and dozens of dips of the feather in the smelly jar, the letter was at last written. The man looked up proudly. "How would you like to sign it?"

Turlough frowned. "What do you mean, sign it?"

"To sign means to tell him whom it is from."

"Isn't it obvious who it's from?"

"Whom."

"What?"

"*Whom* it's from."

"Huh?" Turlough stared at him, bewildered. "Look, he'll know it's from me, won't he? I mean, if he's my brother, I'm his brother too."

The man shrugged and stood up with the parchment.

"No, wait," Turlough said on impulse. "You're right. I do want to sign it."

The man sat back down and dipped the feather into the ink again.

"Write, from your loving brother Turlough."

Endless scratching on the parchment. Impatiently Turlough glanced around, itching to get on his way.

"Tearlach?"

"No. Turlough."

"That's what I just said. Tearlach."

Turlough was dying to leave. "Alright. It's close enough. Just write it. Who cares? Brioc knows my name." He regretted deciding to sign the blasted thing.

"... your ... lov ... ing ..."

Come on, come on.

"bro ... ther ..." The man glanced up, smiling with satisfaction. "Tear ... lach."

Finally!

Turlough whipped the parchment from the scribe's hand and hastily started to roll it up.

The man gasped. "No! No, don't do that!"

"Do what?"

"Roll it up. It's still wet."

Aghast, Turlough unrolled the sheet. Black smudges were everywhere. The man's watery eyes were wide with horror.

"Oh." Turlough heart sank. "Can he still read it? Are the words clear?"

The man stood and examined the smeared symbols, then hesitated. "How intelligent is your brother?"

"Very."

"Then I think he will decipher it."

"Are you sure?"

"Yes. But don't roll it until it completely dries." He pressed his palms together in a begging fashion.

Turlough nodded and held the parchment by its edges. After all this, he hardly remembered what it said in the first place. Maybe he should check one last time. "Can you read it back to me before I leave? I mean, just to make sure?"

"Of course." The man took the letter back, also holding it carefully by its edges. Turlough moved behind him and stared over his shoulder at the bizarre squiggles and dots and lines. How could marks made with ink speak a message? Would Brioc really understand this?

He thought back to the wooden crosses at the graves with the equally weird symbols that Brioc had carved. Yes, Brioc would get this.

"To my brother Breeuck," the man read, "I am trying to save your life. If you don't let me, the king's soldiers will kill you and Liny. Your loving brother, Tearlach." As he read, Turlough desperately tried to memorize the words. What if he forgot what it said? Would it matter?

The man handed it back. "I wish you luck," he said kindly.

"Thank you." Turlough shook his hand and raced out the door with the letter.

48

Dymphna's heart beat with growing worry. She threw another glance at Brioc, who was walking at least ten feet from her horse. He wouldn't even come close enough to lead the animal by its reins anymore. Dymphna was terrified the thing might bolt or rear or take off at an uncontrollable gallop. She would never be able to control it if it did. But it wasn't just her lack of riding skills that filled her with fear. It was Brioc.

In the three days since they'd left the inn, he had hardly spoken. His eyes held a faraway, empty look, which reminded her of when he'd lived at the monastery. And he wouldn't come near her, unless absolutely necessary. Had she offended him? Why was he acting so strange?

Dymphna bit her lip and sucked in a breath. Time to try to say something. *Again.*

"Brioc?"

He glanced over. Oh dear. Each time she saw his eyes, they looked more vacant.

Don't vanish, she begged, *please don't fade away.*

She swallowed. "Father Gerebran will take care of her," she said softly. "And the baby. You know he will."

Brioc didn't reply. Pain flickered in his eyes and he turned away and kept walking.

"God won't let anything bad happen to them. We'll find them in Begerin, perfectly safe, and everything will be fine again." But even as she said the words, Dymphna knew they weren't necessarily true. Sure, they'd all be together again, but they would still be homeless and fleeing for their lives.

Again no answer.

"I bet your baby will be beautiful. I can't wait to hold it." No reaction. "Have you picked out any names yet?"

Brioc threw her a look that warned her to back off and mind her own business. Her lip quivered and she bit it. She'd only wanted to help.

They fell back into silence. She clutched the horse's mane tightly as the upward climb became steeper. Several times the horse nearly lost its footing on the rough, rocky terrain. Dymphna prayed she wouldn't topple off. If only Brioc would come back here and take the reins. But he trudged ahead without a word.

The sun touched the rolling hills on the horizon and turned the sky orange. Soon they'd lose all light. They couldn't keep going in darkness.

When they reached the top of the hill, Dymphna ventured, "Shouldn't we find a place to stop?" Had Brioc even noticed the fading light?

He blinked a few times, as if struggling to pull himself back from somewhere. Dymphna held her breath.

"You're right. You must be tired. We'll find a place to camp."

She let out her breath. At least he had heard her. And answered.

Gazing around, Dymphna searched for a sheltered place. They were high in the hills, the road to Begerin winding like a ribbon far below them. While breathtaking, the view also gave them the vantage point of being able to see for miles. Brioc had wisely decided it was safer to follow the road this way, keeping it in view but without traveling on it. Should that soldier with Sam be on their trail, they would see him coming. At least Brioc was still thinking clearly.

Scanning rocky terrain strewn with huge boulders, Dymphna spotted what looked like a little cave in the distance. It would provide shelter from the rising wind. She pointed. "What about there? That cave?"

Brioc looked where she indicated, then, without a word, trudged towards it.

Dymphna slid clumsily off the horse, grateful to feel her feet on firm ground. Every inch of her body ached. Muscles she never even knew she possessed hurt after every day of riding. Her legs nearly collapsed.

Wobbling, she dragged the horse's reins and followed Brioc.

By the time she reached the cave, he was already clearing an area for a fire and building a pit with loose stones. Before leaving the town, he had bought flint and tinder. Thankfully his strange coin was accepted without trouble. Brioc had purchased a supply of food with another coin too, but they'd hardly eaten. Brioc didn't seem to care about eating, and Dymphna was too worried to have much of an appetite. She prayed that tonight she could convince Brioc to eat something. Prayed that they'd get to Begerin soon. Surely Brioc would return to normal once he was reunited with Ethlynn, wouldn't he?

While he fiddled with the fire pit, she tied their horse to a tree and wandered off to search for kindling. She had learned her lesson. Twigs first. Little dry ones. Logs came later, once the fire was lit. And she had no doubt Brioc would build up the flames into a raging inferno, as he did every night. He would sleep near it — or rather, not sleep at all, near it — and let her stay in the cave.

She tried to focus on collecting sticks and dry leaves into the folds of her skirt. Pushing away the disturbing thoughts, she attempted to turn her mind to prayer, but God seemed so far away. She had never felt so alone and scared in her life. What was wrong with Brioc? He was fading away in front of her eyes.

If only they would come upon a church where she could pour everything out to Jesus. She missed Him so much, missed kneeling in His Presence and feeling His loving protection enclose her. Dymphna felt a twinge of envy when she thought of Ethlynn, wherever she was, attending Mass every morning. But poor Ethlynn deserved consolation more, being pregnant and all. Before they were separated in Méifne, Father Gerebran had offered the Holy Sacrifice for all of them each morning before breakfast. He even allowed them the incomparable privilege of receiving Communion daily. Those brief moments had been Heaven to Dymphna, giving her the courage to keep going.

Now even that was gone.

Her eyes filled with tears. She quickly blinked them back and concentrated on filling her skirt with twigs. When she thought she had enough, she headed back to the cave.

Her heart stopped. Where was Brioc?

She dumped the wood by the fire pit and looked around, fighting back her uneasiness. Brioc was nowhere to be seen. The horse was still tethered where she had left it. Their supplies were inside the little cave.

"Brioc?" she called, as loud as she dared.

No answer.

"Brioc? Where are you?"

The wind whistling through the hills made the only sound. The sky had faded to a heavy cornflower blue. Soon darkness would shroud everything.

Stay calm.

Taking deep breaths, Dymphna scrambled onto the boulders surrounding the cave and carefully climbed higher, hoping to get a better view of the area. He couldn't have gone too far! She had only been collecting wood for ten minutes at the most.

She clambered higher on the rocks, the wind picking up, whipping her hair into her face. Shoving her hair back, she scanned the darkening surroundings with growing fear.

She wound her way around a clump of trees and huge boulders. When she reached the other side, she stopped dead.

Twenty feet away Brioc stood, his back to her. He was on the ledge of a cliff.

Dymphna slapped her hand over her mouth to stifle a gasp. Any sudden sound might startle him and make him lose his footing. She swallowed hard and crossed herself, begging God to let her know what to say, what to do. *Please God, please please.*

She softly cleared her throat. "Um . . . Brioc?"

He spun around so quickly it startled her. One wrong step and — *dear God, it must be a hundred foot drop!*

"Um." Her voice came out tiny. "Don't you think you should, um, maybe move away from there?" She could hardly breathe.

Brioc remained silent. She couldn't see his expression. The light had faded too much.

"Please," she begged. "Would you just . . . come over here? Please?" Her voice broke.

Brioc glanced back to whatever he had been staring at in the distance. Then, to her immense relief, he stepped away from the edge of the precipice.

"I . . . I found some firewood," she said, trying to keep her voice from shaking. Realizing the rest of her trembled, she wrapped her arms tightly around herself in a hug. *Please move farther from that edge. Please!*

"I'll come make a fire," he said. His voice sounded tired.

She waited, but Brioc didn't move. He still stood way too close to the drop. One big gust of wind and anything could happen.

"Well, um, would you walk back with me?" She turned as if to head back to the cave, but watched him from the corner of her eye.

"Dymphna?"

She whipped back around to face him.

"I don't mean to frighten you. But someone's down there. On the road."

Her heart beat so quickly that it seemed impossible any new amount of fear could make it race more. She was wrong. It felt like it would burst. *Was it Daidi?*

Without thinking, she rushed to Brioc's side to see for herself. He grabbed her arm and jerked her back from the edge so fast she didn't even realize how close she'd been.

"Hey! Careful!" he yelled, yanking her back farther, at least five feet away. He held her arm so tightly it hurt. "What on earth are you thinking, Dymphna? That's a ninety-foot drop!" He dragged her back to safer ground.

She stretched her neck, trying to peer over the edge but was too far back to see anything. "Is it Daidi?" Fright seized her. "What are we going to do? He'll find us up here and —"

"Whoa, calm down. I don't even know who it was. Just a few horsemen." Brioc blew out a breath. "I shouldn't have told you. They're miles away."

Was that why he'd been on the ledge, to watch them? Or had he happened to spot them when he was already there to — She shuddered, not wanting to think of it. Suddenly her legs felt shaky. Everything inside her collapsed from fear and exhaustion. Unable to fight back tears any longer, she sank to the ground and cried.

Brioc dropped down beside her. "Hey," he said. "Please don't." He must have realized he was still gripping her arm, because he immediately let go and scooted a few feet away.

She sniffled and wiped her eyes, trying to pull herself together.

"Everything will be alright," he said.

She nodded and looked up. Brioc's eyes were dark. "If it is your father, he's not touching you." Whether realizing it or not, his hand had wrapped around the hunting knife on his belt. It should have been consoling, but instead Dymphna's thoughts flew to the scars on his arms and more fear surfaced. Had Brioc done that to himself? *Dear God, please no. She couldn't handle any more!*

Brioc stood up. "Come on. Let's get a fire going."

She gave a little nod and stumbled to her feet. At least he was speaking. That was something to be grateful for.

She hesitated. "Brioc?"

"What?"

"Will you . . . well, will you eat something tonight? Please?"

He gave her a funny look, like he had no idea where that had come from.

"I mean, you haven't been eating, and . . ." she stared at the ground, feeling heat rush to her cheeks, "well, I'm awfully worried."

Silence.

She risked a glance up. "Please?"

Brioc's eyes squished up with confusion, but then he shook his head and she saw the merest hint of a smile. She took it as a *yes.*

Without another word, he turned and headed back around the boulders towards the cave. Dymphna followed, praying with all her might.

49

"Alright, Sam, this is it. Your moment of glory."

Turlough fished around in his saddlebag and found the letter. Pulling it out, he slid off his horse. He resisted the urge to continue up the hill. He knew Brioc and Lynnie were up there. Their fire, blazing in the darkness, could be seen from miles away. But he couldn't risk riding up there. Brioc would spot him coming and take off.

Turlough realized he was sweating. Was it really a good idea to trust his brother's life to a brainless wolfhound? What if Sam lost the letter on her way up? Worse, what if she lost herself? Could she find her way in the dark? What if Brioc mistook her for a wolf? Then what? Anything could happen.

Turlough ran a hand through his hair and stared at the glow of the distant fire. Three days ago this had seemed like a brilliant idea. Now he wasn't so sure.

He blew out a breath. What was the alternative?

There was none.

"Sam, come here." She padded over and he held out the letter. "Listen carefully. I need you to do something."

She leaped up and snapped her mouth around the parchment. Before Turlough even realized what had happened, Sam raced away with her new toy.

"No!" he yelped. "No!" He ran after her.

She ran faster, thinking it was a game.

"Sam!"

He chased her, scrambling wildly around trees and bushes and rocks.

Two minutes later, Samthann plopped down, tail wagging furiously. She released the letter, clasped it between her front paws, and settled down to chew it.

"No!" Turlough dove to the ground next to her. "Idiot dog, give it back!" He grabbed the edge, trying to wrestle the drool-covered paper from her jaws.

The wet parchment ripped in two.

Sam jumped up and trotted away, half the letter dangling from her mouth. She disappeared through the trees.

Despair washing over him, Turlough sat back on his heels and stared at the torn, slobbery parchment in his hand. Nothing but meaningless blots and squiggles and lines and loops stared back at him.

Were all the words still there? If only he could read! How much of the message was missing? Dare he hope that the part Sam had taken held no writing?

He looked up. "Sam," he called.

A few seconds later she reappeared through the trees, tail swishing. She sat down next to him, her mouth empty.

"Where did you put it? Go get it."

Her tail thumped. Suddenly her tongue was all over his face.

Angrily he shoved her off and pushed himself to his feet. "You have no idea how much I would love to murder you right now." He stormed into the woods to hunt for the missing half. Sam found a stick and trotted after him.

After fifteen minutes of futile searching in the dark, Turlough gave up. The breeze must have blown it away. Or maybe the stupid dog ate it. He hoped she'd get sick. Teach the useless mutt a lesson.

Sighing heavily, he stomped back to his horse. He prayed that the portion of the letter he held contained the whole message. Or at least the important bits. He couldn't even remember what the blasted note said in the first place.

Fuming, he jerked the rope from his saddlebag. He severed a few feet off with his knife, then looked around for Sam.

She sat in the shadow of a nearby tree with the stick in her mouth, waiting for him to play.

"Get over here, right now, before I ram that thing down your throat."

His tone must have given her the message, because she stood and her tail flew between her legs. She dropped the stick and slouched over to him, head drooping in rejection.

Turlough knelt beside her and quickly tied the rope around her neck, resisting the oh-so-sweet temptation to strangle her with it. He added an extra loop to the collar, rolled up what was left of the letter, and tucked it in, securing it to the collar with a tight knot.

"Alright," he said, "hike up that hill and find Brioc."

At the mention of Brioc's name, her ears perked and her tail popped out from between her legs and wagged. Turlough wrestled with her massive body until it was aimed in the right direction, then gave her a whack on the rump.

"Go. Get up there and find Brioc."

Samthann twisted her head around, found his face and licked him good-bye. Then she happily trotted in the direction he'd pointed her. Within seconds, she vanished into the darkness.

Turlough stood and made the sign of the cross, whispering a prayer that the dog understood where to go.

50

As usual, Brioc desperately fought against sleep. Exhausted though he was, he dreaded the nightmares that haunted every moment of his slumber and filled each night with terror. So he struggled to stay awake, loading more wood onto the fire, praying its flames would keep both the wolves and his horror-filled sleep away.

Dymphna's soft, even breathing in the cave a few yards away told him she'd finally dropped off. She looked so tired lately. And fragile, like any minute she might shatter into a thousand pieces. Brioc thought again of the dozen or so riders he'd seen below the cliff. They had been miles away and could have been anyone. But he felt an urgency to get Dymphna as far away as possible. He had to keep her safe, had to get her to Begerin. Then Father Gerebran, or the monks there, or someone — *anyone* — could take over.

But would he last that long? The familiar blackness circled around him, beckoning to him, wanting to suck him back into that deep, silent hole where nothing could touch him, nothing could hurt him, ever again. The thought of returning there both terrified and comforted him, and he longed to be rid of Dymphna so he could slip back to that place where nothing mattered anymore. He'd lost Lynnie. What was left to live for? If it hadn't been for Dymphna, he might have jumped off that cliff.

No, he hadn't drawn back only because of Dymphna. His thoughts had flicked to God. And he knew the gravity of the sin. Though the temptation threatened to overwhelm him, as it had years ago, his heart convicted him. He couldn't give in. How could he both crucify the God he loved and send his soul to Hell?

He couldn't. Simple as that.

But how to keep going?

He glanced at Dymphna asleep in the cave. She was so innocent and vulnerable. He had to protect her. No matter the cost. His own selfish misery couldn't come into this.

Sighing, he tossed another log on the fire and poked it with a stick. His eyelids grew heavier with every passing second. If he could just lay down for a few minutes, maybe he wouldn't actually fall asleep. He could stay awake, but maybe relax a bit, rest . . .

The last thing he remembered was a distant voice carrying on the wind. It should have alerted him to danger, but instead it only blended with his emerging nightmare and became a familiar voice. The voice of his brother. With fangs.

Something warm and damp slid across Brioc's face, likewise becoming part of his frightening dream. A soft whimper, followed by a nudge, then the wet thing streaked his cheek again. A heavy weight burrowed against his side, like a huge, shaggy rug. Fur covered his face.

A wolf!

Brioc's eyes snapped open. The object heaved up and down, breathing. It was alive! He bolted upright, terror surging. His hand flew to his side, heart slamming, and he fumbled for the hunting knife. Ripping it from his belt, he spun towards the wolf and . . . froze.

It wasn't a wolf. It was a dog.

He blinked.

Sam?

How on earth?

His mind whirled. Was he asleep? Was this still the dream? Was he having a flashback? But a flashback of what? The dog beside him looked and felt as real as every wolf in every reliving he'd ever had. Was this real or —

The dog's tail thumped and her tongue found his face again. Her huge body nuzzled against him, warm and comforting and so wonderfully familiar. She barked, then licked his ear.

Brioc slowly let out his breath. It was Sam, and she was real.

She barked again. Brioc wrapped his arms around her and pulled her against him, his heart still galloping. *Calm down. No wolf. Only Sam.* His terror gradually subsided, replaced by relief so great he felt dizzy. He crushed her against him, wanting never to let go. For a few incredible moments the anguish inside melted away. He even forgot about the nightmare.

"Brioc?"

The princess's voice startled him. His gaze flew towards the cave.

Dymphna leaned against its entrance, still half asleep. From the light of the fire, Brioc could see her bewildered expression. Her hair hung loose and uncombed; her shawl was draped around her shoulders, wrinkled from laying on it.

"I heard a bark." She rubbed her eyes and stared. "Is that Samthann?"

In answer to her question, Sam bounded to her, tail swishing, and eagerly licked the princess's hand. Dymphna knelt down and patted her. "Hi Sam. What are you doing here?" She looked up at Brioc, suddenly wide awake, her eyes filled with questions. "How did she get here?"

Brioc's breath caught. In his relief in seeing Sam, he hadn't even thought of where she'd come from or how she'd found him. If she was here, Turlough must be close! This was dangerous. His gaze snapped around in the darkness, looking for a sign of his brother.

"Something's tied around her neck." Dymphna fumbled beneath the shaggy, gray fur. Sam wiggled, trying to lick her hands as the princess struggled to unfasten an object looped in a rope."It's . . . a piece of parchment, I think." Her eyes squished with confusion.

Parchment? Why would Sam be carrying a piece of parchment? And where was Turlough? Not wanting to frighten the princess, Brioc resisted the urge to scan their dark surroundings. He swallowed and walked over to Dymphna, dread filling his every step.

Stay calm. Turlough was nearby, but he wasn't here yet. Brioc instinctively touched the hilt of the knife on his belt. No matter what happened, he wouldn't let his brother return this innocent girl to be violated by her father.

Dymphna managed to free the small folded square. Without looking at it, she straightened and held it out to Brioc with a trembling hand. He took the parchment and stepped closer to the light of the fire. Dare he open it? His own hands shook now too.

He drew a deep breath and unfolded the little scroll. Immediately he saw letters scrawled in black across the page. It was a note. The words were smudged, but decipherable. Brioc's mouth went dry. For a second he closed his eyes, gathering courage, then opened them and silently read.

will kill you and liny. your loving brother, tearlach

The words should not have surprised him, should not have felt like a knife going through him. But they did. That huge black fist reached inside and squeezed the little remaining life from him until he thought he truly might die of sorrow. If he had any doubts before that his brother hated him, there remained no such uncertainty now. Turlough was not the hero he'd worshiped as a child. Turlough had never been that. Brioc's image of him had been nothing but a warped ideal created by a little boy desperate for love. His brother wanted him dead, and had gone to great lengths to get the message across. It came through loud and clear.

"What does it say?" Dymphna's voice came out tiny and scared.

Brioc forced his gaze from the note and looked at her. She stood with her arms wrapped around herself, shivering. Not from cold. Her face was white, fear written everywhere. And his brother would return this girl to the king? Over Brioc's dead body!

"Will you let me read it?"

"No." Unexpected anger surged through him and his fist closed around the parchment, scrunching it into a tight wad. He flung it into the fire. Flames leaped to devour it. The ball curled and sparked, a fiery orange globe. Within seconds it shriveled to nothing and disappeared.

Dymphna stared at the fire, then raised her eyes to stare at Brioc. "What was it? What did it say?"

Sam barked. They both jumped. A faraway voice called from somewhere below the hill, "Brioc? Did you get my note? I know you're up there. I'm coming up, alright?"

Dymphna threw frantic glances in every direction, her arms flying out as if ready to run but not knowing where.

"Brioc? Can you hear me? Is Sam with you? She has a note."

At the sound of both her name and Turlough's voice, Sam went crazy, barking and yipping, her backside squirming nonstop.

Dymphna almost launched into the air. One second she was five feet away, the next she was gripping Brioc's arm so hard it felt like she'd cut off his circulation. "What do we do? It's that soldier! He's coming! He's —"

"Stay quiet." Brioc's head throbbed. His mind reeled. He felt ready to pass out.

"Brioc? Sam? Where are you?"

Oh no, the fire! Turlough would see their fire!

Brioc fell to his knees and urgently shoveled dirt onto the flames. He shook so badly he kept missing, and the dirt landed instead on the rocks of the circular pit. Dymphna crashed down to help him, grabbing handful after handful of soil, dumping them on the fire. Silent tears streamed down her face. Brioc had never seen anyone look so scared in his life.

Sam kept barking, the sound carrying in the suddenly still night. Her tail went crazy.

They had to put the fire out!

"Give me your shawl. Quick."

Dymphna whipped it off and handed it over. Brioc stood and beat it against the flames, again and again, till the blaze died down. Smoke filled the air. Brioc prayed its haze might hide them in the dark.

Samthann kept barking and Turlough kept calling, probably trying to navigate his way up the hill towards the fire's glow. Dymphna raced back and forth, throwing dirt and more dirt on the remaining flames, then rushed into the cave. She reemerged with their waterskin and poured the contents onto the embers. Brioc stomped out the rest.

"Get the horse," he told her. "Hurry." With a frightened nod, she ran off.

Sam alternated between watching Brioc stamp out the remaining sparks and gazing in the direction from where Turlough's voice came. Her ears were perked, her tail wagging furiously. She bounded a few yards forward, then hesitated and came back. She looked at Brioc and whimpered, torn between her equal desires to go meet Turlough or remain with him.

Brioc moved away from the fire pit and fell to one knee beside her. He grabbed the rope around her neck and pulled her close. "Shh, Sam, shh," he pleaded. "Stay. Be quiet."

She excitedly licked his face, then turned back towards the surrounding blackness and barked even more.

"Shut up," Brioc whispered. He wrapped his hands tightly around her muzzle, fighting to keep her mouth closed. It didn't work. She was too strong.

"Brioc! Is Sam with you? Did you find my note?"

Turlough was getting closer. Brioc's chest felt ready to burst. He strained his eyes to see through the darkness, but saw only shadows. Where was Turlough? Sounds were deceiving at night. He might still be far away. *Please, God, please.*

Sam kept barking and whining, dying to be reunited with the other person she loved.

"Sam, pleeeease," Brioc begged. He had to make her be quiet! He squeezed her muzzle shut with all his strength. The dog yipped in pain, her huge head jerking, and broke his hold. She banged her head against his face, licked his cheek, then barked some more.

Horse hooves clomped on the rocks behind him. Suddenly Dymphna appeared. She dropped to her knees and grabbed Brioc's arm. Terror filled her eyes. Her cheeks were wet, tears silently streaming. "Make Sam stop. Please, Brioc, please make her stop. He'll find us, he'll take me back to Daidi, he'll —"

"Brioc! Where on earth are you? Would you just read the stupid note!"

Sam tugged against the rope, trying to break free and run to Turlough. The rope rubbed against Brioc's palm, burning like fire, but he didn't let go.

"Sam, no!" he whispered. "Stay. Be quiet."

"Make her stop barking. Please make her stop." Dymphna's fingers dug into Brioc's arm. Her face was ashen and wet, her body paralyzed with fear.

Shaking, Brioc reached for the hunting knife on his belt. His hand closed around its hilt and he slid it out. Hot tears stung his eyes, and for a second he had to close them, fighting them back. He had no choice. Opening his eyes, he wrapped his free arm around Sam's neck, then jerked her head back, so hard she yelped.

He shoved the knife in and slit her throat.

51

"Brioc?" Turlough called again. "Sam?"

Breathless from hiking uphill over such rocky terrain, he stopped and leaned against a boulder to get his bearings. He'd lost sight of the fire's glow several minutes ago. How had it disappeared so suddenly? Maybe something blocked it from his view. An overhang, or perhaps a cluster of trees. It was hard to tell in the dark. Turlough strained his eyes, but saw no glimpse or hint of flames.

And Sam. Why had she stopped barking? She'd been yapping her head off the whole time, which had been perfect. Turlough had simply followed the sound, knowing it would lead him straight to her and Brioc. But suddenly the dog was quiet, and for some reason the silence disturbed him. Turlough stared at the hills above him, a strange uneasiness settling over him. Brioc and Lynnie were up there, and surely Sam had found them. Brioc must have read the note by now. So why wouldn't he answer Turlough's calls?

And why had Sam stopped barking?

"Brioc?" he yelled again. He swallowed hard, fighting down the fear that something had gone terribly wrong.

Leaves rustled in a sudden gust of wind. Somewhere, far in the distance, a horse neighed. It couldn't be his. He'd tethered his mount below. Holding his breath, he listened intently. A clomping sound, like hooves against rocks, carried from afar, up the hill.

Then suddenly another noise, this time from below him. Turlough froze. A few seconds later the sound came again.

He frowned. Loose stones? Cascading down a slope? He couldn't be sure. It was too soft, too far away.

Was someone climbing the hill behind him? He listened intently, not daring to move. Seconds ticked by. Turned into a minute. Two minutes.

Three.

Nothing. Wind rustled the leaves. An owl hooted.

Turlough slowly exhaled. He was imagining things. Overtired.

He moved forward, picking his way around the boulders, climbing over them, trudging higher up the hill.

If only Sam would bark again. Her silence unnerved him.

His mind spun, trying to figure out what had happened to her. Surely she hadn't been attacked by another animal. Not even a wolf would be bold enough to take on a dog her size. A whole pack, yes, but if that had happened the sounds

210

of snarls and fighting would have carried for miles.

Huh. Maybe she simply fell asleep.

Finally the ground evened out. He'd reached a plateau. A sheltered spot, with trees and a little cave, lay ahead. Orange sparks glowed on the ground near the cave's entrance. Embers of a recent fire. Brioc and Lynnie must have been here, not ten minutes ago. Turlough's heart beat faster. He stepped closer, then spotted Sam stretched out near the fire pit.

Relief flooded through him. He was right — she'd merely fallen asleep. Strange that she hadn't followed Brioc, but at least she was alright.

"Hey, Sam."

He walked towards her. She didn't move.

"Wake up. Where's Brioc? Did you give him my note?"

Even the mention of his brother's name didn't get a reaction, which was unusual. No raised head, no thumping tale. Gosh, she must've been exhausted.

"Hey, wakie-wakie. Time to get up." Reaching her, he gently nudged her with his foot. "We need to find Brioc."

No movement.

Turlough frowned. Was she sick? He knelt in the dirt and tousled her head. "Hey, Sam. You alright?" Her fur felt colder than normal. Her head felt funny too, like it was suddenly too heavy. Why wouldn't she move?

Then he spotted the dark puddle beneath her head.

Oh dear God, no.

With dread, he touched the pooling liquid. *Blood.*

For a moment, he couldn't breathe. It was like some giant vice reached inside him, crushing his lungs.

He closed his eyes, trying to stop the stinging tears, but knew it wouldn't work.

"Sam. Oh Sam. I'm so sorry." He wrapped his arms around her lifeless shoulders and pulled her towards his lap. Her huge head rolled to one side, revealing the deep gash across her throat. Sorrow choked him. Why had Brioc done this? *Why?*

He should check if the note was still tied around her neck. The idea of fumbling around there horrified him. He hesitated, then ran his sleeve cuff across his eyes. Gently moving her head, he probed through her fur for the rope. Within mere seconds, blood drenched his hands. He found the rope but not the note.

So. Brioc had read it. Read it and ignored it.

Then killed Sam, presumably so that Turlough couldn't follow the sound of her bark.

For the first time in his life, anger towards Brioc swept through him, so fierce and unexpected it startled him. He suddenly wanted to walk away and leave his stubborn brother to his fate. Brioc didn't want his help. Fine. Let Daemon kill him.

Turlough stood up, struggling to push back the rage.

Deep down, he suspected his anger came from pain. But that didn't help; it only made it worse. Why did Brioc hate him so much? Turlough would give his life for him! And still Brioc refused to trust him. Alright, so he'd once made a mistake. A mistake with appalling, unspeakable consequences. But he'd only been fifteen, for heaven's sake! Practically a child himself. And he'd been desperate and scared and hurting just as much as his little brother had been that day. Must Brioc punish him for the rest of his life? Couldn't Brioc show an ounce of mercy? *Even one tiny ounce?*

The sight of Sam stretched out dead suddenly made Turlough want to drive his fist into something. Namely, Brioc's face.

The image of Branduff and Raghnall unexpectedly flashed through his mind. They were in Heaven, or at least close to it. What would they think of him now, seething with anger at their youngest brother? Turlough's rage drained as quickly as it had come, replaced by shame. He forced himself to look away from Sam before the temptation came back.

He raked a hand through his hair and tried to decide what to do now. The obvious answer was to head down the hill, get his horse, and go back to tracking. After all, Brioc and Lynnie only had ten minutes on him, fifteen at the most. He sighed. Would this nightmare ever end?

He glanced again at Sam, such a loyal, faithful, stupid friend. How could he just leave her like that? Shouldn't he bury her, or —

A rustle from the shadows made him freeze. Crunching leaves, breathing. Soft footfalls.

Someone coughed.

Turlough's hand flew to the hilt of his sword. Backing into the darkness of the cave, he slid his weapon from its scabbard as quietly as he could. He pressed against the cold stone wall and held his breath.

A cloaked figure emerged from the trees and shuffled towards the fire pit. The man stopped suddenly in his tracks, probably startled by the sight of the dead wolfhound nearby. His back was towards Turlough, the hood of his cloak pulled over his head. A large sword hung at his side. One of Daemon's soldiers?

Turlough silently stepped out of his hiding place. In one swift motion he grabbed the man from behind, spun him around, and slammed him against the cave's entrance. He shoved his sword hard against the other's throat.

Startled eyes looked back at him. Turlough pushed the blade closer against the man's exposed flesh. "One move and you're dead."

The man swallowed, unable to nod. A deep, jagged scar ran the length of his face. Turlough blinked. *Wait, was this —?* He reached up and yanked off the hood. Long dark hair fell to the man's shoulders.

"Neill! What — How did you get here?"

Neill glared until Turlough realized he couldn't speak with the blade against his throat. He instantly lowered the sword.

Still glaring, Neill rubbed his skin where the blade had pressed against it. "That hurt. Thanks a lot."

"What are you doing here?" Turlough asked again, mind spinning.

"Trying to save your backside, what do you think?" Neill squinted. "Do you realize you're covered in blood?"

"Huh?"

"What'd you do, take a bath in it?"

Turlough glanced down at his shirt. The front was streaked red. He hadn't even realized. "Oh, it's the dog's."

Neill made a face. "It's in your hair. How did you get dog blood in your hair?"

Turlough must have smeared it when he ran his hand through his hair a minute ago. To his surprise, he didn't even care. Sam was dead. He'd give anything to have her back.

"Why'd you kill the poor hound in the first place?"

"I didn't. My brother did."

Neill frowned. "Wait. You mean, the minstrel? He liked that dog. It was always with him. Wherever he went, the beast was at his side. Why would he kill his own dog?"

Sadness tore at Turlough. "Because I was too close, and he doesn't trust me."

Neill raised an eyebrow. "He doesn't trust you?"

"No. Look, it's too complicated to explain. My brother hates me. But I'm wasting time. I need to find him. His life is in danger."

"So is yours." Neill glared again. "And now mine too, by the way. Barrf's not far behind us. I managed to sneak off, but it wasn't easy."

Turlough was startled. "Barrf's out here?"

"You're being tracked. Half the army's scattered throughout Ireland, looking for you. Faidh figured you'd lead them straight to your brother."

Turlough should have known! How naive could he have been? That must have been the reason they had let him live!

"They're following me?" Fresh fear for Brioc's safety slammed through him. "How close are they?"

"Close enough you should be having heart failure. As soon as I realized we were tracking you, I knew I had to find you first and warn you."

Turlough was speechless. Before he could think of anything to say, Neill

213

asked, "What in creation did your brother steal from Daemon?"

"I have no idea. Brioc's not a thief. I can't figure it out, Neill. It makes no sense."

"Well, pray you can convince him to give the thing back, whatever it is. Even then, the demon will probably kill him. Not to mention us."

Turlough glanced around, half expecting the king to step out of the shadows. "Daemon's out here too?"

"Yep. With Barrf. Thankfully, he's slowing the party down with his bizarre behavior. That's the only reason I managed to slip away. He's crazier than I thought." Disgust flashed in Neill's eyes. "He stopped some young lassie a few days back, believing she was his daughter. Crazy. I have no idea where he got that idea. The girl was with child."

"I've got to save my brother, Neill. His wife is with him, and she's pregnant too. Brioc doesn't have a clue how to survive out here alone."

"Alright. Let's stop talking and get moving."

"You mean, you're going to help me?"

Neill rolled his eyes. "No. I only hiked up here to admire the view. Looks great in spring. All those flowers. Almost worth getting my throat slit." He stared meaningfully at the sword still in Turlough's hand.

The relief was so great that Turlough slumped against the cave wall, suddenly drained.

Neill stepped forward and kicked more dirt onto the embers of the dead fire. "Well, what are we waiting for? Let's go. My horse is with yours. You can fill me in on the way down."

Turlough nodded and pushed off the wall. His gaze fell on Sam. "No, wait. I need to bury the dog."

"You're going to *bury* her?"

"Yes." Turlough's eyes stung anew. "I can't leave her like that. She . . . she wasn't a bad mutt."

Neill sighed. "Make it fast. Barrf's probably only a few hours behind us. I'll go grab the horses." He pulled his hood back over his head against the chilly breeze and started to walk away.

On impulse Turlough grabbed his sleeve. Neill turned back around.

"Hey, thanks. I mean that, Neill."

Neill rolled his eyes. "Yes, well, let's just find your brother. Hopefully we can figure out a way to save all our skins. Because right now, we couldn't be in deeper water if we tried."

52

Dymphna felt so sad. If only she could stop thinking about Samthann. She should be trying to sleep, not lying here torturing herself with last night's memory.

After hours of riding, they had finally found a safe place to rest, hidden between the entwined roots of three massive trees, where no one could possibly see them, even in the morning light. Dymphna should take advantage of the chance to sleep. Even Brioc had dropped off, doubtless from sheer exhaustion. She closed her eyes again and shifted to a more comfortable position between roots.

The thought of Sam loomed again. Her last heartrending yelp, the way she had collapsed limply to the ground, the look of agony on Brioc's face — *Stop. Don't think of it.*

Dymphna rolled over, blinking back tears. Trying to rest was futile. Sleep would never come, not with that image of poor Sam pervading her thoughts. Maybe if she got up and *did* something, the memory would leave her alone. At least for awhile.

Yes, that's it. She'd distract herself. Keep busy while Brioc slept.

Um. Busy doing what? There was nothing to do.

She sat up and shoved her hair from her face. Yuck. It was oily. She hadn't had a chance to wash it in days. If only she could find a — Wait! They'd crossed a bubbly little brook not long before finding this place. An idea formed. She could sneak to the water and at least wash her hair.

Should she risk it? She glanced at Brioc several feet away. He lay in a heap tucked between roots, deep in sleep. He probably wouldn't stir for hours. Dymphna couldn't even imagine how tired he was. He stayed awake almost every night. Tonight would be even worse, as he wouldn't dare light a fire. Not after last night. *Oh no, here came her tears again. Poor Sam!*

And poor Brioc. If *she* missed Samthann so terribly, how much worse it must be for him. Yet Brioc had only done it for her, to keep her safe from that soldier. What a heroic proof of friendship. She could never repay him for taking care of her at such incredible personal cost. First being separated from his wife, and now Sam. Dymphna's heart stirred with gratitude. God had given her the most noble protector anyone could ever have.

Yet, fear stirred inside her even more. Killing Sam had possibly pushed Brioc straight over an emotional cliff. Physically, he hadn't jumped, as she'd thought he might last night. But mentally, who knew how close he was to the edge?

He hadn't said a word since they'd left the cave. That alone was disturbing, but Brioc had done that before, so Dymphna wasn't too surprised. It was his expression that unnerved her. His eyes were blank now. Completely void, as if he wasn't *inside* himself anymore. Dymphna had no idea how to get him back, other than pray her hardest. Which she did.

But, between all those prayers, it would be nice to wash her dirty hair.

As silently as she could, she rose to her feet and slipped on her shoes. Brioc would never agree to her going alone to the stream. She was positive of that. He wouldn't let her out of his sight. Especially not now, after that soldier had been so close. Dymphna didn't particularly want to wander away without Brioc either. But if she went super fast, she could be back in twenty minutes. Well, thirty. But what could possibly happen in a measly half hour?

She reached for her shawl, then recoiled. The ugly thing had burn spots and reeked of smoke from beating out last night's fire. She'd never liked it, but now the thought of wearing it was penance. Maybe she'd go without, and when they reached Begerin, Father Gerebran would find a way to get her some nicer clothes. Was it wrong to hope so?

As she turned away, an image flashed through her mind of Jesus, crowned with thorns, a purple robe draped around His bleeding shoulders. How horrid it must have been for Him to wear such a revolting garment, covered in spittle and filth. Yes, she would wear the ugly, scorched shawl as a gift to Jesus and offer it for Brioc! Snatching up the shawl, she wrapped it around her shoulders before she could change her mind. The sacrifice brought an unexpected joy.

She stepped quietly over the tree roots. Thankfully, Brioc didn't stir. She was just about to scamper away, then hesitated. What if he woke up and found her missing? She'd better leave a note.

Finding a stick nearby, she knelt in the dirt. She brushed away the leaves and pebbles to make a clean surface to write on. Carefully she etched the words: *Will be back soon.*

There. That should do. Hopefully Brioc would stay asleep and never even read it.

She tiptoed through the trees in the direction she'd seen the stream, praying Brioc wouldn't hear her and wake up. Once she was far enough away, she picked up her pace, eager to reach the water. The quicker she got there, the quicker she could return.

Ten minutes later, she stopped and looked around. Where was the stream? She didn't remember walking this far. A trickle of sweat ran down her back. Maybe this wasn't such a good idea after all. Should she turn back?

But her hair. It was revolting. It would be wonderful to wash it. Maybe she would walk a teeny bit farther.

Another few minutes, and the gentle gurgling of water reached her ears. Whew. Following the sound, she finally spotted the brook through the trees. She hurried to its bank, then stopped. The water would be cold. She had no soap. Should she attempt it? It might be her only chance. She hesitated.

Best to make this quick.

Nervous and alone, she rubbed her arms and stepped toward a flat rock that jutted into the river. She inched up her skirts a tiny fraction to kneel. Her skin crawled and she stopped. What was that? Branches cracked and leaves rustled behind her. Before she had time to spin around, someone grabbed her from behind.

A hand clamped over her mouth. The scream stifled in her throat.

"I'm not going to hurt you. I promise."

She tried to break away, squirming and kicking. The arms held her tighter. Her captor was too strong; she would never get away!

"Stop! I won't hurt you! I'll release you, but only once I'm sure you won't scream."

Everything inside her said she would scream the second his hand left her mouth!

"Just promise me that, and I'll let you go."

She jabbed back with her elbows and kicked him again, knowing she was accomplishing nothing.

"Lynnie, stop. I'm not going to hurt you! I only want to talk."

Lynnie?

Dymphna froze. He thought she was . . . *Ethlynn*?

"Please, just promise you won't scream. Then I'll take my hand away." The man sighed. "I know you don't know who I am. But I'm your brother-in-law." Sadness edged his voice.

Dymphna's mind whirled. Ethlynn's brother-in-law? He must be married to one of her sisters. What was he doing out here? Had he followed them all the way from Méifne? Were Ethlynn's sisters here too?

No, they couldn't be, otherwise they would know she wasn't Ethlynn!

But . . . whoever this man was, he wasn't one of Daidi's soldiers, and that's all that mattered. The terror drained from her so rapidly she went limp. His strong arms holding her up kept her from falling.

"If I let you go, will you be quiet?"

She nodded.

"Promise?"

She nodded again, as vigorously as she could, and he instantly let her go. Her knees buckled and she reached out to the nearest tree to steady herself so she wouldn't collapse. This was just one of Ethlynn's innocent relatives. *Thank you, God, thank you.*

As she turned to look at him, she glimpsed the steel sword hanging from his belt and she gasped. A soldier! He'd tricked her!

Blood stained his shirt and streaked his hair. *He must have killed Brioc!* This time it was she herself who slapped a hand over her mouth. *Don't scream, don't scream.*

"I'm Brioc's brother."

Dymphna stared. Oh my gosh, it was the soldier who looked just like him! Apart from this man's hair being light and Brioc's being dark, the two were nearly identical. This was the soldier who'd been chasing them with Sam.

She staggered against the tree trunk, not sure if her body was about to run or simply pass out.

He must have been thinking along the same lines because he said, "Oh no, don't faint," looking like he wouldn't know what to do if she did.

Her mind suddenly latched on to what he'd said. Brioc's . . . *brother?* Brioc didn't have a brother! His brothers were dead. It was a trap. The soldier obviously realized they looked alike and was using it to trick her. People had probably been telling him for years that he and the minstrel could be brothers.

Besides, he'd murdered Brioc. The blood on his shirt proved it. He must have slain Brioc in his sleep, then followed Dymphna to the stream. Any second now he would tie her up and drag her back to marry Daidi! Her breathing came in quick gasps.

"Lynnie, listen to me, please. Your lives are in danger. King Daemon is hunting you down, to kill you." He glanced over his shoulder, as if half-expecting Daidi to jump out from behind a boulder.

Dymphna backed against the tree.

"Tell me what Brioc stole from the king. Please. If I know what it is, I can help you."

She weighed her chances of outrunning him. They were less than zero. Should she scream? But who would come to her rescue? He'd already killed Brioc. *What should she do?*

"I need to talk to Brioc. Please, Lynnie, you have to convince him I'm on your side."

"You killed him," she said in a tiny voice.

He blinked, bewildered. "Killed who?"

"Brioc." She wondered how she managed to speak at all.

Confusion raced through his eyes. He followed her gaze to his shirt and must have suddenly realized because he said, "No, no. It's Sam's blood. I didn't kill anyone."

Oh, thank God. Relief poured through her. But she was still lost. "Brioc doesn't have a brother. He would have told me if he did. You're lying."

She must be crazy. She should be fleeing for her life, not standing here talking with Daidi's soldier! Daidi was nearby. This had to be a trap. She cast a frantic look at the woods, wondering how to get away.

"I swear, Lynnie, it's true. We're brothers. I . . . I can prove it." He seemed to grope. "Ask me anything." His eyes flicked, his confident air fading.

Before she lost her nerve, she took up his challenge. "His scars. If you're his brother, tell me where they are and what caused them."

The soldier didn't hesitate, not even for a second. "He has scars everywhere," he said. "The worst are on his arms and chest. A wolf attacked him when he was a child."

Dymphna's breath caught. Brioc was mauled by a *wolf*? She was aghast. No wonder he was traumatized!

"It was a couple years after our parents died." The soldier's eyes flickered with deep emotion and his gaze broke away. "When I found him, I was sure he was dead."

Dymphna swallowed. Was this true? If it was, it would explain so much. Brioc's nightmares, why he needed Sam, even his obsession with fire. Wolves feared fire.

The soldier couldn't be making this up, could he? Dymphna wanted to believe him. If fangs had made those scars, then Brioc hadn't mutilated himself, like Daidi. She shuddered. Both images were horrid — being attacked by a wild animal, and cutting oneself unto blood. But at least it meant Brioc wasn't as sick as Daidi.

Yet, if this man was Brioc's brother, why would Brioc run from him? It made no sense.

On impulse, Dymphna said, "Tell me your sister's name."

"Aislinn." Again, no hesitation. He even offered more. "We had four brothers. Branduff, Raghnall, Aedh and Maedoc." He paused and added, "My name is Turlough."

Wait. When Brioc had told her about the day Aislinn was born, he said one of his brothers took him to the festivities. He'd started to say a name, then stopped before finishing. Dymphna was sure Brioc had said, *Tur—* .

This really was his brother!

"Lynnie, please. We're wasting time. You have to tell me what Brioc took from the king."

She was the thing Brioc had taken.

When she didn't answer, Turlough sighed. "Look, I know that whatever he took is holy. I've seen a miracle to prove it." Dymphna flinched, confused. *What was he talking about?* "If you won't tell me what it is, then at least convince Brioc I need to talk to him. Please, Lynnie? "

Dymphna suddenly wanted more than anything to blurt out the whole story and tell him who she was and beg him to help them. His eyes were so kind. And pure, not like the rest of Daidi's soldiers. She'd seen him often at Mass. And he truly was Brioc's brother. How could she not trust him?

Yet something was wrong. Brioc was running from him. Brioc had killed Sam to keep him away!

"Will you fetch Brioc?" Turlough waited for her answer. "I'll wait here."

She nodded uncertainly and took a hesitant step away. He didn't stop her. Daidi didn't leap out from behind a tree. Nothing bad happened.

She walked a few more steps.

Still safe.

She spun and ran. She threw a glance over her shoulder. The soldier stayed behind.

She turned back around and — *Crash!* She bowled straight into someone else, the impact nearly knocking her to the ground.

The man seemed nearly as surprised as she was. He held a dead rabbit in one hand and a dripping knife in the other, as if he'd just returned from hunting. Then Dymphna spotted his heavy sword and she gasped. He was another of Daidi's soldiers!

She recognized him instantly; the one with the scar and long hair. He was always sneaking into the castle to fool around with the serving girls. Her blood froze. He would know exactly who she was!

He stared at her, the expression on his face rapidly changing from surprise to disbelief. He dropped the rabbit and made a move to grab her, but Turlough called out, "Neill! No! Let her go!"

The one named Neill hesitated, confusion stamped on his face. But he obeyed and stepped back so Dymphna could pass.

She bolted from him at a dead run.

53

Brioc stared at Dymphna's message in the dirt. He knew he should worry. Instead, he felt nothing. Lynnie was gone. Turlough vowed to kill him. Sam's blood stained his sleeves. It was hard to care about the princess.

Goodness, how wretched was he?

Trying to conjure up some emotion, and ashamed when he couldn't, he sighed and left their hiding place. The effort to move, let alone search for Dymphna, seemed beyond his strength. He wanted only to give up and die. He would actually find relief when Turlough found and killed him.

No, he took that back. He longed for death, but not by his brother's hand. He couldn't imagine anything worse than the thought of Turlough in Hell.

Besides, he had to stay alive. He had to keep Dymphna safe.

He searched in the soft dirt for her footprints and instantly found them. As he set off towards a line of trees, sounds broke the calm of the woods: a great thrashing and someone panting. A few seconds later, Dymphna burst into view, breathless.

"Brioc, Brioc," she gasped. "I met your brother."

Brioc should have reeled. His heart should have raced. His breath should have caught.

None of those things happened.

He felt nothing. Void.

"He's down at the stream with another soldier." Dymphna's face was deathly pale. "He says he —" She swayed, about to faint.

Brioc grabbed her before she could fall. The action was automatic. He eased her to the ground, then knelt beside her and reached for his waterskin.

"Here, drink this." He handed her the vessel.

"He thinks I'm Ethlynn." Her words poured out. "The other soldier knows who I am, but I don't know if he told your brother yet, and nothing makes sense because you don't have a brother, so he's lying, but he knew all about your family and —"

"Just drink."

Dymphna stopped talking and obeyed. While she drank the water, Brioc's gaze roamed the woods. But it was more out of duty than concern. "Did they follow you?" He didn't feel he cared. His voice came out wooden, even to his own ears.

"No, they let me go." Her color gradually returned. "Brioc, is it true? Is he really your brother?"

Her eyes searched his face. Such helpless, innocent, trusting eyes. How could he lie to her?

He couldn't.

"We had the same parents." He shrugged. "Guess that makes us brothers." Last night, reading the letter and realizing the depth of Turlough's hatred for him, a knife had rammed through his heart. But the blade had already gone through, leaving nothing left for it to pierce. Dead people could no longer be wounded.

Dymphna stared at him. She seemed to grope for words. Or understanding. Or both. "Why didn't you ever tell me he's your brother?"

None of your business. As soon as the rude thought came, Brioc chastised himself for it and, not wanting to hurt her, said nothing. He dropped his gaze, and saw his sleeve. He blinked. *Was that blood?* Confused, he stared at the crimson stains. What did they come from? He couldn't remember.

A memory slammed into him.

Sam. He'd killed Sam!

Dear God, he'd killed her! Pain ripped his insides, so violent he felt for a second he would die. The beast inside stirred and woke and nearly sprang.

Some invisible chain jerked the beast back. The pain and the beast both vanished down the black hole. He was blanking again.

What was Dymphna saying?

He looked up from his sleeve.

Dymphna sat gaping at him. Something like fear fled across her face. "Brioc? Are you even listening to me?"

He forced himself to focus. "Of course I'm listening. You were talking about . . ."

He stopped, unable to remember.

Dymphna's eyes flickered, like she didn't know what to do. She looked ready to jump up and bolt. "Your brother. He wants to talk to you." She floundered. "Will you come with me? Please? He's waiting at the stream."

Turlough was at the stream?

Brioc frowned and ran a hand through his hair. He couldn't follow this.

"Brioc, *please.* You need to speak with him! He's going to help us!"

She was talking about Turlough? No, no, she couldn't be. Brioc must be getting it all wrong.

"Turlough would never help us. It must be someone else. Turlough wants me dead."

"No! He's trying to save us." Dymphna pointed into the woods. "He's at the stream. With another soldier. I don't think the other one will hurt us either. He must be your brother's friend."

"We need to get away from here." Brioc sighed and stood up. His legs felt heavy.

"Wait," Dymphna pleaded. "How do you know your brother wants you dead?"

How *did* Brioc know? He had to think about it for a minute. The letter. That was it.

"Because he told me so. That's what the note said. He plans to kill me."

"The letter said that?"

"Yes." He walked toward their horse, feeling like he was wading through mortar. Every step took an effort.

Dymphna didn't follow. Brioc turned back around. Her expression was confused, her face ashen. She stared in the direction of the stream, visibly torn. It was obvious she didn't know what to do.

"Are you coming?" he asked.

"I . . . I think there's some mistake. His letter couldn't have said that. Please, Brioc, talk to him."

So, now Turlough had convinced her he was on their side. What a liar. Every time Brioc began to trust him, Turlough stabbed him in the back. Yet strangely, the thought brought with it no emotion.

"You can believe me, or you can believe him. Whichever you choose, Princess."

Dymphna hesitated. Just for an instant, but long enough for Brioc to see her indecision. To his surprise, he felt a pang of anguish. Then the sorrow at losing her trust tumbled down the black hole with everything else.

Who even cared?

Dymphna's eyes filled with tears. She threw one more anguished glance over her shoulder towards the stream, then stood up and followed him to the horse.

Brioc almost wished she hadn't.

54

"Well," Neill said, joining Turlough beside the stream, "at least we finally know what your brother took from Daemon." His expression held a blend of disbelief, confusion, and amusement. He shook his head. "Why did you tell me to let her go?"

Turlough frowned. "I gave her my word I'd wait here. But hang on. How do you know what Brioc took? What on earth is it?"

Neill tossed his head in the direction Lynnie had run. "Her. It's obvious."

"Of course he took her. She's his wife."

Neill's eyes widened. "You mean — you don't know who that was?"

"She's Brioc's wife. I just told you that. She's my sister-in-law. Lynnie."

Neill gave him a funny look. For once he seemed speechless. Finally he cleared his throat and said, "I don't suppose you noticed she wasn't pregnant?"

Turlough glanced again to the spot in the trees where Lynnie had disappeared, then back to Neill. Actually, he *had* noticed. It was strange. He didn't know what to think. Had she already had her baby?

"Or that she was awfully young to be married?" Neill folded his arms across his chest and leaned back against a tree. He seemed ready to laugh, like he suddenly enjoyed some secret joke.

Turlough studied him. "Yes, I did spot those things." He'd also spotted how beautiful she was. How could he not? "Are you planning to tell me what's so funny?"

"She's not your sister-in-law."

Turlough's brows knitted. "Of course she is. I've been tracking them since they left Oriel."

Neill pushed off the tree. "You've been tracking your brother and the king's daughter, that's who you've been tracking."

Turlough's jaw dropped. He stared at Neill. "What?"

"Princess Dymphna. That's her. Your brother stole the princess. Remember she went missing?"

Turlough opened his mouth. Closed it. Turned and gaped at the path she'd disappeared down. His mind whirled, trying to process the unthinkable.

Neill strode over and whacked him on the back. "Hey, she's gorgeous. Who can blame him? I'd run off with her too, if I thought I could get away with it."

The comment made Turlough's blood boil. He glared at Neill, suddenly wanting to punch his face. "My brother would never do that! He's honorable and he's pure. Besides, he loves his wife. I know he does." At the graveside, Brioc had been anxious to get home to Lynnie. He'd said she didn't feel well. Same when he dropped off Sam — he was worried sick at the thought that Lynnie might die. No way in the world would Brioc take off with another girl. Turlough refused to believe it.

Yet . . . if that was Dymphna, where on earth was Lynnie?

He raked a hand through his hair, trying to figure it out. "There has to be a logical explanation, Neill. Brioc wouldn't do that. He simply *wouldn't*. Something else is going on."

Neill shrugged.

Think.

Wait! Something Neill had said last night came back.

"You told me Daemon stopped some girl, mistaking her for his daughter. Where was that?"

"Outside Méifne."

"Didn't you say she was pregnant?"

"Yes. No doubt on that score. I think she was about to go into labor. She seemed ready. The archers killed their horse and she fell off."

"*Their* horse? You mean she was on horseback? With another person?"

"She was riding double with a priest."

Turlough remembered the horse chase he'd seen on the hill, right after Brioc raced out of the stable. That must have been them! "Was the girl wearing a pink dress?"

Neill grinned. "Very pink. Pretty too."

Turlough couldn't help smile a little. "The girl or the dress?"

Neill laughed. "Both. The girl more than the dress."

Nice to know Brioc had good taste. Of course he would. "That had to be Lynnie," Turlough said. "Brioc was in Méifne at the same time the couple on the horse took off. They must have gotten separated. I chased Brioc, and the rest of you chased Lynnie and . . . a priest, you say?" He rubbed his chin. "Not sure how he comes into the picture, but the princess must have been with them all along."

Neill scratched his head. "The priest looked vaguely familiar." He thought about it for a second. "He might've been from Oriel too, although I'm not sure. There's more interesting things to watch during Mass." He raised a rakish eyebrow. "Like the pretty things in dresses. Who notices the priest?"

Turlough ignored that last remark. "We need to piece this together. Come on, Neill, help me."

"I am helping." Neill rubbed the back of his neck. "Alright, so far this is what we have. Dymphna goes missing. Next day, so does your brother and his wife. They all end up in Méifne, with a cleric somehow thrown in the mix, and they get separated into pairs. Daemon finds the wrong pair, but obviously recognizes neither your sister-in-law nor the priest. Meanwhile, you're busy chasing your brother, who ended up with the princess."

A fresh worry stabbed at Turlough. "Wait. What happened to Lynnie? Is she alright?" Oh no, something else to deal with!

"Daemon let her go. But like I said, I think she was going into labor. She seemed to be in pain. Maybe contractions." He shrugged. "I gave them some money."

Neill gave them money? Turlough was surprised. And grateful. "Thank you."

Neill laughed. "Thank yourself. It was the money I owed you."

Great. Turlough shook his head. Neill was unbelievable. "Any idea where the priest took her after that?"

"No. But forget your sister-in-law for now. She's in good hands. Let's focus on the princess."

Neill was right. Lynnie could come later. But why was Dymphna with Brioc in the first place? What had started all this?

"Why would the princess run away?"

Neill shrugged. "How should I know?"

"You're always in the castle. Did you hear anything? See anything strange going on?"

That made Neill laugh. "There was never a time strangeness *wasn't* going on. But I haven't been in the castle for ages. We were all up in Cenél Eóghain — remember? — searching for a new bride for the demon."

How could Turlough forget? Hunting women like prey. Sickening. "I wonder if Daemon chose any of them."

"He didn't. I saw Barrf take them away. Not surprising. None of them resembled Odilla in the least." Neill removed his waterskin from his belt and fiddled with the top. "The demon would only marry someone who looked exactly like her. You've finally seen Dymphna. Now you know what the queen looked like. Identical in every way. Dymphna could be her mother's twin." He took a swig.

Turlough's eyes popped. He looked at Neill. Neill frowned, confused, then suddenly his eyes popped too. He choked on the drink, sputtering. They stared at each other with horror.

"You think Daemon — No way," Turlough said. "Not even *he* could be that sick."

"Oh? He's sick alright. Sick as they come. *And* evil on top of it."

"Evil enough to marry his own daughter?" Turlough felt ill at the thought. Why hadn't they thought of this before? His gaze flew back to the route Dymphna had taken when she left them. "We need to go after them. We need to help." He started to move.

Neill laid a restraining hand on his arm. "Do you know where she even went?"

"No, but we can search."

"Bad idea. She knows you're here. If you gave her your word you'd wait, then you had better keep it. Otherwise she'll never trust us. Let her talk to your brother first. I assume that's what you told her to do?"

"Yes, but I didn't know who she was! Brioc is in way over his head, Neill. He can't handle this."

"If you ask me, he's handling it fine. Face it, he's got a whole army after him, and he hasn't been taken yet. Not even by you. Besides, you told me last night he already doesn't trust you. That's why he slit the dog's throat."

Sam. The memory made Turlough's heart clench. Gosh, he missed her. Stupid mutt.

"If he killed his beloved pet to escape you, you can't go barging up there and expect things to go well. And I doubt he'll welcome me either. If we show up, especially with swords, there's no telling what your brother will do."

"Then we leave our swords here."

Neill rolled his eyes. "Turlough, you're not thinking straight. Daemon is out here. So is Barrf. We're dead men walking, just as much as your brother. We keep our swords."

Turlough sighed. "You're right."

"Give Dymphna time. An hour, at least. Hopefully she trusted you enough to not let Brioc bolt."

"An hour's too long!"

"We don't even know how far away their camp is. In fact, an hour might not be long enough."

Would the princess come back? With Brioc?

There was nothing to do but wait and see.

55

Dymphna dropped to her knees in front of the Blessed Sacrament, crossed herself, and folded her hands, her heart leaping with joy. Never in her life had she been so happy to be with Jesus! The moment she'd spotted the bell tower from the road, she had flung herself off the horse, nearly breaking her neck, in her eagerness to run to the church. She all but bowled Brioc over racing past him.

As soon as she knelt, she begged God's forgiveness for her faults, and especially for her sins of vanity and impatience over the last few weeks. Then, as if God had already brushed her failings away, she was tugged into deep and peaceful prayer. Silence and tranquility wrapped around her like a soft, familiar blanket, making everything else disappear. Dymphna was finally home. She was safe here, in the arms of her Spouse.

In some corner of her mind, she became aware of the door opening, then closing again. Someone had entered the church. Footfalls came quietly up the aisle, then stopped several pews behind her. It must be Brioc. He had come in too! Dymphna had so hoped he would. She was worried sick about him ever since he'd killed Sam. But surely Jesus would help him. Because things with Brioc were getting really, *really* bad.

Please, God, she begged. *Please, please, please help him.* She stared at the little golden door behind which Christ hid, and a thought seemed to rush from the tabernacle and bury itself in her mind. Without analyzing it, without flinching, she prayed the thought back to God.

I'll suffer anything. Anything You want, dear Jesus. Pain, death, anything! Just please make Brioc get better again. And take care of his wife and baby. And his brother too! Oh, plus that other soldier who was with him.

The moment the offering left her lips, peace flooded through her. Maybe she couldn't reverse Daidi's illness, but surely, *surely*, if she prayed hard enough, Brioc's messed up brain might be fixed. The thought of God taking her as a victim, little and unworthy though she was, sent a wave of excitement rushing through her. Could offering one's life as a sacrifice be *exciting*?

She frowned. It seemed morbid. So why was she filled to bursting with happiness? It didn't make sense.

She gazed at the crucifix over the altar, and the answer, like a streak of lightning, came to her in a single blinding flash. Jesus had done the same thing! He had offered His life to heal His friends!

Dymphna had always longed to be like Jesus, but she never knew quite how, being only a girl, and especially a princess and all. Suddenly, it became clear. God was asking her life in exchange for her dearest friend. The friend who had risked everything he had, over and over again, to protect her; who had even gone to the extreme of killing Sam solely for her sake. Offering her own life was how Dymphna could both repay Brioc *and* be like Jesus!

The thought of imitating Christ as a victim made her heart throb with such unexpected excitement that she was spurred to even greater boldness. She didn't want to give her life only for Brioc, but for other people too — people she'd never met, but who suffered as he did. There must be hundreds of them, thousands even, emotionally scarred . . . or desperately sick, like Daidi. Dymphna would help them all!

The stronger the idea became, the more her heart swelled, until it spilled over with such joy that she thought she would die right here, right now, in the church.

She closed her eyes and clasped her hands to her chest and waited with eagerness for God to take her to Heaven. This was it. Her last moments on earth. Divine love enveloped her in its folds with such strength it was tangible. She braced herself to die.

A minute passed.

Two.

She was still alive.

Why was God taking so long?

She squeezed her eyes tighter, wondering what it would feel like when her soul departed from her body. Jesus felt so close. His Presence blazed from the tabernacle. Any second now the thread holding her to earth would burst asunder and she would take flight to her Beloved. And in that flash of an instant, Brioc would be healed. She was sure of it!

A scraping noise echoed through the empty church as Brioc shifted in his pew somewhere behind her.

Was he cured already? Dymphna was dying to twist around and look, but that didn't seem appropriate somehow. So she stayed still and forced herself not to open her eyes. Corpses with their eyes open were ghoulish. She'd seen that once and didn't want it to happen to her. Besides, when her eyes were closed, she could more easily think of God.

Why didn't He hurry up?

The church door opened and someone shuffled in. Probably a monk, judging by the slap-slap of sandals across the floor. Dymphna tried to ignore the sound. This was her death scene. She was giving her life for Brioc and knew with certainty it made God happy. If it didn't please Him, why did she feel His love so strongly? Clearing her throat, she briefly unfolded her hands to rearrange her scarf, then clasped them back together. She wiggled to get her knees in the right position, then composed herself again.

Jesus, I'm ready now. Please take me.

The monk, or whoever had entered, suddenly gasped. The sandals slapped back down the aisle, the door crashed open, and he presumably ran out.

What was going on? Was Brioc healed and glowing or something? Maybe Jesus was standing in the church! Oh my gosh! *Should she look?*

No, stay mortified. She squeezed her eyes tighter and prayed even harder.

More minutes ticked by. Her soul didn't take flight, Brioc didn't do anything, angels didn't slip into the pew beside her to whisk her away to Heaven. Nothing happened. Nothing at all.

The supernatural feeling faded, getting weaker and weaker. Then — *poof* — vanished altogether.

Everything inside her deflated. God hadn't accepted her offer after all.

She reluctantly opened her eyes. The church looked normal. Her stomach rumbled and let out an embarrassing growl that Brioc must have heard all the way behind her.

The door clattered open again. The slapping sandals smacked up the aisle, accompanied by normal sounding shoes. Both sets of footsteps stopped where Dymphna guessed Brioc was kneeling. Voices murmured. Footfalls again. Then someone tapped Dymphna lightly on the shoulder. She twisted her head.

Father Gerebran!

Dymphna shot up from the kneeler, her relief so strong that she had to restrain herself from hugging the priest.

"I knew the monks would spot you two." Father kept his voice low, but a smile lit up his face. "They've been keeping a twenty-four hour vigil for me. I knew you were bound to pass this way eventually."

The sandaled monk and Brioc joined them in the aisle. Dymphna's heart sank when she saw Brioc's empty eyes. Her prayers hadn't been heard. The disappointment was so keen that she wanted to cry.

Father Gerebran didn't seem to notice anything wrong. His grin stretched from ear to ear. "Both of you, hurry. Come with me. Ethlynn and I have a wonderful surprise." He winked at Brioc, his eyes shining so bright they seemed to light up the entire church. "You have a beautiful little daughter. She's barely an hour old."

56

Ethlynn couldn't stop gazing at her baby's perfect little face, framed by wispy tufts of dark hair, and the tiny pink hands and itty bitty fingers. Wide doe-eyes stared back at her, making Ethlynn melt. Her daughter was the most beautiful thing she had ever seen.

Laoise was a whirlwind of activity around the bed, fussing with blankets, hot water, and cleaning up the mess, but Ethlynn could only lie there and stare at her baby, this perfect miniature human whom God had plucked from the cupboards of Heaven and given to her in the immensity of His love. She pressed the swaddled bundle against her heart. Her whole life she had dreamed of this day, the day she would be a mam.

But tears blurred her eyes. How could she raise this precious child alone? Why didn't Brioc love her anymore? Would he ever return?

Her bottom lip quivered. She ached to have him back. She missed him so much. If only Dymphna hadn't shown up and ruined their marriage and their lives.

Laoise wafted to the bed and fluffed the pillow. Ethlynn tried to hide her tears as the midwife stopped to gaze at the baby and stroke her downy hair. "What a gorgeous wee girl. And a miracle too. Most babies that come this early are too frail to survive. Yet look at this strong lassie of yours! It's the prayers of that holy priest. I know it is."

Father Gerebran had been storming Heaven for the baby's safe delivery. He had been so kind and considerate, saying Mass every day here at Laoise's so that Ethlynn could attend, allowing her to receive Holy Communion daily, visiting her every free moment he had. He had been Ethlynn's one comfort through this whole ordeal. Her own daid could not have cared for her with more solicitude. When she went into labor, the priest had even paced outside the cottage, staying near, praying and waiting through the long hours. Like Brioc should have been here doing.

Ethlynn sniffed and wiped her eyes. Then, because Laoise seemed to be waiting for a reply, she said, "Father Gerebran's a saint."

"Oh, we can all see that." Laoise smiled and smoothed Ethlynn's sweat-drenched hair, like a mam would do. "Have you thought of a name?"

Ethlynn bit her lip. It should be Brioc who named their daughter. That was the father's prerogative, not the mother's. A name would have to be chosen before the baptism — which Father Gerebran said he could do today — but Ethlynn hesitated to pick one herself.

"I . . . I don't know." She cuddled her daughter closer. "I'll ask Father Gerebran what he thinks."

"He was outside a little while ago. One of the monks from the monastery rushed over and took him away. I'm sure he'll be back soon." Laoise patted the baby's head. "Look at her. Sleeping like an angel. Here, let me get you a drink." She reached for the jug of water on the little table beside Ethlynn, but before she could pour it, someone tapped softly on the door. Laoise placed the jug back on the table and strode across the room.

She cracked the door a few inches.

"Is Ethlynn asleep?"a voice outside whispered.

Laoise laughed. "Alas. If only." She pulled the door wider.

Father Gerebran appeared in the threshold, face beaming. "I brought you some visitors," he said. With a flourish, he stepped aside to admit someone.

Brioc! Ethlynn's heart flipped and she nearly sprang from the bed and into his arms. But before she could disentangle herself from the sheets without dropping the baby, the princess walked into the room.

What! *She* was here too? Ethlynn's heart sank.

"Oh!" Dymphna squealed. "I'm so happy for you!" Her perfect face lit up with a perfect white-teeth smile and she bounced across the room to the bed. "Oh my goodness, oh my goodness! Brioc, come look! She's *beautiful!"*

Just who did the princess think she was, crashing in here as if she were family?

"She's *darling!*" Dymphna gushed. "Look at her hair! Brioc, it's exactly like yours! Come and look!" She clasped her hands. "Can I hold her, Ethlynn? Please?"

Before Ethlynn could even think, she yanked the precious bundle away. "No, you may not."

Everyone froze. Laoise stiffened. Father Gerebran frowned. The baby jerked awake, and started to cry. Brioc stood there with an unreadable expression that Ethlynn had never seen before. Was he mad at her for snapping at Dymphna?

Ethlynn suddenly felt an inch tall. "She's . . . too frail," she mumbled. "You can hold her in a few days." Heat burned her face. Would God forgive her? She hadn't intended to act so mean to Dymphna. Instant contrition poured over her.

Dymphna's gaze had already dropped to the floor. "Oh, I'm sorry," she apologized humbly, making Ethlynn feel even worse.

But . . . why wouldn't Brioc come over here? He stood in the doorway like a slab of carved stone.

Father Gerebran must have noticed that too. He cleared his throat and asked

Brioc gently, "Don't you want to see your daughter?"

It took several seconds for Brioc to react. Dymphna bit her bottom lip and shot Father Gerebran a desperate look, like she wanted to silently communicate something to him. Worry crept into the priest's eyes.

Brioc shook his head a little, as if trying to clear his thoughts, then walked to the bed. Ethlynn still couldn't read his expression. He seemed only partially present, the rest of him somewhere else. Was he daydreaming? He must be. But about what? Princess Dymphna? The thought made Ethlynn feel sick.

He reached the bed. "Lynnie?" he asked, as if unsure it was her.

Did she look *that* bad that her husband couldn't even recognize her? His words stung. After all she had just been through — thirteen hours of labor and unspeakable pain — of course sweat drenched her hair and her gown was stained and wrinkled. What did he expect after childbirth? Did he really have that little compassion on her?

In the awkward silence, Dymphna stepped forward and laid a hand lightly on Brioc's arm. "Brioc, it's your baby," she said. "Don't you want to hold her?"

Brioc didn't move. Obviously, no, he didn't want to hold her. A vice squeezed Ethlynn's heart and she blinked back tears. He didn't even love their daughter!

When Brioc didn't take her, Dymphna stepped forward and eased the newborn from Ethlynn's arms. Ethlynn was too hurt to protest. At the princess's touch, the baby instantly stopped crying, which only added to Ethlynn's chagrin. Dymphna gently handed Brioc the bundle.

Life flickered in his eyes. It was just a spark, but for one fleeting moment, Ethlynn could imagine that he loved his child. He held the bundle close, as if never wanting to let go.

That's when Ethlynn noticed his sleeves were stained with blood.

Before she could react, Father Gerebran said from the doorway, "Have you picked a name?" Worry edged his voice. He must have figured out that Brioc loved the princess. Why else would he sound so concerned?

"You could name her Aislinn," Dymphna suggested, bright-eyed, to Brioc.

Ethlynn's jaw dropped. Who was *she* to suggest a name for their child? Maybe she meant well, but still . . .What nerve!

Dymphna shocked her further by adding, "After your little sister."

Brioc had a sister? Ethlynn reeled. She had never heard about Aislinn in her life! How did the princess know about her?

Brioc said nothing. He wasn't looking at Dymphna. In fact, he didn't seem to look at anything at all. Except maybe their baby nestled in his arms.

Ethlynn couldn't help glaring at the princess, who slapped her hand over her mouth and said, "Oh. Here I go again. I'm so sorry, Ethlynn. Me and my big mouth." Blushing, she backed away.

About time.

She slipped over to Laoise and asked something in a quiet voice. Ethlynn thought she heard the words *hair* and *wash*. Laoise nodded and mentioned something about a clean dress, then the two of them disappeared out the door. Dymphna had taken the hint.

Finally.

Brioc hadn't answered the question yet about a name. He held their daughter, gazing at her for so long that Ethlynn wondered if he intended to reply. Father Gerebran twisted his hands and rocked on his feet, likewise waiting. The baby fell asleep, content in her daidi's arms.

The minutes ticked by.

Finally Father Gerebran cleared his throat and said, "Well, as soon as you have a name picked out, we can bring her to the church. The monks are setting up for her baptism." He attempted a smile, which failed miserably, and excused himself with, "I'll take a little walk and leave you two to decide." Then he, too, escaped the room.

Feeling vulnerable and strangely nervous, Ethlynn had no idea how to act. She lowered her eyes, her cheeks growing hot. Did Brioc even notice her here on the bed? He hadn't said a word to her. Or to anyone, in fact.

An appalling thought belted her in the gut. What if he named their daughter *Dymphna*? Ethlynn held her breath, the thought making her feel ill. She braced herself for the cruel blow, when Brioc softly said, "Brigid."

Brigid? What a beautiful name! Her lip quivered and her heart melted. "Oh it's perfect!" she blurted. She had no idea why he chose it, but she loved it on the spot.

With his finger, Brioc traced a cross on their daughter's tiny forehead and whispered something to her, so softly that Ethlynn had difficulty making it out. She thought she caught the word *cloak*. Then, after holding Brigid for another minute, Brioc carefully placed her back in Ethlynn's arms. As he did, he leaned down towards the bed. Her heart fluttered. Would he kiss her? A few weeks ago, before Dymphna had barged into their lives, he would have. She closed her eyes, waiting.

The door flew open. So did Ethlynn's eyes. Dymphna burst into the room, wearing a pretty green dress. Her hair hung loose and wet, and she clutched that ugly shawl in her hands, yet somehow she managed to be gorgeous even dripping wet. "Brioc!" she cried out like a wounded animal.

He spun.

So much for the kiss.

"Daidi! He's here!" Panic filled Dymphna's eyes. "I saw him on the road!

He's coming to kill you! He'll make me marry him!"

Father Gerebran erupted through the door. "We've got to go, we've got to go!"

Laoise was at his heels, her face white. "The window!" she yelled, herding Dymphna towards the back of the room. "Climb out! Run! Get a boat!"

"Wait!" Father Gerebran ran to the bed and swiped up the pitcher of water. He turned to Brioc. "What's the baby's name? Hurry, hurry!"

When Brioc didn't answer quickly enough, Ethlynn said, "Brigid."

In one swift motion, the priest grabbed the baby with one arm and with the other poured water over her forehead. "I baptize thee, Brigid, in the name of the Father, and of the Son, and of the Holy Ghost." Not even pausing for breath, he said, "Come on, come on, come on!" and raced with the baby to the window.

Dymphna stood speechless, obviously stunned by the lightning speed of Brigid's baptism. Laoise all but had to shove the princess through the window. Father Gerebran climbed out after her, still holding the baby.

Before Ethlynn could react, Brioc scooped her off the bed, blankets and all, and raced after them. For one enraptured moment, Ethlynn was in heaven, carried in her husband's strong arms. Perfect bliss spilled over her.

Then reality took over.

Brioc didn't love her. And they were all about to die.

57

"Turlough. Over there. Below us." Neill pointed urgently to something in the distance.

Turlough shifted in his saddle. The wind slapped his face with salty air. He shaded his eyes against the sun's glare and followed to where Neill indicated. From their vantage point on the hilltop, they overlooked the sea and the town spread along its coast.

Turlough immediately saw what Neill pointed at. He sucked in a breath. "Soldiers."

They were everywhere, swarming through the streets, swords drawn, pounding on doors. Hunting prey, as they had in Cenél Eóghain. Fear for Dymphna's safety pounded through Turlough's chest. He and Neill had to rescue her! Exactly how, he had no idea. But they couldn't let Daemon capture her.

Why-oh-why had he not followed her from the stream and taken his chances meeting Brioc? He should have. Too late now.

"There's Gruagh," Neill said. "By that water trough."

"I see him."

"That stick figure, holding the horses. That's Faidh."

Turlough nodded and tried to identify the others. He spotted Barrf instantly, barging out of a house behind some terrified, screaming girl. But she wasn't Dymphna, so she would be safe. His eyes roved up and down the road. Soldiers moved everywhere. His blood boiled as he watched Cahir draw his sword to intimidate an old man in a wagon, who kept shaking his head and trying to drive away.

It was Cahir, not Neill, who'd told the captain that Turlough had given Brioc money. Cahir was the reason they beat him up; in fact, he had probably been there that night in Turlough's doorway.

Neill asked, "See the demon anywhere?"

"No." Turlough twisted his head to where Neill sat mounted beside him. "What's he wearing?"

"Last I know, his usual cloak." He grimaced. "The one the color of blood. How appropriate."

Turlough returned his gaze to the town, searching. The cloak should be easy to spot.

"There!" Neill leaned forward on his horse. "On the beach. See him? He's running into the water."

Turlough's eyes snapped to the water's edge. The scarlet cloak billowed in the wind. The king plowed into the waves, trying to chase a little fishing boat in the distance, screaming, "Odilla! Odilla!" His voice carried. He waded into the water until he was waist-deep.

Turlough stared at the little boat. Five people huddled in the shallow hull as it sailed away. Two were females. One looked like she might be the princess, although she no longer wore brown. Her dress was forest green. The other girl sat wrapped in a blanket with a bundle on her lap. Lynnie? Of the three men, one steered the boat, another was clothed as a priest. The third, without a shadow of a doubt, was Brioc.

"It's them."

"Are you sure?"

"I'd recognize my brother anywhere."

Neill frowned. "What's the girl holding?"

"I don't know. Maybe Lynnie had her baby."

"Good Lord. A newborn on a fishing boat." Neill broke his gaze from the vessel and looked at Turlough. "They'll never get away. You realize that, don't you?"

Turlough's heart clenched. "They have a head start. Besides, Daemon needs to find a boat. With that many soldiers, he'll need something big. A ship. It could take him days to set out."

"True. But even if Daemon doesn't set sail till next week, it's obvious where your brother's taking the princess. Straight across the sea to Brytenlond." He shrugged. "Wessex, Mercia, makes no difference. They'll be found." He shook his head. "Especially if they continue using those coins you gave your brother. Cahir will recognize them."

Turlough thought, *Just like I did in the tavern.* "What if they go somewhere else?" he asked, clutching at straws.

Neill shook his head, but not without compassion. "Like where? Do they even know what's out there beyond the sea? Do you? Does anyone? I doubt it."

Turlough broke his gaze from the king wading furiously through the water, and looked at Neill. "So what are you saying? Turn around and go home? Walk away and let my brother and his wife be murdered? And what about Dymphna? You want to see her captured and forced to be Daemon's bride?"

"Of course not." Neill sighed. "But it's out of our hands. It's tough, Turlough. Life is tough. But what are we supposed to do?"

There had to be *some* way to save them! Turlough rubbed the back of his neck, trying to think.

A thought slammed into his brain like lightning. "Wait!" In his excitement he grabbed Neill's arm. "Flanders!"

237

"Huh?"

"Flanders! If they sail around Brytenlond and keep going, the king won't know! He'll assume they —"

"Hang on. What makes you think your brother will go to Flanders? Who's even heard of the place?"

"After our parents died, we met an old minstrel. He gave Brioc his harp. I remember him saying he came from some town in Flanders." Turlough frantically tried to remember the place's name. It was on the tip of his tongue. "Brioc always wanted to go there. We both learned the language." He winced. "Well, not really. Brioc did, more than me. I'm sure he knows enough to get by."

"Fine. I'm happy for him. But who says he will think of any of that?"

"Gheel! That's it! The name of the town was Gheel!" Turlough's heart banged in his chest. Brioc *had* to think of it! *He had to*! That's all he'd talked about as a child. Turlough's gaze flew to the fishing boat and he silently begged his brother, *Gheel! Go to Gheel, Brioc! Not Wessex or Mercia! Your life depends on it! And whatever you do, stop using those foreign coins!*

Neill shook his head. "He's already on that dinky boat. You can't suggest a destination to him now. I'm sorry, Turlough. I wish you could."

The memory of the hoof print in the rock flashed through his mind and inspiration hit hard. It was Branduff and Raghnall who had miraculously led him to that rock. Turlough was *sure* it had been them. Maybe he couldn't force Brioc to remember Gheel, but *they* could.

"Come on," he said, grabbing Neill's reins. "Let's hurry! We've got to get a boat!"

"Wait! What are you talking about?"

"We're heading to Flanders." Without explaining, Turlough jerked his horse around and kicked it into a gallop.

If his brothers wouldn't help him from Heaven, what were they doing up there? They would make Brioc think of Gheel. They would make a happy ending to that future legend about the miraculous rock with the hoof print.

They had to.

58

Dymphna's stomach lurched with every wave. She had never been so sick in her life. The choppy sea tossed the tiny boat back and forth in the darkness, and with each heave of the vessel, her insides heaved with it. To her embarrassment, she'd spent most of the ten-hour trip leaning over the side.

At least it was her instead of Ethlynn. Thank God for that. Ethlynn had her hands full caring for Brigid. The last thing she needed was seasickness. Dymphna was happy to be the one to suffer. She was starting to understand that only by suffering could she become more like Jesus, and that's what she wanted more than anything in the world. Besides, all these trials forced her to pray continually, and praying brought peace like nothing else did. It was funny, but Dymphna was starting to look forward to these little sufferings. It had become almost a game, anticipating what God would send next to allow her to prove her love for Him. The thought was exciting. She only wished her seasickness right now didn't render her so useless. She would've loved to hold the baby so that Ethlynn could sleep once night had fallen; instead she was stuck gripping the railing throughout the long hours.

But wait! Were those lights flickering in the distant blackness? Yes, a village was on the shore! They must be nearly there. *Thank you, God.*

She tugged the burnt shawl tighter around her shoulders. It was her reminder to pray. Laoise had insisted she leave the rag behind, but Dymphna kept wearing it as a sacrifice for Brioc. To her sadness, God hadn't accepted her offer in the monastery church. Such joy had seized her at the idea of imitating Jesus by giving her life for a friend. Alas, God had refused. But she could still offer up wearing the ugly shawl. It was *something,* right?

A few feet away, Father Gerebran stumbled urgently to the railing next to her. In the light cast by several lanterns on deck, his face looked as gray as Dymphna's own must be. The whole night he'd huddled, sleepless, against the side of the boat, clutching his stomach. It was amazing that the other three didn't even notice the roiling waves.

The fisherman, a toothless middle-aged man with a greasy gray beard, was obviously at home on the sea. Probably not even a hurricane would unnerve him. His had been the only boat docked when they'd run to the beach and, whether because of Dymphna's begging or because of Brioc's coins, the man had been more than willing to row them to Brytenlond. His attention alternated between steering, rowing and sailing, and he smelled of rotting fish.

When Ethlynn wasn't scooting away from him, probably to avoid the stink, she focused entirely on baby Brigid. Or pretended to. Every once in awhile she tossed an incredibly sad look at Brioc. The lanterns' light revealed tears glistening in her eyes. What was going on between those two?

As for Brioc, he sat silently in a corner of the boat, lost in his own unreachable world. As the hours went by, his expression had changed from pained to empty. Every time Dymphna glanced at him, alarm bells clanged through her head. Ethlynn didn't seem to realize that something was seriously wrong with him, that her husband was slipping away. Then again, Ethlynn hadn't been with them these last several days. Dymphna resisted the urge to cross the hull herself and try to draw Brioc out. But every time she even *looked* at Brioc, Ethlynn would stare her down.

Besides, if she moved from the railing, she might throw up inside the small boat. Then everyone would do penance, like it or not. So she wrung the burnt shawl in her hands and prayed her heart out.

The village lights flickered more brightly. Dymphna struggled to judge the distance in the dark. They must be close. She stared back in the direction of Ireland, an ache growing within her. Would she ever see her beloved homeland again? She blinked back tears.

"We'll be there soon," the boatman announced, breaking into her thoughts.

"Deo gratias," Father Gerebran whispered. "Let's hope we can find an inn."

Brioc sat suddenly forward, surprising everyone, as if something had jarred him back to life. "No," he said. "We can't stay there." His voice held urgency.

Father Gerebran frowned. "Why? Surely we have enough money for an inn?"

Brioc shook his head. "I'm not talking about an inn." His eyes burned with a strange conviction. "I'm talking about Brytenlond. We can't stay. The king will find us."

Father Gerebran's brow wrinkled with confusion. "But where else can we go?"

"Flanders," Brioc said, without missing a beat. He turned to the fisherman. "Can you take us there? I'll pay you."

Dymphna threw a bewildered look at Father Gerebran. The priest looked equally confused. What could have made Brioc come up with this idea out of the blue? Where even was Flanders? Dymphna had never heard of the place.

Father Gerebran turned to Brioc. "Not a good idea. Settling in a country where we don't know the language will be too difficult. I've been to Brytenlond a few times. At least I know their tongue."

"No. We have to go to Flanders," Brioc insisted. "I know the language."

Ethlynn's eyes widened. She opened her mouth, as if to say something, then clamped it shut again. Maybe she remembered she wasn't speaking to her husband.

Brioc glanced from face to face, as if frustrated that no one shared his enthusiasm for the bizarre idea. "Please, Father," he begged the priest. "God wants us to go there. I . . . I'm sure He does."

This time it was Dymphna's eyes that widened. How could Brioc know where God wanted them to go? Yet he said it with such conviction that she felt sure Heaven must've somehow told him. She looked at Father Gerebran, who pursed his lips in thought.

Dymphna held her breath, waiting for the verdict.

Finally the priest nodded. "You have a point," he said to Brioc. "The king will easily pursue us to Brytenlond. He saw our boat, after all. But there is no way he can track us as far as Flanders. There will be no trail for him to follow."

Brioc exhaled in obvious relief. Ethlynn stared at Brigid, pretending to ignore the conversation. Dymphna bit her lip, desperately hoping Flanders could be reached by land. The thought of staying at sea filled her with dismay.

The fisherman cleared his throat. "If we're sailing that far, I'm docking in Brytenlond first for supplies."

That meant they couldn't walk to Flanders. Dymphna's heart sank. Then she immediately thought, *No, that's good. It's more to offer up!*

The man's eyes bored into Brioc. "Laddie, do you really have enough money to buy everything we need for a journey of that length?"

Brioc nodded. He held up a little pouch. Dymphna recognized it.

Inside were the remaining coins Brioc had been using since the tavern.

59

The driver tugged on the reins and the cart rumbled to a halt. He swiveled around in his seat and said something in that strange guttural language that for some reason Brioc recognized. He was telling them that the dirt track ahead of them led into Gheel.

Cramped with the others between wooden crates and bolts of dyed material in the back of the cart, Brioc tried to remember how and when he had learned to speak the language of Flanders. But it remained a mystery. He hadn't learned it at the monastery. No, it was earlier than that, buried farther back in his childhood. But the memory had been swallowed along with Aislinn and the funerals and God only knew how many other things.

Brioc also had no idea why they were meant to go to Flanders, and particularly this one village. But he was certain of it. Branduff had told him.

It had happened in the boat a few days ago. Brioc's thoughts, for some reason, had been tugged towards his four dead brothers. Which was unusual. To his shame, he didn't pray for their souls nearly as often as he should. He prayed for his parents daily. And Aislinn didn't need prayers. So why did he neglect his brothers? Maybe because he didn't remember them much.

What a terrible excuse.

Anyhow, as soon as the four of them had entered into his mind in the boat, he'd started to pray. A bright light had flashed, then an unearthly presence enveloped him, unseen yet so tangible that he'd been seized with a sense of fear. The fear instantly gave way to an incredible peace, and for one soul-soaring moment, Brioc had felt loved. He distinctly heard his oldest brother's voice.

"Gheel," Branduff had said, managing to smile just by his tone, like he'd always done on earth. "Go to Gheel, little brother."

Gheel was in Flanders. Not sure how he knew that, but he did. The supernatural feeling flickered and faded. Then, *poof*, all four returned to wherever they'd come from. Heaven, maybe Purgatory. Definitely not Hell.

No one else in the boat seemed affected. It was just for him. Him alone.

Even thinking of it now sent goosebumps racing along Brioc's flesh.

So, well, here they were. Gheel. As per Branduff's instructions.

Father Gerebran, wedged between boxes across from Brioc, had been dozing on and off during the five hour ride. He awoke when the cart jolted to a stop. Yawning, he stretched and looked around curiously, as if trying to get his bearings. The girls remained asleep, including Brigid. Lynnie cuddled her protectively, pressed against her heart. Both of them were so beautiful in their slumber that Brioc could gaze at them forever. Unfortunately, Lynnie had staked her claim on the opposite side of the cart, as far away from Brioc as possible. She'd hardly spoken a word to him in six days. Not since Laoise's cottage.

Bone-tired and aching, Brioc climbed out of the cart and dropped to the mud-caked road. His body was stiff, his legs rubbery. The noon sun stabbed his eyes in a sky wider than he'd ever dreamed could exist; exotic birds flitted through the branches of odd-looking trees, making strange chirping sounds. Even the air smelled foreign. He glimpsed what must be the hamlet of Gheel down the path and past a row of hedgerows.

A memory stirred deep within him. *Music.* This place had something to do with music.

But . . . how?

Had he visited Gheel before? Lived here? He frowned. No, impossible. Yet he recognized the language. He'd been able to communicate with the driver and the people in Antwerp. Where had he learned about Flanders' existence in the first place? Nothing made sense.

Father Gerebran clambered out of the cart and landed in the dirt beside him, slapping dust from his sweat-stained robe. Dymphna hopped down too, full of wonder, as she gazed around, as if unable to take in the strange sights. Colorful windmills with their whirling blades, slicing the bright blue sky; flat, unchanging fields, riven with narrow canals. Thatched cottages poked between the trees, constructed from materials none of them had ever seen. It was as if they'd stepped off the boat in Antwerp and entered another world. Dymphna had been too tired to notice the scenery then, but now she gasped, mesmerized. Brioc guessed what she must be thinking. Where were the hills and crags and groves of oak and rowan? Didn't thistles and maidenhair grow here? Where were all the shamrocks?

She looked at Brioc, her expression bewildered.

He said, "I guess this is Gheel," and shrugged.

She pulled that charred shawl tighter around her shoulders. For some reason she wore it all the time now. Just as well the princess wasn't here to snag a husband. The shawl alone would make any man think twice.

Except . . . her daid. The thought punched Brioc in the gut. He suddenly remembered why they'd come here in the first place. Fleeing from King Daemon. Unease filled his mind.

Surely Daemon couldn't track them this far. Could he? No, no, his four brothers in Heaven would not have led him to a place where they would remain in danger.

Still, this place felt so foreign.

Brioc suddenly wondered if he'd imagined Branduff's voice in the boat. Doubt came upon him. He had a wife and daughter whose safety depended on him. Lynnie might not love him, but he still loved her and Brigid, come what may. Yet how could he support them in a land he knew nothing about? What had he been thinking when he'd insisted they sail here?

But there was no turning back. They'd spent all the money Turlough had given him, both buying supplies when they'd docked for two days in Brytenlond, and in Antwerp after they had reached port. He'd offered his last coin to driver after driver, asking for a ride to Gheel, but when they saw its strange imprint, all had declined. His foreign accent hadn't helped matters along. He guessed people weren't as friendly here as in Ireland. Finally, when it looked like they would be forced to walk, a merchant heading this direction had taken compassion on them — probably seeing their newborn baby — and told them to jump in the back of his cart.

So. At last they'd reached Gheel. Now what?

Putting aside his doubts, Brioc turned to wake Lynnie. He had taken too long; she was already awake and climbing out. Carefully holding Brigid in the crook of one arm, she reached for the heavy wooden wheel with her free hand, trying to steady herself for the jump. The hem of her sleeve snagged on a nail. She was going to fall!

Brioc's breath caught. In the nick of time, he grabbed her, swooping her into his arms and swinging her safely from the cart. Her sleeve ripped but who cared about the sleeve? Warm emotion rushed through him and for one desperate moment all he wanted to do was kiss her.

Before he had the chance, Lynnie jerked out of his arms and, with cold eyes, clasped Brigid even more tightly. Then she readjusted Brigid's blanket and stepped next to Father Gerebran. Her eyelids flickered, as if she were blinking back tears, but she composed herself and walked — heaven knew where — away from the cart and towards the village. As if she even knew where she was heading.

Once upon a time, Brioc had found it amusing when Lynnie got in a huff. Not that it had happened often, but when it did, her flaming cheeks and stormy eyes made her simply irresistible. Now it only increased his despair. A hollow sadness came upon him, catching him by surprise. What had gone wrong between them?

Lynnie shouldn't even be out of bed, let alone traipsing down an unknown dirt road six days after childbirth. Setting his jaw, he started to go after her, when suddenly a tiny girl flew out of nowhere. She seemed to be racing towards the cart at a dead run.

She collided with Brioc, nearly knocking him to the ground.

60

"A *month*!" Ready to explode, Turlough glared at the boatman in the dingy hut. "We can't wait a month! We need to sail *now*. I told you that yesterday! So why can't your stinkin' boat all of a sudden float?"

"It's not ready." Backing away from him, the man threw his hands up in defense. "It needs repairs." His back hit the wall. He had nowhere left to go. Fear flickered across his face. "It leaks. Everywhere. We'll sink." His tongue zipped across dry lips. "I need time to repair it. I'll have to buy materials and . . ." His voice turned into a squeak as Turlough grabbed him by the collar.

"I suppose it never occurred to you to tell us this *before* we paid you? Like, yesterday, at the dock?" The temptation to punch his lights out overwhelmed him. What a thief!

Behind him, Neill cleared his throat, then stepped into view. "Calm down, Turlough. Another week won't make any difference."

"Week? He said a month. You heard him. He said we can't sail for a month."

"Is there a tavern anywhere?" Neill asked the man, changing the subject. "I think my friend needs a drink. Maybe a wee lassie to take his mind off his cares."

Turlough threw him a death glare, ready to grab *him* by the throat too. "I need to help my brother, that's what I need. Look, I sold my horse to pay this crook."

"You mean *we* sold *our* horses." Neill met his glare.

Turlough huffed and loosened his grip on the man's collar. It was true; Neill was as invested as he was. He should be grateful he wasn't alone trying to save Brioc's life. He released the man, whose hand shot to his throat as he dodged out of Turlough's way.

Neill's face twitched, like he was trying hard not to laugh. He bit the inside of his cheek.

"What? What's so funny?"

Neill began to grin. "They weren't even our horses." His smile cracked wider. "They came from Daemon's stable."

Turlough stared at him.

"We sold Daemon's horses." Neill laughed. "*He's* paying our boat fare. Hadn't thought of that, had you?"

Uh . . . actually, no. Turlough hadn't. Put like that, it *was* kind of funny. But his rotten mood prevented his own smile. They needed to get to Flanders! Daemon had already boarded a ship to Brytenlond with a dozen soldiers. And this stinking man's stinking boat that had cost them a stinking fortune, apparently couldn't even withstand water! He shifted his attention to the owner cowering against the wall, then glanced back at Neill. "Then this thief better give us back the king's money so we can hire another boat." He looked back at the boat owner and touched the hilt of his sword. "One without holes."

The man almost choked on his Adam's apple. "I . . ." His sentence jammed. He tried again. "I . . ." He squeezed his eyes shut. ". . . can't return your money." His doughy face drained of color. Beads of sweat broke out on his forehead and he pushed his back harder against the wall, looking for all the world like he wanted to push clear through and escape out the other side.

Turlough inhaled deeply.

"Oh? And why not? Why can't you return our money?"

The man peeked his eyes open, then closed them again. He pushed harder against the unyielding wall, barely able to breathe. "I — already — sp-spent it." He flinched, as if Turlough had already hit him.

Turlough reeled. "You *spent* it? In just twenty-four hours?"

Neill snorted. "I knew there must be a tavern."

Turlough balled his fist, ready to punch the man.

Neill's hand landed on his arm, preventing him. "Don't. You'll make it worse. It will take him that much longer to fix his leaky boat if he's got broken bones. Besides," — his eyebrows knit and he gave Turlough a funny look — "I thought you were convinced a few days ago that your brother would head to Flanders, where they'd be safe. Either you were right, and they're there already, or you were wrong, in which case they're in Brytenlond." Neill shook his head, but compassion and understanding filled his eyes. "Daemon will track them by those coins, if they're in Brytenlond. We can't save them, even if we sail tonight."

Turlough blew out his breath. Neill was right. They were helpless, even if this man's boat didn't leak. Too agitated to pray, he sent a sigh heavenward. *Please God, let them be in Flanders.*

Neill's expression softened. "We'll still do what we can." He released Turlough's arm and stepped closer to the trembling boatman huddled against the wall. He got right in the man's face, a knife appearing in his hand. "Get that boat repaired," he warned, flashing the weapon under the other's frightened eyes before pressing it against his throat. "Two weeks. If we're not riding the waves by then, you're a corpse."

He stood there a moment, letting that sink in, then flipped his knife in the air, caught it by its hilt, and casually slipped it back into his belt. He wheeled around and slapped Turlough on the shoulder as he headed to the door. "Let's go find that tavern."

61

Dymphna watched as a tiny girl with flying blond braids smacked straight into Brioc's legs. She'd appeared from nowhere. She must have been in the bushes that led into the woods.

To Dymphna's relief, crashing into Brioc didn't injure the child. In fact, it hardly slowed her; she merely giggled, swerved around him, and continued racing towards the cart. She ran with a limp. She bounded directly for . . .

Father Gerebran?

The child threw her arms around the priests' knees, burying her face in his robe. She hugged him as if she'd never let go. Dymphna thought she heard a sigh of contentment come from the material's folds.

With a startled expression, Father Gerebran gently disengaged her arms from around his legs and crouched in front of her. "Well, hello there, little friend." A smile tugged the corners of his mouth.

The girl stared at him, her huge blue eyes blinking in bewilderment at his words but shining with joy nonetheless. Despite herself, Dymphna gasped when she saw the child's deformed facial features. Birth defects? She was the size of a toddler, yet Dymphna guessed her to be at least four or five years old.

"What's your name?" Father Gerebran asked, straightening the wispy blond bangs hanging in her face.

She stared at him, then giggled.

The driver of the cart said something, words that Dymphna couldn't understand. He chuckled, then uttered more nonsensical words. The girl didn't respond; she kept looking at Father as if she'd died and gone to Heaven.

Father grinned. "Don't you have a name?"

Dymphna said, "Um, she can't understand you, Father."

The priest smacked his head. "Oh. Of course. The language. I forgot." He stood up, gently ruffling the child's hair as he did so, then called, "Brioc? Uh, can you help us out?"

Brioc hadn't moved since the little girl had appeared and slammed into him. He stood several yards away, visibly torn between returning to them or following Ethlynn. She had stopped too, farther down the trail, clutching Brigid and watching the scene with curiosity. Ethlynn obviously didn't have a clue where to storm off to anyhow. None of them knew anything about this place.

The driver of the cart let out a laugh, muttered more strange guttural words, then raised a hand in a wave. Father Gerebran turned his head and smiled a *thank you* before the man tugged his horse's reins. Then the cart rumbled away.

The little girl slipped her hand into Father's and tried to haul him towards the prickly-looking bushes she'd come through.

"You want me to follow you?" The priest's eyes twinkled. "Where are we going?" He shot Dymphna a helpless glance, shrugged, and let his new companion lead him a few steps. None of them really wanted to climb through the thorny bushes. But they might have to.

Thankfully Brioc came back over. Like Father had done, he crouched in front of the child. He frowned for a second, as if trying to fetch the right words, then managed a couple sentences in the strange language.

Dymphna's heart leaped a little. It was good for him to be forced to talk. Where he'd learned the foreign language was anyone's guess, but he was the only one who could communicate with these people, so he was obliged to take charge. Dymphna prayed it would prevent him from slipping further away into his own silent, dark world.

He'd seemed a little better since the boat. True, he still hardly spoke, but at least his eyes weren't quite so faraway as after he'd killed Sam. Could her prayers be helping? Instinctively she clutched the ugly shawl tighter around her shoulders, sending a prayer heavenward. If only Ethlynn would be nice to him, maybe he'd be alright after all. Why was Ethlynn being so chilly?

More giggles from the little girl drew Dymphna's attention back to the others. Whatever Brioc had asked her, he'd only received that shy, cute giggle in reply. But the child's face lit up and she snatched Brioc's hand as well. He stood before losing his balance as the child lugged both men towards the woods. Her slower gait revealed her limp even more.

Dymphna gathered up her long skirt, preparing to follow. Down the road, Ethlynn hesitated. Probably realizing she had nowhere else to go, she came towards them.

Poor Ethlynn. Dark circles ringed her eyes. Tears shimmered on her cheeks. Her hair stuck out in every direction. She stumbled as she walked, as if she might collapse from weakness.

Watching her, Dymphna's heart ached. Having a baby under normal circumstances surely was overwhelming enough; this must be a nightmare for Ethlynn. She should be in bed, resting, being waited on and drinking lots of milk with yummy thick cream on top. Not wandering homeless and scared in a foreign land. Guilt gnawed at Dymphna. This was her fault. Why had she run to Brioc's cottage in the first place?

As Ethlynn reached her, she said, "You look exhausted. Let me carry Brigid for you, just for a little while. Please."

As if on cue, the blanket twitched and came alive as tiny feet and fists squirmed and poked within. In a matter of seconds, a piercing *wah-wah-wah* filled the air.

Ethlynn's face crinkled as if she might cry too.

Dymphna reached for the bundle.

Surprisingly, Ethlynn didn't resist. Not meeting Dymphna's gaze, she reluctantly handed Brigid over. She looked so sad and her eyes were swollen, but at least now she could climb through the bushes, hopefully without fainting.

The men had already straggled through and reached the woods. The little girl eagerly pulled them deeper into the forest.

Dymphna navigated the thorny shrubs, hugging the baby to her chest, careful not to snag the blanket on the prickles. Brigid quieted down, and now stared up at Dymphna with the most trusting unblinking eyes. Dymphna could cuddle her forever. It took an effort to watch her step; she wanted only to gaze at the baby.

Ethlynn stumbled behind her, her gown snagging once or twice on a thorn. She didn't say anything; neither did Dymphna. Finally they pushed through the bushes and into the woods. They quickened their pace, trying not to lose sight of the others.

After a few minutes, a slope came into sight. Dymphna wouldn't call it a *hill*. It was nothing like the hills back home. No, it was more like a large mound. It must've been the little girl's destination, because she dropped Father's and Brioc's hands. She pulled aside overhanging branches, took a few steps, and suddenly vanished into thin air. Dymphna frowned. *Where did she go?*

The men exchanged a brief glance, then Father shrugged, ducked his head, and disappeared as well. Brioc followed. They must've come to the opening of a hidden cave. A second later, Dymphna reached the spot, Ethlynn not far behind.

The entrance was so concealed that if Dymphna hadn't seen the others enter, she would never suspect it existed. "Do you want to go in?" she asked Ethlynn. "I'll wait here with Brigid if you want."

Ethlynn stared at the entrance. A huge cobweb filled one corner. "No. I'll wait outside." Still without making eye contact, she took back her baby and wandered to a nearby grassy patch. She sat down to nurse.

Shuddering at the spiderweb, Dymphna tentatively pushed aside the leafy overhang. Then, biting her lip, she bravely crept inside.

Weak light filtered through the leaves and landed on a rough wall only a few feet away. The cave looked tiny, unlike the caves in Ireland. *Where did everyone go?*

A pale flickering glow appeared in the corner of her eye and she spotted a narrow corridor to her left. Goosebumps dotting her skin, she slid along its cold wall until she came to a cramped room. A candle burned on a wobbly makeshift table. Next to it sat a cup spilling with wildflowers, and a carved statue, about six inches tall. Dymphna immediately guessed it was meant to be the Virgin Mary. A lopsided off-cut of material, identical to the little girl's dress, had been draped like a veil over the Blessed Mother's head. It hung at least three inches too long on both sides, the edges wet from the overflow of water in the flower cup.

The little girl knelt before the statue, her hands clasped tightly in prayer, her eyes squeezed shut. Despite the misshapen features, her face held an angelic quality. Dymphna's heart melted. She couldn't resist a smile. Father Gerebran and Brioc had already indulged their tiny friend, kneeling beside her.

Dymphna tiptoed over and joined them.

She hardly had time to bless herself when a young voice at her back made her jump.

"Retha!" The newcomer snapped. The voice belonged to a child, the tone definitely scolding. More stern words followed, none of which Dymphna could understand. She twisted around to look.

A second girl stood at the entrance of the cavity, hands propped on her hips and a scowl on her face. She looked about seven or eight and had the same blond braids as the younger one and a nearly identical pixie face, minus the deformities. They had to be sisters. She huffed, and a new string of guttural reprimands flowed from her lips. The words sounded so strange Dymphna resisted the urge to giggle herself.

The older girl stamped forward and whipped the statue off the table. Catching the word *Retha* several times, Dymphna gathered it was the younger girl's name. The bossy one crossed her arms over her chest, still clutching the statue, and kept going on about something called a *moeder.* The younger one stared at the ground, crestfallen.

Moeder? Could that be the word for mother? Was little Retha somehow in trouble?

Dymphna glanced at Brioc, hoping for a translation. Father looked at him too, expecting the same thing. Brioc's eyebrows squished together as he struggled to follow the older girl's rapid-fire words. Throughout it all, the one named Retha didn't make a sound.

Her sister finished the scolding and seemed to finally notice the rest of them. She must have spotted Father Gerebran's priestly robe, because she slapped a hand over her mouth and her cheeks turned crimson. A new string of words poured from her lips, but this time the tone was apologetic. Then, as if perhaps not knowing what else to do to show belated respect, she curtsied to the priest, over and over, her eyes now glowing with joy and gratitude.

It was so endearing that Dymphna felt herself melt.

Then the girl said something to Father, her tone questioning.

Lost, Father Gerebran turned to Brioc.

"She asked if you're staying here. I guess she means in Gheel."

Father turned back to the girl. "I . . . suppose we are. We just arrived and need a place to stay. Do you know where we might —" The perplexed expression on her face stopped him. He must have remembered she couldn't understand him either.

Brioc took over and managed a painfully halting conversation with the older girl. Dymphna waited, wondering why Retha was in trouble and if it was somehow their fault. Retha herself didn't look worried. She had gone back to holding Father's Gerebran's hand, swinging his arm back and forth with hers, as if they'd been best friends their whole lives.

"Why is her sister mad at her?" Dymphna interrupted, unable to wait any longer.

Brioc didn't answer. He obviously struggled to keep up with the girl's rapid words.

"Is it our fault?" Dymphna persisted.

Brioc raised a hand for silence. He was listening, trying to understand.

The girl kept talking excitedly, hardly pausing for breath.

"No," Brioc answered Dymphna's question. "Apparently Retha sneaks off all the time and her mother's worried sick. Now shush, I'm trying to follow this."

Dymphna shut her mouth.

A few minutes later, the girl stopped talking and Brioc turned to them. "You're not going to believe this," he said. "There's an old church here, dedicated to Saint Martin." He paused, giving the priest a questioning look.

Father said, "Probably Saint Martin of Tours. His cult is popular in nearby Gaul."

Dymphna had never heard of the saint, nor of Gaul. From the look on Brioc's face, neither had he. He continued relaying what Retha's sister had told him.

"If I'm understanding this right, Gheel hasn't had Mass for a couple years. Every once in awhile, a priest will pass through, but not to stay." As he spoke, both girls giggled at his Irish words as much as Dymphna had wanted to giggle at theirs. "Apparently the townspeople have begged God to send them a priest of their own, but so far He hasn't answered their prayers."

That explained why Retha had come running to Father Gerebran and hugged him so fervently, as if she never wanted to let go.

"The church is run down, but there's a room attached where their first priest had lived a long time ago. There's also a tiny hut on the property, not actually a cottage, but big enough for one person." Brioc glanced at Dymphna, obviously thinking she'd make the perfect '*one person.*'

Her heart flipped and beat faster. Maybe she could live there, close to Jesus! Joy burst through her like flames. Her mind raced with ideas. She could start a school here! She would first learn the language herself, then gather the village children and help teach them their catechism. It would be a dream come true.

And living alone, she could do hidden penances! She immediately resolved that if God gave her the little hut, she would begin this very night. No more squishing up her shawl under her head as a pillow. She would learn to sleep on the hard, bare ground, and maybe even give up a blanket as well. The thought of sacrifices was actually exciting. There were so many souls to save! She would start today!

Father Gerebran's voice cut into her thoughts. "But, what about you and Ethlynn?" he asked Brioc with a frown. "We need to find lodging for your family."

Dymphna held her breath. Surely God would take care of them too.

Brioc said, "Anika — uh, that's the girl's name — said their mother might be able to help us."

A smile lit up Father's face. "Well then, what are we waiting for?" He winked at Retha. "Let us then go and meet your parents."

62

Cradling Brigid, Ethlynn tromped behind the others down the road. She tried not to look at the princess skipping gleefully ahead of her, flanked by the two little girls. Ethlynn had learned their names were Anika and Retha. Dymphna held one of their hands in each of her own and all three swung their arms as if they were on their way to a party. How childish. The princess had met them all of ten minutes ago. Must she act like she was their big sister? How did Princess Dymphna do it, become everyone's best friend in the blink of an eye?

Father Gerebran quick-marched beside them, trying to keep up, his hand clasping Retha's free one as she half skipped, half limped along. Brioc walked alone, a few feet behind them. Every once in awhile he stopped, hesitated, and turned to look at Ethlynn. She would immediately avert her gaze, fresh tears threatening. She loved her husband so much. Why didn't he love her anymore?

She stopped walking, struggling not to cry. She squeezed her eyes shut, heroically trying to force the tears to stay inside.

Something tugged on the blankets wrapping Brigid and suddenly the baby left her arms. Ethlynn's eyes snapped open.

"Lynnie, would you just tell me what I've done wrong?"

She couldn't keep eye contact for longer than three seconds. His eyes were so killingly handsome that she would melt if she didn't look away. So she did. Instantly.

Brioc sighed. "Lynnie, say something."

But what could she say? He had hugged Dymphna. She had seen it herself, that night by the fire, right after he'd draped his cloak around her shoulders. Besides, Brioc had always kept so many secrets. How come Dymphna knew he had a sister when Ethlynn didn't? Dymphna probably knew everything about his past. Too many things pointed to the fact that Brioc loved the princess, not her. All those times he left her alone at the cottage and wandered off with Sam, where had he gone? He'd always refused to say. And that faraway look he so often had in his eyes. People looked like that when they daydreamed, right?

Ethlynn risked a glance at Dymphna ahead of them. The forest green dress set off the highlights of her soft flouncy hair. She had no right to be that beautiful. Even wearing that ugly shawl, she was still stunning. It simply wasn't fair.

Ethlynn hardened her jaw. No, she had nothing to say to her husband. She swallowed the lump in her throat and veered away, so he wouldn't walk next to her. Here came her tears again. Her only consolation was that he loved their daughter enough to want to carry her.

As if reading her mind, Brioc said, "I'll carry you too, if you'll let me."

Surprised, she threw him a glance. His eyes held a mixture of vulnerability and . . . yearning? Was he flirting with her? No, he was making fun of her. Nonetheless, her insides fluttered and her heart made all kinds of leaps and flips. For a few seconds their eyes locked. Oh no. Her resolve was melting.

"Brioc!" Dymphna's voice cut through the air, making Ethlynn jump. "Can you come here? Please?"

Something like annoyance flashed across his face. Or was that wishful thinking on Ethlynn's part? How could Brioc be annoyed with Dymphna? With a visible effort, he ripped his gaze from Ethlynn's. He heaved a sigh, shook his head, and called back, "I'm coming."

Ethlynn's heart plummeted.

Dymphna and Father Gerebran stood in front of a rundown yet spacious cottage set back from the others at the end of the road. Ethlynn's gaze traveled to the rows of colorful flowers lining the path to the front door. Across the yard stood a rickety shed with logs stacked against it, the pile so tall it looked ready to topple. Hmm, guess the girls' daid didn't have much time to chop firewood. Behind the shed a lone sheep grazed in a small patch of grass. Ethlynn had never seen the breed before. Even the sheep here were foreign. Beyond the grazing patch stretched dense woods.

Ethlynn returned her gaze to the front of the cottage. A few toys lay scattered on the grass by the open front door. Three tan and black kittens tumbled in play near a bowl of sploshed milk. Anika's voice floated from the open door. She and Retha must have gone inside.

Brioc reached Dymphna, who gave him the sweetest smile. "We need you to translate. We can't understand a single word." Dymphna glanced at Brigid and her face glowed. "I'll hold her if you want."

Ethlynn came up behind them. She couldn't see Brioc's face. Was he smiling at Dymphna? Ethlynn held her breath, waiting to see what he would do.

He said, "Thank you, but I'm fine holding her," and stepped into the cottage, Brigid still in his arms. Ethlynn released her breath.

Dymphna didn't seem offended. She happily bounced into the cottage at his heels. Father Gerebran entered after them.

Ethlynn stepped inside. Despite her depressed mood, a gasp of delight escaped her. Vases of fresh flowers adorned every flat surface of the room, perfuming the air with their sweet scent and giving the cottage an inviting, cozy atmosphere.

An old woman — perhaps the girls' grandmother — stood with her back to the door. Her stark black dress and kerchief seemed out of place in the otherwise cheerful room. Anika handed her the statue she'd taken from the cave and the old lady reached up to set it on a shelf. Then she bent to embrace Retha, the slump of her shoulders showing relief, probably because both her granddaughters were home and safe. Anika excitedly chattered in their strange language. Something she said made her grandmother gasp with what sounded like joy and she instantly whipped around.

It was Ethlynn's turn to gasp. The old woman was . . . not old at all! Despite her somber clothes, the face belonged to someone in her twenties. Was . . . was this the girl's *mother*? If so, she'd obviously given birth to Anika at a very young age. Maybe only seventeen, like Ethlynn. With high cheek bones, cornflower-blue eyes and hair so blond it was nearly white, she was awfully pretty. Why would someone so young and pretty wear black?

When the woman saw Father Gerebran, her face lit up with the same joy the girls had both shown. She rushed across the room and dropped to her knees, her head bent for the blessing which Father Gerebran readily imparted. Blinking back tears of emotion, she crossed herself, kissed the priest's hands, then stood. She spoke to Father Gerebran calmly, peacefully, with a gentle self-control that immediately impressed Ethlynn. Retha silently slipped beside her mother — yes, it *had* to be their mother, she looked like them — and first hugged her, then hugged Father Gerebran's legs. Retha didn't make a peep, just smiled.

It took a moment before their mother figured out the priest couldn't understand her words. Brioc jumped to the rescue and did his best to translate as everyone spoke at once. Ethlynn's mind wandered, her gaze roaming the cottage.

A perfectly scrubbed rough-hewn table with yet another vase of flowers and surrounded by three wobbly chairs dominated the space. Only three chairs? Ethlynn noticed two beds, one messy with scrunched up blankets, strewn with toys and little girls' clothing, and the other tidy yet only big enough for one person. A partially open door led to another room. Ethlynn craned her neck to peek into it from where she stood. Oh. Just an empty stable. No animals, no smell. Being the daughter of a horse-dealer, she could tell it hadn't been used in awhile. Maybe the family had sold all their animals for money.

Her gaze flitted back to the main room. Various articles of feminine clothes, clean but heavily patched, hung from hooks. A crucifix adorned one wall and a loom stood in the corner. Nothing in the cottage remotely hinted at a male presence. Ethlynn frowned. Where was the daid?

Wait. Could the woman be . . . a *widow*? That would definitely explain her black clothes. Ethlynn's heart clenched with compassion. How terrible! She couldn't imagine the hardship of raising a family alone. And what about all the heavy work that a man would normally do? No wonder so many logs outside needed chopping!

"Lynnie, uh, this is Paulien. She wants to meet you."

Huh? Oh. Embarrassed they'd caught her gawking, Ethlynn hurried forward and smiled. "Hello."

Paulien smiled back, her eyes warm and friendly, and returned the greeting in her own strange language. Something about her made Ethlynn like her instantly. Paulien's gaze dropped and lingered on Brigid, asleep in Brioc's arms. Delight flowed over her face, making her even prettier, and her eyes danced with longing. It was obvious she wanted to hold Brigid. Brioc smiled and handed her the bundle. The way Paulien rocked their daughter with such ease brought a rush of comfort and relief to Ethlynn. At last, an experienced mother to help her! With two daughters, Paulien must know everything about babies! Ethlynn hoped they could become friends.

While the girls showed Father Gerebran and Dymphna their three kittens, Brioc resumed his halting, clumsy conversation with Paulien. She repeated the same phrase over and over, as if insisting on something that Brioc couldn't understand. Finally, with an amused sigh, Paulien gave up, clasped Ethlynn's hand and pulled her to the door that led to the unused stable. Brioc followed, bewildered.

Paulien whooshed them both into the stable, plopped Brigid in Ethlynn's arms, and motioned for them to stay put. Then, with a gesture that said she'd be right back, she dashed through the doorway.

Ethlynn dropped her eyes to the floor, nervous to be alone with Brioc. She felt the intensity of his gaze and heat crept up her neck and face. *Please hurry, Paulien.*

A few seconds later she reappeared. Whew. She lugged a chair under each arm. Setting them down, she hurried away again, only to return with an armful of blankets. A pot and an odd assortment of plates and dishes balanced precariously atop the swaying pile. Paulien set the load on a chair, smiled and gestured wildly, trying to make them understand.

She was offering them the stable to live in!

Ethlynn's heart skipped. Gratitude and excitement surged through her. Her gaze flew around the empty room, imagining how cozy it would look with furniture. Brioc could make a table and more chairs, and that corner over there was the perfect spot for a bed and a little cradle! Ethlynn pictured flowers everywhere, like on Paulien's side, and they would become best friends and she'd be so happy and —

"Um, Brioc?"

Ethlynn's gaze shot to the doorway. Dymphna stood in the threshold, her lily-white hand resting against the door-jamb. "Sorry to bother you again. We can't understand what Anika is saying. I think she wants to show us the church."

256

"Oh. Of course. I'll come with you."

Brioc excused himself and left the stable.

Ethlynn's heart dropped to her feet. For those few blissful moments, she had actually forgotten about the princess. Misery and loneliness returned to flood through her. She wanted to cry.

63

The first stars blinked in the darkening sky as the evening breeze chased away the clouds and filled the air with the scent of flowers. Dymphna inhaled deeply as she ambled along the path towards Paulien's cottage. Her heart sang. The fresh, clean air somehow made Dymphna's spirit soar with contentment. The only problem with the sun having set was she now had to be careful where she stepped. She lost her balance too easily wearing the funny wooden shoes Paulien had lent her. She giggled every time she looked down at them. Shoes carved from wood! Who would've thought?

She clasped the red bouquet tighter, imagining how pretty it would look in a vase on Ethlynn's and Brioc's table. Hopefully the brightly colored blossoms would cheer Ethlynn up. Dymphna even knew their name now. Tulips.

She hopped over a little rut on the path, a burst of pride swelling in her chest. Less than three weeks in Gheel, and she'd learned not only the names of all the strange flowers but many other words as well. Not exactly enough to hold a conversation, but enough to understand basic phrases when people spoke to her.

Not that she spent much time with others. She preferred the silence of the church and saved most of her words for Jesus. Gheel was an enchanting hamlet and Dymphna was grateful to be here, but she missed Ireland with an ache that she doubted would ever go away. With each passing day, she longed more and more for Heaven, her true homeland, and to be with God, her true Father. The Father who always took care of her, not like her earthly one.

At the thought of Daidi, the song stilled in Dymphna's heart. Fear prickled her skin. She forced herself to breathe deeply, slowly. Daidi wasn't here. There was no way he could track them all the way to Gheel.

I'm safe. Daidi's hunting me in Brytenlond, not Flanders.

Crickets chirped and more stars peeked out from the blackening blanket in the sky. Dymphna shuddered, fighting to regain the peace of a moment ago. Suddenly the surrounding woods and darkening fields seemed sinister. She quickened her steps and hurried along the path towards Paulien's house, gripping her bouquet so tightly her knuckles turned white. Relief flooded her when she got close enough to hear Paulien's sheep baaing behind the house and Anika's cheerful voice floating from an open window.

Dymphna relaxed a little. She was nearly there. Soon she would be inside Paulien's warm, cozy room. Her fears of Daidi were unfounded here in Gheel. At the sound of Anika's reassuring chatter, a tiny smile crept to Dymphna's mouth.

The girl talked nonstop. She more than made up for her sister, who couldn't speak at all.

Or maybe could . . . but wouldn't.

For some reason, Dymphna wished she knew which. Was little Retha scarred from something in her past, like Brioc? Apparently her daid had been killed in some horrible accident when she was two. Was that why she wouldn't speak? Maybe she'd witnessed it. Or perhaps her daid's death had nothing to do with her silence. Her muteness might simply be part of her birth defects.

More sounds drifted from the open window. Pots clattered to the deep *baa* of the unseen sheep behind the house. Paulien said something, and Ethlynn's voice replied. Both laughed. Ethlynn was obviously picking up the language too, as was Paulien with their Irish. Brigid started to cry in the background, which must have reminded Paulien of Retha, because her laughter instantly stopped. Dymphna thought she heard Paulien ask where her daughter was.

Retha slipped away all the time, continually worrying her already overburdened mother. Since their arrival in Gheel, the child had become Father Gerebran's shadow. She followed him everywhere, nearly every hour of every day. But the priest had gone to a nearby village tonight, to anoint a dying man. He wouldn't have taken Retha with him.

Dymphna glanced around, hoping to spot the little girl. Thoughts of Daidi made her pulse quicken. A trickle of sweat slid between her shoulders. Was Retha safe? The child shouldn't be wandering alone after dark.

A thud and the crack of splintering wood came from near Paulien's shed. Dymphna's gaze shot in the direction of the sound. By the light of a lantern propped on the ground she saw Brioc by the woodpile, sleeves rolled up, an ax in his hands. He swung the ax and another log broke in half and clunked into the dirt.

Hmm. Maybe Brioc knew where Retha had gone. Dymphna swerved off the path and wandered over.

The sheep baaed, which sounded for all the world like an old man's cough.

Dymphna had nearly reached Brioc when the ax came down again, sending a large chunk of wood flying straight at her. Dodging the projectile, she lost her balance and her wooden shoe twisted and slid across the dry wood chips littering the ground. Down she crashed, the bouquet of tulips spilling from her hands. Her arm whacked against the lantern as she fell, nearly knocking it over. She grabbed for it, barely managing to prevent it from smashing on the ground. Whew, thank goodness! With all this dry wood, that could have been disastrous.

Startled by the pandemonium, Brioc spun around. When he spotted her, sprawled on the carpet of wood chips, he leaned the ax against the shed and rushed over. "Are you alright?"

How embarrassing. Heat burned her face, making her blush. Doubtless the lantern light beside her caught the scarlet of her cheeks. "I'm fine." She struggled to sit.

"Let me help you up." He took her hand and pulled her to her feet. "I didn't see you coming. Sorry."

His sleeves were still pushed up. Dymphna's eyes unwillingly locked on the scars on his arms.

"That looked like a hard fall. Are you sure you're not hurt?"

Don't stare, don't stare. Brioc's brother had said the scars were everywhere, not just on his arms. Shock raced through her.

"Hey, are you alright?" Brioc waited for her answer. He didn't notice her gawking. "Did you hit your head or something?"

With an effort, she tore her gaze away. "No, no, I'm fine, really." Mortified, she slapped the dirt and wood chips from her dress.

Brioc dropped to one knee and collected her scattered tulips. She tried not to look at his arms. Across the yard, a door creaked loudly open. Probably Paulien coming outside to hunt for Retha.

"Here. I think this is all of them." Still on one knee, Brioc held the bunch of flowers up to her.

"Thank you." She accepted the bouquet and Brioc stood, brushing off his clothes. Suddenly her thoughts returned to Retha. She twisted her head, scanning the area for the sight of the little girl.

Her gaze paused on the cottage door. Oh. It wasn't Paulien standing on the doorstep. It was Ethlynn.

Dymphna smiled and lifted a hand to wave to her. With her hands full of tulips, the wave came out clumsy.

Ethlynn didn't wave back. She whirled around and stormed into the house. The door slammed so loudly that Brioc nearly jumped out of his skin. His breath caught. "What was that?"

"Nothing. Just the door. Ethlynn came out."

The confused look swiftly changed to hope and his gaze shot to the cottage. The door was closed. He visibly wilted. "I thought you said she came out."

"She did. She went back inside."

His shoulders slumped. "Oh." Sadness filled his eyes and he looked away.

The sheep kept coughing.

Dymphna bit her lip. "Why is Ethlynn always in such a bad mood?"

Brioc blew out a breath. "I have no idea. She never speaks to me." Frustration edged his voice. He stepped back to the wood pile, swiping up the ax. "She spends all her time with Paulien. It's wonderful they get along so well. I want her to have friends. But . . ." He let the sentence trail off. "Just let me finish this, will you? I want to get back inside."

"Should I try to talk to her? Maybe she'll tell me what's wrong."

Brioc positioned another log on the block. "Good luck." He hoisted the ax, stepped back, then swung the ax down with unexpected vengeance. The giant log split clean in half, spraying wood chips through the air. Dymphna jumped back as the two halves clunked to the ground. Before they even stopped rolling, Brioc grabbed another one and swung again. He was clearly in a bad mood all of a sudden.

But . . . being angry was better than being empty, wasn't it? Dymphna instinctively pulled the ugly shawl higher onto her shoulders. She swallowed. "Well, hopefully the tulips cheer her up. I picked them for her."

No reply. Brioc ignored her and murdered a third log.

Uh, maybe it was time to leave. Dymphna turned and took four steps towards the cottage. She stopped, suddenly remembering why she'd come over here. She spun back around. "Have you seen Retha?"

"No." Without missing a beat, he set his next victim on the chopping block. Everything about him warned her to leave him alone.

So, why was her mouth opening? Before she could stop the words, they tumbled out. "Brioc? Do you . . . do you know if Retha can talk? I mean, that she *can* but *won't*?"

The ax paused mid-air. Brioc froze. Brigid cried in the house. *Wah-wah-wah.*

The old-man sheep cleared his throat, then had a coughing fit.

Well, she'd started this, so she might as well finish. She sucked in her breath. "Do you think . . . I mean, um . . . could something awful have happened to her? Something that might've, well . . ." Dymphna squirmed and started again. "Like whatever it was that made you . . ." Oh dear. Why had she plunged into this?

Brioc pulled in a breath and lowered the ax. One of his hands started to tremble. "Like what made me *what*?" He said it almost like a dare.

Heat crawled up her neck and burned her face. She clumsily transferred the bouquet to one hand and with the other clutched the shawl around her shoulders, breathing a quick prayer. "I just thought that, well, if anyone could help Retha, it would be you."

Chilly silence.

Even the woods stilled. The crickets stopped chirping and the lone sheep fell strangely quiet, as if all of nature suddenly feared to breathe.

"Please don't take that wrong, Brioc. All I meant was —"

A bloodcurdling sound rent the air. An inhuman scream of agony.

Dymphna's gaze flew in the direction of the terrifying sounds.

Commotion ripped apart the woods. A frenzy of snarls and growls. Thrashing and leaves rustling wildly. Twigs crackled and branches snapped. A strangled noise as if something gargled blood.

Suddenly footsteps pounded. More snarls. Violent crashing. Hard breathing. A scream jammed in Dymphna's throat and she spun towards the house, wanting to flee from whatever was coming.

Just then Retha blasted through the trees, half-running, half-stumbling towards them. Her face was a mask of terror.

Sheer panic jumped into Brioc's eyes. He dropped the ax and his back smacked against the shed wall as if some giant hand had slammed him into it.

A huge gray wolf exploded through the woods behind Retha. And behind him, came his pack.

64

Turlough huffed. "Gheel can't be more than a mile or two from here. Why can't we keep going?"

"Why?" Neill snorted. "Because it's late. It's dark. I'm tired. We can't even see the road anymore. We've been walking eight hours and . . ." He glared. ". . . frankly, my feet are killing me." He slid his pack off his shoulder and dumped it on the grass. "Go on ahead if you want. I'm stopping for the night."

Turlough raked a hand through his hair in frustration and stared at the tiny dots of light flickering in the distance ahead. That *had* to be Gheel. "Neill, we're so close! Please."

"And what do you plan to do? Knock on every door and wake the whole village up, searching for your brother? Come on, Turlough. He's either there and safe, and has been for nearly three weeks, in which case he doesn't even need rescuing . . . or he's in Brytenlond, already six feet under and helping the daisies grow. And we sure can't rescue him from there."

Did Neill have to be so blunt? "Gosh, thanks for that. Sweet dreams to you too."

Neill unrolled a blanket and spread it on the ground. "I'm only being realistic. You know I'm right."

"But what about the princess?"

"What about her?" Neill tugged off his boots and tossed them aside. Wiggling his toes, he sighed with bliss.

"Well, even if Brioc is —" The word caught in Turlough's throat. "Even if he's . . . dead . . . we still need to help Dymphna."

"How? She's either safe in Gheel and sound asleep in a warm, cozy bed, or she's already been captured by Daemon in Brytenlond."

"Alright, alright, you've made your point."

Much as Turlough hated to admit it, Neill did, in fact, have a valid point. There was no urgency to get to Gheel. After waiting for two and a half weeks, one more night wouldn't make an iota of difference to anyone's future.

Except Turlough was longing to see Brioc. Longing to talk to him and apologize for eleven years ago and try to make things right between them.

Ha! Dream on. How could he ever accomplish *that* when Brioc still wouldn't go near him?

He sighed and unslung the harp from his shoulder, carefully setting it on the ground next to Neill's gear. If he'd been wrong and they didn't find Brioc in

Flanders, he'd be forced to finally sell the instrument. They had no money to get back to Ireland. They had no money to get anywhere at all! Two weeks waiting for the stinking boat to be repaired had completely cleaned them out.

Neill stretched out on the blanket and rolled onto his back. He emitted another blissful sigh. "I could sleep for a year." He drew in a slow deep breath and closed his eyes.

Equally exhausted, Turlough sank to his knees on a soft patch of grass and unwrapped his own blanket from around the harp. He'd been violently seasick and hadn't slept a wink on the boat. Then hardly had he lurched off the deck and onto dry land in Antwerp, when he'd discovered they had a thirty-mile trek to Gheel. Yes, Neill was right; they needed sleep.

Shaking out the blanket, Turlough arranged it on the grass. He pulled off his boots and unsheathed his sword, placing it in easy reach of where he'd lay. He was just about to lie down when screams in the distance made his heart stop. Shrieks and vicious snarling shredded the stillness of the night. Even Neill bolted up, his eyes snapping open.

Horror-stricken, they looked at each other. The sound came from at least a mile away. There was nothing in the world they could do.

Neill held his breath, then said, "Some wolf just found supper." His voice caught. He obviously felt as uncomfortable as Turlough did, listening to a drama they had no power to stop.

Turlough's heart pounded. The memory seared through his mind, what his brother had looked like as a child after fangs had ripped him to shreds by the waterfall. Was that horror happening to someone else right now, this very minute? He swallowed hard. "Was . . . was that human, do you think?"

"The screams, definitely. The prey?" Neill shook his head. "Who knows?"

They waited, frozen, listening. The sounds faded.

An eerie silence settled over the fields of Flanders.

65

The little girl ran in slow motion. Every pump of her legs and every wild flinging of her arms seemed to take place in an invisible sea of molasses, suspending time, defying space. Each detail of the approaching horror seared Brioc's eyes, filling his veins with ice.

Stark terror stamped Retha's face. Her blond braids flew behind her, sticking straight out from the back of her head. She half-limped, half-flew towards the shed, propelled by unimaginable fear.

The gray wolf and his bloodthirsty pack charged through the invisible molasses too. Five wolves, their muzzles smeared with blood. Tufts of fluffy wool, soaked crimson, and grisly fragments of sheep entrails littered a path behind them.

Screams sliced the air. Deafening, earsplitting screams that exploded Brioc's head and curdled his blood. Retha's? Dymphna's? Both?

Everything moved too slowly, completely surreal. Fear glued Brioc's back to the shed wall and clamped his feet in mortar. His lungs refused to work, his heart stopped pumping.

Running in that impossibly slow motion, Retha reached them and plowed straight into Dymphna's arms. The force thrust both girls backwards. Flickers of light from the lantern illuminated the terror on their faces. Red tulips sailed into the air, then fluttered down, scattering like drops of blood among the wood chips and logs covering the ground.

The pack's leader swerved towards Retha, closing the distance, and pushed off its hind legs. It launched into the air, fangs bared, coming in for the kill.

The wall of molasses shattered, jerking everything back into real time.

Adrenaline blasted through Brioc's veins.

Without thinking, he dived into Dymphna, with Retha wrapped in her arms, and rammed them out of the wolf's path. They stumbled back, their screams splintering his eardrums. The wolf crashed straight into him, knocking him off his feet. Together they smashed to the ground.

Weight crushed him; fur smothered his face. The hellish stench of hot breath mingled with blood jumped straight from his nightmares.

From nowhere, the waterfall sprang. Its hissing and roaring melded with the little girl's screams. Ice water sprayed his face. Fangs sharp as daggers sank into his arm. The little girl kept screaming . . . screaming . . .

No, she couldn't be screaming! She was already dead!

He was trapped in two nightmares at once. He thrashed beneath the wolf. Razor-sharp fangs shredded his flesh. Something thudded nearby and a flare of orange shot into the air. Flames burst to life. A yelp of agony rent the air several feet away, turning into an inhuman shriek.

An object smacked into the wolf's face. Twisting with a yip of pain, the animal leaped back, releasing him. A rush of warm liquid poured down his arm. Whatever had hit the wolf's face now thumped into the dirt. A cloud of dust billowed.

A new object whacked against the wolf's back. Startled, it leaped to the side as something square and heavy thudded down. A log? Was someone throwing logs?

The wolf crouched and snarled, baring its fangs.

Yelping filled the air from something he couldn't see. Were there more wolves than one? Orange flames shot higher. Screaming, endless screaming, coming from everywhere. To the side, from the back, from the direction of that little cottage over there. *How did a cottage get near the waterfall? Who was standing on the doorstep?*

Dear God, was that Lynnie?

Where was he? Where was the little girl? He had to save her!

He scrambled to his knees, pain bolting, panic blinding him. *What was happening?* Wood chips and dry kindling exploded into flames all around him. A wall of fire rose up. A few feet away a second wolf writhed and howled, its fur on fire. *Two wolves? Where did —?* Blood pounded in his ears. His heart jammed in his throat.

Another log sailed through the air, barely missing the gray wolf's head. A low rumbling growl came from the depths of its belly. It crouched, trapped by the fire.

"Brioc! The ax! Grab the ax!"

It sounded like Princess Dymphna's voice. How did she get here?

Where even was he?

The gray wolf lunged.

From the corner of his eye, he spotted an ax laying on the ground.

Adrenaline surged and he dived for it. Snatching the weapon, he lurched to his feet.

The wolf slammed into him. The waterfall roared. He slashed the weapon with viciousness born of sheer survival instinct, smashing it straight into the animal's skull. A hefty crack jolted his arm. The wolf crumpled in a limp heap, bleeding. Fire crackled everywhere, heat scorching Brioc's face.

He dropped the ax and spun. Blood poured down his arm. The little girl cowered behind a shed, frozen. Brioc blinked. Why was there a shed? Why was the little girl blond? Was that . . . Princess Dymphna?

Without warning, the woodshed exploded into flames.

Brioc scooped the little blond girl into his arms and ran, the princess at his heels.

66

"Well, this has to be Gheel." Neill stopped on the dirt road and shielded his eyes against the glaring sun, already high in the sky. The village ahead of them was hardly more than a few houses. A faint odor of smoke hung in the air. "Now what? Door to door?"

Turlough hiked the harp higher on his shoulder and stared at the hamlet ahead of them, apprehension twisting his insides. "I guess so."

"Alright. I'll take the houses on the left. You head to the ones bordering the woods."

Turlough sucked in a breath. What if he was mistaken about this whole thing and Brioc had sailed to Brytenlond after all? Daemon would have found him by now and killed him, along with Lynnie and their newborn child. For all Turlough knew, Dymphna was already back in Ireland, forced into a sick, sinful union as her father's bride. Did he really want to enter Gheel and discover he'd been wrong?

"Did you hear me?"

Turlough nodded, his gaze still locked on the hamlet. "I heard you."

He could not spot a single person outside. Where was everyone?

"Then let's move. We'll meet here later." Neill let out a laugh. "If we're lucky, someone might offer us lunch."

Of course. It was nearly noon. Everyone would be inside getting ready for a meal. After last night's terrifying sounds, both he and Neill had a fitful night and slept in late. More wasted time.

Neill gave him an encouraging smile, slapped him on the back and tramped off toward the houses on the left.

Whispering a prayer for resignation at whatever he might find — or rather, not find — Turlough trudged toward a clump of cottages edging the woods. So, Gheel at last. The magical land of Brioc's childhood, where apparently every dream would come true.

If only.

The knot in Turlough's stomach coiled tighter. Why did he feel such apprehension? The tidy houses and colorful windmills gave the place an undeniable charm, making it look cozy and inviting. But to Turlough, it seemed foreboding.

Maybe it was because of last night. His sleep had been haunted with nightmares. The helpless screams and snarls still rang in his ears.

He shook his head a little, trying to push the thought away. Shrugging the harp higher onto his shoulder, he scanned the scattered cottages as he walked, trying to decide which one to first approach. The idea of knocking on a stranger's door and interrupting them in the middle of who-knows-what didn't appeal, so he looked for a person already outside.

Ah. Over there. A woman in a yard, sorting through a pile of burnt rubble. That accounted for the smoky smell. It looked like a small structure had burned down. Not big enough to be a house. Probably a woodshed, judging by the blackened logs on the ground.

Turlough summoned his courage and headed in the woman's direction.

The closer he got, the acrid smell of smoke grew stronger. The fire must have been very recent. Another stench poisoned the area too. Turlough wrinkled his nose. A carcass? Burnt flesh? It couldn't be human; surely no one would have left a dead person laying in the rubble. Maybe an animal had gotten trapped in the fire.

He crossed the small yard, swerving past a few scattered toys and rows of bright flowers that lined the path to the house. He wandered to where the woman worked.

Her back to him, she sifted through blackened logs. Her dress and headscarf were as black as they were. She visibly struggled to lift one, then clumsily heaved it into a nearby wheelbarrow where it landed with a thud. With a loud sigh, she reached up and wiped her brow, then she tackled another massive log. Good heavens, an elderly lady shouldn't be doing such heavy work!

Turlough slipped the harp from his shoulder. The blanket it'd been wrapped in slid off as he set it on the ground. He rushed forward to help the woman. Forgetting that his words would be foreign to her ears, he said, "Here, let me lift those for you."

The woman jumped a little, obviously startled by the sudden voice behind her, and spun around. When she saw his face, confusion raced across her features. She gasped, then stared at him with wide eyes.

He stared back, equally taken by surprise. She wasn't elderly. She was young.

And had the sweetest face he had ever seen.

After an awkward few seconds of gaping at each other, she composed herself from whatever about him had shocked her, and she managed a smile. Her cheeks, smudged with soot, turned red. "Thank you."

"Uh, for what?" His mind went blank. He tried to stop staring at her. She was just so pretty! Not glittery and fake like the girls Neill went for. No, she wasn't glamorous at all. Hers was an innocent beauty, plain, natural, and . . . well, breathtaking, for that reason alone.

Her blush deepened and she dropped her gaze, obviously embarrassed by his staring. He suddenly remembered he'd offered to help. "Oh, right. The logs. Of course."

She barely suppressed a giggle.

He forced his eyes away from her lovely face and stepped to the wood pile. He hoisted a log and — *Hang on.* She'd spoken in his language! She'd understood him and answered. *How on earth?*

His jaw dropped and he turned back to face her, about to ask. But she was already stumbling towards the harp, as if in a daze.

With one hand pressed to her throat as if in shock, she dropped to her knees beside it.

Turlough dumped the log into the wheelbarrow and watched as she ran her fingers gently over the engraved design in the wood of the harp. Her eyes threw him a questioning glance. Then she asked something in her own language which he didn't understand. Her expression was stunned.

"It belongs to my brother," he said, not sure what the question had been.

She frowned, obviously not understanding him this time either.

He groped. "My . . . um . . ." What was the word for brother in her language? He suddenly remembered. "Broer," he tried.

She blinked, her frown deepening.

"What? You recognize the harp?"

She nodded. She pointed to herself, then the harp and said, "Omke."

Huh? What on earth did that mean?

Seeing he was at a loss she repeated it. "Omke." She furrowed her brows, frustrated. "Um . . . Un-kla. My unkla."

"Uncle?"

She nodded furiously, then looked back at the harp. She traced her fingers lovingly over the carvings, her eyes still wide with disbelief, and rattled off more words in her strange tongue.

"Wait. You mean, your uncle . . . made it?" The harp had come from Gheel, after all. Could the traveling minstrel have been her uncle? Under other circumstances, Turlough would have been astonished. But her sweet face and clear blue eyes occupied all his thoughts right now. The harp was the last thing on his mind.

Still, the amazing coincidence gave him the chance to have a conversation with her, even if it was in two languages and they could hardly understand each other. Abandoning the logs, he strode to where she knelt beside the harp. He dropped to one knee beside her, pretending to be interested in the etched designs that so held her attention.

Her hair smelled like smoke mingled with flowers, and unfortunately was mostly hidden beneath that blasted black scarf. The strands that peeked out were soft and blond. The flowers overpowered the smoke.

Turlough cleared his throat, trying again to stop staring. "There was a minstrel from Gheel. He came to Ireland and gave this to my brother." Who cared if she didn't understand a word he spoke? Kneeling close to her made his insides flip around like they never had before.

"My unkla make . . ." She struggled for words. "How you say . . . much . . . insto — instroms?"

"Instruments?"

"Yes! Yes, instroments. He sing." Then, as if to clarify the last word, she trilled, "La la la" in the sweetest voice, making them both laugh. She continued, "He make this." She pointed to the design etched in the wood. "I recognize."

"It's beautiful, isn't it?" He wasn't even looking at it. He wished she wasn't wearing that scarf. "Your uncle obviously went to Ireland. He told us he traveled a lot."

She tilted her head, not comprehending. "You say too fast."

"Ireland." He said the word slowly, pointing first to himself than in the direction of the sea. "Your uncle went there."

She nodded excitedly, understanding. "I am little girl. He go." She blushed, knowing her words came out incorrect.

He smiled. "Don't worry. I got that."

A smile twitched at her mouth too. She couldn't take her eyes off the harp. He couldn't take his eyes off her.

"Did he ever come back? Is he here, in Gheel?"

She shrugged, then giggled. "I understand not."

He slowed the sentence. "Is your uncle here?"

She shook her head, sadness touching her eyes. She bit her lip, searching for the Irish words. "He die."

"I'm sorry." He ran a hand through his hair. " I — I really can't believe this. He gave this harp to my brother. We'd just been orphaned and —" With a ripple of urgency he suddenly remembered what he was doing here in the first place. He needed to find Brioc! How had he allowed himself to become so distracted?

She must have sensed his sudden shift of mood because her eyebrows came together with worry and she asked, "Is you fine?" which he translated to *'Are you alright?'*

"Maybe you can help me. Actually, my brother is the whole reason I'm here. I'm looking for him." Then he remembered she didn't know the word *brother*, so he added, "Broer. My broer. I need to find him. It's urgent."

She smiled. "You look for Brioc?"

His heart stopped.

271

"You mean . . . you know him?"

"Of course." She said it so calmly, so naturally, as if it were the most normal thing in the world.

"He's really here? In this village?" Turlough couldn't believe his ears. He looked around the yard, as if Brioc would be standing three feet away.

An amused smile lit up her face, making her even more lovely, and she laughed. "You look . . . how say? Same." She nodded excitedly. "Very same." She lightly touched his hair, which for some reason sent sparks flying through him. "Except this."

"Do you know where he is? I mean right now?" The combination of knowing that Brioc was close and the feel of her hand on his hair made his pulse race.

She removed her hand and tilted her head, as if thinking. "No. But his . . . um . . ." She cast about for the word. "Wiff?"

"Wife."

"Wife, yes, yes! His wife and . . ." She frowned, then clasped her arms and rocked an imaginary baby. "They in the house." She pointed to the cottage across the yard.

Lynnie was inside? Adrenaline surged through him.

"Turlough!" someone shouted. "Turlough!"

They both twisted their heads in the direction of the voice.

Neill ran, breathless, across the yard. His sword was drawn.

"Daemon! He's here! Soldiers are going through the houses, looking for your brother and his wife."

Turlough bolted to his feet.

Neill didn't even stop running. "Your brother must have left a trail of coins all the way from Brytenlond to Antwerp! Find him. Hurry!" He swerved back onto the road. "I'll find the princess!"

Turlough flew to the house for Lynnie.

272

67

How could he! Giving Dymphna flowers last night! On bended knee! Ethlynn still could hardly believe it. But she'd seen Brioc do it with her very own eyes.

She felt so alone and heartsick.

Tears brimmed and she rubbed them with the cuff of her sleeve. She blinked a few times, trying to refocus on the blurry pieces of material and sewing supplies in her lap. Paulien had given her a basket of scraps from Anika's and Retha's outgrown dresses, insisting she stay inside and do something calming after witnessing last night's traumatizing events. So for the last couple hours Ethlynn had busied herself by sewing a baby outfit.

Well, trying to.

Normally the task would delight her, but she only wanted to throw herself on the bed next to Brigid's cradle, bury her face in the blankets, and cry herself to death. It wasn't the wolves that kept circling in her memory and making her heart clench. It was that beautiful bouquet of red tulips.

It was cruel and heartless, of course, but Ethlynn hardly cared that Brioc's arm had been bleeding so badly after yesterday's attack. And to make everything a million times worse, Dymphna had been the one to bandage his huge gashes. That alone made Ethlynn want to weep.

A tiny twinge of guilt pricked her conscience. Actually, that had been her own fault. Brioc would have let her, if she hadn't fainted. As soon as she'd glimpsed all that blood, she'd passed out cold. Obviously *someone* had to act as nurse. Paulien was out of the question, having her hands full trying to calm her two hysterical daughters. So that left . . . *her.* Everyone's heroine. Perfect Dymphna.

Ethlynn's fingers trembled as she stabbed the needle through the material on her lap and tears blurred her eyes. Where even was Brioc right now? The last time she'd glanced out the window, Paulien had been alone at the shed, salvaging firewood from the burnt pile. Brioc had been helping her earlier, but he'd since disappeared.

Was he with the princess?

Ethlynn swiped at her eyes with sleeve cuff again.

No, wait! Hadn't Brioc said something this morning about building a new shed for Paulien? A spark of hope flickered. Maybe he wasn't with the princess after all. Maybe, just *maybe*, he'd gone to borrow tools from a neighbor.

The front door on Paulien's half of the cottage banged open, making her jump.

"Lynnie! Lynnie! Where are you?"

So, Brioc had come home, had he? She would pretend to ignore him.

"Lynnie . . .?"

She frowned. His voice sounded different.

"Lynnie!"

Why did he stay on Paulien's side? How odd. He knew she'd be in the stable.

A pause, as if for some bizarre reason he was looking around, trying to find her. Then suddenly his footfalls pounded across the cottage floor like he'd only now spotted the door leading into the stable.

A second later, he burst through the doorway. He stood there and —

Ohmygosh, what'd he do to his hair? It was a totally different color!

Her eyes popped.

And how did his bandaged arm get — It wasn't Brioc! It was a complete stranger! Someone who looked just like him! And he had . . . a *sword!*

A soldier!

She screamed and bolted from her chair. The sewing spilled from her lap, material and needles scattering on the floor.

"I'm not going to hurt you! I promise!" The soldier's gaze flew around the room. He spotted the cradle.

Ethlynn tried to scream again, but it wedged in her throat.

The soldier dashed over and scooped Brigid into his arms, blankets and all. "Come on! Come on! I need to hide you!" He ran for the door, then suddenly stopped dead in his tracks at the doorway. He turned to face her. "Wait. You *are* Lynnie, aren't you?"

The scream finally dislodged. It came out at the top of her lungs.

He winced, as if the sound split his eardrums.

Her head grew light. She was going to faint! "Someone save me! Save me! Brioooooooc! Help!"

"Alright, you're her. Let's go!" The soldier darted through the door and into Paulien's half of the cottage.

He was stealing her baby!

Forget about fainting! She had to save Brigid!

Adrenaline racing through her, she chased the villainous kidnapper all the way out the front door and through the yard. He swerved the opposite direction from where a stunned-looking Paulien stood at the shed, and crashed into the woods behind the cottage. He kept running.

Ethlynn ran after him.

"Brioc!" she cried out. "Help me! Help me!"

But even as she screamed the words, she knew with despair that her husband wouldn't rescue her. He wouldn't even hear her.

He was nowhere around.

68

If only Lynnie would stop screaming. Daemon's army could doubtless hear her all the way in Ireland, let alone half a mile down the road. Unless she shut up, they were doomed.

Turlough tore down one path then another, not sure which way to go. He only knew he had to hide Lynnie and her baby, then somehow find his brother. Everything was happening too fast. He had no time to form a plan. There were too many people to save and no way to do it, so he kept barging through the woods and hoping for the best.

Lynnie ran behind him, stumbling and shrieking and making enough rumpus to wake the dead. The baby was the opposite. It lay perfectly quiet in his arms, oblivious to the fact they tore around trees and leaped over bushes, their survival hanging in the balance. Amazingly, every time Turlough glanced down, his niece, nephew, whatever it was, just looked up at him with wide, beautiful, trusting eyes. Him, her, Turlough had no idea. Just don't drop it, don't drop it!

"Give her back!" Lynnie begged, several yards behind. "Give Brigid back to me!" Her voice was ragged, shrill, heartrending. It made him feel like a monster. But they had no time to stop.

"Come on, come on!" He skidded around a tree and dodged a sharp branch out for blood. He had to find a hiding place.

Hang on. Did she just call the baby . . . *Brigid*?

He nearly stopped with shock. A lump jumped into his throat. It was a girl, and Brioc had named her after Mam!

His mind spun back to their conversation at the graveyard and emotion swelled up inside him. He clasped Mam's namesake tighter, feeling even more urgency to save the life of his niece.

And that's when Lynnie tripped.

With a thud and an *"umph!"* and a gasp of pain, down she went. Turlough whirled around. Lynnie lay sprawled in a tangle of roots and leaves several yards away.

He was about to run back to help her when hoof-beats thundered through the forest. Daemon's soldiers! They must be close! Voices droned in the distance.

Turlough froze, mind racing. His gaze darted around the surroundings. He had to hide Lynnie and Brigid, fast! Plus save the princess and find Brioc. He couldn't do it all!

Bushes rustled behind him, then hard, fast footfalls, someone tearing toward them. Something slammed into the back of his legs, the blow crashing him to his knees. It was all he could do to not drop Brigid. His attacker grabbed a fistful of his hair and brutally jerked his head back so hard it felt like it would be ripped off his neck.

Cold, razor-sharp steel pressed against his exposed throat.

The soldier — *was it Barff? Cahir? someone else?* — clamped an arm tighter around Turlough's neck, keeping his chin yanked back with his forearm.

Turlough didn't dare move. Didn't breathe. The blade dug against his flesh.

Lynnie screamed hysterically. Had she gotten to her feet? Was she captured too? What was happening? He couldn't see her with his head pulled back.

Uh, he could really use Neill right now.

His attacker leaned down to speak in his ear. His voice was low, quiet and lethal, sending chills up Turlough's spine.

"I swear, Turlough, I will slit your throat, unless you very, *very* slowly put my daughter on the ground."

He'd finally found his brother.

69

Dymphna hugged her arms tightly around herself and quickened her steps from her little hut to the church. Although the sun hung high overhead and wolves rarely prowled around during the day, she'd had to force herself to step outside today. Last night's experience left her shaky. She'd grown up hearing howls and barking at night outside the castle, but she'd never run across a wolf pack. She'd had no idea until now how terrifying an attack could be.

And those fangs! She shuddered. No wonder poor Brioc was petrified of wolves.

Was his arm alright? Even more, was *he* alright? Imagine going through that twice! Dymphna swallowed. Would last night push him over the edge? He was already on the brink.

With relief she reached the church and tugged open the door. The dim light from the interior and comforting glow of the altar lamp instantly released her tension. She was with God. She was safe.

She was home.

Pulling her scarf over her head, she stepped inside and quietly clicked the door shut. Father Gerebran sat in a pew near the front, a book spread open on his lap. He must be saying his Office. Retha cuddled against him. Dymphna couldn't see her face but could easily imagine the peaceful smile she wore. Retha loved Father Gerebran. Dymphna didn't blame her. Retha probably felt like she was snuggling next to Jesus Himself.

Not wanting to disturb them, Dymphna tiptoed to the nearest pew, genuflected, and slid onto the kneeler.

She crossed herself, her eyes locking immediately on the tabernacle. Tranquility fell like a blanket over her soul. The fear of last night vanished as if it had never existed. She breathed deeply and closed her eyes, her love swelling.

She had much to ask for. So many favors to beg for her friends. But first she must thank God. Thank Him for bringing them safely to Gheel. For giving her such loyal companions. For letting no one die last night. The list was too long, so with a simple sigh of love, Dymphna poured all her gratitude into Jesus's Heart. He would understand.

She sighed again, but this time with longing. If only God had accepted her offer. She would be so happy to die right here in the pew. A heart attack, or an illness she didn't even know she had, or . . . well, whatever. How did people die suddenly? She had no idea. But God could think of something.

He could. But He wouldn't.

Disappointment squeezed her heart and she struggled to find resignation. After all, if God was going to take her to Heaven, He would have done it back in Ireland, right? In that church where she'd first made the offer of her life to cure Brioc. She bit her bottom lip, trying not to let discouragement overwhelm her.

Horse hooves thundered outside. Noises of commotion and yelling suddenly filled the church yard. Dymphna's eyes snapped open.

Father Gerebran twisted his head to look at the door, a baffled frown stamped on his face. He stood, his prayer book still open in one hand. With his other hand, he reached instinctively for Retha's.

The door burst open. Dymphna jumped and swiveled around, following the priest's gaze.

Three men barged into the church. She leaped to her feet and stared.

She recognized them.

Daidi's soldiers.

70

Brioc readjusted his hold on the knife, his lungs constricting. Could Turlough feel him trembling? He better get control of himself, and quickly, because one tiny sign of weakness and his brother would overpower him in a heartbeat. Turlough was a soldier, trained to kill for a living. Brioc was nothing. He'd never fought a man in his life, let alone killed one.

The only things he'd killed were a wolf last night . . . and Sam. That memory still stabbed him with pain. He'd slit her throat to save Dymphna. If he could do *that*, surely he could make himself slit Turlough's in order to save Lynnie and Brigid, whom he loved more than anything. In fact, it would be easier, right?

Um . . . No.

It would be the hardest thing imaginable.

"Put my daughter down," he repeated. His voice shook. His hand shook. Everything shook. "Slowly. Really, really slowly. Put her on the ground."

Turlough hesitated. Brioc pressed the blade harder. Maybe it was a good thing he was trembling so badly. One accidental slip and the deed would be done, intentional or not. Turlough must've realized that too, because he lowered Brigid, inch by painstaking inch. Brioc dropped to his knees so he could keep the knife in place.

Finally Brigid was on the grass. Brioc kept the blade hard against Turlough's throat.

"Lynnie. Get over here and take her. Quick!"

Lynnie had already clambered to her feet, although Brioc had no idea when. She stood a few feet away, frozen in terror, her hand slapped over her mouth. Her face was white as snow, making her look like a statue.

Turlough attempted to talk. "Bri—"

He shoved the knife even closer. His heart hammered a million times a minute. Turlough obediently shut up.

"Lynnie, hurry."

She didn't move. Tears streamed down her cheeks.

"Get over here and take Brigid," he begged. He was weakening. He couldn't do this, couldn't kill his own brother. But Turlough would kill *them*.

"Lynnie! Now!" he ordered. He bore his eyes into her, commanding her.

She snapped out of her stupor. Her gaze darted between Brigid, Turlough, and Brioc with the knife. Silent tears of terror poured down her face. Finally she dashed forward, and snatched Brigid off the ground. She clasped the baby against her chest and froze again.

"*Go!*" Brioc said. "Get out of here! Hurry!"

She stood in a daze, unable to move, looking for all the world like she would faint.

Something rustled in the tress.

"Over there!" a voice yelled. "I see them!"

Footfalls pounded through the forest.

Brioc's gaze shot in the direction of the noise.

That split-second was all it took.

Turlough jammed an elbow backwards into Brioc's chest and with his other hand grabbed Brioc's wrist. Everything happened too fast. Turlough twisted around, fast as lightning, and chopped downward on Brioc's hurt arm. Pain shot through him. The knife flew from his grip and sailed through the air.

Turlough bolted to his feet and whipped out his sword as Brioc scrambled for the knife. *Where was it? Where was it?* Lynnie screamed hysterically, the sound blasting Brioc's eardrums in half.

Footfalls pounded through the forest.

Forget the knife! He had to save Lynnie and Brigid! He spun towards her. "Run, Lynnie! Run!"

She remained rooted to the spot in shock, too petrified to move.

There was only one way to snap her out of it.

Brioc slapped her across the face. Hard.

Way too hard. Lynnie stumbled backwards and gasped with pain. A red mark appeared across her cheek. She jerked out of her frozen stupor, staring at him with stunned eyes. Brioc felt like a monster. He hadn't meant to hit her that hard. But . . . but he'd had no choice. Either hurt her or let her die!

"Get away! Retha's cave! Go!" He gave Lynnie a shove, possibly too hard as well. She lurched, then spun and fled with Brigid.

Brioc had no time for remorse. Two soldiers burst through the trees. One plowed into him, knocking him to the ground and landing on top of him.

Brioc twisted beneath the heavy weight of his attacker. Pain seared through his hurt arm. The man was fumbling to unsheathe his sword. With a surge of strength, Brioc shoved the soldier off, but he couldn't break the other's grip and they tumbled in the grass. What happened to the second soldier? What was Turlough doing during? Brioc kneed the man in the groin, making him falter, then got one good punch to his face.

There were more shouts and running footfalls. The sound of clattering steel against steel filled the air. What was going on?

They rolled again and Brioc glimpsed his own knife in the dirt hardly a foot away. He clawed at the man's face, going for his eyes, while all around him he heard grunting and cursing and clanging of metal.

A shriek, then something heavy dropped on top of him and his opponent. Blood splashed everywhere.

What the —

It was a body.

Brioc felt a sickening jolt as something long and sharp rammed through the torso of the soldier he was fighting. The man made a gurgling sound that belonged in a nightmare, then his body went limp. Warm blood flooded over Brioc's face and chest. *Who had killed the two soldiers?*

Brioc twisted from beneath their corpses and groped for his knife in the dirt. He grabbed it and held on tight.

Fear and confusion pulsing through him, he stumbled to his feet. Blood streamed into his eyes, nearly blinding him. He spied a third man sprawled wounded and unconscious nearby. The grass was soaked crimson beneath him. Then he saw Turlough — wrestling with a vaguely familiar soldier through mud and puddling blood in what looked like a death struggle. Both had daggers. Brioc reeled. What was happening? Whose side was his brother on?

Turlough landed a punch to his attacker's face then managed to shove his dagger up his gut. Brioc watched in horror as the man gasped and slumped, blood spraying everywhere. Turlough rolled out from under him, covered with filth and breathing hard. He staggered to his feet and that's when Brioc recognized the other man. Turlough had just taken out Captain Barrfhoinn.

The captain twitched, then moved. He wrenched the dagger from his own stomach with a moan, aimed the blade straight at Brioc, and whipped back his arm to throw it.

Turlough spun and slammed his sword straight through Barrfhoinn's chest. The dagger dropped from his hand and he crumpled on top of it. Turlough said, "May God have mercy on your soul."

He turned towards Brioc and his eyes widened with alarm.

"Brioc! Behind you!"

Still gripping his own knife, Brioc whirled. His blade caught the midriff of whoever stood behind him, lodging into the man's flesh. Without so much as flinching, the man ripped it out. Brioc lifted his gaze from the man's bleeding middle to his chest, and then up, up, up to his face. Brioc stared in shock. The man stood at least seven feet tall.

Out of nowhere Turlough plowed into the giant.

"Run, Brioc! Get out of here! Go, go!"

Turlough got one decent slash with his sword, which only made the huge man smile. Then the giant unsheathed his own. They instantly fell into a deadly rhythm of steel against steel.

Brioc stumbled out of their way, his chest ready to explode.

Turlough went down. The giant casually tossed his sword to the ground and whipped out a dagger. An animal grin unleashed itself across his face. He strode forward, step by deliberate step, enjoying himself, as Turlough scrambled to get to his feet. Turlough's sword lay several feet away in the dirt, out of his reach.

Brioc couldn't move. His legs wouldn't work. That invisible glob of molasses slurped the scene up, setting everything into slow motion the way it had at the shed last night.

The giant's arm went back with the dagger.

One foot went forward.

The other foot.

Slow. Impossibly slow.

His arm was coming down. Sunlight flashed on the knife in his hand.

Turlough scooted backwards, fear on his face. He had nowhere to go.

The knife was lowering, straight for his —

Brioc flew for the giant's sword on the ground.

Turlough tried to twist out of the way.

The dagger smashed down.

Brioc ran and rammed the sword through the giant's back with all his strength.

With a writhe of agony and an inhuman cry, the man lurched and crashed to his knees. Blood bubbled from his mouth like a fountain. He collapsed, thudding to the ground beside Turlough, the sword impaled straight through his body.

Brioc's heart stopped. *Oh dear God, dear God! He'd killed him! He'd killed a human being!*

"Brioc, run! Get out of here!" Turlough's voice was weak this time, laced with pain.

Brioc's eyes slid from the dead giant to his brother . . . and to the dagger lodged in his left shoulder. Blood poured down his arm. Turlough had his right hand wrapped around the hilt, trying to pull the thing out. His face was pale.

"Go, Brioc. More are coming. Please, just get out of here!"

Brioc's heart hammered. Trembling, he stumbled to his brother and knelt down. Putting his hand over Turlough's, together they yanked out the knife from his shoulder.

Turlough shuddered with pain. Blood ran everywhere. Brioc slapped one hand over the gushing wound and frantically searched for something to bind it with.

"Go. While you still can," Turlough begged. He swayed a little, like he might pass out.

Brioc groped with his free hand for the giant's shirt. He snatched a wad of material but couldn't rip it off one-handed.

"Press on it," he told Turlough, as if a soldier wouldn't already know how to stop a flow of blood. Then Brioc let go, grabbed the dagger, and cut through the dead man's shirt. He tried not to think of it, the fact he'd killed a man. He prayed all this blood wouldn't spin him into a flashback of the little girl.

He turned to Turlough with the strip of material in his hand. "Stay still. Let me do this. I've never done this before."

Turlough's eyes were desperate. "Please, Brioc. Just go."

"No. I can't leave you here. You'll bleed to death."

"Who cares."

Brioc didn't answer. He wrapped the material as tightly and quickly as he could. Then he stood and reached down a hand. Turlough took it and struggled weakly to his feet, his eyes filled with pain. Blood, filth and sweat covered them both.

Brioc searched Turlough's face, a thousand questions racing through his mind. "Why?" he asked.

"Why what?"

"Why didn't you kill me, like you said you would?"

Confusion raced across Turlough's features. "I never said that!"

"Yes you did. Your note."

Turlough's eyes widened with shock. "That's what it said?"

"Of course. Don't tell me you didn't know. It came from you. Your name was on it."

Turlough blinked a few times and ran a hand through his hair, totally at a loss. "No, no! Sam ripped it! Half was missing. I can't read, so I didn't know what part was gone. I sent it anyhow. I swear, Brioc, that's not what it said!"

It was Brioc's turn to be lost. "Then what did it say?"

"That I was trying to save you, and if you didn't let me help, Daemon would kill you and Lynnie. That's all I've been trying to do, Brioc, from the beginning. Save your life."

That made no sense. Turlough had abandoned him as a child. Turlough had never cared about him, never wanted him. Yet the past didn't equate to what Turlough's eyes held now. Brioc saw only love. The same love he'd sensed so strongly pouring down from Branduff and the others when he'd been on the boat.

He looked away, unable to hold Turlough's gaze. "I don't understand, Turlough. I don't understand any of this."

"I know you don't."

Hoof beats thundered through the woods.

Their gazes flew in the direction of the sound. More soldiers!

With a burst of adrenaline, Turlough leaped to the giant's body, planted a foot on his back, and yanked his sword out of the corpse. Then he swiped up the fallen dagger and tossed it to Brioc.

They ran.

71

Seized with terror, Dymphna bolted to the front of the church, tripping over a kneeler and knocking into pews in her desperation to reach Father Gerebran. She barely realized she did it. One second she knelt in the back of the church, the next second she was clinging to the priest.

The prayer book dropped from his hand and thumped to the floor. In one swift motion he dunked Retha down and out of view as the soldiers barged up the aisle. "Hide!" he whispered to Retha. Dymphna glimpsed her scrambling under a pew, where she curled into a tight ball and huddled in fear.

Heavy boots thudding, the three soldiers stormed forward, unsheathing their swords with a *whoosh* of steel that iced Dymphna's blood.

Father Gerebran stepped protectively in front of her, outstretching his arms so they couldn't reach her without veering around him.

Her heart froze in her chest.

"This is a house of God, a place of sanctuary." Father Gerebran's voice boomed with authority. "There can be no bloodshed here. Put your weapons away."

Two of the soldiers glanced at each other with amusement, one rolling his eyes. The third laughed outright. Dymphna recognized his bald head and shaggy beard. He'd taken her shoe when she'd cowered beneath Ethlynn's and Brioc's bed.

"I said, lay down your arms." The priest's tone was strong and unwavering.

The door banged open and Dymphna's gaze shot across the church.

Something resembling a clothed skeleton stopped at the threshold of the church door. Dymphna's breath caught. A split second later she realized the ghoulish figure was Faidh. Daidi's druid. Evil personified.

Trembling overtook her body. Her head grew light.

Faidh halted at the entrance, as if unwilling to step into such a holy place. His hollow eyes roved to the front of the church and landed on Father Gerebran. A tight smile pulled his gray lips into a thin line. For a moment the two priests — one pagan, the other of God — locked eyes. Then Faidh gave a single challenging nod to Father Gerebran and turned his attention to someone behind him. Sweeping his bony hand in a ceremonious ushering gesture, he stepped aside to allow entrance to whoever it was.

Something scarlet flapped at the door as if caught in a breeze, then Daidi stomped into the church. A strangled sound came from his mouth as from a wild animal. His eyes flared.

Dymphna's legs melted. Her knees nearly buckled. She held onto Father Gerebran to keep from falling. Her lungs couldn't pull enough air.

Daidi crashed his way towards them, his face burning with fury. "Dymphna, my bride. I have found you at last. This time you shall not escape!"

Father Gerebran stood his ground. "Leave this place! In the name of God Almighty, in Whose Presence we stand, I order you to get out!"

A whimper escaped Retha cowering beneath the pew.

Dymphna's heart clamped in almost physical pain. *Jesus, Jesus, keep Retha safe!*

Daidi kept coming. "Soldiers, dispatch this priest."

The one with the shaggy beard gripped his sword in both hands. He ran forward, grinning, and with a mighty swing lopped off Father Gerebran's head.

Dymphna screamed. Blood sprayed everywhere. Her hands flew to her mouth in horror. Father's headless body crashed to the floor near Retha under the pew.

Oh dear God, oh dear God! Dymphna turned and threw herself against the altar. *Jesus, Mary, save us!*

Daidi didn't miss a step. His cloak billowed behind him as he strode up the aisle. "I will wed you, Dymphna. Today, this hour, you shall be my wife."

Tears streamed down her cheeks. She backed against the altar, gripping the linens so tightly they slipped to the floor. *Where was Retha? Oh no, had she seen Father's body? Don't look, don't look!*

"Faidh can marry us. Right here in the church." Daidi laughed, emitting a demonic sound straight from hell. "You would like that, wouldn't you, Dymphna? To be wed in your Christian church."

The door crashed open again. Everyone turned to look as someone new burst inside. "No! No!" the newcomer shouted, his sword drawn. Dymphna recognized him by his long dark hair. It was Neill, the one who had been with Brioc's brother.

He tried to run to her but two soldiers grabbed him mid-flight, restraining him.

"Let her go!" he yelled, struggling viciously in their grip. "Let the princess go!"

One of his captors slammed the hilt of his sword into the side of Neill's head and he slumped in their arms. They let him drop to the floor, unconscious.

Daidi laughed. "Faidh, come forward. Our wedding day has arrived."

72

Racing through the woods, weaving around thorny bushes and low branches, Turlough frantically scanned the surroundings for a hiding place. There were too many soldiers, at least half a dozen, thundering behind them on horseback. He and Brioc could never take on that many. His only hope was that the soldiers hadn't yet seen them running.

He spotted a clump of bushes darkened by the shade of several massive trees.

"Over there! Over there!" He shoved Brioc, propelling him into the bushes.

Brioc stumbled to his knees in the thick foliage.

"Get down! Hurry!" Turlough crashed into his back and threw himself on top of him, pushing Brioc to the ground and burying him beneath him. "Shh. Don't move."

Turlough struggled to hold his breath, lungs threatening to explode. Beneath him, Brioc did the same.

"Shh," Turlough whispered again, all his senses soaring into high alert. He gripped his sword tightly, gritting his teeth against the burning agony in his shoulder, and slid his arm around Brioc's head, shielding him with his own body. He listened for the horses, trying to discern how far away they were and in what direction they headed. He could feel his heart thumping wildly in his chest.

A distant voice cut through the woods.

"Where'd they go?"

"Split up. Find them."

Turlough whispered, "Don't move."

As if Brioc needed to be told.

Agonizing minutes ticked by. Birds twitted in the branches above. A lone cricket chirped somewhere in the grass beside them.

Something thrashed through the trees and Turlough glimpsed the legs of a horse through the bushes' leaves. He squeezed the hilt of his sword. *Branduff, Raghnall, please don't let them see us!* A second horse came into view. Beneath him Brioc's body tensed. So did Turlough's. He bit the inside of his cheek to keep himself quiet.

"I don't know," one soldier said. "They're obviously not out here."

"Is Barrfhoinn still looking?"

"Probably. Haven't seen him. But Gruagh's with him. No one can get past those two."

The horses clomped by within three feet of the bushes. Turlough's blood hammered in his ears.

"Then let's head out. I'm tired of this."

"Me too. Hey, wasn't there a tavern in the last village we rode through?"

Their voices finally faded. The forest sounds returned to innocent birds and bugs.

Turlough blew out his breath but still didn't dare move. Neither did Brioc.

They waited, frozen.

One minute.

Two.

No more horses. No more voices. Turlough climbed off his brother and stood, feeling drained. Blood seeped through the bandage on his shoulder, drenching his sleeve. He knew he was losing too much blood. His head felt light and he swayed a little on his feet.

Brioc staggered out of the bushes after him, looking equally a wreck. For the first time, Turlough noticed he had a bandage on his arm as well. Obviously not from today, but blood oozed through the material too. Whatever wounds Brioc had must have reopened, probably when Turlough chopped down on his arm to get away when Brioc had held the knife to his throat. Great. They were both wounded and up against heaven only knew how many more soldiers. Would they get through this alive?

Doubtful. At least not both of them. Turlough took a deep breath. He had to apologize, now, for once and for all, before the grave made it too late. But how? How could he explain what he had done that day on the hillside all those years ago?

He opened his mouth, searching for words.

An idea came in a flash. Was it Branduff and Raghnall from the next world again? Yep, must be them. Turlough said, "You hit Lynnie awfully hard back there. You realize that, don't you?"

Brioc flinched. First confusion, then pain, jumped into his eyes. "I didn't mean to."

"Well, I sure hope she forgives you. Good luck."

The look of pain intensified, making Brioc appear scared. "You mean, you don't think she will?"

Turlough shrugged. "I highly doubt it. That slap would have really hurt her. It left a mark and everything."

Annoyance flared in Brioc's eyes. "I had to," he said, self-defense flying into place. "You don't understand, Turlough. I had no choice."

Turlough put on his most innocent face. "Oh? No choice but to hit your wife so hard?"

Brioc glared. "I had to make her move! Those soldiers would have killed her!"

"She won't know that. She'll think you did it out of cruelty. That you hate her."

Rare anger flashed in Brioc's eyes. He glanced around, as if trapped, as if he needed to defend himself for something terrible that he regretted doing. "As if *you* know about responsibility, Turlough! You have no idea what it means to have someone's actual survival depend on you!"

"Oh? Really? You think not?"

Brioc didn't get it yet. "I had to hurt Lynnie to keep her and Brigid alive! The last thing I need is you telling me that I did the wrong thing!"

"You're right. I take it back." Turlough held up his hands in surrender. "Actually, I do know how it feels. I once did the same thing myself."

Brioc released his breath, calming down a little. "What, you hit someone when you didn't want to?"

"Something like that. Only . . ." He hesitated at the memory. "I did much worse." At the thought of that nightmare day, Turlough's voice caught in his throat. His mouth went dry.

Brioc stared at him, waiting. Confused.

Turlough forced himself to continue, feeling suddenly shaky inside.

"I hit an innocent child. And I hit him too hard. Way too hard." Turlough's chest tightened. "I . . . I pushed him over a cliff. I killed him."

Brioc's eyes widened with horror. "You pushed a child *off a cliff*?"

"Yes. I mean, not a real cliff, but . . ." His eyes stung and he averted them, unable to look at his brother. He hadn't expected his confession to be this hard.

"He was ten years old. I had to keep him alive, but I didn't know how." Turlough bit his lip and looked back at his brother, begging with his eyes. "I was only fifteen, Brioc. Hardly more than a child myself. I . . . I didn't realize what I was doing. Didn't know the damage that I . . ." He stopped, unable to go on.

A dozen emotions chased each other across Brioc's face, as he struggled to take it in, struggled to comprehend. He wasn't stupid. He'd get it. He would know exactly what Turlough was talking about.

After an agonizing silence, Turlough said, "You would not have survived another winter. Neither of us would have. I had to make you stay there, Brioc. I knew no other way. Please forgive me. I truly am so sorry."

Brioc blinked, his eyes misting. He whisked an arm across them. He seemed to grope for words, but nothing would come out.

Words weren't needed. Brioc's eyes said it all.

Before Turlough realized it, he'd reached for Brioc's shoulders. He yanked him hard against him with a desperate squeeze. Then he released him, wiped a bloodied sleeve across his own eyes, and said, "We're wasting time. We need to find the princess."

"She's in the church," Brioc said, as if it was the most obvious thing in the world. Then a pained look crossed his face. "But I can't protect her anymore, Turlough. Lynnie's still in danger. It's her I need to take care of. Her and Brigid."

Turlough didn't want to separate. He never wanted to separate again! But Brioc was right. "Go," he said. "Neill's here too. We'll do everything we can to save the princess."

"Don't get killed, Turlough." Brioc's eyes pleaded. "Please don't. Not now. Not after . . . all this."

"I won't, if you won't. Deal?"

Brioc managed a smile. "Deal."

Hearing Brigid's name a second ago made Turlough remember the statue. "Wait. I have something for you." He fumbled in his pouch and whipped out the tiny Saint Brigid. "Remember this? Mam and her blessing every night?" He offered it to Brioc. "Well, it worked. Saint Brigid has kept us both safe under her cloak. She's got Lynnie and her new little namesake under there too."

Emotion filled Brioc's eyes. With a shaky hand he accepted Mam's statue. He paused, then said, "Our brothers . . . they're . . . well . . . " His voice faltered. "They're helping us too. It was Branduff who told me to come to Gheel." He winced, as if maybe Turlough would laugh at him. "I heard him in the boat. He spoke to me."

Turlough's jaw dropped.

Brioc lowered his gaze. "I know. You think I'm crazy. I'm sick and messed up and —"

"No! No! I'm stunned, that's all." Turlough floundered for words. Then joy swelled in his heart. "I asked him to send you here."

Brioc's eyes shot up with shock. "You — you *asked* him?"

Turlough couldn't stop grinning. "You bet I did. More like begged. And he actually listened to me. I can't believe it! He sure never listened to me when he was alive." He punched Brioc lightly on the shoulder — a motion that pain instantly made him regret but which made Brioc grin too. "You're not the only younger brother in the family, you know." He shook his head. "Let's go save those girls!"

73

Shaking uncontrollably, Ethlynn pressed her back as far as she could against the wall of the pitch black cave. She was afraid to sit, afraid to move, afraid to breathe. Clasping Brigid so hard she was probably crushing her, she silently pleaded with her. *Stay quiet, sweetpea. Please don't make any noise.*

They were going to die. She'd seen all those soldiers in the woods. Brioc was already killed. He could never have survived. Sorrow choked her. Brioc was dead! How could she live without him?

And they would rip Brigid away from her as well! Any minute now, soldiers would crash into this cave; she would hear —

Leaves rustled at the entrance!

Ethlynn whimpered in fear. Tears of terror trickled down her cheeks.

Someone drew branches aside, creeping through the hidden entrance.

A scream rose in her throat. It wouldn't come out. Her body went numb with shock, her insides turning to mush.

More shuffling noises in the dark. The soldier fumbled through the blackness.

She strained to peer into her inky surroundings but couldn't see a thing.

Suddenly something bumped into her.

She screamed at the top of her lungs.

The sound bounced around the dark cave, echoing, blasting across the walls.

A hand groped her face, found her mouth, and clamped over it. "Shhhh!" someone whispered. "Stop! It's only me!"

He muffled her scream, but it still kept coming. She couldn't get it under control. The hand clamped tighter. "Lynnie, it's me! Brioc! Stop! Everything's alright! You're safe!"

Brioc? He was — *alive?*

Her scream stopped. Relief overwhelmed her, making her woozy. She collapsed.

Arms caught her in the dark.

"Lynnie, it's alright." He held her tight, crushing Brigid between them. "It's alright," he kept whispering softly. "You're safe." He lowered her to the floor, not letting her go.

"B-b-brioc?" Her teeth chattered from fright. "I'm so scared, I'm so scared!" She knew she was shivering and shaking, but she couldn't control it. "They'll find us and kill us!"

"No. They won't. I won't let them hurt you or Brigid. I promise."

Brioc held her in his strong arms and let her cry. Little by little, her tears slowed, and her trembling lessened. Brioc didn't let go. She clung to him with all her strength.

Finally, after an eternity, the hysteria passed.

"They . . . they didn't kill you," she whimpered.

"No. But I think you're in shock." He held her tighter.

"What h-happened to-to Dymphna?" she whispered, not sure if she wanted to know. Despite everything, the thought of the princess being captured and forced into a sick, sinful union with her did horrified her.

Brioc hesitated, then said softly, "I don't know what happened to Dymphna. I came here to you as soon as I could."

He . . . he had come to *her*? Not the princess? Truly?

"You — you rescued *me* instead?"

"Of course I did." He sounded confused.

"But . . . but . . . you're in love with her, not me."

Shock rippled through his body. *"What?"* He instantly loosened his grip around her, jerking back as if she'd hit him. "What on earth are you —"

"It's Dymphna you love." She sniffled. "I know you do. She's so gorgeous and brave and perfect. And I'm drab and —"

"Lynnie, I can't believe you're even saying this! Of course I don't love the princess!"

"But you're always with her. And you gave her flowers. I saw you do it. By the wood shed last night."

"No! No, she dropped them! She brought them over for you, to cheer you up, then she slipped and fell. I was only picking them up for her. Honestly, Lynnie, I promise!"

Before she could reply, he pulled her deeper into his arms and crushed her with a kiss, making her melt and —

"Et-lynn . . . Et-lynn? You here?"

They instantly broke their kiss and spun around as the tiny glow of a candle lit up the cave.

Paulien stood trembling a few feet away. Anika clung to her skirt, eyes wide with fear. Paulien didn't seem to have noticed their, um, little romantic moment.

She blurted out something in her strange language, so rapid and frantic that the only word Ethlynn caught was Retha's name.

Brioc must have understood because he shot to his feet. "You mean Retha's missing?"

Paulien nodded. Tears slid down her cheeks, glistening in the flickering candlelight.

Brioc's expression leaped from tender to worried. "Oh no! She must be in the church! My brother won't know! He won't realize!"

His brother? What brother? *You mean . . . that soldier who looked like him was . . . his brother?!*

But before Ethlynn could ask, Brioc yanked out a little carved figurine. He pressed it into her palm. "I have to get Retha. Saint Brigid will take care of you. I know she will."

He bent to give her one more kiss, then was gone in a flash.

74

The first thing Turlough crashed into when he reached the church door was Faidh. The druid blocked the entrance.

"Out of my way, out of my way!" Turlough tried to swerve around the skinny figure. He could glimpse the princess inside at the altar, clinging to it for dear life. Blood splattered her dress, the floor, the altar linens. She had on some old shawl that looked like it had been in a fire. The demon towered over her. Then Turlough saw — *oh dear Jesus! A headless body on the floor!*

"Stay out." Faidh grabbed Turlough's arm. It was the arm he'd been knifed in; fresh agony shot through his shoulder. For such a bag of bones, Faidh's grip belonged to the devil himself. Turlough struggled to get free, his eyes darting into the church. Cahir, a few feet inside, had seen him barge to the door. Cahir's face held a strange look. Fear? Horror? The other two soldiers stood with their backs to him. One's sword was stained red.

Another body lay sprawled on the floor. Turlough's breath caught. It was Neill! Dead or unconscious?

Turlough had to reach the princess! He pulled his sword back and rammed it through the druid's stomach. Before the druid could even fall, Turlough whipped it back out, shoved him aside and ran into the church for Dymphna.

Halfway to her, the other two soldiers grabbed him. The bald one, with the dripping blade, kicked Turlough's sword from his hand. It spun into the aisle and landed with a clatter. The other soldier grabbed him in a headlock. Yet again he felt a blade against his throat.

"You still refuse?" The king's voice boomed through the church with fury.

"I'll never marry you, Daidi! Never!" Tears poured down her face.

"You wish, then, to share the fate of this priest? For that is your choice, daughter." He yanked her to her feet by her hair. She cried out in pain. "You shall become my wife or die!"

She gulped for air and her hands wrung the shawl she was wearing. Suddenly, for some reason, as soon as she did that, the sheer terror on her face faded. Her features evened out with a look of . . .

Peace? Calmness?

Joy?

"Then kill me, Daidi. I forgive you if you do. Jesus is my Spouse. I am His bride and shall never be yours!"

Daemon spun in a rage. "Behead her!" he screamed.

No one moved.

Turlough held his breath.

Cahir averted his eyes and shrank back. The other two froze.

"Do it!" The king shrieked.

Dymphna's gaze traveled to each soldier in turn. Heavenly joy radiated from her face. Her calm dignity, her courage, arrested them all. Everyone remained frozen.

Her eyes met Turlough's. She blinked, recognizing him. Then she smiled the most beautiful smile he'd ever seen and silently mouthed the words, *'thank you.'*

The king howled like a wild beast, unsheathed his sword and whirled around. With one violent blow he did the job himself.

He took off his daughter's head.

Turlough jerked away from the sight, squeezing his eyes shut. Something warm and wet splashed onto him. Onto his wounded shoulder.

The pain vanished, as if it had never been.

The blade against his throat loosened, then dropped. Both soldiers released him. He opened his eyes and saw the horror in theirs. Everyone stared in shock at the dead princess on the floor.

Daemon collapsed beside her, shrieking and wailing hysterically. He ripped at his hair, clawed at his face. No one helped him. No one went near.

The door burst open and someone crashed inside. A pause, then Brioc yelled, "Nooooo!" He ran forward, blindly towards the altar and the horror.

Turlough grabbed his arm, yanking him back.

From nowhere, a little girl shot into the aisle, hysterically pounding across the church towards them. Turlough bent and caught her in his arms. She must have been under a pew by the altar! Her clothes were splattered with blood. Good God, she'd been there the whole time! She'd witnessed the brutal murders! His heart clenched with anguish and he crushed her tight against him, trying to shield her from the gruesome sight she'd already seen.

She buried her face in his neck, gasping out words in the strange foreign language, words that he couldn't understand.

Beside him, Brioc's breath caught in shock. "Retha's never spoken before!" He reached over, prying the girl from Turlough's arms and taking her into his own. "Retha, everything's al—" He stopped and gasped. "Your — your face!"

Confused by Brioc's reaction, Turlough looked at the child's face. What was wrong with it? Nothing that he could see. In fact, it was the most perfect, flawless face he'd ever seen on a child. She looked like an angel. And her expression was not panic-stricken at all. Exactly the opposite! Despite the horror she'd just seen, hysteria hadn't made her blurt out whatever she was saying. Excitement had. And . . . *happiness?* Turlough reeled, uncomprehending.

Brioc's eyes widened even more. He listened to what Retha told him. He swallowed hard. At her words, peace fell over his features.

"What is she saying?"

Brioc said, "Shh. Wait." The child's story was still bursting forth.

Daemon's clamor made it hard to hear. He rolled on the floor in despair, screeching and tearing his hair and clothes. No one paid attention. Cahir and the other two soldiers sheathed their swords and slunk from the church with shame and disgust, knowing that the king was a beast.

"What's Retha saying?" Turlough asked again, dying to know.

Brioc waited till she finished, then looked at Turlough with stunned joy. "She saw them go to Heaven." His eyes grew moist. "Both of them, Father and the princess. Angels carried them. She said they . . ." A single tear slid down his cheek. ". . . they looked down at you and me with special love."

Turlough stood speechless. Emotion swelled through him.

"They knew we tried our best."

Turlough gazed at the two martyrs by the altar. Their sacred blood had splattered everywhere, including his knifed shoulder, and this little child who had never spoken before today.

Brioc nudged him and with a hint of a smile nodded at something on the floor. "Him too. Retha says they smiled at him too."

Huh?

Turlough swiveled his gaze. It fell on Neill.

Neill sat on the floor in a daze, clutching his head, looking ready to murder someone. He didn't seem to have a clue what was going on. But he'd obviously heard Brioc's last words because a scowl crossed his face.

"Someone was smiling at me unconscious? Thought it was funny, did they?" He looked around with glazed eyes and a death glare. "Tell me who and they're dead."

75

Turlough crossed himself and reluctantly rose from his knees in front of the sealed entrance to the cave. Heart heavy with sadness, he slapped the dirt from his trousers and sighed. The princess was in Heaven and eternally happy now, but he couldn't help wish they'd been able to save her. He'd only met Dymphna once — the time he'd mistaken her for Lynnie — but that brief encounter, and her smile to him the moment before she died, would stay etched in his memory forever.

The priest would not be forgotten either. Turlough couldn't count the times he had attended Father Gerebran's Mass back in Oriel. He'd always regarded the kindhearted priest as a saint. Everyone had. Turlough hadn't even realized Father Gerebran was a part of all this until after the murders.

Beside him, Neill clambered to his feet as well. "I still think it was a strange place to bury them," he grumbled. "In a cave. It's a bit silly if you ask me. They're martyrs. They deserve better."

"I know, Neill, I know. But the villagers were too frightened of Daemon. They wanted to hide the bodies quickly. At least that's what Paulien told my brother."

Paulien. Even speaking her name made him tingle inside. Sweet Paulien with her hair scented of flowers and her breathtaking blue eyes. Try as he might, Turlough couldn't shake her from his mind.

But she'd already been married, already lost the one man she'd loved. Continuing to wear black three years after her husband died sent a clear message. She wasn't interested. Not in him, not in anyone. Forget Paulien. That was the safest thing to do.

Besides, he'd soon be back in Ireland. After a few days, she wouldn't even remember his existence.

Neill hoisted his bundle over his shoulder. "Ready to head out?"

"Might as well. No point hanging around." Turlough swiped up his own pack from the ground. The kind villagers had not only given them the last two nights' lodging, but had pitched in with money and supplies for their journey home. Turlough dreaded the boat ride. It'd be a relief to get the seasickness over with.

Neill said, "I'm dying to get back. Did I tell you about the lassie I met up in Cenél Eóghain?"

"You might have. I don't remember. Surely you can't expect me to keep track of them all."

Neill laughed. "Actually, I have you to thank for this one. She was one of the beauties you hid from Barrf."

Turlough looked at him with surprise. "Really? Well, glad I could help." He inwardly rolled his eyes. Neill and his sweethearts.

"I've been thinking about it and I'm going to look for work up there. We obviously can't go back to Oriel, so Cenél Eóghain is as good a place as any." Neill hesitated, shifting uncomfortably. After a moment he confided, "I'm going to ask her to marry me."

Shock rendered Turlough speechless. Neill, settling down? The thought was mind-boggling.

Then again, why should it be? The princess and the priest were no doubt busy in Heaven. Their blood had miraculously cured Retha and healed his own wounded shoulder. Why should it surprise him if they'd turned their attention to Neill as well?

"Neill, that's wonderful. I'm so happy for you." Turlough meant it. Neill wasn't such a bad fellow. He'd take good care of a wife. Might even make a good daid.

"Come on. Let's go," Neill ordered, as if not wanting to admit his roving days were over.

"I need to say good-bye to my brother. Give me five minutes. Go on ahead if you want. I can catch up."

"Nah. I'll come with you."

"Thanks." Turlough appreciated the moral support. His heart clenched at the thought of saying good-bye. After all this, he hated to lose Brioc again. The wide sea would lay between them for the rest of their lives.

Neill cast one last look at the huge stones blocking the cave and shook his head. "Guess that little girl needs to find a new place to play." He snorted. "Burying martyrs in a cave. Who would have thought?" He walked past Turlough and slapped him on the shoulder. "Come on. Quick partings are best."

Turlough gazed at the cave for another long moment, whispering a silent prayer to the two saints within, asking them for the strength he would need. Then he blessed himself again and followed Neill.

They walked in silence down the dirt track to Paulien's house, every step filling Turlough with a new degree of nerves. How could he get through this?

When they reached the little path lined with flowers, music drifted to them through the open window. Music from a harp. Turlough halted, unable to go further. His eyes stung.

He recognized the melody — Brioc's favorite as a child. It was a bouncy, happy piece — the type that would make Brigid coo with delight once she was old enough. Turlough had known Lynnie for barely two days, but he could easily picture her swirling around the floor, her baby cradled in her arms.

Neill went ahead of him and knocked on the door. He twisted his head around. "You coming?"

Turlough blew out a breath and headed up the path. Best to get it over with.

Paulien opened the door and Turlough did a double-take. She didn't wear black! Her dress was somber but colorful, and her hair was uncovered. A beautiful blond braid fell over her shoulder. Turlough tried not to stare.

As soon as Paulien saw them, a smile lit up her face and she said something in her strange language and motioned for them to come in. The music stopped. Through the doorway Turlough caught a glimpse of Lynnie. Sure enough, she had been dancing across the floor with Brigid.

Neill stepped in and Turlough followed. Paulien kept smiling at him. His legs nearly melted and his vocal chords vanished altogether.

When he didn't say anything, Neill gave him a funny look and took over. "We're heading out. Just came to say good-bye."

Across the room, Brioc shot out of his chair, nearly dropping his harp. Confusion raced across his face. "What? Where are you going?"

Turlough regained his power of speech. As long as he didn't look at Paulien, he'd be alright. "Back to Ireland. Where else?"

"You mean . . . you're *leaving*?" Something unreadable flashed through Brioc's eyes. Could it — could it actually be sadness? All of them were sorrowful about the deaths, of course, but could Brioc be sad to lose *him*?

Brioc blurted, "I thought you'd stay. I mean, I just assumed —"

Lynnie said, "Don't go. Please don't leave." She bit her lip. She'd spent all yesterday apologizing to Turlough for how she'd acted when he'd swiped up Brigid and ran from the cottage. She must have apologized a thousand times. And when she wasn't apologizing, she was crying. She couldn't forgive herself for apparently having thought poorly of the princess. Brioc had tried everything to calm her down. Finally he'd found a way: playing happy music on his harp.

That had done the trick. And just in time, because Turlough didn't think he could handle any more tears. Lynnie had been crying, Paulien had been crying, Anika had been crying. He and Brioc felt like it too, and even Neill had blown his nose more than normal. Retha was the only one yesterday who wasn't sad. In fact, she'd been filled with joy and kept telling them how happy the two martyrs were in Heaven.

She should know. She'd seen them there.

Lynnie said again, "Please don't go back to Ireland. Please."

And just then the door banged open. Anika and Retha exploded inside.

"Moeder! Moeder!"

They flung themselves at Paulien with excitement, chattering at once.

Watching Retha, Turlough found it hard to believe she had been crippled and disfigured a few days ago. She ran faster than her sister now.

Each girl held something wrapped in a blanket. The contents squirmed and wriggled. Paulien peeked inside Retha's and gasped in surprise, her lovely blue eyes lighting up.

"What is it?" Brioc asked, moving across the room.

Lynnie set Brigid on the bed and rushed over to see too. Everyone crowded in. The girls put their treasures on the floor, giggling with delight.

From each blanket a tiny puppy face peered out. They couldn't have been more than a few weeks old. They looked almost identical, except one had dark fur and the other had light.

Anika launched into an excited explanation. Turlough caught a few words of their strange language, and what he didn't understand, Paulien beside him tried to translate with her broken Irish. It reminded him of their first conversation by the woodshed. Surprisingly, Brioc didn't step in to translate. He simply watched as if trying not to smile but failing miserably. Could he tell that Turlough liked Paulien? Was that why he left them to struggle through their clumsy conversation?

Turlough actually had little problem piecing the girls' story together. He wished it had been harder so that Paulien would talk to him longer, but alas. Apparently the girls had found the pair of puppies huddled together in the woods, hungry and abandoned.

When Brioc heard that part, he knelt on the floor and unwrapped one from its blanket, visibly overcome with emotion. For a moment he closed his eyes, as if in pain. Turlough knew why, and anguish shot through him too. The monks had told him that was how Brioc had found Samthann, alone and starving in the woods. Brioc spoke, for the first time in six years, just so he could get food for Sam.

Brioc reopened his eyes and picked up the pup he'd unwrapped. He stroked it gently and held it close to his face. Its tiny tongue found his cheek and started to lick him. The second puppy managed to flop out of its blanket on its own and Brioc scooped it up too.

Turlough's heart stopped.

They were wolf pups.

Oh no! Brioc didn't even realize!

Turlough rushed forward and dropped on his knees beside Brioc. He had to get them away, fast, before someone said —

"They're wolves."

Thanks a lot, Neill.

Brioc blinked and jerked back.

Turlough managed to snatch one wolf away, trying to hide it. Brioc would have a flashback, right here in front of everyone!

"Really?" Brioc said. His voice caught, but only a little. "They're . . . they're so cute. Lynnie, come here. Come hold one."

Turlough couldn't believe his ears.

Anika and Retha bounced up and down all around Paulien, clasping their hands and begging. They wanted to keep them.

Paulien's eyes found Turlough's and she asked him, "Can they . . . how say? Pain us?"

He answered, slowly, so she could understand, "At this age, they're perfectly harmless."

Neill added,"Not sure if it's true, but I've heard wolves can be tamed if you get them young enough. I mean, by someone who really knows dogs." He grinned. "Or someone who has powerful friends in Heaven, who really know dogs."

Brioc was hardly listening. He and Lynnie were too busy cooing over one of the pups. It was licking Brioc everywhere.

Paulien smiled and knelt next to Turlough, making his temperature rise. He offered her the tiny wolf in his hands.

Paulien said, "They look very same." She giggled. "Like you and Brioc."

"What, you mean we look like animals?"

Everyone laughed.

Paulien blushed and frowned, not comprehending. "I . . . I say some ting wrong?"

Neill whacked Turlough on the head and said, "She means the color of their fur, you idiot. Mind you, come to think of it —"

"Alright, Neill. Shut up."

Neill crouched and pet one of the wolves. "Both males. I wonder what happened to their mother."

"She must have been one of the wolves Dymphna and I killed." Brioc said it calmly, like he killed wolves every day. Turlough raised an eyebrow, but Brioc and Lynnie kept petting the squirming puppy.

Paulien nudged Turlough and asked, "What Neill say? Males? What's that?"

"Broers," Turlough said, instantly remembering the word this time.

She smiled. "Brothers?"

"Yes."

She remembered the word too.

She looked up at her daughters, still smiling that incredible smile of hers. "We keep," she told them, for some reason still speaking in Irish. "We keep both." Anika and Retha clapped with glee amid squeals of *danks* and *dankewols.*

Paulien's gaze returned to Turlough's, then traveled to Brioc and back again. "They broers. Broers must stay together. Always together." She nodded with a seriousness that made her more lovely than ever. "It is how the good God made tings."

Brioc looked at Turlough. His voice caught. "I think so too. Don't you, Turlough?"

Turlough's heart swelled.

Brioc had been right all along.

Gheel truly was a land where dreams came true.

afterword

Several years after the murder of Princess Dymphna and Father Gerebran, the villagers of Gheel decided to move their remains from the humble cave to a more suitable burial place. When the entrance to the cave was unsealed, however, the bodies were no longer wrapped in the simple shrouds they had been buried in. Instead, the workmen discovered both martyrs resting within beautiful snow-white coffins. There was no explanation, except that the stone coffins had been carved by angels.

When the one holding Princess Dymphna was pried open, the villagers found a red tile upon her heart. On it was written the words: "Here lies the holy virgin and martyr, Dymphna."

Her remains were moved to a small church, and miracles immediately started taking place at her tomb. Those who suffered from mental and emotional disorders seemed to be the ones the princess favored from Heaven.

News of miraculous cures spread from country to country, and Gheel soon became a place of pilgrimage for the mentally afflicted. So great were the crowds that flocked to her tomb that eventually a magnificent church was built in her honor on the site where the bodies were first buried. Her relics still repose there in a beautiful golden reliquary.

Saint Dymphna's feast day is May 15th.

Saint Gerebran's relics were taken to Germany, where his cult remains popular to this day.

Whether King Daemon was ever cured, or converted, by his daughter's intercession shall be known only in Heaven.

Did you know that reviews sell books?

If you have enjoyed this novel of Saint Dymphna, or any of my other books, would you consider leaving a review on Amazon or Goodreads? Even a line or two would be awesome and so very appreciated. Thank you and God bless!

with Gratitude

So many people helped with this novel that it would be impossible to name them all. I owe an enormous debt of gratitude especially to my wonderful friend, fellow author and editor, Theresa Linden, whose help went over and beyond at every step of the way. A huge thank you also to author Gary Ludlam, my invaluable critique partner, whose insights helped shape the story in ways I had not originally planned.

To my beta-readers, and my amazing friends from the Catholic Writers' Guild, whose generosity with their time and expertise knew no bounds and who were always willing to dive in and help me at the drop of a hat, thank you.

I extend my deepest gratitude to the several victims of Post-Traumatic Stress Disorder, who wish to remain nameless, but who shared their personal traumas and experiences with me in an attempt to make the character of Brioc as realistic as possible. These unsung heroes and heroines even took the time to read and offer suggestions for the chapters containing PTSD flashbacks. May Saint Dymphna bless them all.

A giant thank you to Sister Mary Roberta, whose enthusiasm and help cannot even begin to be measured. Father Antonio of the Immaculate Conception, O.S.F. and Brother Leo were incredibly generous with their time and support, and I'm sure Sister Josephine Marie's prayers in those last frantic moments made all the difference!

My kids have been awesome, putting up with an author for a mom, and bearing with all the mess, chaos, unwashed laundry and heat-n-eat meals that go with it. You guys are the best and always will be!

And last but not least, my wonderful husband, Jeff, writer extraordinaire, who not only wrote the Introduction, but gave me the best line in this book. Without his years' long patience, moral encouragement and material support, this book could never have been a reality.

Made in the USA
Monee, IL
02 April 2021